P9-DWT-007

CALGARY PUBLIC LIBRARY

NOV   2015

TOWER OF THORNS

TOWER OF THORNS

A BLACKTHORN & GRIM NOVEL

Juliet Marillier

A ROC BOOK

ROC

Published by New American Library,
an imprint of Penguin Random House LLC
375 Hudson Street, New York, New York 10014

This book is an original publication of New American Library.

First Printing, November 2015

Copyright © Juliet Marillier, 2015
Penguin Random House supports copyright. Copyright fuels creativity, encourages diverse voices, promotes free speech, and creates a vibrant culture. Thank you for buying an authorized edition of this book and for complying with copyright laws by not reproducing, scanning, or distributing any part of it in any form without permission. You are supporting writers and allowing Penguin Random House to continue to publish books for every reader.

Roc and the Roc colophon are registered trademarks of Penguin Random House LLC.

For more information about Penguin Random House, visit penguin.com.

LIBRARY OF CONGRESS CATALOGING-IN-PUBLICATION DATA:

Marillier, Juliet.
Tower of thorns: a Blackthorn & Grim novel / Juliet Marillier.
pages cm.—(Blackthorn & Grim; book 2)
"A ROC BOOK."
ISBN 978-0-451-46701-0
I. Title.
PR9619.3.M26755T69 2015
823'.914—dc23   2015019510

Printed in the United States of America
10 9 8 7 6 5 4 3 2 1

Designed by Laura K. Corless

PUBLISHER'S NOTE
This is a work of fiction. Names, characters, places, and incidents either are the product of the author's imagination or are used fictitiously, and any resemblance to actual persons, living or dead, business establishments, events, or locales is entirely coincidental.

Penguin
Random
House

For my granddaughter Jamaica

acknowledgments

My heartfelt thanks to the team at Pan Macmillan: Claire Craig, Libby Turner and Brianne Collins; and to Anne Sowards and her team at Penguin U.S. I have found their support invaluable. A very special thank-you to Arantza Sestayo for capturing the spirit of the book so wonderfully in her cover painting. My agent, Russ Galen, has believed in this project from the first, and that is more valuable than I can put into words.

My daughter Elly has been a valuable brainstorming partner and beta reader, creative, honest and patient. The wise and serene Tamara Lampard was my sounding board for matters magical and uncanny.

The central characters in this book have been seriously damaged by past trauma. In preparation for writing the novel, and the series, I read a lot about the effects of PTSD (post-traumatic stress disorder) and strategies for coping with the condition. I should mention two brilliantly written books by Pulitzer Prize–winning journalist David Finkel: *The Good Soldiers*, about the experience of a U.S. infantry battalion in Iraq during the so-called "surge" of 2007, and *Thank You for Your Service*, Finkel's follow-up volume dealing with the fallout for those servicemen and their families after their return home.

CHARACTER LIST

This list includes some characters who are mentioned by name but don't appear in the story.

At Winterfalls

Oran:	prince of Dalriada
Flidais:	Oran's wife
Donagan:	Oran's companion
Deirdre:	Flidais's chief handmaid
Nuala:	maidservant
Mhairi:	maidservant
Seanan:	man-at-arms
Blackthorn:	wisewoman, formerly known as Saorla (seer-la)
Grim:	her companion
Emer: (eh-ver)	Blackthorn's young assistant

At Cahercorcan (The Court of Dalriada)

Ruairi:	king of Dalriada; Oran's father
Eabha:	queen of Dalriada; Oran's mother
Sochla:	Eabha's sister
Master Caillín:	court physician
Rodan:	man-at-arms
Domnall:	senior man-at-arms

| *Eoin:* | man-at-arms |
| *Lochlan:* | man-at-arms |

At Bann

Geiléis: (ge-*lace*, hard *g*)	the Lady of Bann
Senach:	steward
Dau: (rhymes with *now*)	manservant
Cronan:	manservant
Caisín: (ka-*sheen*)	seamstress, married to Rian
Onchú:	senior man-at-arms
Donncha:	man-at-arms
Rian:	man-at-arms, married to Caisín
Mechar:	man-at-arms (deceased)
Ana:	a cottager
Fursa:	her baby son

At St. Olcan's

Father Tomas:	head of the monastic foundation
Brother Dufach:	one of the monks
Brother Fergal:	gardener
Brother Ríordán: (reer-dawn)	head archivist
Brother Dathal: (do-hal)	assistant archivist
Brother Marcán:	infirmarian
Brother Tadhg: (tīg)	a tall novice
Brother Eoan: (ohn)	keeper of pigeons

At St. Erc's

Brother Galen:	scribe and scholar (deceased)
Bathsheba:	his cat (deceased)
Brother Conall:	a novice

In Geiléis's Tale

Lily:	a young noblewoman
Ash (Brión):	a young nobleman
Muiríol: (mi-*reel*)	Lily's maidservant

Others

Mathuin:	chieftain of Laois
Lorcan:	king of Mide
Flannan:	a traveling scholar
Ripple:	Flannan's dog
Conmael:	a fey nobleman
Master Oisín: (a-*sheen*)	a druid
Cass:	Blackthorn's husband (deceased)
Brennan:	Blackthorn's son (deceased)
Brother Gwenneg:	an acquaintance from Geiléis's past
Cú Chulainn: (koo *hull*-en)	a legendary Irish hero

TOWER OF THORNS

PROLOGUE

Rain had swollen the river to a churning mass of gray. The tower wore a soft shroud of mist; though it was past dawn, no cries broke the silence. Perhaps he slept, curled tight on himself, dreaming of a time when he was whole and hale and handsome. Perhaps he knew even in his sleep that she still kept watch, her shawl clutched around her against the cold, her gaze fixed on his shuttered window.

But he might have forgotten who she was, who he was, what had befallen them. It had been a long time ago. So long that she had no more tears to shed. So long that one summer blurred into another as the years passed in an endless wait for the next chance, and the next, to put it right. She did not know if he could see her. There were the trees, and the water, and on mornings like this, the mist lying thick between them. Only the top of the tower was visible, with its shuttered window.

Another day. The sun was fighting to break through; here and there the clouds of vapor showed a sickly yellow tinge. Gods, she loathed this place! And yet she loved it. How could she not? How could she want to be anywhere but here?

Downstairs, her household was stirring now. Someone was clanking pots, raking out the hearth, starting to make breakfast. A part of her considered that a warm meal on a chilly morning would be welcome—her people sought to please her. To make her, if not happy, then at least moderately content. It was no fault of theirs that she could not enjoy such simple pleasures as a full belly, the sun on her face, or a good night's sleep. Her body was strung tight with waiting. Her heart was a constant, aching hurt in her chest. What if there was no ending this? What if it went on and on forever?

"Lady Geiléis?"

Senach tapped on the door, then entered. Her steward was a good servant, discreet and loyal. "Breakfast is ready, my lady," he said. "I would not have disturbed you, but the fellow we sent to the Dalriadan court has returned, and he has some news."

She left her solitary watch, following her man out of the chamber. As Senach closed the door behind them, the monster in the tower awoke and began to scream.

"Going away," she said. "For how long?"

"King Ruairi will be attending the High King's midsummer council, my lady." Her messenger was gray-faced with exhaustion; had he traveled all night? His mead cup shook in his hands. "The queen will go south with him. They will be gone for at least two turnings of the moon, and maybe closer to three."

"Who will accompany them? Councilors? Advisers? Friends and relations?"

"All the king's senior councilors. Queen Eabha's attendants. A substantial body of men-at-arms. But Cahercorcan is a grand establishment; the place will still be full of folk."

"This son of King Ruairi's," she said. "The one you say will be looking after his father's affairs while they're gone—what manner of man is he? Of what age? Has he a wife?"

"Prince Oran is young, my lady. Three-and-twenty and newly married. There's a child on the way. The prince does not live at Cahercorcan usually, as he has his own holding farther south. He is more a man of scholarship than a man of action."

"Respected by his father's advisers, those of them who remained behind?" A scholar. That might be helpful. "Is he a clever man?"

"I could not say, my lady. He's well enough respected. They say he's a little unusual."

"Unusual?"

"They say he likes to involve all his folk in the running of household and farm. And I mean all, from the lowliest groom to the most distinguished of nobles. Consults the community, lets everyone have a say. There's some at court think that odd; they'd sooner he just told folk what to do, as his father would."

"I see." Barely two turnings of the moon remained until midsummer. After the long, wearying search, the hopes dashed, the possibilities all come to nothing, she had been almost desperate enough to head south and throw herself at King Ruairi's feet, foolish as that would have been. Common sense had made her send the messenger first, with orders to bring back a report on the situation at court. She had not expected anything to come of it; most certainly not this. Her heart beat faster; her mind raced ahead. The king gone, along with his senior advisers. The queen absent too. The prince in charge, a young man who would know nothing of her story . . . Could this be a real opportunity at last? Dared she believe it? Perhaps Prince Oran really was the key. Perhaps he could find her the kind of woman she had so long sought without success.

She'd have to ride for Cahercorcan soon—but not too soon, or she risked arriving before the king and his entourage had departed. It was the prince she needed to speak to, not his father. How might she best present her case? Perhaps this scholarly prince loved tales of magic and mystery. She must tell it in a way that would capture his imagination. And his sympathy.

She rose to her feet. "Thank you," she said to the messenger. "Go to the kitchen; Dau will give you some breakfast. Then sleep. I'll send for you later if I have further questions." Though likely he had told all he knew. She'd sent him to the royal household in the guise of a traveler passing through and seeking a few nights' shelter. There'd be limits to what a lad like him could learn in such a place. "Senach," she said after the messenger was gone, "it seems that this time we have a real opportunity." At last. Oh, at last! She had hardly dared to dream this might be possible. "You understand what this means?"

"Yes, my lady. You'll be wanting to travel south."

"I will, and soon. Speak to Onchú about an escort, will you? In my absence, you will be in charge of the household."

"Of course, my lady." A pause, then Senach added, "When do you plan to depart?"

"Not for a few days." Every instinct pulled her to leave now, straightaway, without delay; any wait would be hard to bear. But they must be sure the royal party had left court. "Let's say seven days. That should be long enough."

"When might I expect you to return, my lady?"

Her lips made the shape of a smile, but there was no joy in her. She had forgotten how it felt to be happy. "Before midsummer. That goes without saying. Prepare the guest quarters, Senach. We must hold on to hope." Hope, she thought, was as easily extinguished as a guttering candle on a day of spring storm. Over and over she had seen it tremble and die. Yet even now she was making plans again, looking ahead, seeing the way things might unfold. Her capacity to endure astonished her.

"Leave it to me, my lady. All will be ready for you."

Later still, as her household busied itself with the arrangements— horses, supplies, weaponry—she climbed back up to the high chamber and looked out once more on the Tower of Thorns. All day its tenant had shouted, wailed, howled like an abandoned dog. Now his voice had dwindled to a hoarse, gasping sob, as if he had little breath left to draw.

"This time I'll make it happen," she murmured. "I swear. By every god there ever was, by the stars in the sky and the waves on the shore, by memory and loss and heartbreak, I swear."

The sun was low; it touched the tower with a soft, rosy light that made a mockery of his pain. It would soon be dusk. There was just enough time.

With her gaze on that distant window, she began the nightly ritual. "Let me tell you a story."

1

BLACKTHORN

I sat on the cottage steps, shelling peas and watching as Grim forked fresh straw onto the vegetable patch. Here at the edge of Dreamer's Wood, dappled shade lay over us; the air held a warm promise of the summer to come. In the near distance green fields spread out, dotted with grazing sheep, and beyond them I glimpsed the long wall that guarded Prince Oran's holdings at Winterfalls. A perfect day. The kind of day that made a person feel almost . . . settled. Which was not good. If there was anything I couldn't afford, it was to get content.

"Lovely morning," observed Grim, pausing to wipe the sweat off his brow and to survey his work.

"Mm."

He narrowed his eyes at me. "Something wrong?"

A pox on the man; he knew me far too well. "What would be wrong?"

"You tell me."

"Seven years of this and I'll have lost whatever edge I once had," I said. "I'll have turned into one of those well-fed countrywomen who pride themselves on making better preserves than their neighbors, and give all their chickens names."

"Can't see that," said Grim, casting a glance at the little dog as she hunted for something in the pile of straw. The dog's name was Bramble, but we didn't call her that anymore, only Dog. There were reasons for that, complicated ones that only a handful of people knew. She was living a lifelong penance, that creature. I had my own penance. My fey benefactor, Conmael, had bound me to obey his rules for seven years. I was compelled to say yes to every request for help, to use my craft only for good, and to stay within the borders of Dalriada. In particular, Conmael had made me promise I would not go back to Laois to seek vengeance against my old enemy. I'd known from the first how hard those requirements would be to live by. But my burden was nothing against that borne by Ciar, who had once been maidservant to a lady. For her misdeeds, she had been turned into a dog. Magic being what it was— devious and tricky—she had no way back.

"Anyway," Grim went on, "it's closer to six years now."

"Why doesn't that make me feel any better? It doesn't seem to matter how busy I am, how worn-out I am after a day of applying salves and dispensing drafts and giving advice to every fool who thinks he wants it. Every night I dream about the same thing: what Mathuin of Laois did to me, and what I'll do to him. And the fact that Conmael's stupid rules are stopping me from getting on with it."

"I dream about that place," Grim said. "The stink. The dark. The screams. I dream about nearly losing hope. And when I wake up, I look around and . . ." He shrugged. "The last thing I'd be wanting is to go back. Different for you, I know."

I wanted to challenge him; to ask if there weren't folk who'd wronged him, folk he might care to teach a lesson to. Or folk who'd once loved him, who might still be missing him and needing him to come home. But I held my tongue. We didn't ask each other about the past, the time before we'd found ourselves in Mathuin's lockup, staring at each other across the walkway between the iron bars. A whole year we'd kept each other going, a year of utter hell, and we'd never shared our stories. Grim knew some of mine now, since I'd blurted it out on the day fire destroyed our cottage. How Mathuin of Laois had punished my man for his part in a plot against injustice. How he'd burned Cass and our baby alive, how he'd ordered his guards to hold me back so I couldn't reach them. Grim knew the dark thing I carried within me, the furious need to see justice done. And Conmael knew. Conmael knew far more than anyone rightly should.

"Pea soup?" Grim's voice broke into my thoughts.

"What? Oh. Seems a shame to cook them—they taste much better raw. But yes, soup would stretch them out a bit. I'll make it."

"Onion, chopped small," he suggested. "Garlic. Maybe a touch of mint."

"Trying to distract me from unwise thoughts?" I turned my gaze on him, but he was busy with his gardening again.

"Nah," said Grim. "Just hungry. Looks like we might have company in a bit."

A rider was approaching from the direction of Winterfalls. From this distance I couldn't tell who it was, but the green clothing suggested Prince Oran's household.

"Donagan," said Grim.

The prince's body servant; a man with whom we shared a secret or two. "How can you tell?"

"The horse. The white marking on her head. Only one like that in these parts. Star, she's called."

"You think the prince's man will be happy to eat my pea soup?"

"Why not? I always am. Need to start cooking soon, though, or he won't get the chance." Grim laid aside his pitchfork and straightened up, a big bear of a man. "I'll do it if you want."

"You're busy. I'll do it." Since I didn't plan on standing out front like a welcoming party, I headed back into the house. Donagan was all right as courtiers went, but a visit from a member of the prince's household generally meant some sort of request for help, and that meant saying yes to whatever it was, however inconvenient, because of my promise to Conmael. The most reasonable of requests felt burdensome if a person had no choice in the matter. If I was to survive seven years, I'd need to work on keeping my temper; staying civil. I only had four chances. Break Conmael's rules a fifth time, and he'd put me straight back into Mathuin's lockup as if I'd never left the place. That was what he'd threatened, anyway. Maybe he couldn't do it, but I had no intention of putting that to the test.

Grim stayed outside and so did Donagan, whose arrival I saw between the open shutters. Once he'd tethered his horse, he leaned on the wall chatting as Grim finished his work with the pitchfork. That gave me breathing time, which I used not only to prepare the meal, but to put my thoughts in order. Step by small step; that was the only way I'd survive my time of penance. My lesson in patience. Or whatever it was.

Donagan had brought a gift of oaten bread. It went well with the soup. Dog sat under the table, feasting on crusts. Our guest waited until we had all finished eating before he came to the purpose of his visit. "Mistress Blackthorn, Lady Flidais has asked to see you, at your convenience."

Nothing surprising about that, since Lady Flidais, wife to the prince, had been under my care since she'd first discovered she was expecting a child. The infant would not be born before autumn, and thus far the lady had remained in robust health. It was typical of her, if not of Donagan, that this had been presented as a request rather than as an order.

"I can come by this afternoon, if that suits Lady Flidais," I told him. "I have one or two folk to visit in the settlement." This had to be more than it seemed, or they'd have sent an ordinary messenger, not the prince's right-hand man. "Is Lady Flidais unwell?"

"The lady is quite well. She has a request to make of you."

There was a silence; no doubt Donagan felt the weight of our scrutiny.

"Can you tell us what it is?" I asked. "Or must this wait until I see her?"

"I've been given leave to tell you. King Ruairi and Queen Eabha will be traveling south soon for the High King's council; they and their party will be away from Dalriada until well after midsummer. The king requires Prince Oran to be at court for that period, acting in his place."

My thoughts jumped ahead to an uncomfortable conclusion. Lady Flidais and the prince both loved the peaceful familiarity of Winterfalls. I was quite certain they'd rather stay here than go to the king's court at Cahercorcan, some twenty miles north. But although Oran was not your usual kind of nobleman, he wouldn't refuse a request from his father, the king of Dalriada. And where Oran went, Flidais would be wanting to go too. The two of them were inseparable, like lovers in a grand old story. If they needed to be at court for two turnings of the moon or more, that meant . . . My guts protested, clenching themselves into a tight ball.

Grim said what I could not bring myself to say. "The lady, she'll be wanting Blackthorn at court with her. That what you're telling us?"

"Lady Flidais will explain," Donagan said. "But yes, that is what she would prefer. Lady Flidais does not place a great deal of trust in the court physicians." He fell silent, gazing into his empty soup bowl. Grim and I stayed quiet too. There was a long, long list of reasons why the prospect of going to court disturbed us; not all of them were reasons we could share with Donagan or indeed with Lady Flidais.

"Inconvenient, I know," the king's man said eventually, still not meeting my eye or Grim's. "Your young helper would need to act as healer here in your absence. And . . . well, I understand this wouldn't be much to your liking." Now he glanced across at Grim. "Lady Flidais's invitation extends to both of you. Since it's for some time, there would be private quarters provided."

"Invitation," echoed Grim. "But not the sort of invitation a person says no to, coming from a prince and all."

Donagan gave Grim a crooked smile. I had come to understand that he had a soft spot for my companion, though what exactly had passed between them during that odd time when Grim and I had stayed in the prince's household I was not quite sure. I knew Grim had been in a fight and had hurt another man quite badly. I knew Donagan had

helped get Grim out of trouble. So it was possible that Donagan realized how hard it was for Grim to sleep without me to keep him
company—not the sort of company a man and a woman keep when
they're wed, more the company of a watchful friend, the same as we'd
had when we were in that wretched place together, before I'd understood what friends were.

"True enough," Donagan went on. "Still, I imagine you will say
yes, not because you feel obliged to, but because Lady Flidais trusts
you. And because you have her welfare at heart, as we all do."

It was a pretty speech. No need to tell him that if I said yes, it
wouldn't be for that heartwarming reason, but because I was bound to it
by Conmael. Court. Closed in by stone walls, surrounded by highbred
folk quick to judge those they deemed their inferiors. I imagined myself
embroiled in petty disputes with the royal physicians, who could only
resent Lady Flidais's preference for a local wise woman over their expert
and scholarly selves. Court, where every single activity would be subject
to some sort of ridiculous protocol. Morrigan's curse! I'd found it hard
enough staying in the prince's much smaller establishment. Grim would
loathe it. And what about Conmael and our agreement? He'd ordered me
to live at Winterfalls, not at Cahercorcan. So complying with one condition of my promise would mean breaking another. A pox on it!

I rose to my feet. "Thank you for bringing the message. I have
some herbs to gather before I head over to the settlement, but please tell
Lady Flidais she can expect me around midafternoon." I thought I did
an excellent job of sounding calm and unruffled, but the look Grim
gave me suggested otherwise.

"How soon?" he asked Donagan. "When's the king leaving?"

"At next full moon. It's a long journey to Tara, made more challenging by the fact that Mathuin of Laois is stirring up trouble in that
region. And the king will want Prince Oran settled at court before he
leaves."

"Doesn't give us long," Grim said. His hands had bunched themselves into fists.

"You'll be offered all the assistance you need for the move. Horses, help with packing up, arrangements put in place so young Emer can continue to provide a healer's services to the community."

"Emer's been under my guidance for less than a year," I protested. "She may be quite apt, but she can't be asked to step into my place. It's too much to expect."

Donagan smiled. "I'm sure a solution will be found. Lady Flidais will discuss that with you. Now, I can see you are both busy, so I will make my departure."

When he was gone, we sat staring at each other over the table, stunned into silence. After a while Grim got up and started gathering the bowls.

"Court, mm?" he said.

"Seems so. But what if Conmael says no?"

"Why would he?"

"The promise. Go to Winterfalls. Quite specific."

"Then you tell Lady Flidais the truth," Grim said.

"What, that the wise woman she trusts with her unborn child is actually a felon escaped from custody? That the only reason I help folk is because I have no choice in the matter? That the person I answer to is not even human?"

Grim fetched a bucket, took a cloth, wiped down the table. He spooned the leftover soup into a bowl for Dog. "Thing is," he said, "she knows you now. She's seen what kind of person you are. She's seen what you can do. That's why she trusts you; that's why the prince trusts you. And you did get them out of a tight corner."

"You mean we did."

"Something else too," said Grim. "Escaped felons. We may be that, and if we went south we might find ourselves thrown back in that place or worse. But Lady Flidais is hardly going to take Mathuin's side. He's her father's enemy."

The thought of telling Flidais the truth—of telling anyone—made me feel sick. "Trust me," I said, "that is a really bad idea. What lies in the past should stay there. I shouldn't need to tell you that. Let word get out about who we are and where we came from, and that word can make its way back to Mathuin."

"Mm-hm." He poured water from the kettle into the bucket and started to wash the dishes. After a while he said, "Why don't you ask him, then? Conmael?"

"What, you think he's going to appear if I go out there and click my fingers? I need to know now, Grim. Before I go and see Flidais."

"Mm-hm." He looked at me, the cloth in one hand and a dripping platter in the other. "What were the words of it, the promise you made to the fellow? Was it *live at Winterfalls*, or was it only *live in Dalriada*?"

I thought about it: the night when I'd been waiting to die, the terrible trembling that had racked my body, the way time had passed so slowly, moment by painful moment, Grim's presence in the cell opposite the only thing that had stopped me from trying to kill myself. Then the strange visitor, a fey man whom I'd never clapped eyes on before, and the offer that had saved my life.

"I'm not sure I remember his exact words. One part of the promise was that I must travel north to Dalriada and not return to Laois. That I mustn't seek out Mathuin or pursue vengeance. Then he said, *You'll live at Winterfalls.* Or, *You must live at Winterfalls.* He told me that the prince lived here, and that the local folk had no healer. And that we could live in this house; he was specific about the details."

"Maybe you don't need to ask him," said Grim. "Isn't part of the promise about doing good? Looking after Lady Flidais, that's doing good. Sweet, kind lady, been through a lot. And her baby might be king someday. If it's a boy."

"Some folk might say a future king would be better served by a court physician."

"Lady Flidais doesn't want a court physician," Grim said. "She wants you."

"Why are you arguing in favor of going? You'll hate it even more than I will."

"Be sorry to leave the house. And the garden. Just when we've got it all sorted out." Grim spoke calmly, as if he did not care much one way or the other. His manner was a lie. It was a carapace of protection. He had become expert at hiding his feelings, and only rarely did he slip up. But I knew what must be in his heart. He had spent days and days fixing up the derelict cottage when we first came to Dreamer's Wood. He had labored over both house and garden until everything was perfect. Then the cottage had burned down, and he had done it all over again. I wasn't the only one who would find going away hard. "But it's not forever," Grim said. He tried for a smile but could not quite manage it. "Lads from the brewery can keep an eye on the place. Emer could drop in, make sure things are in order."

I said nothing. A lengthy stay at court would be miserable for both of us. We had a natural distrust of kings, chieftains and the like, based on our experience with Mathuin of Laois. That Oran and Flidais were exceptions did not mean a stay at Cahercorcan would be easier, since the king and queen would leave a good part of their household behind. We preferred to be on our own, Grim and I, which was why Conmael had suggested the cottage as a likely home for us. Conmael, a stranger, had somehow known that living at a distance from the settlement was the only way I was going to cope with being a wise woman again. At Cahercorcan, private quarters or not, we'd be right in the middle of things.

And there was another complication. The baker, Branoc, whom we'd helped bring to justice after he kidnapped and abused a young woman, was serving out his sentence as a bondsman to the king. He would be living in the household at Cahercorcan. I doubted Grim's capacity to be so close to the man without killing him.

"So, you going to ask him?"

"You mean Conmael?"

"Mm-hm. I know you don't much like the fellow. Me neither. But he's had his uses. And he did save your life."

I hesitated. If Grim was right, and the promise had been only to stay in Dalriada, then going to Cahercorcan would not be breaking my vow. On the other hand, if Conmael had bound me to stay at Winterfalls, then heading north would put another year onto the term of our agreement and lose me one of my four chances. That was a sacrifice I was not prepared to make.

"Brew?" asked Grim. "Ready when you get back."

"What makes you think Conmael will be there when I need him?"

"Came when I needed him, didn't he? The day you took it into your head to rush off south on your own."

There was no arguing with that. I had believed a lie that day, and I'd let anger guide me, not common sense. Although there were times—more than a few of them—when I'd have preferred my own company to Grim's, there was no doubt that he had the ability to steady me, and that was not something to be lightly set aside. "I'll look. But he won't be there."

The herbs had been an excuse to get rid of Donagan; I had no immediate need to gather anything. I went into Dreamer's Wood without my basket and knife, and without any real expectation that Conmael would make an appearance. Dog came with me, pattering along behind as I walked down the pathway toward the shadowy, fern-fringed pool that lay within the woodland. She had not yet learned the way of being a creature, and did not venture far from the path in pursuit of interesting smells or rustlings in the grass. I felt for her, though as a woman she had done Lady Flidais a great wrong. If Flidais's own experience was anything to go by, Ciar still had her human understanding while trapped in her canine body. No wonder she was sometimes ill-tempered. Who would look after her if we went to court?

I reached the strip of pebbly shore where, last autumn, I had witnessed a sudden death and a strange transformation and had not fully understood either. One thing I had learned from that experience—I would never dip so much as a single toe in the waters of Dreamer's Pool. I might frequently despise my wretched, inadequate self, but I far preferred this body to that of, say, a dragonfly or trout. In Dreamer's Pool things were apt to change, and not always in the way one would wish.

I sat down on the shore, not too close to the water. Dog retreated into the undergrowth and hunkered down to wait for me. The wood was hushed; the birds knew it was a place of deep mystery, and within the shade of these trees they did not sing. So, how to summon Conmael? When Grim had needed our fey friend, he'd cursed him, shouting. I was disinclined to attempt that approach.

I was considering the right words to use when my skin prickled, I looked up, and there he was, two paces away, tall and pale in his dark cloak, gazing down at me with an expression of mild amusement. I rose in a measured fashion, not wanting to show that he'd unnerved me.

"Conmael."

"Blackthorn. You need me?"

Could the man see right into my mind, every moment of every day? "I have a question for you, concerning our agreement."

"Ask it, then."

I explained what Donagan had told us. "While I have absolutely no desire to spend time at court, let alone that much time, under the terms of my promise to you I am bound to assist Lady Flidais if she asks for my help."

Conmael made no reply, simply fixed me with his deep blue eyes and lifted his brows as if well aware that this was only part of the truth. He was handsome after the manner of the fey, his features high-boned and haughty, his nose straight, his mouth thin-lipped but not devoid of humor. His crow's-wing hair was not loose today, but gathered at the nape by a silver cord. His long fingers wore shining rings worked with signs I could not decipher.

"I have a great deal of respect for Lady Flidais," I added. "I would help her even without the obligation under which you've placed me. But I believe our agreement included a requirement that I live here at Winterfalls. A lengthy stay at Cahercorcan would seem to break the terms."

"You wouldn't enjoy court," said Conmael. "All those folk, all those rules."

"I don't need reminding of that."

"Why go, then? Are not the king's physicians capable?"

"Conmael. It is a simple question. Would my spending two or three turnings of the moon away from Winterfalls constitute a breach of our agreement?"

Conmael gave a wintry smile. He folded his arms. "If my memory serves me well," he said, "the requirement was to stay within the borders of Dalriada and not to travel south toward Laois. To stay away from Mathuin. And, yes, to live at Winterfalls, but that part of it is not binding—provided you do not leave Dalriada, I see no reason why you should not travel about, going wherever there is a need for your services. I would expect you back at Winterfalls on the fourth full moon, if not before."

"Or . . . ?"

"Surely I need not spell it out for you, Blackthorn."

"The term of our agreement becomes longer. And my chances fewer."

He smiled again. "Walk with me awhile."

"I have patients to visit. And Lady Flidais to see."

"Indulge me a little." He cupped my elbow as if to guide me to the path; I could not help flinching, and his hand dropped away. "You are strung tight," he observed.

"I don't take kindly to folk putting their hands on me without asking first." I made myself take a steadying breath. "I'd like to say a year in that place of Mathuin's didn't leave a mark on me, but I'd be lying."

"Then let us sit here side by side, not touching, and talk awhile. Not about our agreement. Not about the past; at least, not the painful past."

I sat down again, and he settled beside me, a careful arm's length away. His cloak made a pool of liquid darkness on the stones.

"You have done well," he said quietly.

"I thought you said we wouldn't talk about the agreement."

"Ah. You came close to breaking it, when you fled south on the strength of a foolish lie. That was the day when I realized your guard dog does indeed have his uses."

"I'd appreciate it if you didn't use that name for Grim. He's a man like any other man. If Prince Oran can treat him with respect, so can you."

"You measure me by the yardstick of a human prince."

"Oran is a good man. It irks me to admit that, but it's the truth. And I have no other yardstick to use."

"When I say, *You have done well*, I mean in the matter of solving Prince Oran's puzzle. Your solution pleased me. It was bold, risky, clever, ingenious. Everything that I would have expected of you, Blackthorn."

"I would say *thank you*, but I am wary of compliments. They so often come with requests attached."

There was a silence, as if he could not think how to answer this. Then he said, "You do not believe I have asked enough of you already?" His voice was oddly constrained.

"I believe you please yourself. I think that may be typical of the fey. But what would I know?"

"More than some of your kind."

"Because I was once a wise woman? A dealer not only in potions and cures, but in spells and charms?" I glanced sideways at him, and caught an odd expression on his face. For a moment he looked . . . softer. A little less fey; a little closer to human. Something stirred in my mind, a fragment of memory, gone before I could grasp it.

"You never ceased to be a wise woman, Blackthorn," Conmael said. "You simply lost your way for a while. As for the spells and charms, they may not come as readily to your fingertips as they once did, but that is only a matter of practice. On the night when you helped Lady Flidais return to her own form, did you not hold back the rain in order to assemble those you needed here at the pool? That was no easy matter."

I grimaced. "And there was I thinking maybe you'd had something to do with that." It was pleasing to know that my use of natural magic had been effective; that the success of that night had owed nothing to fey intervention.

"I?" Conmael's elegant brows shot up. "I trust you. Possibly more than you trust yourself. Why do you imagine I offered you the lifeline I did? It was not out of a wish to play some kind of game, I assure you. I did so because I knew you could make something better of your life."

"Then why the conditions? Why not just free me and let me go my own way?"

"Hatred was devouring you. The only thing left in your heart was the will for vengeance. You wouldn't have survived a single day. Even now, the desire to go back to Laois, to see your enemy face justice, tugs at you constantly. That is your great weakness. Give in to it, and you will disappoint me."

"I cannot think why your disappointment should matter to me in the slightest, Conmael."

"You will also disappoint yourself. And that, I think, would matter."

"Rubbish. If there's one thing I want to achieve before I die, it's to see Mathuin brought to account for his crimes. Nothing else matters. Nothing."

"Your expectations of what you can achieve are unrealistic. Hence my conditions and their term. Seven years: long enough to reclaim the woman you once were. Long enough to complete a journey."

"What journey?"

"To wisdom."

"Morrigan's curse, what are you, some hoary old mentor teaching a half-grown girl? First you say you trust me; then you tell me I'm still bound to your rules. What sort of trust is that?"

"Did I not say you could travel to court?"

"But not be my own woman."

He sighed, moving his graceful pale hands in a gesture suggesting helplessness. Which was ridiculous; whatever game we were playing, Conmael held all the pieces. "You will always be that," he said.

"Bollocks, Conmael. You saw me in Mathuin's lockup. I'd lost any vestige of the woman I was before. That place hammered me flat. It wrung out every drop of kindness. It turned me into a . . ." Why was I telling him this? "Never mind. I will go to court, I will keep to your wretched rules. I wish you'd explain what it's all about. I wish you'd explain why my small human life is of sufficient interest to you that you believe you should take control of it."

"The reason is of no importance." Conmael was not smiling now. "If it were, you would remember."

"Remember what?"

He rose to his feet, elegant as always, and reached out a hand to help me up. I did not take it.

"Remember what, Conmael?"

"As I said, it is of no importance. And now you must be getting on. Did you not say you had folk to visit, places to go? Make sure you are back in Winterfalls by the fourth full moon. And be mindful of your promise." He did not wait for me to say good-bye, but in characteristic fashion faded and vanished before my eyes. Wretched fey! There was no making sense of them. The only thing certain about this day was that I'd best hurry if I wanted to partake of Grim's brew before I headed off to the settlement. As for the looming stay at court, Grim and I would have to grit our teeth, breathe deeply and somehow get through it.

2

GRIM

Thought it would try us hard, stone walls shutting us in, folk everywhere, no room to breathe. Turns out I was right, more or less. King and queen have taken a whole bunch of folk south with them, guards, councilors, grooms, the queen's ladies and so on. Even so, the place is packed. As for stone walls, these ones would keep out the strongest army in all Erin. They're high and thick, with walkways along the top and guard posts everywhere. On the north side, a sheer cliff to the sea. Good thing, that; sort of an escape. Not talking about climbing down there on a rope—a man would need to be a fool or set on killing himself to try that. Been both in the past, but death's not on my mind now. Blackthorn needs me. Not going anywhere without her.

Thing is, from up there a man can get a grand sea view. The guards on watch can't miss boats coming in. The men-at-arms from Winterfalls, the ones who've come with Prince Oran, are doing guard duty with the rest, and they know me. So I can go up there anytime I want some peace and quiet. I like the spot. Pretty, with the sun on the water. Like a pathway to the end of the world.

When I need to come down and make myself useful I keep that

picture in my head, the sea, the sky, birds flying over. Helps me breathe. Helps when there are too many folk around, filling up my head with their noise. So yes, an escape.

Donagan makes things easier. Never thought I'd be grateful to that fellow, but he's kinder than he seems. Clever too. Sorted things out for me pretty well at Winterfalls when I got in trouble, and keeps an eye on me here too, though he must have better things to do. Donagan made sure Blackthorn and me had our own quarters. And they're roomy, though not the same as home, of course. We're tucked away in a tower, and she's got a stillroom down below, shared with one of the court healers, fellow called Caillín. We've left Dog back at Winterfalls, at the prince's house. Lady Flidais left one of her maids, Mhairi, behind. She's looking after Dog. Not sure how that'll work out.

Wasn't looking forward to staying at court. But it's not so bad. Word is, the healer that went off south with the royal party is a difficult sort. Grumpy. Caillín's all right. No pricklier than Blackthorn. She grumbles, but she'll cope. And me? Donagan said if I wanted work—guard duty, he meant—I just had to say the word. I won't, though. Want to be free for Blackthorn if she needs me.

The fellows who've come from Winterfalls treat me like I'm one of them. Always a welcome in the guard room or up on the wall, and nobody asks why I'm there. Nobody mentions that time I half killed Seanan for saying bad things about Blackthorn. Funny, that. Instead of getting me kicked out of the prince's house, that earned me respect.

Lot of rules in this place; who eats when and where, who has to step back to let who pass, who's allowed to go into some parts of the fortress and so on. Apart from that it's like the prince's place at Winterfalls, only bigger. Too full and too noisy. Food's good.

Blackthorn's soon busy. Caillín should be happy. She's doing half his job for him. Lady Flidais doesn't need her much, just wants to know she's close by, Blackthorn says. And me—I keep an eye on Blackthorn, make sure she's safe, make sure she remembers to eat. I keep our quarters clean and tidy. And work comes my way without being asked for. When something needs doing, I do it. This and that. Unblock a clogged drain, fix a few tiles back in place, load a cart, help muck out a stable. May as well be useful—why not?

One good thing. The prince must have known I couldn't be in the same place as that godforsaken bastard Branoc without doing him violence. He's sent the wretch away somewhere. Not coming back until we've gone home to Winterfalls. Good choice. Otherwise Prince Oran would have had a murder to explain to his father when the king got back. I'll never forget seeing that girl chained up. Branoc didn't even understand that what he'd done to her was wrong. I've seen a lot of bad things in my time. Done some too, and been sorry for it. But a man like that never comes good. Doesn't have it in him.

Feel like I'm waiting for something, don't know what. After all that's happened to us, to Blackthorn and me, seems like our path's never going to be simple and straight. Be good if it was—the two of us staying in our cottage, getting on with our work and minding our own business. Peaceful, that'd be. Don't think it's going to happen, somehow.

I'm up on the wall one day, talking to a few of the lads, when some riders come into view—we're on the landward side, looking roughly west.

"Nobody expected. At least, nobody I've been told about," says Domnall, narrowing his eyes as he looks down. He was chief guard at Cloud Hill, where Lady Flidais came from to marry the prince. Led her escort. Good man. "Eoin, go down and find Lochlan, will you? Tell him there are folk coming, and ask someone to alert the steward. Is that a lady riding in front there?"

"Escort's armed to the teeth," I say as Eoin heads off down the steps. Can't tell if the rider in the lead is a lady or not; big cloak covering most of her. Or him. If it's a lady, she's tall. Blue tunics on the men-at-arms, some kind of emblem on them, too far away to see what. They're hung about with swords and clubs and knives and bows like they've been expecting trouble. "Thought the roads were pretty safe in these parts."

"They are," says Domnall. "Could be they've come from farther afield. Beyond the border." Meaning the border with Tirconnell, which has its own king and maybe isn't as peaceful as Dalriada.

The riders get closer. After a bit, some of the king's guards appear down below, heading out to meet them. They're armed too, taking no chances. Though folk don't attack a place like this with a force of nine or ten, and that's all this lady's got. Yes, it is a lady; she's pushed back her hood and made that plain. Sitting straight in the saddle, head held high, got a proud look about her. Youngish. Hair the color of ripe corn, all done up in plaits.

Both parties halt. The lady says something. Waves her hands around a bit as if she's upset. The fellow heading the king's guards answers, and after a bit the guards escort the visitors in. "Must be a friend," I say. A lady who's ridden to Cahercorcan with her own men-at-arms isn't here to see Blackthorn or me. But I get a funny feeling all the same. I'm thinking this could be the start of whatever it is I've been waiting for.

Not sure why I go down to the courtyard then. But I do. So I'm there when the lady's party rides up to the steps. Someone's told the prince he's got visitors, and he's all ready to welcome them. The lady gets down from her mount, not looking as stiff as you'd expect after a long ride. Groom takes hold of the bridle. Prince Oran walks forward, but before he gets a word out the lady's thrown herself at his feet, clutching onto his leg and babbling like she's crazy. I move forward quick, thinking she might be up to no good. Prince's guards get there before me, grab the lady's arms, lift her up, pull her away. Prince looks a bit white, as well he might. The lady's men-at-arms draw their weapons. It's not looking good.

"I need your help!" The lady's sobbing. "Oh, please, please listen! I have nobody else to turn to!" She goes on like this for a bit. Face all wet with tears, cheeks flushed red, hair tumbling down. The prince tells his guards to let her go, and they do.

"Please compose yourself," says Prince Oran. "Whatever has happened, I give you my promise that you will be safe here. Come, this is best discussed in private. First you need rest and refreshment."

He gives some orders, the grooms lead the horses away, the guards sheathe their blades and one or two waiting women, the ones that haven't gone south with the queen, help the lady indoors. She's still crying and carrying on, but she's quietened down a bit. I'm wondering what it's all about. But I've got no real business following them, so I go off to talk to Blackthorn instead.

Turns out this visitor doesn't want to wait for rest and refreshment before she tells the prince her story. Blackthorn and me are sitting in the stillroom enjoying a brew when there's a knock at the door and there's Deirdre, Lady Flidais's handmaid. Looks a bit flustered.

"Oh, Mistress Blackthorn, you're here, thank goodness," she says. "The prince and Lady Flidais want you to come to the small council chamber—I'm to take you there. Grim too."

"Now?" says Blackthorn, not getting up. "Why?"

"There's a lady here with a story to tell, a strange one, and the prince thinks you should hear it."

Blackthorn looks at me; I look at her. Feels too soon for another adventure. Hardly had time to get over the last one. But we're at court, and though Oran's the king's son and Flidais is his wife, they're our friends. Anyway, you don't say no to a prince.

Not long after, we're in the small council chamber, so-called. There's a table long enough for twelve, and another table with writing things, and two chests with lamps on. But there's only four people here, apart from me and Blackthorn and Deirdre: the prince, Lady Flidais, Donagan and the visitor, who's wiped her face and tidied herself up. Looks calmer now. Prince Oran tells us to sit down. There's a jug of ale and a platter of honey cakes on the table. Donagan pours ale for us. Deirdre asks if she should leave, and Flidais tells her no, she should sit down with the rest of us. Donagan walks over and shuts the door. Couple of the fellows are standing guard out in the hall.

"Mistress Blackthorn, Grim," says the prince, "this is Lady Geiléis of Bann. We believe you may have some insights into the situation she is facing. That's why we've asked you to join us. Lady Geiléis, please tell your tale in full, from the beginning. Take your time. I would have waited until tomorrow, since you've had such a long ride to reach us. But I understand your need to have this heard straightaway." He looks over at us. "We've already been told part of the story. We thought it best to call you in before Lady Geiléis went further, since we believed we would not find answers for her on our own."

I catch Blackthorn's eye. We're thinking the same thing. I know it. This is going to end up with her getting asked for help. And she'll have a problem.

Lady Geiléis's face is still puffed up from crying. She's got a little handkerchief crumpled in her hand. "My lands are bordered to one side by the river Bann," she says. "They take their name from that body of water. I have grazing fields, a tract of forest, my house and outbuildings, a scattering of farms and small hamlets whose folk look to me for leadership. I inherited my property from my father, and I have never wed. Across the Bann lies Tirconnell, territory of the northern Uí Néill. My holding is in Dalriada. A bridge spans the river some miles farther north. It is too far away for my folk to use. But at a certain point, where the Bann runs along my border, there is a ford, passable at all times save in severe flood. It lies in a wooded area, the trees growing densely on either side of the river. In the middle is an island, and on that island stands a tower."

"The Tower of Thorns," murmurs Blackthorn.

"You know of it?" Lady Geiléis sounds surprised.

"I remember the name from somewhere," says Blackthorn. "It may be mentioned in an old tale, in connection with the river Bann. I do recall some mention of the ford and the tower together."

"The Tower of Thorns," says Lady Flidais. "That does indeed sound like something from a tale of magic and wonder. How did the place get its name, Lady Geiléis?"

"There are thornbushes growing on the island; it is a forbidding place. The tower is tall and lonely. For many long years, it has stood empty."

"And now?"

"It is empty no longer. Something has taken up residence there. A . . . a presence. Since its arrival a kind of curse has fallen over the district. I cannot find any way to break it. I am at my wits' end."

Blackthorn's bursting to ask more questions, plain to see that. But she keeps quiet.

"My home is isolated," the lady goes on. "The folk who live within my borders are spread thin. We have neither wise woman nor druid. There is a monastery—St. Olcan's—but this is hardly a matter for monkish intervention. The brethren know of the difficulty. Prayers have been offered up in their chapel for the banishment of evil spirits, but to no avail."

Monks. I'm liking this less all the time. I swallow down bile, make myself take slow breaths.

"The tower is not easily accessible," says the lady. "Not only is it in midstream, but there are the thornbushes, growing densely all around the base. The place was built so long ago that nobody can remember who set it there."

"If the Tower of Thorns stands all alone, out of folk's way," says Prince Oran, "why does this represent such a threat, Lady Geiléis?"

"The island on which the tower is situated lies close to the ford. That ford is the only safe river crossing on my land, and indeed the only crossing of any kind for long miles up- or downstream. The banks are heavily forested; to approach the ford, one must walk, or ride, or drive stock along quite narrow ways through those woods. Since the arrival of this . . . creature . . . those ways are no longer safe."

We're all caught by the story now, whether we want to be or not. A monster in a tower. It's like one of those old wonder tales Blackthorn's so good at telling. Only this one's true. Has to be. Why would the lady come all this way and then lie to us?

"The creature does not come out; it does not attack. By day, it makes noises—howling, wailing, crying—from the top of the tower. All day. Every day. When darkness falls it becomes quiet. But . . . it is not only the sound, terrible as that is. The monster has brought with it a curse. A strangeness has fallen over my lands in the summertime. Folk set out on straightforward errands, and some hours later find themselves in unknown parts of the wood, confused and exhausted. Stock wander into deep water and drown. Cattle drop dead calves. Hens will not lay. This continues right through the summer, just when crops should be growing and stock fattening. By the time it stops, when the season changes, the damage is done. I have never encountered anything like it. My folk turn to me for answers, but I have none for them."

"It stops when the season changes?" says Blackthorn. "So this thing has been there for more than one summer?"

"This is the second. When it fell quiet last autumn I believed it gone. But alas, it returned with the first summer days."

Odd that she's waited this long to ask for help. Not for me to say, though.

"The monastery you mentioned earlier," Blackthorn says. "Where is that in relation to the tower?"

"My home lies between the monastery and the tower. St. Olcan's is a significant foundation; the brethren there are widely known and respected for their tradition of scholarship. The monks have been helpful, to the extent they can be. But I do not believe this is a demon to be driven out by Christian prayers. It has been suggested to me—this will sound odd—that the creature may be a manifestation of the Otherworld. Something old and dark, whose influence cannot be broken by ordinary means. My folk are frightened, Mistress Blackthorn. Burdened; weighed down. I do not know how to help them."

"Does this curse, if that is what it is, lie over the monastery too?" asks Blackthorn. "Can the brothers travel these paths unaffected? And what about their stock, house cows and the like?"

"Their grazing field lies at some distance from the ford, and thus far their cows have been spared. As for the fell magic that disturbs the minds of men and animals and causes them to stray from the paths, the monks too are susceptible to it if they wander into the area close to the tower. To travel west with any degree of safety, one must go by circuitous ways. So this is difficult for St. Olcan's too. They are accustomed to accommodating traveling scholars, and to making visits to other monastic houses. It is fortunate that the brethren keep pigeons for the purpose of sending and receiving messages; otherwise they would be quite isolated."

"What about the owner of the land on the Tirconnell side of the river?" Donagan asks. "Has he taken any action to drive this thing out?"

"A chieftain of the Uí Néill oversees that district. I sought help from him some time ago, and my concerns were brushed aside as a madwoman's ravings. His stronghold is located at a significant distance from the river, and his folk generally travel by the main road and the bridge, farther north. As far as he was concerned, not only was I out of my mind, but it was a Dalriadan problem and not his responsibility."

"Two summers, you say. How did this thing come to the tower?"

"Nobody saw it arrive, Mistress Blackthorn. One day the tower was empty; the next the woods were full of screaming. Soon after, the misfortunes began."

"It sounds like something from an old tale," says Prince Oran. "And that makes me wonder if there are precedents. Mistress Blackthorn thought she remembered the Tower of Thorns from a story. Have you looked in the lore for answers, Lady Geiléis?"

For a bit, the lady doesn't say anything. My guess is, she doesn't want to tell us this part, whatever it is. "I have done some investigation, yes," she says. "There are no tales about the Tower of Thorns. Only snippets, fragments. Rumors about the woods by the Bann. They suggest that something similar may have happened before, long ago. The same creature; the same enchantment or curse. The same misfortune. Endured not only once, but several times over by my forebears."

We're all staring at her. My guess is, I'm not the only one wondering if she really is a bit wrong in the head.

Blackthorn asks a good question. "Do these snippets include anything about what folk did the last time it happened, or the time before? The creature must have gone away, then returned for some reason. That's if it really is the same one—it would have to be rather long-lived, if it's been around since the time of your forebears. How was it driven out?"

"Ah." Lady Geiléis looks down at her hands. "There are no clear answers on that point. It does seem that if anything is to be done, it must be done on Midsummer Eve. On that day, the thorns that bar entry to the tower are said to yield somewhat; a brave soul armed with a sharp ax might force a way in."

Really is like one of those old tales, a good one. Or would be good if it was only a story, not real. *Can* it be real? "Tried to get through, have you?" I say. Seems fair enough to ask, seeing as she's said this thing was there last summer too.

"I set foot on the island, last Midsummer Eve," the lady says. "I attempted to slash a way through the thorns, though I did not know what might lie within the tower. The rumors, such as they are, tell us nothing about what a quester might encounter there, or what that person should do on encountering the creature. I knew only that I must bring an end to the terror and confusion brought by the tower's strange tenant. But I fell short of achieving that. For a certain distance the thorns did indeed give way to my blade. But before I had gone far, the thing in the tower began an eldritch moaning, perhaps a kind of singing, and the branches began to snap back around me. Had I not retreated speedily I would have been trapped within the thicket of thorns; I would have perished there like a fly caught in a spider's web. I had brought two guards with me, but neither could make any impact on the fearsome barrier; they tried ax, hatchet and knife to no avail. Mine was the only blade that could cut the stems. And as I said, that success was short-lived."

There's a silence; then Blackthorn says, "Forgive me, Lady Geiléis, but attempting such a feat on your own seems . . ." *Crazy.* That's the word she wants. But she says, "It seems misguided. Why didn't you send in your men-at-arms? What were you planning to do, fight the creature to the death on your own?"

I'm thinking the same thing. Fact is, though Lady Geiléis is tall for a woman, and well built, she's hardly a warrior. Monster would likely snap her in half before she got two steps inside the tower.

"I thought . . ." The lady's struggling for words now. "I believed that once I saw the thing face-to-face I would know what to do. Kill it, yes, I was prepared to do that. Or drive it out."

"All by yourself," says Blackthorn.

Lady Geiléis bows her head. "I was desperate, Mistress Blackthorn. I would do the same thing again, if only I could make a way into the tower. To silence that voice, to rid my lands of the curse, I would do almost anything."

"Mistress Blackthorn's right," says Donagan. "It would make more sense to send in a warrior. Or several."

"I had two armed men with me when I attempted to hack a way through; I told you. Neither of them made any progress, and both were hurt trying to save me from the thorns. Perhaps that should tell us something. I wish I knew what."

"That it's a job for a woman?" suggests Blackthorn.

Lady Geiléis gives her a look. "It is suggested in the old fragments of story that only a woman can prevail against this creature. It seems I am not that woman."

Not liking the sound of this at all. Wish the prince would tell the lady to fix her own problems and leave the rest of us out of it. Wish Blackthorn hadn't said what she's just said. I can see where this is going, plain as plain. So although I don't want to, I speak up again. "This sort of thing's trouble," I say. "And not the kind of trouble you can fix by running at it with a weapon in your hand."

"I'm in complete agreement with that," says Blackthorn. "A body doesn't meddle lightly with such matters. Even if you're right about Midsummer Eve, Lady Geiléis, marching in to confront this creature—to destroy it—could be disastrous, whether it's one woman doing it or a whole troop of guards. Only a fool uses human means to combat the uncanny.

Besides, the thing may not be evil, only . . . misguided. Frightened, perhaps."

"You believe the tenant of the tower is fey."

"If it were anything else," Blackthorn says, "you'd have solved your problem long ago, one way or another. That's if your account of matters is full and accurate."

"Why would I lie to you, Mistress Blackthorn?"

"I didn't say you were lying. But the story feels incomplete. How does this thing survive up in the tower on its own? What does it eat, birds plucked from the sky in midflight? Spiders and moths?"

"Someone—*something*—must supply its needs. What, I cannot say."

For a bit it's quiet. I can see Blackthorn thinking hard, choosing the right words, the safest words.

"You could call in a druid," she says. "If there are none in your district, I think Prince Oran could find someone for you."

"To do what?" asks Lady Geiléis.

"To cleanse and bless the land. To ask for the goodwill of whatever spirits dwell in that place."

"Could not you fulfill that same task, Mistress Blackthorn?"

That's come sooner than I thought it would. The lady hasn't quite asked for Blackthorn's help. But she's come close; too close for comfort.

"A wise woman could do it, yes," says Blackthorn. "But not this wise woman. I have work here. I can't travel." She waits a bit, then says, "When I suggest a ritual of that kind, Lady Geiléis, it doesn't mean I'm certain it would achieve the end you desire. The fey don't see the world in the same way as you or I might. To deal with them is to walk a perilous path, full of twists and turns, byways and dead ends. The fey have little comprehension of human feelings: love, friendship, loyalty, selflessness. That makes it hard for their kind and our kind to work in true cooperation. But the fey understand nature in ways humankind cannot; every part of their being is attuned to it. To bless the woods that lie under the curse, to cleanse the isle where the tower stands . . . I do not believe the ancient inhabitants of Bann would look unkindly on such a ritual." She takes a breath, then says, "It is for that reason that I do not suggest something that might seem obvious: the use of fire."

Things go quiet again for a bit; then Prince Oran says, "Astonishing." Could be talking about what Blackthorn just said. Could mean the whole thing. *Unbelievable* would be another word.

"You're very wise, Blackthorn," says Lady Flidais with a smile. "Lady Geiléis, I understand why you might want Mistress Blackthorn to do this for you in person. But we need her here at Cahercorcan. Or, to be more precise, I do. She's acting as my personal healer until our child is born. And after that, she has work at Winterfalls. An entire community depends on her skill."

"If you believe it might help, Lady Geiléis," says the prince, "I could certainly summon a druid to assist you. But it would take some time; we'd need to send a message south. I believe Master Oisín would oblige, provided we can find him. I could not promise he would be at Bann by midsummer."

Lady Geiléis bows her head. "I see," she says. Her voice is wobbly, like she's holding back tears. I start to feel sorry for her, though I don't want to. She's trouble for us, for Blackthorn and me. I knew it as soon as I clapped eyes on her.

"It is so hard, I don't know if I can go on," she whispers. "And yet I must."

Donagan's been pretty quiet. He gets up now, pours more ale for everyone. Deirdre, who's been even quieter, hands around the platter of cakes. But nobody's eating.

"Why not send for Master Oisín anyway?" Donagan says. "The wait would give Lady Geiléis the opportunity for a well-needed rest—you and your escort could be easily accommodated here, my lady—and in the meantime we could apply our minds to other solutions for you. As Grim pointed out, this isn't a problem that can be solved by a show of force."

"Even if it were," says the prince, "I would be reluctant to send men-at-arms to Bann for the purpose. That kind of action is too easily misunderstood by neighboring chieftains, and Lady Geiléis's land lies right on the border with Tirconnell. Wars have broken out over less."

"It is a frail hope," says Lady Geiléis. "To wait for this druid, while time passes and midsummer draws closer . . . and then, perhaps, to bring him west only to find his blessing no more effective than Father Tomas's well-intentioned prayers . . ."

"Sometimes," says Blackthorn, "answers take time to find. A long time. Druids know their lore; they spend years and years committing it to memory. Somewhere in that body of learning, there may lie an answer to your difficulty. Meanwhile, consider what we already know. This being has taken up residence in the tower. It is disturbed, distressed, perhaps angry. Since it came, some kind of spell has fallen over the land all around. The question I would be asking, if I were you, the key to the whole dilemma, is *why*?"

3

GEILÉIS

Tonight, as on every night, dusk would be heralded with a story. No matter that she was miles from home. She would tell the tale anyway, as she had over and over since she had first found herself trapped in the endless nightmare. She would tell it before her mirror, here in the guest quarters at Cahercorcan, with the door closed against the intrusions of Prince Oran's serving folk. She would tell it in a whisper. Even if she had stood on the high walkway of the king's stronghold and shouted at the top of her voice, he surely could not have heard her. He was too far away; beyond reach. But she would remain faithful. She would keep her promise. So, the nightly ritual.

Onchú stood watch outside her door. He would ensure she was undisturbed. She stood quite still in the center of the chamber. By the light of flickering candles she whispered the story: the old, old story. Each time it was a little different, for she twisted and turned it according to her mood. But no matter what the manner of telling, the tale was cruel as a knife; bitter as gall.

Long ago and far away, across valleys and over mountains, there lived a noble couple. Theirs was a prosperous holding, with many farms and settlements. There was a wide tract of woodland in which many creatures roamed. There was a broad river brimful with fish. On all sides there were peaceable neighbors.

The couple had but one child: a daughter. When she was a babe, her doting parents had used a pet name for her: Lily. As she'd grown older, the name had stuck. At sixteen, Lily was tall and straight, with long hair the color of ripe corn and wide eyes as blue as the summer sky. Folk thought her beautiful. She was a quiet girl, sweet and biddable, and all in that household loved her.

Now, in those days, the fey walked the land of Erin more openly than they do now. In the forest close by her father's holdings, Lily would sometimes glimpse a cloaked woman moving between the great oaks, or a tall man clad all in green, bending to converse with his own reflection in the water of a woodland pond. She was not sure what it was about such folk that told her they were fey; she simply knew, and knew instantly. Lily was cautious; she had heard tales of men and women wandering into mushroom circles, or venturing into caves at twilight, or taking other risks that led them into a world from which there was no returning. Her mother had warned her that the fey were tricky, dangerous, not to be trusted, and in general Lily did her best to avoid them.

But after her sixteenth birthday, a restless spirit grew in Lily. No longer content with embroidery or spinning or playing with her mother's lapdogs, she snatched the chance, when she was supposed to be resting in her bedchamber, to slip out the window, climb down by means of a conveniently placed oak tree, and head off into the forest alone. This was quite against the rules—her handmaid and a guard were supposed to accompany her anytime she ventured out. That was only common sense. Had her parents known of Lily's solitary expeditions, they would have been deeply disturbed.

A river flowed through these woods. In the river was an island, a lovely place all covered with wildflowers, and on the island stood a tower. That tower drew Lily as a selkie's song draws a lonely fisherman. It fascinated her; it had done since she was a small child and had been told by her parents that the place was dangerous and that she was never to go there. It had not been explained what the danger was, but as Lily grew older she heard folk talk about rotting wood and crumbling stones, sudden steep drops and hidden wells. She heard hints about magic. And she noticed that nobody, nobody at all, ever seemed to set foot on the island. No wonder birds thronged there, and insects on the blossoms. For them, it was paradise.

Nobody knew who had built the tower; nobody knew how long it had been there. The ford that lay quite close to the island saw daily traffic of many kinds: horsemen, oxcarts, herds of goats, folk on foot with bundles held over their heads. A person could not reach the island from the ford without wading into quite deep water; to do so without being seen was well-nigh impossible. Should a goose girl or swineherd or carter spot Lily attempting it, word would soon get to her father, and her father would make sure that was the last time she visited the tower.

But Lily, that good, obedient girl, had found another way across. It was the day of Beltane when she made her discovery. Folk were sleeping off the effects of a night of revelry, and nobody was about. The road was quiet, the ford deserted. The fair isle called to her, with its greensward and its flowering bushes and its tower rising to the sky in an elegant sweep of moss-softened stone. But the river was flowing high. Trying to wade across would be a foolish risk. Besides, how would she explain her wet clothing when she got home? Maybe there were stones to balance on, or a fallen tree, or some other way to get over. Lily went along the riverbank, picking a path through the dense growth of shade-loving plants. Once, she slipped, and in clutching at the nearest stem to stop herself from falling in, she bloodied her palm on thorns. Muttering an oath, she forced a way through to find herself on a tiny strip of level shore, covered in neat round pebbles, all shades of brown and gray and green. They were remarkably uniform in shape.

Lily found a handkerchief in her pouch and used it to bind up her bleeding hand. Already, her mind was fashioning explanations. She knew that just a season ago, she would not have dreamed of deceiving her parents thus. But something had got into her; something had changed her. Perhaps it was all part of growing up.

She used her teeth to tighten the knot in the makeshift bandage. It was as she did so that she spotted the boat. Had it been there a moment before? She could not say, but now it bobbed in the shallows as if waiting for Lily to climb aboard. The little craft was shaped like half of a walnut shell, and was just big enough for one young woman to sit in and row herself to the island, had there been oars. Oh, but she wanted to go across. She wanted so much to climb that tower, climb to the very top where she could look out over the dark expanse of the forest and the long, silver winding of the river, and catch a glimpse of the mysterious lands that lay beyond. Although she knew it was foolish, she felt she might give almost anything to do that.

Perhaps there was a stick she could use as a pole, or a piece of bark for a paddle . . . She cast around for something useful.

"What will you give me if I take you over?" spoke up a wee little voice. And there on the sward was a wee little man not much higher than Lily's knee, and clad all in green like the folk in the old tales. The diminutive fellow doffed his hat and gave Lily a bow. "You want to use the ferry, you pay the ferryman."

"Ferry?" echoed Lily. "It's rather small, isn't it?"

"I think I can count up to one," said the little man, "and one of you is what I see. Room for you, room for me. What will you pay?"

Now, Lily did not carry silver pieces or coppers or anything of the like when she went walking in the forest; why would she? Besides, she'd been taught not to trust the fey, and though all the fey folk she'd seen before had been tall and stately, who was to say they did not come in all shapes and sizes? Either way, she knew she should be careful. "What is the usual fee?" she asked, thinking of an old and disturbing story in which an unwary passenger found himself obliged to act as ferryman until he could convince someone to take his place. No matter how badly she wanted to explore the tower, she must not fall victim to a trick of that kind.

"A coin, a kiss, a tale, a promise. A bag of magic beans, a feather from a singing bird, a hair from your head."

A hair. That should be simple enough. She was already plucking it when doubt came over her. "Why would you want a hair?"

"Pretty," said the wee man. "Like gold."

"And that really is all you want? Will one hair get me over to the island and back again?"

"It will, and more besides."

She plucked the hair, coiled it into the shape of a ring, and gave it to the ferryman, who did not put it on his finger, but slipped it into the leather pouch at his belt. Yes, Lily was foolish. But she was sixteen years old, and the rising, capricious tides of Beltane were flooding through her body and spirit. Such things happen.

She stepped into the little boat, and the ferryman got in after her, with a long pole in his hand, and took her on a bobbing, uneven course out onto the river. The ferry was not the most comfortable of boats, but the wee fellow knew what he was about. In next to no time they reached the island, and Lily disembarked onto another pebbly shore.

"You will wait for me, won't you?" she asked. "I want to have a look at the tower. Climb up, if I can."

"When you want me, do this." The wee man stuck his fingers in his mouth and delivered a piercing whistle.

"When I want you, I'll call 'Ferryman!'" Lily said. "I have never learned to whistle like that."

"Useful skill," observed the ferryman. "Off you go, then; take a look around. You never know what you might find in a spot like that." He jerked his head toward the tower, but did not quite look at it.

So, at last she was here. Such a lovely place, all grown over with a profusion of flowering plants, here and there a small tree—a hawthorn, an elder—and the air filled with a wonderful sweet scent. Patches of soft grass seemed to invite a traveler to lie down and dream awhile; flat stones provided perfect spots to sit and listen to the singing of birds, the rippling of the river and the sighing of the wind in the trees. But there was the tower, standing at the highest point, and Lily set her steps toward it, not letting herself linger. Who knew how soon her small ferryman might grow tired of waiting and head off on his own business?

The base of the tower was broad; it took some time to walk right around it. Mosses clothed the pale stones in a soft garment; flowers grew everywhere, a bright carpet. The voices of birds made a high music. And ah! here was the door at last, and it stood open. Within, all was shadow.

Lily drew a deep breath and squared her shoulders. She was not afraid; not really. But her heart was beating like a drum, and her palms were suddenly clammy. It was so dark in there. She took a step inside, and another step. There was a spiral stair against the tower wall, stretching up, ladder-steep, into the shadows.

Very well. She tucked her hem into her belt and up she went, treading with care. Spiders had colonized the tower's interior; their webs were everywhere, catching at her hair, tickling her fingers, covering her skirt with filmy white strands. Things scuttled and scurried and whisked out of sight. The darkness was not complete; had it been so, she would indeed have been risking her life on this stair. From somewhere above, a faint light filtered down. There must be a window, an opening up there, Lily thought. She might be able to stand at the top looking out, as she had dreamed.

The stair came to an end, and she stepped forward into a round chamber. There was indeed a window, but its shutters were drawn together; between them a narrow gap admitted a thin bar of light, which fell across the wooden floor. It was cold in the chamber; the chill sent a shiver through Lily, and she hugged her shawl around her. The empty room seemed somehow a disappointment, though she was not sure what else she had expected. Still, there were those shutters, and the view outside. But she hesitated; she did not rush across to throw them open. Something felt wrong here; what was it that set her on edge? Lily stood quiet a moment or two, and in the quiet she heard *something. A sound so faint that it would have been easy to miss. A sound softer than the creak of the floor under her feet, softer than the rustling of mice in the wall, softer than the distant murmur of the river, down below the shuttered window. The sound of breathing.*

Almost, she turned and fled back down the precipitous stair. But no; this was an adventure, like something from an old tale. She must be brave.

She walked steadily to the window, lifted her hands to the shutters and flung them open. In the chamber behind her, nothing stirred. It seemed, now, that the breathing had ceased. She turned.

There was a man in the tower room. He lay sprawled on the floor, clad in little more than a torn linen shirt and leggings. His face was ghost white in the light from the window; his hair was as dark and glossy as a crow's wing. His eyes were closed. He might have been dead, or merely asleep. He was the most beautiful young man Lily had seen in her whole life. All sixteen years of it.

Her heart hammered. What should she do? Slip away without a sound? Touch him, try to move him? Scream for the ferryman? Run back home, admit that she had broken the rules, fetch help?

Be calm, she told herself. What was it that drew you here, but this? She went over to the young man, crouched down and bent close, so close that surely, if he breathed, she would feel it against her cheek. Let him not be dead, she prayed. Please, let him live.

And there it was, slow and steady; the soft whisper of his breath against her skin. Her heart leaped. In that moment, her whole world changed.

Darkness had fallen; it was night.

"Tomorrow," Geiléis whispered. "I will tell more tomorrow." Oh, if only the story could end there, in that moment of wonder. If only it could end with youth and innocence and hope. "Sleep now, until the morning."

4

BLACKTHORN

Grim and I were in our chamber preparing for bed. "No sign of Lady Geiléis at supper," I said. "That was something of a relief."

"Long ride from Bann," said Grim. "Four or five days, the fellows were saying. She must be tired out. And upset. Hoped for more from the prince. Made that plain enough."

Geiléis's arrival had set me on edge. Perhaps that feeling was a warning. Perhaps it was only the anticipation of change. I knew Grim felt the same, and I had learned that his judgment was reliable. His appearance and manner might once have earned him the name Bonehead, but beneath the blockish exterior and straightforward manner was a person of sharp instincts and natural wisdom. It had taken me a long time to see that fully.

"The prince can do whatever he wants for her," I said. "As long as nobody asks me to help. Going to Bann and dealing with this monster is not the way I planned to spend the summer."

"The prince won't want you heading off. Not with Lady Flidais and the child and all." Grim's was the voice of common sense. "He'll wait for the druid. No need to worry."

He was wrong, and he knew it as well as I did. A magical puzzle to be worked out; a task only a woman could perform. An entire district depending on the problem being solved by midsummer. Lady Geiléis clearly desperate for a solution . . . Surely it was only a matter of time before she asked me directly to help her and put me in an impossible situation. Oddly enough, part of me wanted to set things right for her. The story of the screaming monster in the tower intrigued me. But I couldn't go. Getting involved in a matter right on the border would be asking for trouble. I had promised Conmael I would stay in Dalriada. Take one step into Tirconnell and I'd be bound to my fey mentor for an extra year. A river, an island . . . It would be all too easy to take that step without even realizing I'd done it.

Besides, if this was an uncanny curse, a doom that might have been in place, on and off, for years, it would not be easily lifted. It could not be up to me, or indeed to any ordinary person, to do so. I knew in my bones that the cleansing ritual, though it might help, would not be the complete answer. Someone needed to find out what had brought that being to the tower.

"You could ask Conmael," Grim said.

"You reading my thoughts now?"

He smiled. "Nah. Just having the same ones. What do you think?"

"Conmael's not here."

"Can't he pop up anywhere he wants? By magic? Remember when we were on the road. Him and his friends did that when it suited them."

"When it suited *them*. Not us."

"Seems to me," Grim said, "that fellow's on your side, even if he's been hard on you. Wants you to get on, you know? Don't much care for him, myself, but he's been a help. You can't say otherwise."

"I don't want to ask him. And I don't want to go to Bann. I want to stick to his wretched rules and get the seven years over." *And then I'll go back to Laois and make Mathuin pay.*

"Mm-hm."

"I'll stay out of Geiléis's way. I'll keep as busy as I can. You can help by warning me if you see her coming, so I can avoid her. With luck

Master Oisín will get here soon, and she'll be off home again before she has a chance to ask me outright for help."

"Mm-hm."

"Stop saying that! It sounds as if you're saying yes and meaning no."

"Night, then. Sleep well."

"Hah!" Neither of us ever slept well. Our nights were a tangle of bad dreams, the ghosts of the past come back to torment us. "You too, Grim."

I was not best pleased next morning when, just as I was at the most difficult stage of preparing a salve, there was a polite tap at the still-room door. I swallowed the snarling *Go away* that sprang to my lips. That kind of knock might mean Flidais or one of her attendants, Deirdre or Nuala. "Who is it?" I called.

The door opened and there was the Lady of Bann, clad in a gown of russet red with her hair in cunningly interwoven plaits. So much for avoiding her. I could feel myself scowling. "Lady Geiléis. Did you need something?"

"To speak with you, if you permit. May I come in?"

"I'm busy. If I interrupt this preparation, the mixture will curdle and be spoiled. Sit on that bench, over there."

Geiléis sat. If she thought me unmannerly, she gave no sign of it. I took my time with the preparation. Rushing it was likely to see a botched result, which meant good ingredients wasted. So I stirred the mixture in its little pot on the brazier, tested it from time to time, eventually took it off the heat, added further components, stirred again and waited until it was well thickened. I spooned it carefully into a sturdy jar. My visitor waited in silence while I washed pot, ladle, spoon, knife and chopping board in the bucket and wiped them dry.

When all was to rights, I dried my hands on my apron and addressed Lady Geiléis. There had been plenty of time to rehearse the right words in my mind. "I'm hoping you have not come to ask me if I can travel west with you, my lady. I understand how difficult things are for you, and I have some sympathy. But I've given Lady Flidais my word that I will stay here and look after her. She needs me."

"You take your calling seriously."

"Why would I not?" Impossible to sound anything but sharp.

"I meant no offense. Watching you work is an education."

"I work better on my own. Was there something else you needed? Were you seeking some kind of remedy?"

"Your opinion only."

"I'm a healer, not a councilor."

I saw Geiléis school her features. Thinking, no doubt, that I sounded hostile and wondering why.

"All I ask is that you listen awhile," she said. "I seek nothing further from you."

"Very well. You'll excuse me if I get on with my work while you talk." I busied myself, wondering what was coming.

"You are a wise woman, Mistress Blackthorn. A wise woman is generally well versed in ancient lore, or so I understand. And . . . I believe it is usual for your kind to be more open than most to the strange and uncanny. More precisely, to the fey. Some folk do not believe they exist outside the old tales. But you were quick to suggest the creature in the Tower of Thorns is not of this world. Tell me, in the course of your years as a healer, have you yourself encountered beings of that kind?"

She could hardly have chosen a question better calculated to annoy me. My past was not for discussion. Not with anyone. "I do know a great many tales, and the fey are in most of them."

"But beyond the tales, in the world where you and I walk? Have you met beings that are neither the wild creatures of forest and hills, nor human men and women, but Other?"

"That question strikes me as somewhat intrusive, Lady Geiléis."

"Then let me put it a different way. Are you open to the idea that such beings may exist? That they still walk the secluded places of Erin alongside our own kind?"

"It's possible."

"Some have suggested the creature in my tower is simply an animal that has wandered into the place and found itself trapped; or a flock of unusual birds out in the woods; or, indeed, a figment of my imagination. My requests for aid have been greeted with ridicule."

"Mm-hm." It was all too easy to imagine how that had felt: to tell her tale, perhaps to the northern ruler she'd mentioned, only to be scorned and laughed at. It brought back Mathuin and the way he had scoffed at my attempt to challenge him; how he had mocked me when I spoke the truth. I willed myself not to feel sympathy for Geiléis. My decision was already made. Whoever went to help her, it wouldn't be me. Couldn't be. I returned my attention to knife and chopping board, attacking the bunch of comfrey leaves with more violence than was strictly necessary.

"You know of the Tower of Thorns," Geiléis said. "And yet I'm told you are not from these parts."

Told? By whom? She'd been snooping around, asking questions about me. Why, when I'd already made it clear I would not go? "I find your dilemma interesting, my lady, but it's for someone else to deal with. I don't understand why you've come to see me. I've heard the story already. I've given you what wisdom I have to offer."

Grim loomed suddenly in the doorway. He gave Geiléis a look, then turned his attention to me. "Fetch you something to eat?"

"Thanks." I tried to convey with my eyes that he should come back promptly; I did not want Geiléis prodding me with her difficult questions any longer.

"Won't be long," Grim said, and headed off toward the kitchens, where no doubt he had already made useful friends. He'd done that with remarkable speed at the prince's house in Winterfalls. Which was one of the many ways in which Grim was not like me.

"You are close," Geiléis remarked. "Has he served you a long time?"

I held on to my temper, though it was fraying fast. Why couldn't she just go away? "Grim is not my servant. He's my friend and traveling companion."

She smiled. Perhaps she thought she understood. But nobody could understand what Grim and I were to each other. I wasn't sure I did myself.

"I don't know what you came here to ask," I said. "More than my opinion on the existence of the fey, I imagine. I'm busy, so if there's another question, please be quick with it."

"You are rather direct."

"I see no reason to wrap the truth in flowery garments. Please just say whatever it is. Unless it's a request that I travel to Bann; I'm not going to change my mind on that matter."

"Very well," Geiléis said. "Since you limit your answers to your knowledge of lore, I will ask you a question about that. Do you believe in happy endings?"

Lost for words, I stared at her.

"The tales are full of them, of course," Geiléis went on. "But can such an ending exist outside the confines of a tale? Given patience and belief and endurance, do you believe true love can eventually triumph over the odds, no matter how great they may be?"

This was the last thing I had expected, and I could not think how to reply. She had revealed more of herself in that speech than perhaps she realized. Such a question deserved an honest answer. But I saw on her face, now, a naked need for that answer to be *yes*.

"I'm not the right person to ask," I said.

"But?" She was gently insistent. "Is a wise woman not allowed a personal opinion?"

"There's no rule against that. But it is wiser, surely, for such a one to do the work folk expect of her—healing, counseling, telling suitable stories, laying the dead to rest and welcoming new life into the world. Personal opinions can lead to trouble." Now I'd said a little too much; inwardly, I kicked myself. How could I answer a question about true love? In my mind was Cass, my lovely man, blinking in the sunlight as he emerged from his workroom, his russet hair on end where he had run his fingers absently through it, his steadfast gray eyes fixed on me as if I were the loveliest woman in all Erin. In my thoughts was Brennan, my sweet baby, who would be a young man of fifteen now if he had lived. "True love breaks your heart," I said. "If you want my opinion, there it is." *Go away. Go away without another word.*

"Oh, yes," breathed Geiléis. "And yet, it is surely better to have had such a love and lost it than never to have known the joy of it at all."

I drew an uneven breath. "I couldn't say, my lady."

"I think you could, Mistress Blackthorn, but I will not vex you further. I know when I am not welcome. Perhaps, another time, you will give me an answer to my question."

"Can true love triumph over the odds? The only answer I have for that is sometimes yes and sometimes no." In the case of Prince Oran and Lady Flidais, it was a resounding yes, though their happy ending had not been achieved without cost. My own story had ended in sorrow. Cass and Brennan were dead; they were never coming back. And I was broken beyond repair.

"Then the story could end either way," said Geiléis. Her voice had shrunk to a whisper. "Thank you for your time, Mistress Blackthorn."

I closed the door after her, then leaned on it with my eyes shut, trying not to see Cass and Brennan in the fire, trying to block out the smells and sounds of that day. Wretched Geiléis! She knew I wasn't going to help her, so why did she have to come prying with her silly questions and waking up the nightmare? True love and happy endings, pah! I paced, resisting the urge to throw something and the equally strong urge to burst into tears. Three strides this way, three strides that way. One fist striking the other palm as I went. Mathuin. It all came down to Mathuin. I shouldn't be here; I should be in Laois, in the south, making sure that man paid the price for his crimes. Making him atone for Cass, for Brennan, for all the women he hurt and shamed and abandoned, for all the poor wretches locked up with us in that foul prison, for Grim, for me, for everyone he wronged. I could curse Conmael too, for holding me back. Only I couldn't, because if it hadn't been for him

I'd be dead, and the dead can't wreak vengeance. Unless it's a wonder tale, of course. There was nothing wonderful about my story. "A pox on it!" I snarled, striding toward the door.

And there was Grim, balancing a heavily laden tray. "You talking to me?"

Somehow we avoided crashing into each other. I retreated to sit on the bench, and he entered to set his burden on the table. Suddenly the stillroom was full.

"No. And don't ask me what Geiléis said. I just want to sit here in the quiet."

One of the qualities that made Grim bearable to live with was that I didn't need to tell him anything twice. If I wanted him to shut up, he shut up. If I needed him to talk, he talked. If I was in a foul mood, as now, he made a brew, gave me a cup, then got on with his own business. Often I didn't need to tell him at all. The only time he'd done something I didn't want was the time I tried to go back south on my own, and he followed me and stopped me. I couldn't blame him for that. It turned out he was right; if I'd gone then, I'd have made a mess of things. The scary part was, that time he'd seemed to know me better than I knew myself. If anything was uncanny, that was.

He set a cup beside me. "I'll be off, then."

"Stay," I said. "If you want." And, after a bit, "She asked me about happy endings. The kind you get in tales. Whether I believed in them. Whether they could happen in real life."

"Mm-hm." Grim filled a cup for himself, sat down, passed a platter of bread and honey. "Upset you."

"I'll live. I just hope she's done with her efforts to get something out of me that isn't there in the first place."

"Eat," suggested Grim. "It'll make you feel better." So I did, and it did. And eventually, when we had made considerable progress on the bread and honey, he said, "About happy endings. Folk like a story to finish well. Doesn't matter if that's true to life or not. Helps to hear about folk being content. About good folk getting what they deserve.

While you're listening you can believe, for a bit, that you're good too. Worth a happy ending."

I dashed away a sudden treacherous tear. "You're saying they do only exist in stories."

"Thing is, the story's like a different world. While you're in it, anything can happen. The stupid get wise, the ugly get handsome, the poor find pots of gold, the swineherd marries the lady of the house. Only, as soon as the tale's over, that's all gone. You're back in this world. And you're still poor or stupid or ugly or all three, and folk like Mathuin are still getting away with murder."

"You knew I was thinking about him."

"Not hard to guess."

I wondered if Grim thought he was stupid or ugly or both, but I didn't ask him. "You once said a person has to have hope or it's not worth going on," I said. "But maybe hope's the same as believing in happy endings."

"Job to do," Grim said succinctly. "Duty. Enough to make it worth going on."

"Justice. The same."

"Vengeance?"

"On its own, not enough." I would not be satisfied with an assassination. I needed to see Mathuin face up to his ill deeds publicly and pay the penalty under the law. Many folk had suffered because of him. Without justice, we would remain forever what he had made us: victims. "Vengeance and justice, together."

"Family," said Grim. "For them that have got one."

"Comrades," I suggested. "That's what men fight for, not for some grand cause."

We sat quiet after that, each of us sunk in memories. Until a man-at-arms came to the door and asked, in an embarrassed mumble, if I knew how to lance a boil in an awkward place. He had a friend with him who was trying hard not to laugh. I was tempted to give him a smack.

Grim put everything back on his tray. "Better?" he murmured.

"I'll do."

5

GRIM

For a while we're both on edge. Thinking Lady Geiléis might talk to the prince or Flidais, convince them Blackthorn's the one to go to Bann with her and solve her problem. Convince them she needs Blackthorn more than they do. But days pass and nobody says anything. The prince has sent for the druid, Master Oisín. So Lady Geiléis is waiting.

Blackthorn goes to give Flidais a check-over, make sure the baby's growing right. Looks happier when she gets back. Flidais has said she'd never ask Blackthorn to go somewhere if she didn't want to, and nor would the prince. Just as well. If they did, Blackthorn would have to tell them the real reason she couldn't go, which is Conmael. And that story's not getting told. Once it's out, folk will know who we are and where we came from. Only one step from there to Mathuin finding us. That bastard wouldn't care about me. But sure as sure, he'd try to stop Blackthorn from talking.

Once I hear what Flidais has said, I'm happier too. Though not as happy as I'll be when Lady Geiléis is gone. Still got that funny feeling about her, the feeling I get when I know trouble's coming. Blackthorn says not to worry, she's not going to take a foolish risk by heading off to the border. Turns out she thinks a ritual won't make things much better at Bann anyway.

"It'll take more than that," she says. "Master Oisín will have to stay up there and work it all out. Talk to people. Listen to their stories. Find out what brought the creature to the tower and why it's stayed there. Who drove it out the last time, and how, and why it came back."

Seen that look in her eye before. "You're interested," I say.

"Not interested enough to risk my whole future. And don't tell me I did that once already. I've learned my lesson."

"Mm-hm," I say. Keep the rest of my thoughts to myself. We're cursed, her and me. Cursed to a life full of nasty surprises. Soon as you start thinking it's plain sailing ahead, the worst storm in the world blows up. Still, a man can hope. If not, what's the point of going on?

Thought I knew Blackthorn pretty well: how she's feeling, whether I should stay around or leave her alone, what she needs doing. How she'll be if one thing happens or another. Then another visitor comes to court, and I find out how wrong I am.

We're out beyond the walls. Blackthorn wants to gather an herb that grows down on the rocks near the sea. Little crawling plant with flat leaves, looks like it's trying to hide in the cracks and chinks. Easy to miss. Blackthorn says she can use it in a salve for sore joints. Lots of folk ask her for that, so she's planning to make up a big batch. Gather it first, then soak the leaves to get the salt out, then grind them up and mix them with a lot of other things. Littlefoot, the herb's called.

She's busy gathering. Not an easy job. Has to find the stuff first, then make sure she doesn't take too much from one plant. Doesn't want to kill it. She's crouched down, picking and muttering to herself. Can't quite catch the words, but I know it's a kind of prayer, thanks for letting her take the herb and sorry at the same time. I've offered to help but she says no, my job is to keep an eye out for trouble. So that's what I'm doing when the traveler comes in sight. Walking along the road toward the fortress with a dog at his heels, big handsome thing, shaggy gray. Fellow's got a pack on his back, a staff in his hand, no weapons I can catch sight of. Wearing a scholar's robe. Looks harmless, but you never know. Dog sees us first and heads in our direction. Fellow clicks his fingers, calls it back. He gives me a nod, then catches sight of Blackthorn, who's on her haunches with her back to him. Traveler freezes on the spot, staring. That's a surprise. Her and me, we try not to catch the eye. I'm big, she's got that bright red hair, but we're not as startling as all that.

"Man on the road," I say, under my breath. "Looking at you."

She straightens. Shields her eyes, gives the man a look back. I see a smile break out on his face. Looks like he knows her, and that can only be bad.

"Saorla!" he calls out. "Is it you?"

Blackthorn makes a word with her lips, only she doesn't say it—the fellow's name?—and then she's walking forward, and he's opening his arms, and she's running to him before I can say watch out, be careful. They throw their arms around each other; he's got his hand on her hair; she's crying. Dog's jumping around them barking its head off. I'm shocked. Can't think straight. This is not Blackthorn's way at all. It's like she's turned into a different woman.

For a crazy moment I wonder if it's her husband, Cass, somehow not dead after all. Who else would she hold on to like that? Who else's shoulder would she cry on? Makes me feel odd, all mixed up inside. Then I'm next to the two of them, putting a hand down for the dog to sniff, waiting for them to notice me. Blackthorn moves back but keeps hold of the fellow's hands. She's staring at him with her face all tears. Looks like she hardly believes what she sees. "But how is it you're here?" she's saying. "I thought you were dead with the others; how did you escape? Where have you been all this time?"

"I might ask you the same," says the fellow. Looks a bit shaken up himself. "Where are you living? Close by here?"

"At the Dalriadan court, for now. It's a long story." Blackthorn remembers me suddenly. "Grim, this is Flannan, a very old friend.

From back in the . . . A friend of Cass's and mine." She turns back to the newcomer. "Grim is my—traveling companion."

"Greetings, Grim," Flannan says, smiling. "Any friend of this lady's is a friend of mine."

"Fine hound you have here," I say. "Good company for the road."

"This can't be Tempest," puts in Blackthorn. "She'd be ancient by now."

"Tempest's long gone. This one's Ripple, from the same bloodline. She's a fine friend; she's walked a long way with me. My work takes me from one house of prayer and learning to another, Grim. I'm a traveling scribe and scholar. That is how Saorla knows me."

"I don't use that name now," she says, quick sharp. "You should call me Blackthorn." Flannan's a well-made fellow, tallish, maybe five-and-thirty, got some muscle on him, not what you'd expect for a scholar. A friend of Cass's, she said. She's hardly spoken her husband's name since the day our cottage was set on fire. That night she told me the story of how Cass and her son were burned to death when Mathuin's men torched her house. So Flannan's from the south and he knows her story, some of it anyway. Enough to put her in danger, most likely. But here she is, clutching his hands and smiling, face all wet with tears. I fish a handkerchief from my pouch and hold it out to her. She doesn't even see me.

"Where are you heading?" she asks him.

"West, toward Tirconnell."

"In a hurry?"

Flannan smiles. "Monastic business is generally not conducted in great haste. I'm intending to study some manuscripts; I'm writing a book of tales, and they may provide good material. I'll tell you more later. For now, if you think the court of Dalriada would accommodate me for a night or two, I'll come with you. If that was what you were about to suggest."

"I was," says Blackthorn. "The king's away. Prince Oran is presiding at court. He's something of a scholar, and very fond of tales. His wife's the same. My guess is, you'll be welcome to stay there as long as it suits you."

The three of us walk back together, me carrying Blackthorn's basket with the herbs, which she's forgotten all about. The hound, Ripple, pads along beside us. Flannan's trained her well. He only has to move a finger or murmur a word and she does what she's meant to. Nice to watch, that. Makes me think how good it would be to have my own dog, a proper one, I mean.

Nobody talks much on the way back. Flannan hadn't expected to walk into his old friend here in the north, and she's shocked to see him. There's a story behind this. For some reason she thought he was dead, and he isn't. But they don't talk about the past now. I'm guessing Flannan doesn't know yet if he can trust me. Doesn't want to talk with me around, which is fair enough. As for Blackthorn, she still hasn't got her head straight. But one thing's plain: she's happy. Happy deep down, like I've never seen before.

6

GEILÉIS

W hen would word come from the druid? Midsummer Eve was drawing ever closer. She cursed herself for agreeing to wait; she should have dismissed that idea straightaway. Now precious time was being wasted, and for no good reason. She didn't want a druid. She wanted a woman. More precisely, she wanted Mistress Blackthorn, who had made it quite clear she was not interested. The wise woman was the prince's friend. Moreover, she was clever and cautious. Not to be coerced, that one. What argument would influence her? What was it this healer wanted most in the world? Could it be that curiosity alone might draw Blackthorn west? Geiléis spent her days pacing as she thought up one unlikely approach after another and discarded them as quickly. At night, in her dreams, the thorns closed around her in a piercing, bloody embrace. Perhaps time would weigh her down until she went entirely mad.

Each evening, at dusk, she told the story. Over and over she told it: the young woman in the forest, the mysterious tower, the precious day of discovery . . .

He stirred, his dark lashes fluttering, his slow, steady breathing becoming a sudden gasp. Lily shrank back. The young man might have the appearance of a handsome prince, but that did not mean he was a good person. It did not mean he would not hurt her. It came to her, rather too late, that she was alone in the tower with a complete stranger, that she had told nobody where she was going, and that she had no weapon with which to defend herself. The tiny ferryman was unlikely to be much help if this man decided to attack her.

He opened his eyes. Ah, such eyes! They were deep and dark, and there were shadows around them, as if his sleep—if indeed it had been only sleep—had been troubled by unwelcome dreams.

"I don't . . ." he murmured. "I can't . . ."

"Are you all right?" Lily could not stop staring. The voice of common sense urged her to get to the stair, to be ready for a speedy departure, but she could not make herself obey. Oh, she gazed and gazed, and her whole body trembled with new feelings. "Are you hurt? You were lying there so still, I thought you were dead."

The young man struggled to sit up. His torn shirt revealed rather too much of his well-muscled body, which bore bruises and scratches as if he had been in a fight. Belatedly, Lily remembered her good manners and dropped her gaze.

"Who are you?" the man said. "I thought . . ."

"They call me Lily. I live nearby. What has happened to you? I can fetch help—"

"No!" Such was the urgency in his voice that she looked at him once more, and saw a matching panic in his eyes. "No, don't tell anyone I'm here, please!"

"But you're hurt—"

"I'll be fine. See?" He pushed himself to a sitting position, then tried to stand. A woeful effort, as it turned out; his legs failed to support him. Lily was quick to kneel beside him, but hesitated to touch. "Really," he said, "you had best just go away and leave me. As you see, I am fit for nothing right now."

Lily felt a pang of disappointment. Worse than disappointment. Was this mysterious stranger no more than some local lad who had taken too much strong drink and got into trouble with his friends? Had those friends perhaps left him in the tower as a rather cruel kind of joke? Now was the moment to step away, to go home safely and leave him to sort himself out. But she had not smelled ale on his breath. "What is your name?" she asked, sitting down on the floor a safe arm's length from him.

For the first time, the young man looked at her; really looked. He smiled, and her heart turned over anew. "If you are Lily," he said, "then I am Ash."

"Ash." It could not be his real name, any more than Lily was hers. This felt like being five years old again and playing a game of pretend. But different. There was a wanting in it that left her breathless. "I have a water skin with me. Here." She took it from the little bag she was carrying on her back and handed it to him.

Ash drank deeply, as if he had been long thirsty. "By all the gods, that tastes good. Tell me, Lily, what brings you up into this chamber? This is not a place where a young lady should be wandering all on her own."

She found that a little annoying. He was not so old himself. Besides, look at the trouble he'd got into, with those bruises; it was hardly for him to give her advice as if she were a child. "I live here," she told him. "This is my father's land. I can wander where I like."

"How did you get across to the island?"

"By boat." Let him make what he wanted of that.

"Best if you don't stay. Best if you go home. Best if you never see me again."

Lily found a courage she had not known she had. "Nonsense!" she said briskly. "You're hurt, you're confused, you're too weak to stand up. And you don't seem to have any supplies here, not even water. I could turn my back and go away, but that would be irresponsible. Either let me fetch help, or let me bring you what you need. At least tell me where you came from, so I can send word to your family."

"No! Please!"

Already sickly pale, he turned still whiter, and Lily wondered if he might faint away. "You should eat," she said, trying to be practical. What would she do if he expired right here in front of her? Whom could she tell? She had no idea who he was or where he came from. "I have bread and cheese; here." She divided the small supply she had brought with her and handed him half. "And an apple for later." Gods, how silly she sounded! What would he think of her? "Try some, please. It will make you feel better."

Ash nibbled at a corner of the bread. After a while he said, "You are a kind girl. Too kind for your own good."

"What do you mean by that?"

He managed a smile; it made her heart skip a beat. "Truly, you would do better to leave me on my own. Forget you found me."

"Why?"

His gaze dropped. "Because you can't help. I thank you for the food and water, and your kind words, and . . . and your goodness. You are a lamp in the dark; a fair flower in the shadows. But this is no place for you, and if you wish to find a friend, or more than a friend, you should search anywhere but here." His eyes gave his words the lie; he could not stop looking at her. And her eyes returned that look a hundredfold. Something had happened between them; it was already too late to stop it.

"More than a friend," echoed Lily, feeling strangely bold. "What are you suggesting?"

"You are the daughter of a nobleman," said Ash, "if what you told me is true. You are of an age to be wed, if not now, then surely soon. I suggest nothing improper, Lily. Only that your father must be looking about for a husband for you. Perhaps you are already promised."

"Perhaps you are already promised," she said, as quick as a flash. "In fact, I am not; my parents are not over-keen to see me leave home just yet."

"But sometime soon?"

She felt her cheeks flush. "Maybe."

"Then you should not be here with me, alone."

"I did not know you would be here when I climbed the tower,"
Lily said, quite reasonably, she thought. "And how can I go away and
leave you when I cannot be sure you can get home safely on your own?
Given the choice, my father would surely want me to take good care of
a stranger in difficulty rather than run away in order to preserve my
reputation. Just tell me where you live, and I can at least get word to
your family."

"No!"

His answer was too forceful, too full of terror for this to be a sim-
ple case of a young man who had taken more strong drink than was
good for him, and been led astray. "You're scared of something," Lily
said quietly. "Is that why you're in here? Are you hiding?"

"I can't tell you." Ash wrapped his arms around his drawn-up
knees. "It's safer if you know nothing. Safer if you just go. I want you
to go, Lily. Please, just do as I ask." His voice was rich with feeling. He
looked at her as if she were the last good thing in his world. She knew
that, in his heart, he did not want her to leave him. But she had not
entirely lost sight of reality. When rest time was over, her handmaid
would come looking for her. If she could not be found, Muiríol would
tell her mother, and her secret expeditions would be over. If she wanted
to see Ash again—and she did, oh, so much—she must leave him now.

"Farewell, then," she said, rising to her feet. "I hope you will soon
be recovered." It sounded stilted and formal, and in no way conveyed
the feelings in her heart. "I wish you would let me help."

"You cannot help," said Ash. "But I will treasure the memory of
our meeting; I will hold it close when you are gone. Good-bye, Lily."

She made her way down the stair with her thoughts in turmoil; she
had hardly a word for the wee boatman as he ferried her over from the
island. She ran all the way home, and was just in time to clamber up
the tree and in her window before Muiríol came to wake her from her

nap. All through supper time and afterward, she could think of nothing but Ash: his pale skin, his dark, dark hair, his sorrowful eyes. His sweet words and the way he had looked at her.

Tomorrow, she resolved, when it was night and she was at long last alone again. Tomorrow I will take salves and soft cloths and some proper food and drink for him. Tomorrow I will find out who he is and why he is in the tower. Tomorrow . . .

7

BLACKTHORN

Even when I was young and content and thought life would bring good things for me and mine, I didn't believe in miracles. Magic, maybe, of the kind wrought by the fey. But that wasn't the same. Magic could seem to deliver the remarkable, the impossible, the stuff of wild dreams, but such gifts all too often came with hidden tricks, nasty surprises, the drop of poison in the golden chalice, the venomous lining in the silken garment. A real miracle, such as the survival of a dear old friend whom one had believed long dead, was truly wondrous.

Close on thirteen years. That was how long it had been since I'd last seen him, when he'd waved Cass and me farewell and headed off on one of his scholarly expeditions, the one that had ended up saving his life. When disaster had struck us and our fellow conspirators, Flannan had been far away in Mide, working in some monastic scriptorium and, in effect, out of Mathuin's reach. Not that the chieftain of Laois wouldn't be able to track someone across Mide and Ulaid and Dalriada if he chose to—I still lived in fear that one day he would find me. But he wouldn't remove a man by force from within a house of prayer. Not if that house lay within King Lorcan's borders. Lorcan of Mide was married to the High King's daughter.

Those thirteen years had marked both of us. Flannan's dimpled smile came less often than it once had, and his green eyes were not as limpid as they had been in the younger man. His hair bore traces of gray. But he was still himself. Flannan, my friend. Flannan, who had introduced me to the man who became my husband. Flannan, whom I had known since I was a child growing up in the south. His return was indeed a miracle.

For a while, after he'd been made welcome by Oran and Flidais and had settled into the men's quarters at Cahercorcan, we simply enjoyed the remarkable gift of finding each other again. Our talk was of the good times past: the way Flannan had introduced me to Cass, his friend and fellow scribe; the long arguments the two of them used to have over obscure points of law or calligraphy; the fierce debates we three had conducted in lowered voices as it became more and more apparent that the new chieftain of Laois was both cruel and unjust.

Flannan had heard of Cass's death, and Brennan's. He had not known whether I had survived. I gave him the bare bones of the story. That I had been in Mathuin's prison, though not because of the plot that had seen Cass punished so terribly. It had been later, after I'd fled south near-unhinged by grief, then, after a time so dark I could not bear to think about it, had come back to confront my demons. I'd faced up to Mathuin. Or tried to. I'd sought a hearing and spoken up for the women he'd wronged. For my pains, I'd been laughed at and thrown into the lockup.

"You were in that place?" Flannan was shocked—it was well-known that few survived incarceration there. "For how long? And how did you get out?"

"For a year. Me and Grim. The details don't matter. I'm out now and making my life again." I held back from telling Flannan any more, though I knew he was trustworthy. Grim's story was his own to tell, and as it had been tangled with mine since the day Conmael's magic freed us, I would not share either. "Strange, isn't it? After everything that's happened, here we both are. You and me."

"Here we both are, safe, well, and out of Mathuin's reach." There was an odd quality in Flannan's voice as he said this, something that made me look at him more closely. But his gaze was turned on the floor. "And I feel ashamed," he said.

"Ashamed? Why? We've all made errors. We've all done things that are uncomfortable to own up to."

"All this time," he said. "All these years, and I never went back. Not once." His hands were clutched tightly together. He looked up, not at me, but across the chamber to the spot where Grim's big cloak and my smaller one hung side by side from pegs on the wall. He was avoiding my eye. "Messages came from Laois. I heard that the others had been taken into custody. I knew what that meant; knew none of them would survive Mathuin's attempts to force information out of them. What could I have done to help them, all on my own? I got on with life, as you have. I spend my time between one house of learning and another, copying, writing letters—safe, innocuous letters—reading, discovering, making notes."

"Notes?" It was a short enough tale after nearly thirteen years of silence.

"For a book. A collection of old tales with a scholarly commentary. In Irish, not Latin. Magical stories related to the elements."

I grimaced. "And how do your monkish hosts view such an un-Christian project?"

"You'd be surprised," Flannan said, flashing a smile that brought back the young man in an instant. "Many of them have a love for the old tales, the kinds of stories druids and wise women told more widely before the brethren brought their new teachings to these parts. They're well practiced in shaping the old stories to fit Christian rituals and beliefs. I may be providing more grist for their mill. For me, the exercise is to preserve this ancient lore before it is forgotten; to record it for posterity."

I held back my opinion that such tales were better passed on from mother to daughter, from father to son, from elders to community. Fixing them with pen and ink felt wrong to me, like forcing a flowing river into confines it would always fight to escape. But he was a friend, and he meant well.

"A woman came here recently with a very odd tale," I told him. "Lady Geiléis of Bann. She's still at court. Brought a sort of petition to the prince, one he had no real answers for. I'd never heard the story before, though I thought I remembered the Tower of Thorns from somewhere. Is that name familiar to you?"

Flannan frowned. "I can't say it is. Bann—that's close to the monastic foundation of St. Olcan's, isn't it? Quite some distance west of here?"

"That's what she said, yes. Have you been there?"

"Not yet. What was this tale?"

I gave him the bare essentials: the tower, the howling monster, the hedge of thorns, the so-called curse that had set a blight on the land all around and made the ford impassable. "Lady Geiléis mentioned the monks using birds to carry messages. But what's happened makes travel difficult, especially to the west of her holdings. There's a roundabout way, but it's long and inconvenient. The oddest thing was that Lady Geiléis seemed to think this had all happened before, in the time of her ancestors. Possibly more than once."

"You're intrigued by the tale. I see it in your eyes."

"You do?" Flannan had been in the habit of teasing, back in the old days; it had been hard, sometimes, to tell whether he was serious or not.

"I recognize that look. You always did like a challenge."

I dropped my gaze. "That was a long time ago. I'm a different woman now. Lady Geiléis must find help elsewhere. I'm looking after Lady Flidais; I've promised to deliver her child." It wasn't a lie; just half the truth. Nobody knew about my promise to Conmael—nobody but Grim—and I planned to keep it that way.

There was a silence. Then Flannan said, "Even with my limited knowledge of such matters, I can see that Lady Flidais's child is unlikely to be born for some time. Would you not be able to go to Bann, sort out the monster, and return before her confinement?"

"Sort out the monster? Who do you think I am, Cú Chulainn?"

"I feel sure this puzzle would not be beyond your considerable abilities," Flannan said. "Cass once told me he believed you could do anything you wanted to."

Sudden tears pricked my eyes. "He was wrong," I said. "If I'd been able to do anything I wanted, I would have saved him. I would have saved Brennan. That's where my so-called abilities led me—into losing everything I cared about. Into letting that foul wretch Mathuin defeat me."

Flannan's look was painfully direct. "You're defeated? Or merely delayed on your quest? Which is it?"

This was close to the bone. It was uncomfortable. "I don't have a quest. And I wasn't expecting an inquisition."

His manner softened straightaway. "I'm sorry. I have spent too long on my own, poring over books; forgotten my manners." He rose to his feet, ready to leave.

"I don't need manners from an old friend. Only honesty. I can't go to Bann because I gave Lady Flidais my word. And there are folk back at Winterfalls who rely upon my being there to look after them. And . . ."

A silence; he was giving me time to collect myself.

"I've been beaten down over the years, Flannan. Hammered flat. Every time I picked myself up, there was a bit less of me left. I've been through things nobody would want to hear about. It's the same for Grim. Lady Geiléis's monster in the tower intrigues me, yes. But experience tells me getting involved would be complicated. I don't want a quest. The life I've got now is enough. Let the druid help Lady Geiléis. He'll do as good a job of it as anyone can."

I thought Flannan was going to leave the room without another word. But in the doorway he paused to look back at me. "Have you really changed so much?" he asked. "The woman I knew was all courage. A taker of risks. A seizer of opportunities. She'd never have been content with the life of a village healer."

"But that's exactly what I was back then." I spoke through clenched teeth. The truth hurt sometimes.

"If you believe that," Flannan said, "either your memory is faulty, or you're refusing to face reality. What happened to Cass was terrible; I don't deny that. But—"

"Stop. Just stop. That woman you knew would not have broken her word to go rushing off on a wild quest to deal with a monster. And there's nothing wrong with my memory. The day my husband and son were burned to death before my eyes is as clear now as it was then. I wish time had blurred those images. I wish it had muted their screams. Now go, please. I have work to do."

"I'm sorry." Flannan's voice was shadow-soft. "There's more for us to talk about; much more. But it can wait."

I wasn't proud of what happened after that conversation. I did try to keep calm. I knew I shouldn't give myself time to brood. That would only make me angrier, not with my old friend but with Mathuin and his ill deeds and my inability to do anything about them. Mathuin held such power. A woman on her own had next to no chance of exposing his crimes, let alone of bringing him to justice. Even supposing I got an unlikely opportunity to stand up and accuse him at a council, chances were his fellow chieftains would laugh at me exactly as Mathuin himself had done before he locked me up in the dark. Maybe, if Flannan knew the whole of that story, he'd think me brave after all. But in truth, I'd been a fool. And now there was my vow to Conmael. It bound me to leave Mathuin alone for seven years. And it held me close to home, if you could call Winterfalls home. Lady Geiléis and her monster in the tower might be a quest, but they were not my quest. I couldn't tell Flannan about Conmael. If that meant he thought I was a coward, so be it.

I went to the stillroom. Just as well nobody was waiting to consult me, as I was in the foulest of moods and liable to snap off someone's head if they so much as looked at me. I cursed the day I had told Grim the tale of how I lost my family. I cursed Flannan for reminding me of it; for implying that I was somehow betraying Cass by choosing the life

I had. For a man whose friendship I had always valued to say those things made them doubly painful.

I closed the door, stood completely still and made myself count up to ten, then commenced preparations for the most complex distillation I could think of, something so tricky it would take all my concentration. I willed the memory of that long-ago day into the locked compartment of my mind where I had kept it secure until the fire at our cottage at Winterfalls had seen it burst from its safe confines. Cass. Brennan. They'd been dead for close on thirteen years and they still tore at my heart. Grim had told me once that Cass was watching over me, cheering me on, admiring my courage. But I had seen the pitiful mass of bone and ash that was all the fire had left of my husband. Cass had died crouched over our baby, trying to shield Brennan from the flames. I wanted to believe that his spirit was still here with me; I wanted to believe that the two of them were together, and that they forgave me for not saving them, and for not dying alongside them, and for not bringing their killer to justice. But wanting something was not enough to make it real. Needing something to happen didn't mean it ever would. Instead of letting herself be eaten up with longing, a person should just get on with things. As for Flannan, he'd hardly lived the life of a questing hero himself. How dared he accuse me of cowardice?

My hands were shaking; the mixture slopped over the side of the flask onto the worktable. Old friends, trusted and true friends, did not lie to each other. Perhaps I really was a coward. Perhaps I should have done what I'd intended when I first agreed to Conmael's terms—told him I would keep my side of the bargain, then broken it as soon as his back was turned, and headed south to face up to Mathuin, despite what Conmael had threatened. Perhaps I should have died fighting.

A knock on the door. The flask fell from my hands and shattered on the floor, splashing its contents all over my skirt. I swore, loudly, as Grim pulled the door open. A pungent smell filled the little chamber. As he came in, I picked up an earthenware vessel and hurled it at the wall. It broke with a satisfying smash, making Grim wince.

"Came to see how you were." He squatted down and began to gather up the pieces.

"Leave that! You're not my servant! I'll clean up my own mess."

He went on calmly tidying, leaving me no choice but to get down and help him. "Put them in the bucket, over there," I said. "Then you'd better go." After a moment, I added, "I'm not fit for company. As you see."

He dropped the shards into the bucket. "Want to tell me what made you so angry?" he asked.

"No. I want you to stop being so understanding and leave me on my own. I just said so."

"Planning on breaking any more pots?"

"I'll break all the wretched pots I want!"

He rose to his feet, turning a particular look on me. "It's just, these are your work things. Useful things. Also, they belong to Cahercorcan, not us. Might be cross with yourself later."

"I don't want to talk about it. Not to you and not to anyone."

He simply stood there, a big solemn presence, making me feel like an ill-tempered child screaming over some thwarted desire. I seized a cloth and began to mop up the worktable. In my current state, I had no more hope of completing this distillation than I had of becoming the woman I had been, the one Flannan seemed to think I still could be. Or should be.

"He's upset you," Grim said. When I made to speak, he went on. "I know—you don't want to talk about it. But he's upset you."

"It's my business, Grim."

"Don't like to see you angry. Not like this, throwing things and cursing."

I smiled, surprising myself. "Really? You put up with it all right in the lockup. A whole year of it."

"Different in there," he said, fetching the millet broom from its corner to deal with the smaller fragments. "We needed it, the rest of us, to keep us going. Reminded us we were still alive. Stopped us from giving up."

I examined my skirt; those stains would be hard to get out. "I wonder if it was worth it," I said. "Staying alive. Getting through that hellish year and the time before. I wonder what the point of it was."

Now I had really shocked him. I had even shocked myself.

"Start thinking like that," Grim said, "and you lose hold of hope. Hope's all we've got. You taught me that, remember?"

"Mm." I was realizing that I had just made an exhibition of myself for no good reason. I had broken some perfectly good crockery and ruined a perfectly good gown. I'd lashed out at Grim, who had committed no offense beyond walking in at the wrong moment. And all because Flannan had brought not only himself but the ghosts of the painful past. "He implied I was a coward," I said, rubbing at invisible traces of the spillage on the table. "A lesser woman than I once was, because I said I wouldn't go west and deal with Lady Geiléis's monster in the tower. He said Cass believed I could do anything I wanted to. What he meant—what Flannan meant—was that if I stayed here, stayed safe, I was proving Cass wrong."

Out of the corner of my eye I saw Grim's big hands clench into fists and wished I had not spoken. A moment later, he let out a breath and relaxed them.

"Cass was right," he said. "Had faith in you. Me too. And other folk. Lady Flidais and the prince. All the people you look after. Flannan hasn't seen you for—what, twelve, thirteen years? What would he know?" A pause. "Throw some more stuff if you want. If it makes you feel better. Go right ahead—don't mind me."

"Maybe not," I said. "I don't want to bring in an audience. And I can't afford to lose any more of these crocks. Though they do make a satisfying noise when they smash. I suppose I'd better go and change this gown, try to scrub the marks out."

"Salt," said Grim. "Might do the trick. Don't let him upset you again, eh? Meant well, most likely, but he should watch his words."

"He was telling the truth, as he saw it. I expect he'll be gone soon, more monasteries to visit, more lore to study. Lady Geiléis too, once the druid comes. Flannan being here—it's got to bring the past back; it can't be otherwise. And that brings a flood of bad feelings. Sorry I shouted at you. And . . . thanks."

"What for?"

"Talking sense." It was far more than that; so much more, I hadn't the words for it. Nobody else could break through that rage when it overwhelmed me.

"Anytime."

8

GRIM

The day after they've had their argument, I see Flannan walking in the garden with the dog, Ripple. Looks like he's got a lot on his mind. So much he's not seeing what's around him. Upset, and who wouldn't be? They're old friends, him and Blackthorn. Old friends don't fight right after they've found each other. They don't call each other cowards. Flannan sits down on a bench, bent over like he's got a weight on his shoulders, and Ripple leans against him, puts her head on his knee. That dog's the best-trained creature I've ever seen.

I was angry before, when she told me what he'd said. Now I feel sorry for both of them. I go over and sit down beside him. Flannan doesn't say a word, not even *good morning*.

"Don't suppose you want my advice," I say after a while. "But you need to make your peace. Thing is, she's not often happy these days. Been through some dark times. That smile on her face, when she saw you, that was a rare thing. Most likely you don't know how rare."

Flannan looks like he hasn't had much sleep. He strokes Ripple's ears and stares across the garden. Couple of fellows digging, too far away to hear us. "So she told you what I said."

"Some of it, yes."

"I didn't think she would do that. Betray a confidence."

"Whatever was said, it'll go no further than me," I say. "Her and me, we're careful with our words. You need to talk to her again. Explain yourself to her. Hard to believe you think Blackthorn's a coward. That's what she told me. She's the bravest person I've met in all my life."

"Would she listen, Grim?" He's looking at me now, looking properly. He's just as upset as she was.

"She might throw things. Talk to her when she's not busy—that's my advice. And say what you mean straight-out."

He nods. Still looks weighed down.

"You've brought back the past," I say. "That's good for her. And it's bad. Talking about Cass and her little boy . . . It hurts her. You'd want to tread softly."

"I shouldn't have come," he mutters. "I'm doing no good here."

Know that feeling all too well. "If you can put that smile on her face again, you'll have done more good than you know," I say. "She'll be working now. I'll take you to meet some of the fellows, show you around the place if you want. Big maze here, easy to get lost. Start with the garden, mm?"

Turns out this is a good idea. Walking around gets him out of his gloom. He asks questions, not about the past, just about my garden and the work I do at Winterfalls, thatching and carting and so on. Then I take him and Ripple to meet some of the prince's guards, the ones I'm friendly with. We share some ale and tell a few stories. And later on, by the time he goes to see Blackthorn again, he's in a better mood and so is she. If she's happier, I'm happier. Job well-done.

The two of them have got things to talk about, private things. That's plain enough. So I keep out of their way and let them talk. That stuff, it's none of my business. One thing worries me, though. Flannan's come from the south. He's from Blackthorn's past, and the past's dangerous. Hope he understands why we don't want anyone knowing where we are.

I ask her about this, one night when we're in bed but still awake. She snaps at me across the chamber.

"Of course he understands! He's in the same position as I am. Flannan was part of the whole thing, the letter denouncing Mathuin, the plan to confront him. But he was away a lot; his work often took him across the border. He was in Mide at the time; that's why he wasn't taken in when the rest of them were. That's how he escaped torture and execution. And afterward he just never went back."

"Not as brave as the others, then."

"What was he supposed to do, walk straight into Mathuin's clutches saying, *Oh, you forgot me?* Not a sensible idea unless you believe in heroic sacrifice, which I don't."

I'm thinking that's exactly what she was planning to do last autumn when she started off for Laois all by herself. But I don't say so. She was sensible enough to stop when I caught up with her. Something I'll be glad of until the day I die.

"I'm going to sleep," Blackthorn says. "No more talk about this. It'll only give me nightmares."

The next morning she's cast off her bad feelings, and she's walking around with a smile in her eyes and a spring in her step again. Makes me wonder what I was worrying about. Seeing her this way's like magic, not spells and curses but a good kind of magic. Like spring flowers and sunshine and children laughing. I do miss sitting with her, just the two of us chatting the way we did before Flannan came. I used to drop in when she was free, bring her a brew, pass the time of day until she started work again. Makes me sad that we don't do that now. If anyone drops in to see her, it's him, not me. But how can I want things any different, with her so happy?

Tempted to ask Domnall if I can do some shifts on guard, just to keep me busy. But I don't ask him. Lady Geiléis is still here waiting for the druid. I see her pacing around the place, wound up tight as a bowstring. Something tells me, *Don't get too busy. Blackthorn might need you.* But a lot of the time I feel out of place, like an extra finger or toe that's not wanted.

At night, when we're back in our quarters, she's not so keen to talk as she was. Her mind's away, off somewhere else. In the past, most likely. Know that feeling. Know it better than I want to, the dark things that never go away, the sunny, precious things that go all too soon. With him here, there's talk of Christian houses of prayer he's visited, scholarly monks he's learned from. When I hear that, I'm straight back to that day I'd like to wipe away forever. The day of blood and death. The day when I wasn't strong enough. That's one story I'll be keeping all to myself.

9

BLACKTHORN

After our argument, Flannan stopped talking about Laois and Mathuin and the failed plot. We spoke instead about the distant past: our shared childhood. Or we chatted about this and that—the court musicians, the passing season. He told me about his work and the discoveries he was making in the royal collection of books and manuscripts. The prince and Lady Flidais both liked him—no surprise, since he was a friendly, open-minded sort of man, and loved scholarship—and there was plenty to keep him occupied in Cahercorcan's extensive library.

He offered no apology for upsetting me. He did not retract his words about my lack of courage, or my failure to be true to myself or to the memory of Cass or whatever it was he'd meant. And, not wanting to find myself cursing and throwing crockery again, I acted as if that difficult conversation had never happened. I did not forget it. His words had stung hard.

Time passed and although Lady Geiléis was still at court, waiting, I began to believe things would go according to plan after all. The king would return from the south, we would go back to Winterfalls, and with my help Lady Flidais would deliver a healthy baby. Flannan would travel on to his next monastery, and Lady Geiléis would head home for midsummer, with or without the druid.

More fool me. My life and Grim's were never going to follow a straight path. Fate loved to spring surprises on us. Mostly unwelcome ones.

I was in the stillroom, dressing a knife wound suffered by one of the men-at-arms during combat practice. Another man hovered, anxious for the friend whom he had accidentally wounded.

"It will heal cleanly," I told them. "Twelve days. Don't pick at the stitches, don't be tempted to take them out yourself, and under no circumstances try to use your arm for anything more than wielding your spoon at supper time, understand? If your master-at-arms raises any objections, tell him to come and talk to me."

Grim appeared in the open doorway. "Got news for you."

"We're almost done here." I tied off the ends of the bandage. "Keep this clean and dry, Rodan."

"Thank you, Mistress Blackthorn." It was the patient's friend who replied. He helped Rodan up, and the two of them went off together.

Grim came in and closed the door. "Just spoke to Deirdre," he said. "She told me a message came in from the druid. Says he'll be happy to help Lady Geiléis, only he can't get there until after midsummer. Flidais just told the lady."

"And how did Geiléis take it?"

"Badly, Deirdre said. Floods of tears."

"Tears or no tears, there's nothing I can do to help her. Another midsummer will come around; she can try again then."

"Mm. Oh, and Flannan was looking for you. Told me to tell you he's in the library."

"He'll have to wait. Maybe he's forgotten I have work to do."

"Go and tell him that, will I?" Grim was smiling.

"He knows where to find me."

"Mm-hm. I'll be off, then. Couple of the fellows are working on unarmed combat. Said I'd go and watch."

"Maybe you can stop them doing each other serious damage. I'm getting tired of patching up their mistakes."

"See you later," said Grim, and was gone.

The next knock on the door would be Lady Geiléis, no doubt. Pleading for me to change my mind. Wanting me to sort out her monster and set her world to rights. Thinking that because she was nobly born she could bend me to her will. I would give her a firm no, as I had before. If Conmael challenged me about it later, I would tell him that Flidais had asked for my help first, so I wasn't technically breaking his rules.

But when the knock came, it was Flannan's, and what he said to me turned everything upside down.

10

GRIM

"Y ou've what?" I'm shocked. Too shocked to hide it.

"I've changed my mind," Blackthorn says, calm as calm, though she's set my head spinning. "I'm going to Bann to deal with Lady Geiléis's monster."

It's late, after supper, and we're in our chamber. Haven't talked to her since the afternoon, when I passed on Flannan's message. Been busy with the lads in the practice yard, then talking to some other folk at supper, and haven't had the chance. She was looking pale at supper time and she still is. On edge about something. That makes two of us now.

"But . . ." I can't get the right words out. There aren't any right words. "But you said . . ."

"I've spoken to Flidais. She's given me permission to go provided I come back straight after midsummer, and Lady Geiléis has agreed to that. The baby's not due until autumn; Flidais will do perfectly well under the care of Master Caillín."

Plenty I could say. Thought she'd decided, thought *we'd* decided going to Bann was too risky, right on the border and all. Thought she wanted to stay with Lady Flidais right through, and Lady Flidais wanted her. Thought she was counting the days till we could head home, same as me. Seems I was wrong. Bonehead. Only . . . that's what she *said*, before. Why would she change her mind so quick?

"Mm-hm," I say, trying to be calm like her though I'm a jumble inside. "Made up your mind, then."

"I have." Sounds like she doesn't want questions. Got no answers, maybe.

"When do we leave?"

Blackthorn's been fussing with some things on the bed, taking a long time to fold them. Now she turns and looks at me properly. "Grim," she says in a voice I don't like much, "you don't have to come. Not if you don't want to. Not if you think I'm doing the wrong thing."

I look straight back at her. "You saying you don't want me to come?" Had to happen sometime. But I'd started thinking it wouldn't, stupid me.

She folds her arms, looks at the floor now. "No. Just that Flannan's coming with me, so I won't be on my own."

Nothing to say to that. So it's him—he's what changed her mind for her.

"He's going to this monastery, St. Olcan's," she says. "There's some work he can do there. And since it's right next to Lady Geiléis's holdings, it makes sense to travel together. Besides, Lady Geiléis came with an escort. There'll be plenty of protection."

"So, no need for me."

"Not as a bodyguard. Grim, don't look like that. I want you to have the opportunity to make up your own mind about it, that's all. If you think it's a bad idea, and I can see you do, you shouldn't feel obliged to come. You could go home to Winterfalls, wait for me there."

"Mm-hm." Me at the cottage, on my own, and her at Bann with this monster. Ha! She's crazy if she thinks I'm going along with that.

"You won't, though, will you?" she says. Not so crazy after all.

No need to answer that. She knows I'll follow unless she orders me not to, and maybe even if she does. It's my job, looking after her. It's what keeps me moving from one day to the next. So I'll go even if I think it's the worst idea she's ever had. "What about him?" I ask. "Flannan. Planning to help you kill the monster, is he?"

She heaves a big sigh. "I imagine he'll be with the monks at St. Olcan's, studying their famous collection of manuscripts and consulting their esteemed scholars. Nothing to do with Lady Geiléis and her creature in the tower."

Monks. For a bit I'd forgotten them. "Where would you be staying?" I ask her.

"Not at the monastery. That'll be men only. I think Lady Geiléis can accommodate me. Us. That's if you're coming."

"Looks like I am," I say. "Better pack up, then. Not sure what a fellow needs to deal with a monster."

"Courage," says Blackthorn. "Sharp wits. Imagination."

"Mm-hm." Courage, I might be able to find, though if I have to visit this monastery that could get hard. Not strong on sharp wits and imagination. But then, she's got more than enough for two.

11

GEILÉIS

By all the gods! She hardly dared believe it true. So late, when hope had seemed all but lost, Mistress Blackthorn had suddenly changed her mind. Of her own volition, she was coming to Bann.

Geiléis pushed down the wild excitement that was rising in her, threatening to undo the whole enterprise. She must be cool, calm, every bit the lady, even when her inner voice was shouting, *Yes! This time it's really going to happen! This woman is clever, she's brave, she's open to the strange and uncanny. She's not like the others. This time, this time* . . . There must be none of that. The very strengths that could help Blackthorn complete the task could also be the quest's undoing. A clever woman could solve puzzles. A fearless woman might ask difficult questions, seek answers in places others would shun. A woman who understood magic might see what an ordinary person was blind to.

. This must be carefully controlled, every step of the way. She must feed the information to Blackthorn drop by drop, giving her enough to hold her interest, but not so much that the healer would balk at the task ahead of her, or question Geiléis's sanity as others before her had done. This must be calculated perfectly.

First things first. She bade Prince Oran and Lady Flidais farewell in the privacy of the royal council chamber. She thanked them for their hospitality and for lending her their valued wise woman. She promised to ensure that Mistress Blackthorn returned to court straight after Midsummer Eve, whether or not she was successful in banishing the monster.

The healer was bringing both the hulking bodyguard and the scholar with her to Bann. Neither was required for purposes of safety; Geiléis's own escort was more than adequate. But Blackthorn had simply stated that both men would be accompanying her. Since Blackthorn's cooperation was essential, Geiléis had agreed without demur. A little inconvenience could be endured in order to keep the woman content.

The guard, Grim, was all muscle and no wits. Loyal to his mistress, certainly. But lacking in intellect and subtlety, and therefore no real threat. The scholar would be quickly absorbed at St. Olcan's, as others of his kind were. He would become enmeshed in his studies; blind and deaf to the outside world. The illuminated manuscripts in the monastic collection were considered the finest in all Erin. Provided Master Flannan stuck to what he knew best, he would not present a problem. She might send one of her guards ahead to have a word with Father Tomas. Best if the fellow was accommodated in the monastery guesthouse, safely out of the way.

They rode out in the early morning. Cahercorcan had provided horses for Blackthorn and her two men.

"I should have explained, perhaps," Geiléis said to the healer, "that when we stop along the way—the journey takes almost five days—we do not seek out the hospitality of chieftains or princes. My men carry rudimentary supplies for camping. We sleep under the trees. We wait until the horses can go on."

"That's fine with Grim and me," Blackthorn said. "What about you, Flannan? You may be more accustomed to sleeping with a roof over your head."

"Not at all," said the scholar, who was riding close to Blackthorn. "A great deal of my life is spent traveling. Provided I can keep my writing materials dry—and they are well wrapped against possible damage—I have no objection to a few nights in the open, Lady Geiléis."

"Call me Geiléis, please, Master Flannan." She favored him with a smile. "You must do the same, Mistress Blackthorn. On the road we may dispense with convention, surely."

"If you say so." Blackthorn glanced over her shoulder. The men-at-arms were in their usual formation, three at the head of the group, three at the rear, one on either flank and one free to move about as required. The healer's man, Grim, was riding with those at the back of the party. "That goes for Grim too, I take it?"

"If you wish." What was the fellow to her? Not a lover, surely—there seemed nothing of passion or tenderness in either of them. Indeed, they appeared singularly ill-suited to each other. Even a beaten-about sort of woman like Blackthorn could surely do better than that slow-witted lump of a man. But perhaps she liked her pleasure quick and rough, with no sentiment attached. "We'll ride as far as Cormac's Crossing today, all being well. My men will set up shelters, cook a meal, provide all that is required."

"Mm-hm."

"A long ride for you," Geiléis said.

"We'll cope. And as for the camping, we're used to managing with very little. No need to apologize for the lack of amenities. Cormac's Crossing. Who is, or was, Cormac?"

"It's an old name; I know nothing of its origins. You'll find the spot perfectly suitable for an overnight camp. I thank you again, from the bottom of my heart, for agreeing to do this. Your courage is exemplary."

"More curiosity than courage. Grim and I like a mystery. Yours is particularly challenging."

Geiléis would have said more; would, perhaps, have ventured a question or two about where Blackthorn had been before she came to Dalriada. But the healer let her horse drop back and the opportunity was lost. There was a story behind the woman's combative eyes and sharp manner. There was a story behind her unlikely friendship with her hulking protector. Not that it mattered, unless it got in the way of the task ahead. She'd watch them carefully, and set others to do so when she could not. Make sure her guests saw what she needed them to and nothing else. Make sure they heard only what was required to ensure the fulfillment of the task.

"Question for you." Blackthorn had come up beside her again, jolting her out of her thoughts. "You still want a cleansing ritual, yes? That should be the first thing I do when we get there. But you've spoken of these monks as if you're on friendly terms with them. Since you're happy to have my assistance with your problem, I assume you're not of the Christian faith."

"That is not a question, Blackthorn."

"What is your own spiritual path?"

Geiléis felt her mouth twist into a bitter smile. "You think Father Tomas and the brethren might object to a ritual of the old faith conducted so close to their house of Christian prayer?"

"One might expect that."

"We are all desperate for answers, Blackthorn. The creature's screaming is enough to send the sanest of folk witless. Father Tomas may not be best pleased by your arrival, but I am chieftain of Bann, and what happens on my land is my business. As for my faith, ill fortune has all but snuffed it out."

"But not entirely?"

"If it was quite gone," Geiléis said, "I would not have waited so long for the druid. As it is, I am prepared to try anything. When we reach Bann, you will understand why."

12

BLACKTHORN

The landscape passed me by unseen. The voices of my fellow travelers might have been the babble of a brook or the sighing of the wind. I held my tongue. The secret within me, the perilous secret Flannan had shared with me, was so huge that I feared it would burst out and ruin everything. One wrong word might betray me. One wrong word— *Mathuin* or *south* or *plot*—might alert Grim or Geiléis or even Conmael, if the man really could appear wherever he liked. And once they had an inkling of what had made me change my mind, they would start asking questions, and then stop me. And that would be wrong this time, because what Flannan had told me meant I wouldn't be on my own confronting Mathuin; I would be part of a much wider strategy, a plan that had been years in the making, a plan involving many folk. With so many voices raised, the chieftains would surely listen this time. Mathuin would face justice for his wrongdoing. At last we would make it happen.

When Flannan had first told me, I'd refused to believe him. False hope was a cruel thing, and this had reeked of it. We'd tried, hadn't we? We'd tried, and my husband and child and a whole lot of other folk had been killed. I'd tried again, years later, and where had I ended up? Incarcerated in Mathuin's cesspit. Powerless. Hopeless. Silenced as effectively as if I too had died. The plot Flannan spoke of sounded just like that first one, only weaker, because Flannan himself had not gone back to Laois and spoken in person to his fellow conspirators there. He'd relied on messages carried by pigeons from one monastery to another, messages that could then be passed on to other trusted allies. Why would I break my word to Lady Flidais and my promise to Conmael and rush off south on the strength of that?

Flannan had come to find me in the stillroom while Grim was off watching combat practice. Even so, with just the two of us behind a closed door, Flannan had dropped his voice to a whisper as he'd told me. This was not like the old plot, he'd said. There were sympathetic folk, folk who knew the secret, strategically placed in every chieftain's stronghold and in every Christian monastery in Laigin and the south of Mide. There was a network of reliable informants; a growing number of stalwart supporters. All were ready to stand up and be counted. Their number included folk of considerable authority—councilors and nobles. It had taken Flannan and his loose fellowship years to set it all in place. The birds were vital to the enterprise; every monastery had its pigeon loft. Monks could write in Latin, or use coded messages only decipherable by scholars.

"Stand up and be counted when?" I'd asked, fighting back the urge to say yes. "Where?"

"At the council."

"The High King's council? Is the plan that you and I sprout wings and fly to Tara? Even if we could be there in time, the moment any of Mathuin's cronies recognized me, whether as the wife of the traitor scribe from years ago or the troublesome woman who wouldn't stop talking about his misdemeanors, I'd be silenced. Permanently silenced. Either killed or thrown back in that hellhole and left to rot." I'd made myself unclench my hands; forced myself to take a few deep breaths. "Why have you waited so long to tell me this?"

"You'd made it pretty clear you weren't interested in taking risks anymore," he said flatly. "I didn't think it was worth asking."

It had been like a slap in the face. Had I really changed so much? Had I truly become the coward he'd called me? "Well, you've asked now," I'd snapped. "So explain how we're supposed to get to Tara before the council."

"I don't mean this autumn's council," Flannan had said. "Not only would you and I lack the time to travel so far south, but others, too, could not be assembled by then. The plan is that we—all of us—make our ways separately to Mide, to the court of King Lorcan or its environs, or to one of several monasteries that lie close by. We would make our move at Lorcan's next spring council. The High King should be in attendance. They are kinsmen, as you probably know. At least two of Lorcan's councilors are sympathetic to our cause. It's been suggested, indirectly, that the king of Mide would not be averse to seeing Mathuin removed from his position of authority, since he stirs up constant trouble on the border."

It had taken me a while to find words; my thoughts had been conducting a minor battle among themselves. "Make our move," I'd said eventually. "What move?"

"Stand up at the council. Make a statement of Mathuin's crimes, supported by evidence, including the accounts of witnesses. Request that he be formally charged. In the presence of both the High King and King Lorcan, Mathuin will not be able to do what he did last time. At the very least, he'll need to answer to the accusations."

"Witnesses. You must be out of your mind." But my heart had been racing, my thoughts leaping ahead. "What witness would be prepared to come forward? Everyone knows that would amount to suicide. Or worse."

"It's the weakest part of the plan, I would be the first to agree." Flannan had reached out to take my hands in his. "But you could help. What I thought was that you might find some of those women you told me of, the ones whose cases you tried to draw to Mathuin's attention. You could talk to them, persuade them to speak out."

"You're crazy. Why would those women risk everything, after what happened to them? Not only were they assaulted, they were then publicly shamed and ridiculed. Some of them have got Mathuin's little bastards to raise. Some of them were thrown out by their families—they may be destitute. And you're asking me to drag them all the way to Mide so they can stand up and perhaps face another dose of the same? I can't do it. I won't do it. I've made promises to folk here in Dalriada, Flannan. Promises I mean to keep, one of which is that I won't try this again." I'd refrained from telling him what I thought about his expecting me to walk back into Laois as if I had no fear of what Mathuin might do to me. I'd held back my opinion on Flannan's expectation that I would do this when he wasn't prepared to go back there himself.

He'd turned a very direct look on me. I'd waited for another accusation of cowardice; waited for him to say I was no longer the woman he'd known and admired before my life turned to ashes. But what he'd said was, "I won't ask who extracted that promise from you. As far as I'm aware there's only one man in these parts who knows your story, and he's got a vested interest in keeping you in the north."

For a moment I'd thought he meant Conmael, though there was no way Flannan could know about the bond that held me in Dalriada. Then I'd realized he was speaking of Grim. "It makes no difference who it was," I'd snapped.

"Shh. Keep your voice down." Flannan had glanced toward the closed door of the stillroom.

"Flannan, I have to be honest. The way you set it out, my part in this sounds ill-conceived. I'm assuming you dreamed this up once you found I was still alive. It's hard to believe you would ask it of me."

"I ask it because you're brave," he'd said. "You've always been brave. I can't promise the plot will succeed this time; nobody can. But it gives us the best chance we're likely to get of seeing justice done. Yes, your part in it would be risky. I wouldn't insult you by pretending otherwise. But I believe you can do it."

"What happens if this plot fails as the last one did?" I'd whispered, tempted despite all my reservations. Knowing that if I acted sensibly and said no, I would always regret the missed opportunity. "What if all the conspirators make their way to Mide, or to Laois to gather witnesses, and Mathuin's henchmen find out what's being planned before this council of Lorcan's gets a chance to happen? It only takes one person to get scared and whisper in the wrong ear. It only takes one careless word, one misstep, and the whole thing comes tumbling down, and us with it. You know that." One shaky breath. "And don't you dare tell me this is what Cass would want me to do, or I swear I'll hit you."

Flannan had been silent after that, leaning against the wall and looking at me with that same expression, the one that told me he knew how much I wanted to say yes, and how hard I was wrestling with my demons. Not a word about Cass; not a word about being brave or standing up to be counted. He'd simply waited.

The words had been all ready. *I won't be part of this. Not under any circumstances.* But what had come out was, "I can't go anywhere without Grim. And I can't tell him about this."

Still Flannan had stayed quiet. His brows had lifted a little in question.

"If I did go south, I'd have to slip away, not tell Lady Flidais, not tell anyone."

A nod from Flannan.

"Only there's no slipping away from Grim. Where I go, he follows. And I wouldn't want him drawn into this. He has as much to fear from Mathuin as I do. Besides . . ." Grim was the only one prepared to tell me, honestly, if I was making an error of judgment. The only one who could make me listen when a certain mood came over me.

"Besides what?"

I'd found myself suddenly reluctant to give Flannan further explanations. "I'm just saying that even if we went covertly, he would come after us. And if we went openly we'd invite the possibility of someone alerting Mathuin. He sent men after us, after Grim and me, when we . . . when we got out of the lockup."

"Ah." Flannan had moved to sit down on the bench. "I have a plan, though I confess I had not thought to include Grim. We would not head south straightaway, but would leave court on the pretext of aiding Lady Geiléis with her monster in the tower. Or rather, you would; I would offer to ride with you in order to pay a perfectly plausible visit to the monastic foundation at St. Olcan's. To make our movements still more convincing, you might actually assist Lady Geiléis with her problem. While you did so, I could spend time studying a certain manuscript I've heard they have in that collection. We could move on from Bann after midsummer—that would still allow sufficient time for what must be done. I could make use of the messenger pigeons at St. Olcan's to check on the progress of our fellow conspirators. And we could head south by a different path, bypassing Cahercorcan entirely."

"We could? What path?"

"Farther west into Tirconnell, then down through the pass from the north. That's provided we can get across Lady Geiléis's ensorcelled ford. Don't look like that, Saorla. There are friends all the way. I have learned to be careful, I promise you. The fact that I am still alive and my own man proves it."

"You call me by that forbidden name and say you're careful? This sounds . . . It sounds fragile, Flannan. Like a rope woven too thin, that would snap under the least strain."

"The rope is woven from courage, comradeship and hope. It is strong enough to bind an evildoer and bring him to justice. I promise."

No denying it had sounded good; inspirational, almost. Enough to make a woman turn her back on her other allegiances and march forward with the flag of justice held high, disregarding common sense entirely. Enough to make offending Lady Flidais and deceiving Grim unimportant. But something in the detail had troubled me, even so. "Flannan?"

"Yes?"

"When Grim and I met you on the road, were you really on one of your usual trips between monasteries? Did you encounter us purely by chance?"

"How could it have been otherwise, since I didn't know you'd survived? If I had known, I'd have gone looking for you in the south, not here. When I saw you down on the shore . . . When I realized who it was . . ." I'd seen a look in Flannan's eyes then that startled me. Had my survival truly been such a miracle for him? "Finding you again—it was a gift, pure and simple."

For a while I'd fallen silent, for his eloquence had made it hard to go on arguing. "All very well to talk of being brave," I'd said eventually. "But I suspect you haven't thought this out properly. I was only in the lockup a year." *Only.* Hah! It had been the longest year of my life. "What about before? Yes, I went south after Cass died. Stayed away years. But I came back. I told you before, I was in Laois for months, talking to the folk Mathuin had wronged, gathering what evidence I could, until eventually I confronted the man in public and got myself incarcerated. Why did nobody tell you about that? Even if they didn't know we'd been friends before, I made enough of a stir to have folk talking. Or I thought I did. Surely someone in your network must have known about it."

"Mathuin is expert at making his enemies disappear. I don't need to tell you that, surely. Besides, I imagine you were not using the name I knew. No word came to me at all, either from the community or from my fellow plotters. Nobody would have had cause to associate you with me. To all outward appearances I am a mild-mannered scholar, a quiet person who keeps out of harm's way."

"Seems I made less of a stir than I'd hoped to." All for nothing. All of it. Could I bear to go through the struggle all over again, perhaps with as little success?

Flannan had made no comment. Into the silence had come the sounds of footsteps passing, conversations, the distant ringing of a bell beyond the closed door of the stillroom. Only a matter of time before someone interrupted us. "I knew, you see," Flannan had murmured, "that you'd want to be part of it. Need to be part of it, once you heard. I knew how you'd feel if we confronted Mathuin at last and you weren't there to add your voice. You were always so fierce in your quest for justice, even before Cass died. It was one of the things he loved about you. That your spirit burned as brightly as your hair."

A knock on the door.

"I need some time," I'd said.

"It can't be too long."

"I'm not stupid, Flannan. A day or two, that's all. And if I do say yes, I can't tell Grim."

"So he wouldn't be coming with us?"

"It's complicated. Just don't say anything to him, all right?"

"Not a word."

I didn't need the day or two I'd asked for. The next morning I went to see Flidais. Being less than honest with her made me feel bad, but there was no other way. So I said that I was moved by Geiléis's distress, knowing very well what it was to be a woman and to feel powerless, and that I wanted leave to travel to Bann and conduct the cleansing ritual Master Oisín could not perform in time. While I was there, I would see if I could find other solutions to Geiléis's problem. I would return straight after midsummer, I told Flidais, whether or not I succeeded in banishing the monster from the tower. That part was the lie, or the half lie. If I decided to go south with Flannan, if I decided to walk that perilous path, I would never be back. Not to court, and not to Winterfalls. Saying what I did felt like stepping off a cliff. My stomach was churning with nerves. It was hard work maintaining a calm face. Flidais knew me well, and she wasn't stupid. But she gave me her blessing to go. The truth was, the court physician, Caillín, would do a more than adequate job of delivering the baby, provided there were no complications. But Flidais wanted me, and I had promised to be there.

I told Lady Geiléis I would come with her and was thanked with a beaming smile. Before I'd even left the room she was sending for Onchú, her head guard, to make plans for our departure. And then I told Grim I'd changed my mind about going to Bann. He'd known already that something was up. I'd had a restless night, full of dark memories. If one of us couldn't sleep, the other generally stayed awake too. At one point Grim had gone downstairs to make a brew, and had asked if I wanted to talk, and I'd said no. He hadn't pressed it; we understood each other too well for that.

I told Grim nothing about the new plot against Mathuin. And I did not tell Flannan that for now, my *yes* went only as far as riding to Bann and attempting to deal with the monster in the tower. Geiléis's home was remote, isolated—hard to reach even without the monster making the ford impassable. I would be safe there while I made up my mind; it was far from Mathuin's clutches. And who knew? I might even succeed in banishing the creature. A small victory beside the one I so longed to achieve, but worthwhile all the same. Hadn't Conmael bound me to use my talents for good?

I would not let myself say an impetuous *yes* to Flannan's plan. I'd nearly made a bad mistake last autumn when I'd rushed off south without thinking things through. I had to consider this soberly, when the thrill of terrified excitement had died down. I needed to weigh up the risks and advantages of each course of action. I could come back to court after midsummer. I could honor my promise to Flidais and respect my vow to Conmael. I could set aside the burning need that had kept me alive all those years since Cass and Brennan died, and all those filthy, desperate days in Mathuin's lockup. Or I could choose to slip away with Flannan, turn my back on Dalriada, seize the unexpected gift of another chance. How likely was it, really, that Conmael would make good on his threat to send me back to the lockup if I went south? I could bear witness as Mathuin faced justice; I could have vengeance for my dear ones at last.

As for Grim and what would happen to him if I chose the second course, I would face that difficulty when the time came.

So we rode out: Geiléis and her men-at-arms, Flannan, Grim and me, with the dog, Ripple, running alongside. Geiléis had told us the journey would take five days. I discovered at the end of the first day that the lady's idea of camping was to have her men erect a tentlike shelter for her, make a fire, prepare her a meal and generally attend to all her needs. The men-at-arms had brought all the materials for a camp, either on the pack horse or in their saddlebags. They set everything up with such practiced efficiency that it did not feel right to offer help, though Grim did knock in a few tent pegs. Geiléis offered me a shelter of my own for the night, along with soft bedding, and I declined.

"We're used to sleeping in the open. And the weather's dry. We'll find ourselves a spot by the fire. But thank you," I made myself add, thinking how odd it felt to be treated like a lady, even though Lady had been Grim's name for me in that place, when it had been more or less the opposite of what incarceration had reduced me to.

Cormac's Crossing, where we'd stopped, was at the edge of some woodland, with a sizable stream nearby. We'd been well supplied from the royal kitchens, but from force of habit Grim and I dropped lines in the water and, somewhat to our surprise, caught enough fish for everyone to have a share. Grim cleaned them and cooked them over the fire; Ripple stayed close to him, eager for scraps. I gathered a supply of edible greens to make it into more of a meal. Flannan didn't have much to say. He watched us with what appeared to be amusement, making me even edgier than I already was.

"Your job's washing the dishes," I told him, though I suspected Geiléis's men would do that as efficiently as they had made camp.

One thing they didn't do much of, and that was talking. There was no storytelling around the fire. They didn't share jokes and songs. They fed and watered the horses, cleared away the meal, laid out their bedrolls and organized a watch with hardly a word exchanged even among themselves. Lady Geiléis retired to her tent as soon as she had eaten; before dusk. Somewhat later, the men who were not taking first watch settled to sleep. I had thought that the awkwardness of lying between Grim and Flannan, even at a discreet distance, might lead to a restless night, but I was so exhausted from the long ride that I fell asleep quickly and did not wake until the first birds began to announce the new day's dawn.

The weather stayed fair. We made good speed across farmland and through woodland, encountering few folk on the road. Some of the way was high ground, giving fine views north over the sea and south over hills and valleys fading into distant blue and brown and purple. Somewhere in that shadowy realm was Laois, and my enemy. Somewhere in that haze was the place where my man and my baby lay under the earth, still holding each other close. *What would you want me to do, Cass? See justice done, or get on with my life in peace? Try to stamp out evil whatever the cost, or simply do good and keep out of trouble?* The shade of my husband had nothing to say, which was entirely as I'd expected. Grim had once suggested Cass was watching over me, proud of my achievements. I was more inclined to think that on the day he died, my husband's spirit was snuffed out forever, leaving no more than the pitiful pile of bone and ash the flames had reduced him to. I had buried him— buried them—with my own hands. That day, I had sworn that I would never shed tears again. The promise had been beyond me to keep.

With Geiléis and her men close by, not to speak of Grim, I had no opportunity to talk to Flannan privately along the way. That was probably just as well. For all my good intentions—of taking time to decide, of weighing all the arguments—the secret still burned hot inside me. So I limited my conversation to the everyday. Grim, not a talkative man at the best of times, had become almost as silent as Geiléis's retainers.

So four days passed, and on the afternoon of the fifth, Lady Geiléis informed us that we should reach her holdings just before nightfall. "The creature will be growing quieter as the sun sets," she said, "but you may still hear its voice. I should warn you. It can be . . . disturbing."

I had not given much thought to the monster. Flannan's plot had squeezed it out of my mind, and I had almost forgotten that in order to retain credibility with Grim, at least, I would actually need to attempt the task Lady Geiléis had entrusted to me. As we rode, I pondered what the word *monster* really meant. Monsters in ancient tales were often a disconcerting mixture of man and creature. They rose from swamps or lurked in dark forests, ready to leap out and sink their teeth into the unwary traveler. Monsters were ugly, fearsome, strange; they tended to attack without asking questions first. They might be dragons that demanded tribute in the form of young women to devour, or giant dogs that enveloped folk in dark clouds of nothingness. Every storyteller knew the tricks for making such creatures as terrifying as possible. But in my book, the vilest and worst was the human monster: a man like Mathuin of Laois, whose actions made it clear he was devoid of any good qualities. Compassion, for instance. Kindness. Fairness. Justice. The ability to put himself in someone else's shoes. All humankind was flawed; I'd learned that over and over. We all had times when we failed to display those fine qualities. But they existed in us, provided we could dig deep enough. They seemed entirely lacking in Mathuin. Did that make him less than human? Or could even a monster like him somehow find a better self? It was hard to believe.

"All right?" Grim had ridden up alongside Flannan and me. "Long ride."

"I'll live. You?"

"Be glad to get there, monster or no monster. Sure you're all right? Looking a bit white."

"I'm fine. Tired, that's all."

Lady Geiléis must have heard me. She reined in her mount and announced that we would stop for a brief rest before tackling the last part of the ride. We were close by a sizable body of water, almost a small lake. Ducks swam, wading birds foraged in the shallows, and willows dipped their long branches into the water.

The men-at-arms moved into their practiced routine, laying blankets on the grass for us to sit on, unpacking food and drink, tending to the horses, and as usual saying very little.

"Come, sit with me," Geiléis said, patting the blanket beside her. "You look exhausted."

"I need to stretch my legs first. I'll walk a little way along the shore."

"Don't stray too far, Mistress Blackthorn."

I set off without replying. Grim made to follow but checked himself. He'd be assuming I was heading off to relieve myself in private. This was not like the times when he and I had been on the road together. Where each of us might once have stood guard in turn on such occasions, in present company that would cause eyebrows to be raised, not only Geiléis's but most likely Flannan's as well. Clearly, my old friend had not yet worked out what Grim and I were to each other.

I was squatting behind an elderberry bush when my skin prickled. A chill; a sense of strangeness. Had I heard a distant cry, a voice neither human nor animal? It was gone now. I tidied myself up and rose to my feet, senses alert. The small birds that had been chattering in the trees and searching for insects in the grass had fallen abruptly silent.

When I got back to the others, a fire had been kindled and water set to heat. There was no sign of Grim. "That was quick," I said to one of the men, but he made no reply beyond a nod. I sat down next to Flannan on one of the blankets. I still wasn't used to letting Geiléis's men wait on me, but the respite was welcome; I had aches and pains all over. At a certain point Grim reappeared, but did not come to sit by us. Instead he leaned against a tree on the far side of the small encampment with arms folded. He looked relaxed, off guard. I knew that pose; it was deceptive.

I accepted cold salt meat and a dried-out hunk of bread, softened with water from the stream.

"You're very quiet," murmured Flannan.

That moment of strangeness was still with me, though I was starting to wonder if I'd imagined it. I wasn't prepared to ask outright if anyone else had heard something odd. One thing I did notice: Ripple, who should have been exhausted after the long day's walk, was instead on high alert, ears pricked, body tense as she scanned the area around the camp. Obedient to Flannan as always, she stood beside him, but her unease was plain.

"Lady Geiléis?" I asked.

"What is it, Mistress Blackthorn?"

"The birds stopped singing all at once; did you notice?" I let that remark fall into the silence. She could make what she wanted of it. To me, the hush around us signaled the presence of the uncanny. I'd noticed it before, at Dreamer's Wood. Dreamer's Wood was full to the brim with magic.

"You are acute, Mistress Blackthorn," Geiléis said. "Of course, we are drawing closer to Bann, though we have some miles to travel before the tower comes into sight. Its voice—the monster's voice—carries a long way, and creatures have better hearing than ours. It has the power to silence them. Or so I believe."

"Extraordinary," said Flannan. "It sounds like something from an ancient tale. I heard nothing at all."

There was a note of doubt in his voice, which surprised me. "Every ancient tale has truth at its heart," I said. "That's what I've always believed, anyway. But after years and years of retelling, the shape of those old stories changes. What may once have been simple and easily recognized becomes strange, wondrous and magical. Those are only the trappings of the story. The truth lies beneath those fantastic garments."

Geiléis was gazing at me with apparent interest; she had set aside her food almost untouched. What unusual eyes she had, of a light gray-blue with a darker rim. The sort of eyes that belonged in just such an ancient tale as we were discussing.

"But Lady Geiléis's monster exists now," Flannan pointed out. "And it sounds as strange and wondrous as the oldest tale in the world."

"Indeed, Master Flannan." Geiléis's tone was cool. "When we reach Bann, you can assess for yourself how accurate my description was. Though you, I suppose, will continue on to St. Olcan's. You will find Father Tomas hospitable." She frowned. "But perhaps you have visited that foundation before in your wanderings."

"I have not, Lady Geiléis, though it has long been known to me by reputation. I look forward to spending some time there." Flannan glanced at me. "And to assisting Blackthorn with her quest, should she need me."

"You are old friends, I gather."

"We knew each other long ago." I hoped my tone would cut off further questions. "As for assisting me, Flannan, it would certainly be useful if you spoke to the monks at St. Olcan's about the monster. The older men in particular. You may dismiss ancient tales as fantastical, but they often contain the solutions to puzzles; the answers to mysteries. One of those monks may know something that will help us."

"I have spoken to Father Tomas about this, of course. On numerous occasions." Lady Geiléis rose to her feet, brushing down her skirt. "He had nothing to add to what I already know. Rumors, whispers suggesting this is not the first time the creature has haunted the Tower of Thorns. Hints that it can only be driven away on Midsummer Eve. Those snippets did not come from the brethren at St. Olcan's, but from folk out in the community."

"I'll be talking to them as well," I said. "As will Grim. The more we can find out before midsummer, the better our chances of success." Grim had contributed nothing at all to this conversation. He hadn't moved from his spot under the tree.

"Of course, your man would also be welcome to stay at St. Olcan's." Geiléis gave Grim a brief glance. "He could ask his questions there while you did so more widely. No doubt you'll receive requests for your services as a healer. As I mentioned, we have neither wise woman nor druid close to Bann. If folk ask, you must say no. We have so little time."

"It's up to Blackthorn if she says yes or no." Grim spoke at last, making no concessions to courtesy. "That's her job, tending to sick folk. What if a babe was wrong way round, or someone got a nasty kick in the head from a cart horse? You wanting her to say, *Sorry, I'm too busy to save your life?*"

"You defend her with some passion." This time Geiléis's gaze stayed on him longer, and he flushed.

"Just saying."

"He's right." I hated to see that look on Grim's face, the one that appeared when folk treated him like a simpleton or doubted his judgment. He was all too ready to believe their assessment of him true. "Under circumstances like those I would feel obliged to help; that's what a wise woman does. I understand the need to find a solution for you before midsummer, Lady Geiléis. And yes, time is short. But I can't make any promises other than that Grim and I will both do our best. I've already made that clear. And as for accommodation, it's more convenient if Grim and I are housed together. That rules out St. Olcan's." In fact, if I decided to go south with Flannan, having Grim stay elsewhere could make evading him easier when the time came. But I wouldn't suggest that now—it would alert him to something not right. We always stayed together. He couldn't get through the nights on his own.

"Should be moving on," muttered Grim. "Time being so short and all."

"Indeed," said Flannan, rising in his turn. "Quite apart from that, I'm becoming somewhat saddle weary. The relative comforts of a monastery are starting to sound quite appealing."

13

GRIM

I t's hard. No chance to talk to Blackthorn on her own, no chance to tell her what I've seen. Hoping when we get to Bann we'll have a spot that's just ours, bit of privacy. She'd want to know. Odd, it was. Oddest thing I've seen since we've been on the road together. Odder even than Conmael and his cronies popping up out of nowhere the way they do. And it could be useful.

Don't know if she heard what I heard. A howling, long way off, sad enough to bring tears. Reminded me of looking down at Strangler's face after I'd heaved him out of the lockup and hauled him to safety in the woods. Looking down and seeing his dead eyes. Reminded me of . . . No. Won't think of what's coming and the bad dreams that'll come with it. Got to be strong. Got to set all that aside. But this sound was sad as sad. Was it the monster? No knowing. Only after I heard it the birds all went quiet.

Turned back for the camp thinking I'd tell Blackthorn. Then I saw something. Long grass moving a few strides from me, like there was a creature there, a rabbit or squirrel. Reached for my knife, thinking of fresh meat for supper. Thing started running, and I got a better look. Wasn't any sort of animal, at least not one I've got a name for. It was something in a fur cloak with a hood. Little thing with a basket. Going on two legs. Only as high as my knee. There, then gone. Didn't see its face. Gave me the creeps. Gave me that tingling feeling I get in Dreamer's Wood. The fey. Only not Conmael's kind. Something else.

Can't tell her, though. Flannan's right beside her, talking and waving his hands around, and there's Lady Geiléis listening in to everything. Can't come straight-out and ask if the fey live around here, and if some of them are tiny folk. You'd think she'd have said. So I keep my mouth shut.

After a bit we ride on. The lady sends two of her men ahead to tell her folk we're nearly there. Whatever it was I heard, it's stopped now. We take a winding way past some farms and some woods. Nobody comes out to pass the time of day. Feels odd. So quiet here, not a soul in sight. Glad to see smoke rising from a hearth fire and a couple of cows heading into a barn, so I know we haven't wandered into some different world, an empty one.

The track passes through a beech wood. Pretty spot, little stream gurgling by, afternoon sun through the leaves. Path gets steeper. Big rocks under the trees. We slow down. Don't want any horses going lame.

"When we ride clear of these woods," says Lady Geiléis, "we will be on a rise, looking down over my holdings. You will see the forest, the river, the tower in the distance. And you will hear the creature's voice. My men will ride in front and behind; I will be beside Mistress Blackthorn, with Master Flannan and Grim close after. Do not let the crying distract you. Be assured, we can reach my house without entering the area that is . . ." She trails off, not finding the words.

I don't tell her I've already heard the monster. If that's what it was.

"Enchanted?" Blackthorn says.

"It could be put that way. You will be safe if you do not break from the formation."

The crying comes again, and Blackthorn's face tells me she's hearing it too. Louder here, and sadder. Fit to shake up a man's bones and chill his blood. Like before, it brings the bad times, the sad times, the times I've failed, the times I haven't matched up to the man I should be. I'm guessing Blackthorn'll be thinking of Cass and Brennan burning and how she couldn't save them. She'll be thinking of standing up to Mathuin and being laughed at. Flannan—can't tell if he can hear it. Don't know a lot about the man. But he'll have something in his past that he wishes was different, same as us. Doesn't everyone? This monster, it makes a man feel like a dog kicked out the door on a winter day.

I want to say I'll ride with Blackthorn, but I keep quiet and do as I'm told. Truth is, with all those men-at-arms she doesn't need me right now. Deep down, though, I know I'm the only one who can really keep her safe. If that makes me a fool, then I'm a fool. Bonehead, that's what they called me in that place of Mathuin's. Meaning stupid. Stupid to think I can do better than a team of armed guards who know the lie of the land. But that's just what I do think.

Up the top of the hill this bit of forest comes to an end, though not for long. We're looking down over a river—the Bann, must be—and there's a bigger forest between us and it, oaks mostly. Glimpse of farmland, a bit farther away. Just got time to take a breath or two and the sound comes again, loud as loud. Nobody could miss it.

"Halt!" calls Onchú, who's in charge, and we all rein in our horses. Onchú dips into his pouch and brings out what looks like a wad of wool.

"The sound is hard to bear, even for those who are accustomed to it," says Lady Geiléis. "For you, it will soon become intolerable. You should block your ears."

Onchú's pulling the wad into smaller pieces. He passes a couple to Blackthorn.

"Once dusk falls, of course," the lady says, "the creature will be silent. Be glad of that. To hear that sound both day and night would drive you out of your wits."

Flannan rides forward, takes the wool Onchú's offering and brings it back. Hands half to me.

"What about you?" Blackthorn's looking at the lady, brows up. "And your men?" None of them're blocking their ears. Though they're not looking keen to ride on either. Ripple's got her tail between her legs.

"The passage of time has enabled me to develop some resistance." Lady Geiléis is a nasty shade of white. Looks worn-out all of a sudden. "The wailing still has its effect," she says, "but I have learned to withstand the worst of it, as have the members of my household. It would be impractical to go about with one's ears blocked all day, every day. But you are new to this. You are here to help me, Mistress Blackthorn, and you will not be able to do so if you fall victim to the spell."

"If I did fall victim," says Blackthorn, "what would happen?"

"The sound would not only hurt your ears and give you a severe headache, it would also fill your mind with unwelcome thoughts. Recollections of past failures. Memories of sorrow and loss. If you traveled unguarded, you would soon find yourself swept away in a tide of self-reproach. The curse would leave nothing of you. Only a hollow shell in which regrets rattled about like dry seeds in a gourd."

Makes me wonder why Prince Oran hadn't even heard of this lady before she turned up at court. Nobody knew about her or the monster or any of it. Such a strange tale, you'd think everyone in Dalriada would be telling it. And the lady did say it had been going on for a while. Long enough for word to get out, I'd have thought. But what would I know?

"This has actually happened to folk?" says Blackthorn. "The sound has turned them witless? Are the effects permanent?"

"The effects are long-lasting," Lady Geiléis tells her. "Believe me, you and your friends should block your ears."

Blackthorn turns a look on her. "If you want me to solve your mystery," she says, polite as if she was asking Geiléis to pass the salt, "you must allow me to make my own choices. I will carry the wool. That's only common sense. If I think I need to use it, I will. Grim can make his own decision. We will remain with the escort; I give you my word." She looks across at Flannan. "You should stop your ears from the start, Flannan." She speaks softer when she's talking to him. "Nobody's asked you to investigate the monster; no reason to put yourself at risk. But I must be able to hear. Time is short for this quest. I should listen and learn."

Lady Geiléis is not having this. Doesn't like anyone else trying to take charge, that's plain. "But, Mistress Blackthorn—"

"Past failures, you mentioned. Memories of sorrow and loss. Grim and I are accustomed to those. They walk with us day and night." Blackthorn glances over at me again, not quite smiling. "Besides, I've been hearing your monster's voice clearly for some time now. It started while we were halted by the lake. You?" It's me she's asking.

"Mm-hm." Not saying any more than that. I put my share of the wool wadding in my pouch. Blackthorn's right about sorrow walking beside us. Surprised to hear her speak up about it, though. Got a weight of bad memories, the two of us. Doubt if a wailing monster could make it much heavier.

Lady Geiléis signs to her men to ride on, and we all move forward. I'm behind the lady. Her back's stiff. Angry, but holding it in. Or upset. Because she hasn't blocked her ears any more than Blackthorn and me have. She's hearing what we're hearing. And that's a sound that's getting sadder with every step the horses take. My animal's shivering under me. And Ripple doesn't want to walk on; Flannan has to keep calling her. Why didn't we block *their* ears? I want to ask, but I don't. Didn't the lady say, in her story, about cows dropping dead calves? Stock wandering into the river and getting drowned? But maybe these riding horses are used to it, same as the men. Not the animals we've brought from Cahercorcan, though. Seems a bit cruel to put them through it.

We get down the hill, ears full of the wailing, and the escort picks up the pace. Light's starting to fade. Nightmares in my head. Finding Blackthorn's red kerchief neatly folded on my bed and thinking she was gone forever. Our house burning. Hearing her screams and thinking she was trapped inside. And farther back, Strangler and the other lads and that place of Mathuin's. The stink, the sounds, the pain, the dark. The way I failed the others.

Blackthorn hasn't blocked her ears, so I'm not blocking mine. Job to be done. Need to match her, help her. Listening. Solving a puzzle. Back in Mathuin's lockup, when the bad things got too loud, I shut them out with words. Worked sometimes. Not always. I try it now. Keep my voice down, though the monster's making enough racket to drown out anything. *Dominus regit me, et in loco pascuæ id . . . ib . . . ibi me collocavit.* Funny how it comes back. Been a long time. Still there, though, tucked away inside. *Super aquam refectionis educavit me.* Steady and soothing, the words are. Even when a man's long ago lost his faith in gods.

Maybe Flannan's ears aren't stopped up tight enough. Keeps glancing over at me. I drop my voice to a whisper. *Nam, et si ambulavero in medio umbræ mortis, non timebo mala: quoniam tu mecum es.* Walking in the shadow of death. Been there. Know it like I know my right hand. Feel myself shivering; make myself breathe strong, be the man I should be. Should have been. *Et misericordia tua subsequetur me omnibus diebus vitæ meæ.* Mercy. Fine thing. Wish I could believe in it. Tears in my eyes. Stupid fool.

Getting darker. The monster's voice is not so much of a wail now. Sounds more like a child who's been crying so long he's all out of strength. Harsh, rasping sort of sound. Sobbing. Like he's defeated, giving up. Makes my throat hurt to hear it. For just a bit, I wonder if this monster's not yelling threats and curses, but calling out *Help!* In my head there's a little boy fallen down a well, or shut up in the dark, or stuck up a tree with night coming, and nobody to hear him.

"Look through that gap between the trees," says Lady Geiléis to Blackthorn, "and you will see the tower."

I look too, and there it is. Eerie, with the light starting to fade. Made all of pale stone, taller than the trees, and they're old oaks, some of them. Window at the top. Can't see if the shutters are open. Can't see if the creature's there, but the sound's still coming, cracked and broken. Wisps of mist coming up from the river, creeping between those big trees, making a shroud for the place. Of course, it's on an island. That's what the lady said. Woods are so thick around the tower, all I can see of the river is a gleam here and there.

Birds, suddenly. Birds all around the tower, a dark cloud of them. The sun's sinking; nearly dusk.

"Ride on," says Lady Geiléis.

"Wait!" Blackthorn's not moving, and even though she's not much of a rider, her horse keeps still too.

"We must move on, Mistress Blackthorn. The path is not easy; we must reach our destination while there is still sufficient light."

Blackthorn's not hearing her. She's staring at the tower, the birds, the window that might or might not be open.

"Mistress Blackthorn!" Geiléis is sharp now. "We must move on."

Those birds; if they were making a sound, could we hear it? Or are we too far away? Could be it's like Dreamer's Wood. Full of magic, dangerous stuff, so birds know to keep quiet. One thing I can guess, looking at that tower. Whatever's in it is uncanny. Or it's something trapped there by a spell. A spell so strong, even I can feel it.

The lady reaches out to grab hold of Blackthorn's bridle and haul her away, which I could tell her wouldn't be a good idea at all.

"Give her a moment, my lady," I say, speaking loud so she can hear me over the monster. "Could be important."

Don't much like the look Lady Geiléis gives me. Chilly as a lake on midwinter morning. That look tells me what she really thinks—that I'm too stupid to take any part in this, and that she can't understand why Blackthorn lets me tag along.

Flannan takes the wool out of his ears. "Holy Mother of God," he says. "That's the saddest sound I heard in my life."

"Mm," murmurs Blackthorn. "I want to wait here until the sun sets, Lady Geiléis." Seems she did hear after all.

"Impossible. The track would be far too dangerous in the dark."

"You said the crying stops at sunset. I want to hear that. I want to see what those birds do when it ceases."

"The birds? What part can they play in this?"

"I don't know. But I'm here to find a solution for you, and I cannot do so if you restrict me." Got that note in her voice, the one that means trouble's coming.

"We could come up another day," I say. For once, I think the lady's right. Makes no sense to risk the horses just because Blackthorn's got a bee in her bonnet about something. "On foot. Wait for the sunset. Bring a lamp for the way back."

Geiléis looks at me again, not so chilly. "Indeed."

The horses are restless, picking up their feet, twitching their ears, ready for the home stable and a good feed. Even Blackthorn, with her eyes fixed on the tower, can't miss it. "Very well," she says, and turns her horse. "Either here, or somewhere else with a good view of the top."

"Ah," says the lady. "For that, there is no need to venture so far. The tower is clearly visible from a certain spot in my house. Now come. The power of that place and its inhabitant is far greater than you imagine. We must not linger here."

Turns out Lady Geiléis's house has its own tower. Small one, on the corner. Built all of stone, like those old fortifications you find here and there. The rest of her house is stone too, big dressed blocks that would have been hard to lift. Looks as if it's been there a few generations. Moss growing all over; thatch darkened with the wet. Forest all around, couple of old oaks growing up right beside the house. Someone's lit torches by the entry to show us the way in. Monster's stopped its wailing. I'm guessing it went quiet right when the sun dipped out of sight. Couldn't see, riding through the woods. The birds—there's no knowing what they did, though there are birds in the trees around the house, making the little chirps, peeps and hoots that mean good night. Could do with a sleep myself. Blackthorn's got a look in her eyes that says her temper's holding by a thread. She needs food, quiet, rest. Soon. Hope Lady Geiléis can see that.

We go in through a gate in the wall and stop in a courtyard, nothing grand. I make sure I'm down quick enough to give Blackthorn a hand. She looks like she might have trouble standing on her own.

That's when I remember Flannan isn't meant to be staying here at all. But here he is, with his dog, and it's almost night.

"Master Flannan," says the lady. Her men-at-arms are leading the horses away. The house door's open and a fellow with a lamp is waiting to see us in. "It is too late for you to ride on to St. Olcan's tonight. Please accept my hospitality until the morning; one of my folk will take you there after breakfast."

Makes sense. Trouble is, if he's around, I'll get no chance to talk to Blackthorn on her own until bedtime. Maybe not even then.

Flannan thanks her and we go indoors. The fellow at the door is Geiléis's steward. Name of Senach. There are other serving folk around, waiting to be told what to do.

"Grim and I need our own chamber, with two beds," says Blackthorn. "I imagine Master Flannan will be happy with a place in your men's quarters." She's trying not to let everyone see how the journey's worn her out.

"You'll be weary, all of you," Lady Geiléis says. "Senach will arrange for a light supper to be sent to your quarters; we don't stand on ceremony here. Time enough to talk again in the morning." She gives Blackthorn a direct sort of look. Blackthorn meets it, as steady as a rock, though I know she's dropping with tiredness. "You're sure you would not prefer a chamber all to yourself, Mistress Blackthorn?"

"Quite sure, Lady Geiléis. Can your household not accommodate my request?"

"Senach," says the lady, "show Mistress Blackthorn and her . . . friend to the guest quarters. Dau, take Master Flannan to the men's quarters, and arrange for all of our visitors to be provided with hot water for bathing. The dog will need to be fed; I'm sure you can find something suitable." She looks at Blackthorn again, then at me, but holds back whatever it is she wants to say. I'm guessing she doesn't want to offend Blackthorn, because she needs her problem solved. And if she didn't know Blackthorn had a mind of her own when we left court, she must know now. "I wish you a good night's rest."

"Just one thing."

"Yes, Mistress Blackthorn?"

"The stairs to that higher level of the house—where are they?"

"The high chamber is accessible only through my private quarters."

"I see," says Blackthorn, maybe not so tired after all. "Since I was unable to watch and listen as the creature fell quiet at sunset, I would like to be present in the morning when it wakes. Shall I knock on your door a little before dawn?"

Something funny going on here. Beyond me.

"Let us delay this one more day, Mistress Blackthorn. That was a long ride. I, for one, intend to sleep late tomorrow."

"We don't have a lot of time," Blackthorn says. "As you've pointed out."

"True; but one day will make no great difference. Besides, you'll be wanting to take breakfast with Master Flannan before he leaves, since the two of you are old friends." Never mind that the creature starts its noise at dawn, according to the story, and Flannan's not going to be rushing off to this monastery as early as that. Though the brothers will be early risers. That I know.

"The day after tomorrow, then," Blackthorn says. "I've no wish to disturb you in your private quarters, but if that's the only stairway to your tower I'll need to do so, more than once. I want to hear how it starts and stops. I want to see if anything changes."

"I have watched it over and over, Mistress Blackthorn."

"And learned nothing from it," Blackthorn says, blunt as ever. "Isn't that why I'm here?"

"We are all weary," says the lady. She looks it, same as Blackthorn. Pale as pale, her eyes all dark shadows. "I will accommodate your needs in due course. Now I'll bid you good night. If you need anything, ring the bell in your quarters and my folk will attend you."

14

GEILÉIS

It seemed to Geiléis that the mirror lied. The woman in the polished bronze was every inch a queen. Her golden hair was plaited into a crown. She held her back straight and her head high. Nobody would have doubted that she held control of her own destiny.

"Who are you?" Geiléis whispered. "Pretender! I do not know you."

Her reflection gazed back, eyes wide, brows lifted as if in silent mockery. Behind her the bedchamber was quiet, shadowed, a single lamp casting soft light from the chest in the corner, by the little stairway to her tower. Up there, the shutters had been closed for the night. She had come too late for dusk. Across the forest in his own tower, he would be sleeping. A blessed time of respite, until tomorrow's dawn.

"This is impossible." Despite her best efforts, her voice shook. By all the powers, could she not keep a rein even on that? She made herself breathe deeply; tried to hold herself tall, as that other woman did. "It is intolerable. I look at you and I see—I see weakness. I see falsehood. I see failure."

Perhaps the woman in the bronze smiled just a little. It was hard to tell.

"The healer—this Blackthorn—she will be as useless as the others, and you know it," Geiléis muttered. "They've all been useless. Nobody can do it. Who but a fool or a half-wit would undertake such a task willingly? Blackthorn is neither. Indeed, I believe she may be altogether too astute."

A tap at the door. She flung the cloth over the mirror, veiling the lying mask of her reflection. "Come in!"

Senach, with a tray. "My lady, your supper."

"I can't eat."

"Perhaps later, my lady. I will leave it here." Her steward set the tray down on a chest carved with oak leaves and acorns. "Your guests are settled. All that you requested has been provided for them. And word came from Father Tomas. He will send one of the brothers in the morning to escort Master Flannan to St. Olcan's."

"Thank you, Senach." He was a good servant. It was too easy to take him—to take all of them, patient and loyal as they were—for granted. "You have done well."

He bowed his head in acknowledgment. They expected little from her. Which was as well, since she had little left to give.

"There are times when it is near impossible to go on, Senach. When the flame of hope might be extinguished by the merest sigh. I do not think I can bear another failure."

A silence.

"Nothing to say?"

"It is not for me to express an opinion, my lady. I serve you. I serve your will."

"And if I told you my will is as fragile as that flame I spoke of? That I look at myself in the mirror and see beneath the surface an old woman, weak and exhausted?"

"Then I would say, my lady, that Midsummer Eve is not far away. Whatever is needed to keep that flame burning, we will do it for you. We would give our lives for you, Lady Geiléis. Every one of us."

"I know." She drew a deep breath; released it in a sigh. "And what choice is there, when it comes to it? Very well; here are my instructions, for now. The woman, Blackthorn—she is inquisitive, Senach. Clever. Observant. Not like the others. I don't want her discovering the full truth too early, or she may turn tail and run. But we mustn't appear to be impeding her investigations. I persuaded her to come to Bann on the grounds that she might find a solution for me, and we must allow her to take what steps she thinks appropriate. We should let her learn enough to hold her interest until the time comes. But not too much. She is the kind of person who might want to meddle. Already she shows a desire to take control of the situation. That we cannot have."

"And the fellow, Grim?"

"I don't believe such a man can present any threat, save in his devotion to the woman. I doubt the fellow will observe anything that the healer misses. Let him trail along behind her until we near the end."

"Yes, my lady."

"Mistress Blackthorn has expressed a wish to observe the activity of the birds at the tower; I cannot imagine why. She can be admitted to my chamber at dawn, if she insists, but not at dusk. You might instead offer to take her and the man up the hill to a spot with a clear view. Make sure she does not see anything else, Senach. No activity on the ground. Nothing untoward in the woods. Make sure the word goes out."

"I will attend to it, my lady." Her steward paused; cleared his throat. "I hope you will take a little of the supper. It will give you strength."

"That will be all for tonight." She waved a hand toward the door.

"Yes, my lady."

Alone once more, Geiléis used her lamp to light a candle. Then, step by careful step, she climbed to the upper level. Never mind that dusk had fallen some while ago. She must keep faith. Her folk believed in her. They still had hope, even after so long. Senach was right; Midsummer Eve was drawing ever closer. Perhaps, against all odds, this time she would succeed. Perhaps this healer with her shock of flaming hair and

her prickly ways would be the answer she needed. Perhaps, perhaps . . .
And in the meantime, although he slept, the story must be told . . .

*Lily slept little that night. Her mind was alive with Ash: the way he
had looked at her, the brief touch of his hand, the whisper of his breath
against her cheek. His words: You are a lamp in the dark, a fair flower
in the shadows. Nobody had ever spoken to her like that, and it made
her feel quite odd. Why had she left him in the tower all alone? Why
had she not run to her father or to the household steward, explained
the situation and asked for help? Yes, that would have meant confessing
she had been out in the woods without any companions, and that
would have led, without doubt, to her being prevented from going
back, and that meant, almost certainly, that she would never see Ash
again. But what if she returned to the tower tomorrow and he was lying
dead, when she could have saved him?*

*Next morning she endured an hour of embroidery, an hour of prac-
ticing the harp, an hour of exercising the lapdogs in the courtyard and
kitchen garden, where they dug a deep hole while she sat on a bench
and dreamed of Ash. She returned the dogs, filthy but in good spirits, to
her mother. She went to the larder and helped herself to a slice of mutton pie, two apples and, on further consideration, a small bag of sweetmeats. All this she smuggled to her bedchamber. It helped that her
maid, Muiríol, was fond of one of the grooms, and welcomed any
excuse to make a trip out to the stables or to the field where the horses
were exercised. But it startled Lily to discover her own talent as a dis-
sembler and thief.*

*She found another water skin, though she hoped Ash would, at the
very least, have regained enough strength to get down the stair to the
island, where the river could provide as much water as anyone could
possibly want. Perhaps the little ferryman would have brought him
back over. Indeed, the more she thought about it, the more obvious it
became that Ash would have gone home, wherever home was. He was
surely tall enough to wade to shore with no difficulty. Of course he
would be gone. He would have been braver than she was. He would*

have faced up to his family and told them he'd been out late, and had drunk too much, and had fallen down and hurt himself, and had then found himself in a strange place, and had suffered disturbing dreams . . . He wouldn't be there, she told herself. And that was a good thing. But she would still go, just in case.

She found bandages and salve in the stillroom, making sure she slipped in and out while her mother was occupied with bathing the lapdogs. Back in her chamber, she packed everything into a bag and, hearing Muiríol's voice from the hallway as her maid returned from the stables, thrust it under her bed. She waited, trying not to think of him and failing miserably.

Then there was the midday meal to get through, and a conversation during which she made brief responses while barely aware of what her parents were saying. The meal seemed interminable. Her mother commented that Lily seemed out of sorts; perhaps she was unwell? Lily agreed that it was time for her rest, and that she might stay abed a little longer than usual. She retired, telling Muiríol to take the afternoon off. She closed her bedchamber door.

Then it was bag on her back, shutters open, down the oak tree, out through a tiny door in the outer wall that only the kennel boys used, and away through the forest to the tower. Lily was certain nobody had seen her go; she had made herself as swift as a shadow.

Today the sun was veiled by clouds, and the river flowed sullen and gray. Lily made her way along the bank to the little pebbly beach, but no small craft bobbed there in the shallows. There was no sign of the ferryman. Should she call out? What if her voice alerted the wrong person to her presence—a traveler heading north across the ford, or even someone from home, who would surely tell her parents she'd been in the woods alone?

"Ferryman?" She dared a soft call. "Are you there?"

No reply. Even the birds had gone quiet.

"Ferryman? Will you take me to the island?"

Nothing. The wee man was not there, and nor was his boat. Common sense said go home, climb up and slip back in the window, try again another time. But Ash . . . What if he was still up in the tower, on his own and needing her help? She could not turn her back and walk away. That would be wrong; cruel. But she could not shout his name. Her father's swineherd took his charges out to forage in the woods most days. If not him, then someone else was sure to hear.

There was another way. She could hitch up her skirts and wade to the island. The bag was secure on her back; if she trod carefully, she should get over. If she did not spend long in the tower, she could be quickly back home and in dry clothes before anyone saw her.

Without taking time to consider the pitfalls of this plan, Lily tucked her hem into her belt and headed back along the bank toward the ford. The best approach, she judged, was to wade halfway over in that shallower water, then strike out for the island at the point where the distance was least, which meant right in the middle of the river. She must hope that she wouldn't need to swim. Go, she ordered herself. It was easier to do alarming things if one did not think about it too much beforehand.

The ford was deeper than she had expected, and the pebbles slipped and slid underfoot as if they had minds of their own. The water was icy cold. Ash, she thought. I'm doing this for Ash. But another voice within her said, He'll have gone home by now; why would he stay up there? You'll have got wet and cold for nothing. And then you'll have to wade back again.

She reached the middle of the ford; from here, the island seemed not so very far away. Its gently rising sward and bright wildflowers seemed to call to her; it was easy to imagine herself and Ash sitting there together, hand in hand, perhaps whispering such sweet remarks as those he had made to her the day before. Yes, he had told her to go away. But . . .

She took a step into deeper water. Gods, it was cold. The current tugged at her clothing with insistent fingers. A shiver ran through Lily. Perhaps she should go back. She could feel the power of the river, and it frightened her.

Birds rose suddenly from the tower, a cloud of them, and beneath the susurration of their wings came another sound. Was that a voice, calling her name? Now silence; only the river spoke. Ash, thought Lily, and took another step.

It was fast; oh, so fast. Her foot slipped, she fell, the water came over her, she could not breathe. It swept her downstream, and as she came up, gasping for air, trees and sky and bushes and riverbank rushed past in a dizzying confusion. "Help!" she shrieked in the moment before she went under again. I'm going to die, she thought. And it's all my own fault.

Then someone was in the water with her, someone whose arms came around her, strong and sure, and she could breathe again, almost, and someone was half dragging, half carrying her out onto the bank. Onto a grassy sward dotted with flowers. She was on the island. No, she was dead and this was some sort of vision . . .

"Lily! Lily, speak to me!"

It was real. He was here, soaking and shivering in his torn shirt, and she was on her hands and knees, coughing, spluttering, retching up river water, her gown dripping, her chest heaving.

"What were you doing? I thought you had drowned!"

Through her discomfort, she heard the desperate note in Ash's voice. "I'm sorry," she choked. "I brought you some food, some other things . . . but they'll be all wet." She snatched a breath; managed to sit up. Eased the sodden bag off her back. Realized that the soaking had rendered her gown somewhat transparent and crossed her arms over her chest. "You're still here," she said. "I thought you might have gone home."

"Just as well I didn't, or you would be far down the river by now. You scared me, Lily. I haven't run so fast in a long time. And now you're wet through and freezing cold, and I have neither warm hearth nor blanket to offer you."

She was indeed cold. The island might be a pretty spot, but the day was cool and her clothes were wet through. "I'm sorry," she said again through chattering teeth. "The ferryman wasn't there. And I didn't want to go home without checking that you were all right." He seemed to have more bruises and cuts than before; had that damage been done in the water?

"What ferryman?" Ash asked.

"The little ferryman. The . . . I don't know what he is. A small fey person."

Something changed in Ash's face; something closed up. Did he think she would lie to him?

"There are fey folk in these woods. I see them sometimes. But that was the first time I had spoken to one. He was . . . friendly. Helpful."

"Not today."

"I'm sorry," she said once more, not sure whether she felt embarrassed or guilty or furious or all three at once. "I . . . I needed to come over. I needed to be sure you . . . I mean . . . You saved my life, Ash." She was shivering so hard now that she could barely speak. She had indeed been foolish. How was she going to get home?

"Here," said Ash, and drew her into his arms. "I have no hearth fire, but I'll warm you the best I can."

It was an awkward sort of embrace, made more so by the fact that the two of them were wet through, but Lily felt his body strong and warm against hers. She laid her head on his shoulder, and knew that if her whole world had not changed the moment she first saw him in the tower, it surely had now. His hand came up to stroke her hair; his fingers were gentle, brushing back the wet strands from her face. Through a rent in his shirt, her cheek touched smooth bare skin.

"I'm—" she began after a little.

"Shh," whispered Ash. "Don't say you're sorry you came. I am not sorry at all, only glad that I did not fall and break my neck in my headlong rush to reach you. Glad that I still have you." There was a lengthy silence, during which his hand came down to caress the back of her neck, while her fingers moved tentatively, then lingered in the strands of his crow-dark hair.

A few paces away, someone cleared his throat. Lily and Ash released each other instantly and struggled to their feet, awkward in their wet garments. Before them stood the ferryman, holding an armful of dry wood and regarding them with a quizzical expression. "Kindle you a wee fire?"

"Oh, yes!" said Lily, and at the same moment, "No!" said Ash.

"Young lady might perish from the cold."

"No fire," Ash said. "Unless you can make a fire without smoke. Smoke would draw unwelcome attention."

He was right, of course. Smoke rising from the island was sure to bring curious onlookers, since it was well-known that nobody ever set foot over here.

"I can," said the little man, and proceeded to do so, every twig set just right, the whole arrangement circled by white stones that he seemed to find without really looking. When the wood was in place he crouched over it, and a moment later the heap was ablaze, crackling heartily. There was no smoke at all.

"Thank you," Lily said, crouching close to the flames and reaching out her hands to warm them. "I brought you something, but I'm afraid it will be spoiled." She unfastened her pack and reached inside for the sweetmeats. Curiously, the little bag that held them was quite dry, and when she peered in, the contents looked entirely unharmed by their dunking in the river. "Here it is."

The ferryman accepted the small bag, opened it and sniffed deeply at the dainties within.

"It's not meant as a payment," Lily said. "More of a gift."

"Tasty," said the little man, and slipped the sweetmeats into his pouch. "Kind girl. Warm up quick and I'll ferry you back over. No harm done."

What was to be said? She had nearly drowned. She had endangered not only herself, but the man her heart told her was her one and only, her destined true love. If the ferryman offered safe transport, she had no choice but to accept. As for why he had not helped her before, when she needed him, the answer was simple. The wee man was fey. The fey did not think the way humans did; everyone knew that. "Thank you," she said, feeling her eyes fill with foolish tears.

She unpacked her bag. Her plan had been to tend to Ash's wounds herself, to salve and bandage them. But now that he had held her close, now that she had felt the thrill of that in her body, deep and dangerous, she thought it best not to offer. "I will leave these things for you. There's food and drink too."

Ash had gone oddly quiet. He sat staring into the small fire, his handsome features as somber as if someone had indeed drowned. What had she said to upset him? Was he angry with her for being so foolish? Perhaps she was quite wrong about this. Perhaps those feelings of longing were entirely one-sided.

"Ash," *she said after some time.* "You could come too. Leave the island, go home, be safe. Will you tell me who you are? Who you really are? I could help you."

"You said you'd seen the fey in these woods." *He did not look at her, but kept his gaze on the flames.* "When? Who did you see, small folk like him, or . . . ?"

His tone troubled her. It was as tight as a bowstring.

"I see them quite often when I'm out walking, though never very close, and never for long. Not wee folk; these are more like human men and women. Only . . . only I can tell they're different."

"Have you seen a—" *Ash began, then fell silent once more.*

"I should go," *Lily said. But she did not rise.*

"Rain coming," *put in the ferryman after a while.* "Go soon, yes?"

Rain. Rain might be useful, Lily thought. "Ferryman," *she said,* "could you take both of us back over? Ash and me? I know the boat is small, but you could ferry us one at a time."

"What will you pay?"

"I will pay," *said Ash before Lily could answer.* "For her to go safely across, and for you to see she gets home unharmed. Here." *He held out his hand with something on the palm; a small, shining thing that must have been concealed in his clothing, or around his neck perhaps, for there was a fine cord attached.*

The wee man examined it. "Sure?" he asked, turning a beady stare on Ash. "Quite sure?"

"I've nothing else to offer. Please take Lily safely home."

He did not want to come with her; he did not want to leave the island. And yet he'd sounded distraught at the idea of losing her to the river. Lily wondered if young men thought quite differently from young women. She surely did not understand this one. First he put his arms around her and filled her up with warm feelings; then he sent her away.

"It's best," Ash said now. "My presence imperils you, Lily. Look what just happened—you were a hair's breadth from drowning. If I came with you, danger would follow us both. There's no escaping it."

"I don't know what you mean. All I want to do is help you. I—" No, she would not say, I love you. She had known him only a day. But she said it in her heart, and with her eyes.

"Just let him ferry you across, and go home, and don't look back," said Ash. "Promise me."

This was cruel indeed. And unfair. "I won't promise," she said with such firmness as she could muster. "I can't turn my back and forget this ever happened. Not unless you can tell me, truthfully, that you never want to see me again."

Ash looked down at the ground. He said nothing at all.

Lily reached out and took his hands in hers. "Let me help you," she said. "Please. Whatever the danger is, I will face it with you."

Ash drew a deep breath and let it out in a kind of shudder. "I can't, Lily. I can't go, and I can't explain. I'm sorry; sorrier than I can say. Go now, please." He released her hands; took a step back. Now he was looking at her, and his eyes returned the feelings that were in her own heart. "Please, Lily. Leave the island; forget me."

"Best be moving," put in the ferryman, glancing up at the clouds, which were darkening even as he spoke. "A wet walk home, I'm guessing."

Her pride would not allow her to beg, to cling to him, to shed tears.

But walking away broke her heart all over again. "I'm not giving up,"
she murmured. "I'm stronger than you think."

What could it be that held him in such fear? This must be far more
than she had thought at first. No young man was in such terror of his
parents that a night of carousing would leave him unable to return
home at all. Surely an apology, a promise to do better in the future and
an acceptance of appropriate punishment would be all that was re-
quired. The answer must lie in finding out who he really was. Someone
must know; someone, surely, must be looking for him. She would find
out, even if it meant breaking secrets. She would find out and she
would save him.

The little boat made its way across to the shore, every dig of the
pole taking her farther from Ash. He stood on the island as she left, his
arms wrapped around himself, his face all shadows. It seemed to Lily
that she would need hope enough for two.

The rain came as the ferry reached the shore: droplets that soon turned
to a steady downpour. Lily stepped out. She could see barely an arm's
length ahead. "There's no need to walk back with me," she said, remem-
bering that Ash had, in effect, paid for her to be escorted home. "Thank
you for your kindness, ferryman."

"Kindness, is it? There may come a day when you won't thank me.
But you're a fine girl, and I hope it won't happen. Off home with you,
then, and may good spirits watch over you."

"And over him, I hope," said Lily. "Ash, I mean."

The wee man offered no reply. With the rain roaring down as if to
punish all in its path, Lily turned and sprinted for home.

15

Geiléis's household provided Grim and me with good accommodation—a roomy chamber, its stone walls softened with embroidered hangings; two comfortable beds well supplied with woolen blankets; and, best of all, our own small hearth with logs and kindling set by in a basket. Not that we'd have much time to sit by the fire sharing a brew, but it was good to have the means to make one if we felt so inclined. A second door led directly to a yard with a privy and a well. We could hardly have asked for better.

Soon after our arrival, servants brought us a small tub and jugs of hot water for bathing. Geiléis's retainers were efficient and, for the most part, curiously silent. There was no screen in the chamber. While each of us in turn bathed, the other went out into the yard. Our domestic arrangements were what they were: too complicated to explain to folk who did not know us well. And none of their business anyway. Grim would rig something up for privacy. He was good at these things.

After the long ride and that welcome bath, and with a full stomach, I anticipated a good night's rest. But the decision that lay before me, along with the knowledge that I had kept the truth from Grim, turned my belly into a churning mass of disturbance. When fitful sleep did come it was attended by dark dreams. I did not make any noise—at least, not that I was aware of—but Grim knew, all the same, and stayed awake with me. He asked me once or twice if anything was wrong, and I said, *Nothing worth talking about*, which was a kind of lie, but not the bare-faced one that an outright *No* would have been. Geiléis and her monster troubled me less than perhaps they should have. I would deal with them and move on. I would send the creature in the tower packing or I wouldn't. It was Flannan's mission that tangled up my thoughts, the mission I longed to say yes to, in spite of all my reservations. It was the only thing that counted. The only thing I cared about. What Flannan had said, about my not being true to Cass if I held back from bringing Mathuin to justice, stuck in my heart like a prickly burr that could not be dislodged. Yet I knew going south would be a reckless choice, even with all those like-minded folk ready to stand up alongside us. Mathuin was powerful. He was ruthless. Some chose freely to serve him; others did so out of fear. He was quick to punish the disobedient and was ingenious in his cruelty. Yes, Flannan's network was extensive, but I doubted, now, that anything less than a challenge by other leaders could overthrow the chieftain of Laois.

Last autumn I'd walked away from Winterfalls and headed south alone. Back then, my furious desire to see justice—the same passion I'd felt burning in me when Flannan had first told me his plan—had overwhelmed my common sense. If Grim hadn't come after me and talked me out of going, who knew where I would be now? Back in Mathuin's lockup, maybe, either thrown there by his henchmen, or magically transported there by Conmael. Though Conmael had given me five chances to get this right. So he might simply have appeared when I reached the border, made a comment about my poor judgment, and told me to go home. And although it galled me to admit it, he would have been right.

So why couldn't I let go of this? Why couldn't I tell Flannan straight-out that under no circumstances would I be part of this plot? In my dreams, brief, disturbing dreams, I saw Cass, a man whose goodness had shone from him, a husband who had loved me despite my faults, a father whose son had filled him with joy. I knew in my heart that Flannan was right—if Cass had lived, he would still be fighting. His greatest weapons had been his pen and his intellect. He would have found a way to go on using them. There were other dreams too. The lockup. The dark, the screaming, the thud of a whip on naked flesh. The filth, the things they did to me, the way I became so accustomed to being abused that I almost didn't care anymore. The faces of those men who shared the place with us. Strangler. Poxy. Dribbles. Frog Spawn. Poor sods.

And Grim. Grim who had stood by me when I was at my worst. Who, in those foul days and nights, had always called me Lady, as if I were above it all. Grim who had saved me from myself, over and over. Who had his own terrors, which meant he could not sleep on his own. If I said yes to Flannan, I would have to leave Grim behind. There was no way I was going to risk leading him back into that hellhole.

I ordered myself to go to sleep. I shut my eyes tight, rolled the blanket around me and buried my head in the soft goose-feather pillow. But my thoughts still roiled and swarmed like angry bees, setting my whole body on edge.

Once, during the night, I heard Grim muttering to himself from the darkness of his own bed. The words were unclear. Maybe nonsense, maybe not. It made me sad. It took so little to send him—or me—right back to that place, with the stink and the crying and the last spark of hope all but crushed. In the dark. Among the others, but alone. Almost alone.

"Grim."

A movement across the darkened chamber as he sat up abruptly. "What?"

"You all right? Just, you were talking to yourself."

"Sorry. Keeping you awake. Need your sleep."

"Not as if I'm not used to it," I said. "And I was awake already." And would not be sleeping; that had become quite obvious. I got out of bed, wrapped my shawl around me and went over to the hearth. It didn't take much to coax the ash-covered coals back into flickering flame, thanks to the handy supply of wood. I settled on the bench close by, letting the warmth soothe me. After a bit, Grim got up too and came to sit opposite me, his blanket around his shoulders. The light flickered over his plain, strong features, showing me the small, sad eyes, the heavy jaw, the nose that looked as if it might have been broken more than once. What would happen to him if I did go? Back at Winterfalls there was work for him, a home, friends who knew he was a good man. Maybe he'd be better off without me.

"Why did you change your mind?"

The question came out of the blue, startling me. "What do you mean?"

"About coming here. Leaving court, leaving Lady Flidais. Taking the risk. What changed your mind?"

He hadn't asked me before. I'd thought he wouldn't. "I don't want to talk about it. I just decided it was something I should do, that was all."

"Mm-hm." A weighty silence. Grim was hunched over, looking down at his linked hands. "It was him, wasn't it? Flannan. He changed your mind for you."

Too close to the truth. "Not exactly. But it did make a difference that he wanted to visit St. Olcan's, yes."

The silence filled with unspoken questions. Grim and I didn't talk about our past. We didn't ask each other about our lives before the time when we met as fellow prisoners. Only, if one of us wanted to talk about that time, the other one listened. I didn't want to now, but it felt necessary. I couldn't have him putting the pieces together and guessing the truth.

"Flannan and I are good friends. Having him survive, salvaging something worthwhile from that terrible time . . . I knew he'd be moving on at some point. That's his life now. Coming here instead of staying at court—it means I can spend a bit longer in his company, yes."

"Mm-hm. So you turn your back on another friend and go off to fight a monster. Something nobody else has managed to get near."

"What do you mean, another friend? Are you talking about Flidais? She gave me permission to go. Don't make more out of this than it merits, Grim. We're here now, we have a job to do and we'll do it. And . . ." I couldn't say, *Then we'll go home*. "And don't say *Mm-hm* again or I'll scream and wake up half the household."

Instead, he said nothing.

"A brew would be good," I said after a while. "Tomorrow I'll ask that steward for a pot and a couple of cups. And I'll gather a bit of this and that in the woods. We can head out after breakfast and have a look around."

"Something I forgot," Grim said. "Something I was going to tell you. Saw a little person, when we stopped by that lake. One of *them*, you know. Only not like Conmael's folk. Even stranger than them. Tiny. With a basket. Scurrying away across a field. Thought it was a squirrel, but no. Wearing a cloak with a hood. Like something out of an old tale."

"Not a child?"

"Not a human child. All wrong for that."

"Why didn't you say?"

He twisted his fingers together, not looking at me. "Didn't feel right to speak up, when all of them could hear. Not as if they know about us and Conmael, is it? Didn't get a chance to tell you on your own." After a little he added, "Sounds as if Flannan doesn't believe in the fey, anyway. He'd have thought I was crazy."

"Perhaps not. Nobody could visit this place without feeling the— the strangeness. That touch of the Other. And that's even without the monster wailing. Little folk with baskets might be the least of the surprises." I glanced at him. "You must be feeling it. The same as at Dreamer's Pool, only more so. Magic everywhere, and I can't tell if it's good or bad."

"Both, maybe," said Grim, who was a lot wiser than folk gave him credit for. "Could be what a body makes of it. One thing I know. That crying makes a man sadder than an old house with the roof half gone and the rain coming in."

"Mm." He was right, of course. And it wasn't as if Geiléis hadn't warned us. Could be my churning stomach and warring thoughts owed as much to the monster's influence as to anything else. "Sadder than a dog watching over its dead master," I said.

"Sadder than a pot of porridge with nobody to eat it."

"Sadder than a sausage left to go cold in the pan."

"I'm partial to a cold sausage, myself," said Grim, making me smile.

"I daresay Geiléis's retainers could oblige, if we asked them," I said. "They seem helpful, though not exactly given to chat. We'd better try to sleep. In the morning we'll brave those woods, if only to gather the makings of a brew. You keep an eye on me; I'll keep an eye on you. Just in case this curse inclines one of us to wander into the river and drown, or stray into some trackless part of the forest, never to be seen again. As for the curse addling folk's thoughts, mine feel addled enough already."

"Easier to fall asleep thinking of a sausage than that."

"True. Good night, Grim."

"Night."

Nobody could have slept past dawn in this household. As the sun rose, the crying began anew. Although the thick stone walls damped the sound, nothing could have shut it out entirely. If I had not fully understood Geiléis's desperation before, now it made a terrible sense.

We rose and dressed, observing modesty by the simple means of turning our backs to each other. I was heading out to the privy, thinking to draw water from the well for a brisk wash, when a servant came to our door with a jug of hot water, a bowl and a soft cloth. Another manservant. I realized I had not seen any women here yet, save Geiléis herself.

"What is your name?" I asked the man.

"Dau, Mistress Blackthorn."

"Have you been working in this household long?"

"A good while."

He looked no older than eighteen; a clear-eyed, golden-haired lad. "Does the creature's crying trouble you? Or are you used to it by now?"

Dau set down jug, bowl and cloth on the bench. "We serve the lady," he said. "The creature is what it is." He gave a little bow, then left the room. Whether he meant yes or no, I had no idea.

Another serving man came to the door not long afterward, offering to escort us to the dining chamber. There, breakfast was laid out on a long table with benches to either side. A platter held fragrant loaves; cold meat was fanned out in tidy slices. In addition there were several kinds of cheese, a dish of porridge, and a jug of ale. No sign of Lady Geiléis, but Flannan was there before us and rose to his feet as we came in. Ripple came out from under the table to greet us.

"Good morning." Flannan sounded in excellent cheer. "I hope you slept well."

I grimaced. "Could have been better. You?"

"Best night's rest I've had in a while. I daresay tonight will be less comfortable; monasteries are generally somewhat austere in their accommodations. Come, sit here. The steward said we're not to wait for Lady Geiléis. She'll be breakfasting in her own quarters."

The men were hungry and ate well. I drank some ale and made myself consume a bowl of porridge, though I was strung too tight to enjoy it. The servant had slipped silently away. But even with the three of us alone together, I found it hard to sustain anything like a normal conversation. I was relieved when the steward, Senach, came in to ask whether we needed anything.

"The breakfast is very good, thank you." I forced a smile. "Might I borrow a basket? I plan to gather some herbs this morning. And we'd like a kettle and some cups for our bedchamber. Grim and I don't sleep well; it's useful for us to be able to make a brew when we need it."

"You need only ring the bell, Mistress Blackthorn, and one of our folk will bring you whatever brew you wish, no matter how late the hour."

"What, wake folk in the night to wait on me? I don't think so, generous as the offer is. Just the things I've asked for, Senach, nothing more." Plainly this fellow didn't understand that boiling the water, tending the fire, chopping the herbs, all helped to settle restless minds and quiet tormenting voices in the night. No obliging servant could replace that.

"Of course, Mistress Blackthorn. Consider it done. As for going out to gather herbs, you should wait until Lady Geiléis has risen. I believe she may advise against wandering into the woods. She has told you, I expect, that folk often go astray in these parts. And there is the . . ." He glanced toward the shuttered windows, beyond which the monster's wails could be heard, faint but distinct.

"Keep the shutters closed all day, do you?" asked Grim.

"Only when we have visitors to the house," said Senach. "Those who live here are accustomed to the sound."

"Open them if you want," I said. "We're here to investigate Lady Geiléis's problem, after all. We can't do that very well if folk are constantly shielding us from its influence."

Senach regarded me gravely. "I would require Lady Geiléis's permission for that. Let us wait for her. I am sure she will wish you to take an escort." He turned to Flannan. "Speaking of escorts, Master Flannan, yours will be here soon. With your permission, I'll send someone to pack up your belongings."

"No!" Flannan got abruptly to his feet, then checked himself. "That is, I have very little with me, and I prefer to pack for myself. My writing materials, you understand—they are somewhat delicate, and I'm happier if nobody else handles them."

Senach managed, with the slightest lift of the brows, to convey that he thought this about as ridiculous as guests wanting to brew their own tea in the middle of the night. "As you wish, Master Flannan. When the monk arrives, I will let you know. Meanwhile, please ring the bell if there is anything you require." And he was gone.

"Odd old place," muttered Grim.

"No odder than any house where serving folk tend to grand lords and ladies," I said. Though that was not entirely true; Winterfalls was different. Prince Oran conducted the business of his household in an unusual spirit of equality. He treated his serving people, and his community, with a friendly respect that belied his status as crown prince of Dalriada. He let everyone have a say, yet when it came to the hard decisions, he was not afraid to make them. A pity there weren't more like him. When his time came, he would make an interesting king.

"We might walk part of the way to St. Olcan's with you," I said to Flannan. "Surely Geiléis won't object if we have a monk as escort. Grim and I can come back through the woods, gather an herb or two and have a look around on the way."

"So, not quite breaking the rules?" Flannan flashed a grin.

"They're not my rules. We'll be fine if we exercise common sense. Stick to the path. Stay together. Head for home if anything odd happens. And don't let the screaming get to us."

"I'd best go and pack up my things," Flannan said. "I don't quite trust that fellow to leave well alone, and I suppose the monkish escort will be here any moment. I'll leave you to your breakfast."

When Flannan was gone, Grim put down his spoon and looked across the table at me.

"What?" I said, unable to sound less than snappish. I was tired. I didn't especially want to say good-bye to Flannan, even if he wouldn't be far away. And I didn't want the complication I could see was coming. Grim looked uneasy. Almost unwell. "You disagree with the plan?"

"No need to go to the monastery. You want to find herbs, you want to have a closer look at the tower, we should go the other way. Toward the river."

"It'll be useful to know the way to St. Olcan's," I said. "We'll be wanting to talk to everyone in the district, monks included. Someone must know more about the monster and how it came to be here. Monks know a lot of old stories." He really was pale. "Are you all right? You look terrible."

The door opened, and in came a youngish man with the part-shaven head of a Christian cleric. His homespun habit, his rope sandals and the wooden cross at his belt completed the picture. "Oh," he said, looking around the chamber. "My apologies; I was looking for Master Flannan, the scholar."

Since, as far as I knew, the fellow had never seen Flannan before, this was a backhanded insult to Grim. "Gone to pack up his belongings," I said. "You're the escort, I presume?" If he could be rude, I could be ruder.

"So sorry—my name is Dufach. Yes, sent by Father Tomas to accompany Master Flannan to our foundation at St. Olcan's. And you are . . . ?"

"Blackthorn. A healer. A wise woman." Just to make it quite clear. If Father Tomas's community was going to object to me, best get it over quickly. "This is Grim. We're friends of Flannan's. But we'll be staying here with Lady Geiléis."

The monk gave a nod. The expression on his face told me he had no idea what to make of us. Perhaps Lady Geiléis had few visitors. Though if what she had told us was correct, St. Olcan's must see many linger within its scholarly walls. Or must have done, before the monster came.

"Are your devotions much disturbed by this creature at the ford?" I asked him. "I know you are a little farther away, but its voice is loud. Lady Geiléis has told us of a curse . . ."

Dufach was about to reply when Grim got up abruptly, mumbled something, and bolted out of the chamber. "Excuse me," I said, and followed him; I knew those signs all too well. He wasn't in the hallway. He wasn't in our bedchamber. I went outside to find him doubled over in the yard near the privy, bringing up his breakfast with some violence.

I drew water from the well; filled the cup that stood on the rim and brought it to him. "Should've told me you were feeling sick."

"Be fine in a bit. Nothing wrong with me." He straightened, wiped his mouth on his sleeve, accepted the water and drank. He was shivering.

"I'm a better judge of that than you are. If you were my patient I'd order you back to bed. You look appalling." I surveyed him as I would any person showing signs of illness. "Though not quite as bad as you did before. Sometimes all it takes is to empty your stomach."

"Waste of a good breakfast." He drank again, then went to refill the cup. "I'm all right."

"We'll see. Sit down awhile. That came on rather suddenly."

"I'll be fine. I said so."

There was no arguing with Grim on this sort of thing. There was no leaving him behind if he believed he should be with me. So I went off to collect a basket from the kitchen, and a few provisions in case we got hungry while gathering herbs, and when Flannan reappeared with his belongings the four of us set off together: the scholar and the monk, the so-called wise woman and . . . If this were an old tale, what name would I give Grim? The bodyguard? The companion? The protector, the keeper? The friend? He was all of those and more.

It seemed that one bout of vomiting had rid his stomach of whatever had disturbed it. But he still looked pale, and there was a tightness about his features. I'd seen Flannan eat the same breakfast as Grim, but he had not been visited by the same sudden sickness. Whatever had caused it, it was not the food.

The path to St. Olcan's led up a rise, under a fine stand of old oaks. We passed under an arching canopy of green. Ripple danced along beside us, making short forays from the path when interesting smells drew her attention. It would have been a lovely walk, had it not been for the creature's voice, ringing through the woods, piteous and terrible in its sorrow. The sound not only assaulted the ears, it crept into the very bones.

As he walked, Brother Dufach recited a prayer under his breath; at least, I assumed it was a prayer. My knowledge of Latin was limited to what I needed as an herbalist and healer. Since I had given up believing in gods of any kind, I would not use prayer to distract me from that dreadful voice, not even a form of prayer that had once had meaning for me. And it might seem insulting to the monk if I suggested we tell a story. The look on Grim's face was worrying me. It was bringing back memories I had no wish to revisit.

We reached the top of the rise.

"Might stop to catch my breath a moment or two," I said, fishing out the water skin I had brought in my bag. "Drink, Grim?"

He took it; his hand was shaking.

"Go on if you like," I said to the others, trying to sound offhand. The last thing Grim would want was for me to draw attention to what he would see as weakness. "How much farther is it, Brother Dufach?"

"A mile or so. Down through the beech wood, along by the stream and up over another hill. You'll see a copse of willows by a drystone wall. That is the edge of the monastery land. Then you simply follow the wall around to the gate." The monk glanced at Grim, who had his back turned to the rest of us. "If you wish to come all the way, we can offer you refreshment before you return to Lady Geiléis's residence. We have a guest area where women can be received." He paused. "Our establishment is far enough from the ford to render the creature's voice much less troubling. Within our walls it can barely be heard."

"And that, I imagine, is why you and your brethren, and your animals, are not affected by it in the way others in the district are," I said, thinking to give Grim what time he needed to recover himself. "Lady Geiléis told us your cows are still producing healthy calves. And it seems your work continues undisturbed."

"The power of prayer is great," said Brother Dufach. "God holds us in his hand. That is not to say this does not try us hard. We did not invite visitors this summer, and will not do so again until the creature is gone. As a result, our work does not progress as it used to. Our scholars are looking forward very much to spending time with you, Master Flannan." A pause. "Forgive me, Mistress Blackthorn, but I had heard . . . I had heard that Lady Geiléis brought you here to . . . deal with the creature. Is that true?"

"Something like that, Brother Dufach. Though if your God has not managed to rid the district of the scourge, who am I to attempt such a feat? Let's just say I'm here to find out as much as I can about the creature and why it does what it does. Shall we walk on?"

Grim had turned to face me. There was a little more color in his cheeks. Still, he was plainly not himself. Perhaps he'd benefit from a rest at the monastery, time away from the constant crying. It was enough to bring the sunniest of folk to tears.

"How about a tale?" said Grim, working hard to make his voice steady. "Got one for a day like this?"

"A good idea, if Brother Dufach has no objection." For the life of me I couldn't think of anything appropriate, though I had a rich fund of tales. Any story that came immediately to mind was full of loss, heartbreak, failure. Like my own life.

"Clurichauns," murmured Grim.

"Clurichauns, very well. You might have to help me." I glanced from the shivering Grim to Flannan, who wore a puzzled smile, to Brother Dufach. The monk was serene, waiting patiently for us to go on. "And we should keep walking as I tell it. Long ago and far away there lived two tribes of clurichauns . . ."

It felt distinctly odd to tell a tale of Otherworldly matters to a party containing a Christian monk. As we made our way through the woods, I had the clurichaun tribes fall out over the ownership of a certain pony. "Such a fine creature had never been seen throughout the land of Erin," I said. "Snowdrop was her name, and such was the dazzling whiteness of her pelt that when she passed by, folk thought the moon herself had come down from the sky to visit the earth in the guise of a creature.

"Each of the clurichaun kings—there were two tribes, the green and the blue—wanted Snowdrop as a gift for his daughter. You'd think, wouldn't you, that they might have got together to discuss the matter and reach some kind of agreement to share the creature. But no; clurichauns being what they are, there was no compromise to be made. There was only one way to settle the matter: war."

"These clurichauns," said Brother Dufach, sounding not the least disturbed by the story, only interested, "they are combative in their very nature, then?"

"Did your parents not tell you tales like this when you were a lad?" I asked him. Monks must start their lives as ordinary boys, with ordinary lives. As did, say, druids. Even as I thought this, memories of my own childhood came back, memories I had long ago shut away. I made sure I did not meet Flannan's eye, though I could tell he was looking at me.

"I suppose they did, Mistress Blackthorn, but not quite in the manner you do. You have a gift for bringing the story to life."

"So far, so good," I said, somewhat surprised. "Battle scenes are not really my strong point. If I were telling this in a prince's hall to entertain the crowd, at this stage I'd ask if anyone wanted to help."

"I doubt if any of us could match you," said Flannan.

"Fought from daybreak to nightfall." Grim spoke up, surprising me. He still looked shaken and pallid; I wondered how he was managing to walk on, let alone tell the story as he went. "Blood all over the woodland; children wailing, old folk wringing their hands, wives and sweethearts yelling encouragement, if they weren't out fighting alongside their men. Wise women of the blue and green tribes watching on, side by side, thinking they'd be lucky if anyone was left at the end to be patched up. Then into the middle of it all comes Snowdrop the white pony. Wondering what the fuss is about." He glanced at me. "Could end in sorrow for all of them. Or not. Better if you finish off."

Yes; this could indeed be fashioned into a cautionary tale, the beautiful pony killed on the battlefield through no fault of her own, and half the clurichauns slain for no good reason. And, of course, the bag of silver wasted. But, clurichauns being what they were, if I ended it that way I could not say they had learned their lesson.

"The king of the blue tribe did not see Snowdrop coming," I said, "and slashed out with his sword—a weapon of sharpened oak wood, and very fine—just as she passed by. There was a sharp scream from the pony, and sharper ones from the two princesses, who rushed onto the battlefield heedless of danger. 'Retreat!' yelled the blue king, and 'Lay down your arms!' shouted the green king, as their daughters pushed a way through the melee to the mad-eyed animal. One snatched the halter; the other grabbed hold of Snowdrop's mane."

Before I could draw the tale to a close by accounting how the warriors obeyed their leaders' commands, the battle ceased, the horse suffered only a scratch and the two girls became fast friends, Grim spoke again.

"Pony was hurt and scared. Reared up. Hoof struck one girl on the brow and she fell to the ground. 'My daughter!' screamed the green king. 'Your accursed creature has killed my daughter!' Threw back his head

and howled like a banshee. Leaped forward, knife in hand. Slit Snowdrop's throat. Blood spurted out. The princess's white gown turned red."

"Grim," I said quietly. We had stopped walking, the four of us.
Grim's face was like a death mask; he was no longer with us, but somewhere else entirely.

"Fighters went mad all at once. Like they were deaf and blind. Like
they'd forgotten everything but the weapons in their hands and the
enemy waiting to be killed. So it went on, men falling, maimed, hurt,
dying, dead. Screaming. Such screaming. On and on. Couldn't stop
them. Couldn't save them. Not strong enough—"

"Grim! Stop!"

He was as white as chalk, his eyes gazing on the unspeakable. If I
slapped his cheek to bring him out of the trance I risked being hurt; he
would not know who I was. Flannan took a step forward as if to lay
hands on him.

"No, Flannan." I kept my voice soft and calm, though my heart
was thumping. "Grim, I'm getting tired. I want to go back now. You
come with me; Brother Dufach will take Flannan on to St. Olcan's."

"But—" began Flannan.

"Come on, Grim." I took a step closer, praying that he wouldn't
turn on me. "Best if we head for home now. Grim?" I laid a cautious
hand on his arm.

He started as if struck, and dashed my hand away with such violence that both Flannan and Dufach protested, moving toward us.

"No!" I snapped.

Grim rubbed a hand over his face, blinked a few times. "What?
What did I . . . ?"

"We were just telling a tale to pass the time," I said, fighting to keep
my voice steady. "But the story's finished now. I'd like to go home."

"Are you sure—" Brother Dufach fell silent as I gave him a slight
shake of the head.

"Said something wrong," Grim muttered. "Didn't I? Did something bad." And without a further word, he turned his back and strode away from us. At least he was heading in the direction of Geiléis's house.

"I'd best go." I attempted a calm tone. "He's not well. Flannan, good luck with your studies. Brother Dufach, thank you for your forbearance."

"He seemed quite—are you sure you'll be all right on your own?" Flannan protested. "He looked as if he might . . ."

"The effect of the curse," said Brother Dufach quietly. "I've seen it before. It can turn a man's thoughts down dark pathways. It can show him the worst of himself. Will you be safe, Mistress Blackthorn?"

"I'd better come back with you," Flannan said in the manner of a man who has decided to take charge.

"You'd better not." I gave up pretending to be calm. "I'll be safer without you. I understand this; you don't."

"Then I will walk down tomorrow. Or this afternoon. I need to know you are safe."

"Just leave it, will you? I have to go."

Flannan said nothing more, but I saw a question on his face, one I had no wish to think about. *You're only here to cover your tracks before we head south. Why does any of this matter?*

I turned my back and walked briskly after Grim. Looked over my shoulder once, twice, three times, until Flannan and the monk were out of sight. Then picked up my skirt and ran.

16

GRIM

C an't seem to catch a breath. Eyes wet, nose running, feel like a
child who's been hit. Noise won't go away. I put my fingers in my ears
but I still hear it. Head down on my knees, arms up over my head, the
words, the words, try the words . . . *in medio umbræ mortis . . . non
temp . . . non timb . . . non timebo mala . . .* Shadow of death's over me.
All around me. Creeping inside me. Words seeping away, all away . . .
Non timebo. Non timebo mala . . . I fear no evil. A lie. A big lie. Fear's
got its teeth sunk deep in me.

I'm curled up tight against a fallen tree, fighting to hold on to the
words. Someone touches my shoulder and my heart near bursts out of
my chest. I yelp like a stuck pig.

A little hand reaches out toward me, with a little cup in it. "Drink,"
someone says in a tiny voice. "Feel better." My jaw dropped; my eyes are
most likely out on stalks. Thing's no higher than my knee. Hooded cloak
all of fur. Skinny, knobbly fingers. Long nose; eyes like black currants.

"Drink," the creature says again. "Friend."

Stupid, maybe, but I take the cup and drink what's in it, which is
not much at all, since the thing's so small, but whatever it is tastes very

good and not like anything I know. Stupid, because the creature's not human, and not animal, and that means . . . Well, it could mean all sorts of things, and some of them are trouble.

"Better," says the small one. "Yes?"

Take a deep breath, and a few more. Try out the bits of myself, since they're feeling as if they don't belong together. Stretch arms, then legs. Wipe snot and tears from my wretched face. Think I might be sick again, but no. "Thanks," I say. Look up and see the hooded one isn't alone. I'm in some part of the forest, right off the path, in under the trees. Eyes watching from the shadows. Shapes, small ones. Not animals. Not children. "Better, yes." Not sure if I am, though. Can't remember what happened. Only Blackthorn looking worried. And a monk. There was the monster. Crying. Still crying.

"Who are you?" I ask the little fellow. He—I'm guessing it's a he—looks right at me, and I get a better look at him. Face like a tiny man's, only not quite right. Eyes too round, nose too long, mouth too wide. Those knobbly fingers, like twigs. Hair under the hood, mossy green. Brown boots, look like bark. No need to ask if he's fey. Question is, why would one of them help me?

"Who are *you*?"

"Name of Grim. Traveling through. With my friend."

"Friend is looking. Searching high and low. Searching up and down. Not finding you anywhere."

I get to my feet. Clumsy giant, beside the little one. "Blackthorn—she's searching for me? Can you show me where?"

"Better you go home."

"We're staying at the big house, by the ford. Lady Geiléis's house. Need to find Blackthorn first. Need to hurry." She might get lost, looking for me. Might wander, the way the lady told us could happen. Folk went missing. Got drowned. Never came home. "Can you show me where you saw her? Please?"

"Better you go home, you and your friend. Sad place, this. Crying place. All tears."

No arguing with that. The monster's voice is everywhere. Feels like it's right inside my head. "Please. Will you help me find her?" Have a feeling there are things I should ask. Things Blackthorn would be wanting me to ask. Can't think straight, though. Did I do something bad? How did I get here?

"Come," says the small one. He walks; I follow. The others, the ones under the trees, have melted away. "Not far."

But it is far. What have I been doing? Starts to come back; being sick after breakfast, walking up with Flannan and that monk, and then . . . nothing. Only that feeling, the one I get when the red's come down and I've done something bad. But different somehow.

"Where did you find me?" I ask the little one. "Back there, where you gave me the drink? Or somewhere else?"

"There. Sad. Lost."

We go on walking. Feels like we're going deeper into the forest. Start to wonder if it's a trick. In the old tales, you drink or eat fey food and you're trapped in the Otherworld, can't ever get back home. Blackthorn would have said no. But I do feel better. Feel like, if I hadn't drunk whatever it was, I'd be going right down in the dark.

More walking. Uphill, downhill. In between rocks, some places a squeeze for me. Makes me wonder what would happen if I got stuck. Under bushes. Across a stream. I do it in a long stride. Little fellow jumps. Like a cricket. Like he weighs nothing at all.

"Heard somewhere your kind don't like giving your names," I say by way of conversation. "Sorry I asked, before." That's what it says in the tales, some of them.

"Grim," says the little one. "Not your real name."

That shakes me. How could he know anything about me? "It is now."

He nods. "My name, too tricky for your kind," he says.

I remember a bit more. Blackthorn telling a tale as we walked, something about clurichauns. Don't think this is a clurichaun, though.

I'm wondering if the walk's going to take all day, and worrying about Blackthorn, when we come into a clearing. The little one hasn't

taken me to find her at all. He's tricked me. He's led me into a trap . . .
or maybe not. I take a proper look around and I see why he's brought
me here. Another tree's fallen. A dead tree. Not a big one, but big
enough. And all along one side of it are small folk like my one, lined up
and pushing hard, grunting with effort, but the tree's not budging an
inch. Which is bad because someone's trapped underneath. "Get me
out! Help!" comes the scream, high and shrill, loud enough to cut
through the monster's crying.

I roll up my sleeves and move forward. The wee folk let go the tree
and scatter in fright. Close up, I see a small arm sticking out from
under the log. Takes me right back to Mathuin's lockup and Slammer
crushed under a heap of stones. Push that picture down. "Move back,"
I say, though they have already. "I'll do it."

Need to be careful. One wrong move and the little one underneath
will be crushed to nothing. Surprised it's not dead already. I squat
down, lift quick and clean so one end's on my shoulder and the other
on the ground, pivot the trunk around and lay it down again in a safer
spot. Doesn't take long. Dust off my hands on my trousers. Wish Blackthorn was here. She'd be the one to patch up any injuries, like she did
the time I lifted a cart off a fellow. Feels like long ago.

"My friend," I said. "Blackthorn. The one I'm trying to find. She's
a healer. She could help you."

"No need." The little man, the one that brought me here, is back
beside me. "We can mend. Moving trees, not so easy."

Some of the wee folk put the injured one onto a very small stretcher,
then carry him off into the forest. Some of them thank me; some nod
their heads; some smile. They're quickly gone. All but the first one.

"You could have said," I tell him. "Straightaway, I mean. I'd have
been happy to help."

"I find your friend, you lift the tree," the little man says. "I help, you
help."

"I would have helped you anyway. But yes, it would be good if you
could find Blackthorn."

"Not far," he says. "You will find her. That way." He points in a direction that feels completely wrong. "Secret," he says. "All secret. Not a word."

"I don't keep secrets from Blackthorn," I say. "And what's this *you'll find her*? Didn't you say you'd—"

Then I hear her voice. And the little fellow's right—she's not far off. "Grim!" she's calling. "Grim, where are you, you foolish big man?"

"Here!" I yell. Almost before the word's left my mouth, the wee man's gone. Not bolted; not strolled away; vanished. Like Conmael does when he's had enough of talk.

Never mind that. I'm going fast through the undergrowth to find Blackthorn, who's shouting, "Over here! This way!" Know she's been worried. Only calls me names like that when I've given her a real fright. I come out into a clearing and there she is. Looking upset. Can't tell if she's scared or cross or just tired out. Could be all three.

"Sorry," I say. "Must've wandered off the path. You all right?" Plainly she isn't. But I can't wrap my arms around her like I want to. Way she looks, I'd get my head bitten off.

"Am *I* all right? You were the one who went rushing off by yourself. You were the one who . . ."

I wait but she doesn't finish. "What did I do?" I make myself ask.

"Gave me a fright. Twice over. You mean you can't remember what happened?"

"You tell me."

"You were sick after breakfast. We walked up to St. Olcan's; we told a story on the way; you turned the story into . . . something else. Something that upset you. You bolted into the forest. I made some excuses and came to find you. Only you weren't so easy to find." She's staring at me. Seems to be thinking hard.

"And?" Know whatever it is can't be good. "What did I do?"

"You were talking nonsense. You weren't really with us. I touched you on the arm and—well, you lashed out and almost hit me."

See through that straightaway. I hit her—that's what she's saying. I hit Blackthorn.

"Don't look like that, Grim. You gave me a fright, that was all. And it was you I was frightened for, not me."

When I don't say anything at all, she starts walking. "We should get back," she says over her shoulder. "Or Lady Geiléis will have search parties out looking for us. Not the best impression to make on our first day. I haven't gathered a single herb. Hope I find one or two between here and the house. If ever a day called for a good brew, this one does."

"What did I say? In the story, what did I say? Did they hear me?"

"Who, Flannan and Brother Dufach? They could hardly not hear you—they were right there." She waits for me to catch up so we can walk together. "You made the clurichaun battle end in bloody slaughter. Warriors who'd forgotten everything but the weapons in their hands and the enemy waiting to be killed—I think those were your words. You tell a good story, I'll give you that. But this was . . . it was different. Almost uncanny. Brother Dufach suggested it was the curse affecting you. The crying getting into your head and . . . well, taking over."

I could tell her different, but I don't. The monster crying was part of it, that's most likely true. But the bloody slaughter was in my head already. No shaking it out. No shutting it down. And kindly Brother Dufach's part of the problem. "Sorry," I tell her. "Sorry I messed things up."

"Forget it," says Blackthorn. "If we think this through, maybe we can learn something. Where were you, all this time? I went right back to the house, looking for you."

Secret. But I can't keep secrets from her. Be like one half trying to lie to the other half. "Something happened," I say. "Something strange."

"Tell me."

"Thing is," I say, "maybe it wasn't real. Could have been what that monk said, the crying getting to me. Making me see things that weren't there."

"What things?"

"One of those little folk. Like the one I told you about before. He talked to me."

"Saying what?"

"*Sad old place.*" Not going to tell her the wee fellow offered me a drink and I drank it. "There were more of them. In the woods here. Dozens of them."

Blackthorn looks around as if she might see little folk popping up everywhere. "Why aren't I surprised?" she says. "Was that all he said?"

"They needed something lifted. I helped them. He showed me where you were, more or less. And . . . well, he said it was secret."

"But you've told me."

"Mm-hm."

"Could have been your imagination, I suppose, brought on by the monster's voice. Though you seem all right now. I suggest we don't go rushing in and telling Geiléis about this. Or anyone. I do plan to ask Geiléis about the fey again, in a general sort of way. This is an odd place, Grim. Even odder than I thought it would be."

I mumble some kind of answer. Maybe I did a good deed just now, with the wee folk. Still, I hit her, and I ran away, and that little man found me blubbering like a baby. Balance that up, and the good deed doesn't count for much. "Sorry I ran off," I say. "Sorry about before."

"Stop saying sorry, will you? Chances are none of it was your fault. Especially if this curse works the way we've been told it does. Next time we leave the house, you're blocking your ears. And don't argue."

"Wouldn't dream of it."

17

GEILÉIS

"Ah," she said, opening her door to meet Blackthorn's steady gaze. "You're here."

"As you see."

This healer was the kind of woman who would stick to her plans, Geiléis thought. Even when it came to being here before dawn on the sort of chilly morning when most folk would welcome the chance to stay under the covers a while longer.

"Come, then." Geiléis led her visitor up the steps to her high chamber, where the shutters had been thrown open. Below them, the forest lay in shadow still. That was the point, of course; what Blackthorn wanted was to see dawn break over the Tower of Thorns. "Warm enough? I can lend you a shawl."

"I'm fine." A lengthy pause. "But thank you."

"Your man is not with you this morning?"

Blackthorn gave her a sharp look. "I thought you might consider it inappropriate, since these are your private quarters and the rest of the household is still abed. Given the choice, he would have come with me."

"He's loyal."

"As you say."

"A loyal servant is a fine thing. We forget, sometimes, how much they do for us."

A little frown creased the healer's brow. "I did explain. Grim and I are friends. Traveling companions."

Geiléis let it drop. It was of no matter what they were to each other. The plan required only that Grim be absent at the critical time on Midsummer Eve. There were many ways that could be ensured. "You wish to observe the birds," she said. "There is a good view today. Often, mist obscures the tower almost completely. I do not know what birds can tell you."

"Perhaps nothing," murmured the healer. "But perhaps something. I have wondered if this creature is all alone in the tower, and how it survives. The birds might provide a clue. It's all part of the pattern."

So close to midsummer, the time of true dark was short indeed. Soon enough, a warm gold light washed over the land, and all at once a great cloud of birds arose from the tower, calling and crying, circling and swooping against the lightening sky. As if that were a signal, the shutters covering that other window were opened. Geiléis's throat tightened. She clenched her hands; felt the nails digging into her palms. It never got better. It never got easier. No matter how many times she saw it. No matter how many times she heard it. Today, she must not shed tears. Not until Blackthorn was gone and the door was closed fast behind her.

The sun's edge showed rosy-bright; below them, through the trees, the river glowed in response. As one the birds fell silent, winging their way to the shelter of the forest. She could not breathe. *This time*, she prayed as she always did, knowing it was useless, knowing she was thinking like a child, *oh, please, this time let it not happen; make this be the time when it is different . . .*

Blackthorn stood steady beside her as the wailing began. As the sun rose fully, and the forest awoke, and the last of the mist dispersed. As the lament went on and on, punctuated now and then by brief silences during which Geiléis imagined him sucking in a desperate breath. Where did he find the strength to go on?

Something made her turn her head. Blackthorn was no longer watching the tower; the healer's gaze was fixed on her as if she would read Geiléis's very thoughts. Which was ridiculous. This woman was no seer. Folk who gave themselves the name of wise woman might be skilled in herbal healing and good at birthing babes or setting broken limbs, but those were ordinary human talents, nothing more.

"This disturbs you very much," Blackthorn observed.

"It would disturb anyone. Obviously."

"But you choose not to stop your ears. And you said you had become used to it, you and your household."

"Believe me, I have no reason to lie to you on such a matter. I have learned to tolerate the sound, yes, as have all of us who live here. That does not mean I am any less troubled by it. It does not mean I would wander unguarded in those woods during the summer. That would be foolish indeed. The crying alone is bad enough. But I believe that even if it were silent, the monster would still affect everything close to the tower: people, livestock, wild animals, the land itself. This place is slowly dying, Blackthorn."

The healer's gaze, already intense, sharpened further. "What do you mean?"

Geiléis reached to close the shutters. Today, she could not keep her morning vigil. *I'm sorry*, she thought, as the Tower of Thorns with its distant window vanished from view. *At dusk I will be here. I promise. I will tell the story.* "Let us talk further over breakfast. I will join you soon."

They sat at the table, the healer, her man and Geiléis, with Senach a discreet presence by the door.

"Ask your questions," Geiléis said. "This place must seem strange to you. Tell me how I can help." She hoped she could find answers that would serve.

"Strange," echoed Blackthorn. "It is that, certainly. One question immediately springs to mind. You said the place was dying. When you told your story at court, you mentioned failing crops and sick animals. Yet here we are, sitting down to an ample breakfast. Where do your supplies come from?"

"Much of this comes from St. Olcan's. The monastery gardens are extensive. The brethren also have grazing fields and their own house cows. And Father Tomas is generous; he does not judge me for the oddity of my situation."

"A strange curse indeed," observed Blackthorn, "that lies over your own land and that of your nearest neighbors, but does not affect these monks at all. Do you believe Christian prayer has the power to protect folk against this creature's influence?"

"On that, I can make no comment. It is a matter of belief. I myself put little credence in gods of any persuasion."

Blackthorn smiled. "And yet you put your faith in a cleansing ritual, to be performed by a druid. And now, by myself."

Ah. She had made an error; for the moment, she had forgotten this. "To be quite truthful, Blackthorn, my faith in the ritual is limited. But I am desperate. Anything that may serve to quiet the creature, or to bring some reassurance to the local people, I am happy to try." The healing ritual would at least keep the wise woman busy for a while. "You must let us know what we can do to assist with your preparations."

Blackthorn crumbled a piece of bread in her fingers. "How far away are your farm communities? Villages or settlements? All the folk that live on your holdings should be invited to attend the ritual. We'll need to give them time to get here. Maybe you could ride out with the message, Grim. One of Geiléis's guards could go with you. And I'll need to walk down through the forest and have a look at the tower."

Geiléis's heart clenched tight. She made herself draw a deep breath before she spoke. "The local people . . . yes, of course they must be

invited, but I do not think many will come. The presence of the creature . . . it is like a malady that creeps into the very hearts of folk and
robs them of good purpose. It turns hope to despair; it steals away the
future. So many of our young men have traveled away, seeking better
opportunities, and have chosen not to return . . . Those left behind have
become disheartened; they have lost the will to keep trying. It has become
harder and harder to keep the animals healthy, the houses watertight,
the crops sown and harvested in season. Fences, bridges, pathways are
not maintained. One must travel many miles to find a blacksmith or a
thatcher. We have no druid or wise woman. That is what I meant by
dying. In just such a way may an entire community vanish."

They were both staring at her now, Grim with a spoonful of porridge
halfway between bowl and lips. He set it down uneaten. "Monster's only
been here a year or two, hasn't it?" he asked. "Seems a bit soon to be giving up. Though it is hard to take. The creature crying, I mean."

"Geiléis did ride all the way to court to ask for help, Grim," said
Blackthorn.

"Fair enough," the big man said. "Still, not long, is it? Since the creature came?"

"Believe me," Geiléis said, "it feels like an age. But no, it is not so
long. I understand you may find it startling that such a blight has been
cast so quickly. Only . . ."

"Only it's been here before," said Blackthorn, quick as always. "And
some of the effects of the curse might lie over the land even during the
times in between this creature's visits. Might that be so? Were your parents here before you, Geiléis? And their parents before them?"

Geiléis had been waiting for that question. Answering in a convincing manner would be a test. She'd been relieved that nobody had asked
about her family while she was at Cahercorcan, though she'd had the
answer ready even then. If King Ruairi had been at court he'd have
asked. His father might have told him the story when he was a boy. For
once fate had done her a favor. "My parents died when I was quite
young," she said. "I do not recall either of them speaking of the mon-

ster. If they had done so, I would have thought it a fanciful tale devised solely for my amusement. Nobody in the neighborhood has any memory of the tower being tenanted before last summer. There are only those half-forgotten stories I spoke of. But . . . you are astute, Blackthorn. When I was a child, this place was my whole world. If there were oddities, I took them as simply the way things were. If an unusual number of young men left the district never to return, if an unusual number of folk chose to end their own lives, if there were some parts of the woods where I was not allowed to go, I accepted it."

"Were you allowed to go to the Tower of Thorns?" asked Blackthorn. "Did you explore the island where it stands? Folk must have passed close by it all the time when the ford was still open."

"Main road to the north and all," put in Grim.

She fought down a sudden wave of impatience. "How can this make any difference?"

"You've asked me to solve your problem." Blackthorn had a rather blunt way about her. Perhaps she too was impatient. "I can't do that unless you give me the information I ask for. I won't know if it makes a difference until I put all the pieces together. If it helps, anything you tell us is confidential." She glanced at Senach, who had remained at his post, quite silent.

"My parents did not let me run wild in the forest. But yes, I crossed the ford, both on foot—possible only if the water is unusually low— and on horseback. I walked between this house and the river, though only on those paths I had been told were safe. As a child, I was forbidden to go to the island. The tower was seen as dangerous, though the reasons for that were never clear. You know already that last year I ventured to that place on Midsummer Eve and tried to cut my way through the hedge of thorn. Tried and failed. Woefully."

Blackthorn and Grim exchanged a look.

"These safe paths," Grim said. "Could you show us? Be good to take a look at the tower soon. A close-up look. We'll be needing to get across to the island."

A shiver ran through Geiléis. If there was one thing she was sure of, it was that she did not want these two to go tramping about on the island. She did not want a living soul to approach the tower. But how could she forbid it? She had invited them to Bann on the strength of the story she had thought most likely to make an impression on Prince Oran. While that story had not exactly been a lie, it had been far from the complete truth. Blackthorn believed she was here to rid the tower of its unwelcome resident by whatever means she could find. She must therefore be permitted to move about and look at things. A refusal would only make her suspicious, and then she might decide to turn tail and flee. That could not be allowed to happen. "The island," she said. "Yes, if you wish. It is not easy to reach, but my men-at-arms could escort you over." She took a steadying breath. "You are not planning to conduct your ritual there, I trust? That would present severe difficulties, as you may imagine."

"I'll need to pay the place a visit before I make that decision," Blackthorn said.

"Senach," Geiléis said, not turning her head, "have a word to Onchú about this, will you?" Her folk were well aware of the risks; they would take adequate precautions. They knew what Blackthorn could be allowed to see and what must remain hidden.

"Yes, my lady."

"Another thing," said Blackthorn. "I'll be wanting to talk to the local folk, find out if anyone remembers more than those snippets you mentioned. About this being a job for a woman, and about Midsummer Eve being the time to drive the monster away, I mean. There has to be a whole story there; I can't believe it's completely lost."

"I fear you will be disappointed," Geiléis said.

"Perhaps we could offer refreshments after the ritual, either here in the house or in the courtyard," Blackthorn went on, as if Geiléis had not spoken. "That would provide a good opportunity to talk to people. I want to meet the old folk especially."

Gods, the woman was brimming with plans. It would be a challenge to keep her under control until it was time to give her the truth. As much of the truth, that was, as she would need to perform the task. "I have asked the local people about this already," Geiléis said. "You know that. Nobody remembers anything. They are all weighed down by the monster's presence, its constant crying. To press them further on this matter would be . . . burdensome. And fruitless."

Blackthorn subjected her to a level gaze; Geiléis could almost see the wise woman thinking.

"I know old folk can be forgetful," Blackthorn said. "And when a person cannot remember, for instance, how to make porridge or tie up their apron strings or play a tune on the whistle, you might assume they will never be able to do those things again. But that is not necessarily so. One day that old man or old woman will hear a lark singing, or smell dried lavender, or see a fair-haired rider on a white horse, and suddenly the old skill is back, for a short while at least. The memory of youth returns. The tale is remembered by the hands, if not fully by the mind."

"A pleasing theory," Geiléis said. "But in this case, not apt. I am quite certain nobody in the district can remember this particular tale."

"Thing is," put in Grim, "tales get old. So old you don't hear them around the fire anymore. Sad, that is. But even then, there's always someone who knows parts of the story. A bit here, a bit there. Something about pigs. Something about a ladder or a kerchief. Seems nonsense—then you start putting the bits together and . . ."

"And suddenly you've got the answer you were looking for," said Blackthorn, giving one of her rare, brief smiles. Most times, her mood ranged between touchy and somber; Geiléis had observed already that her guest was not the warmest of souls. If the healer ever wed and had children—Geiléis judged Blackthorn not yet too old for that—heaven help them. That would be a loveless hearth.

"So," said Grim, "stories. The ones folk think they've forgotten. That's what we'll be looking for."

"And quickly," said Blackthorn, "since by my reckoning we have less than a turning of the moon until Midsummer Eve, and the ritual will take time in the planning. A good first step would be for us to talk to everyone in this household. Senach, I hope you can help us with that." She glanced at the steward. "I'm not sure how many folk live here or where we might find them."

This, at least, should be entirely safe. "The men-at-arms have their own quarters up near the stables," Geiléis said. "A fair walk away. This house has seven retainers, including Senach. Speaking to them should not take you long."

"Good," said Blackthorn, rising from the table. She seemed to have forgotten her breakfast. "And while I'm doing that, Grim can talk to Onchú about a visit to the tower and a ride out to the settlement. Is there only one on your holdings?"

"One close by. Two others at a distance. Farms scattered here and there, some quite isolated. It would be difficult to get the word to all. And, I fear, pointless."

"That's for me to decide, Lady Geiléis." Blackthorn looked at Grim, who had got up when she did. "We'll talk to the household now. Visit the tower this afternoon, if that suits Onchú. Riding farther afield can wait a day or two. We'll start issuing invitations once we know where the ritual will be held. And the day and time—I need to think about what is most appropriate. It will have to be before dawn or after dusk, or nobody will hear anything but the creature's screams."

Geiléis found herself uncharacteristically lost for words. Once Blackthorn decided to take the reins, it seemed she was blind to anything that might stand in her way.

18

I spoke with the household servants and learned very little. Unusually, none of them had family living nearby. Dau, who did the cooking, mentioned a grandmother in the south who might be still living, though he had not seen her for some time. Geiléis seemed to like youngish folk around her—even Senach, who was more or less in charge of the household, appeared no more than five-and-twenty, and the rest were younger. There was only one woman among them: Caisín, a slender, quiet girl who did sewing and mending and looked after the household linen. She was married to one of the men-at-arms, Rian. Nobody had much to say about the monster, save that it tried Lady Geiléis sorely, and that they were doing their best to make things easier for her, since she was such a good mistress. They believed what Geiléis believed: that midsummer was the only time the thorns would yield, and that perhaps only a woman would succeed in cutting her way through. None offered a theory about what that woman was supposed to do when she entered the tower—battle the monster and kill it, talk to it kindly and send it on its way, answer riddles, sing songs . . . With my fund of lore, I had plenty of ideas to suggest. They listened with courtesy and made minimal comment.

Seven seemed to me a small number to run such a large establishment and to do it well, even with Geiléis as the only occupant other than themselves. Senach supervised; the others, among them, cooked, served, cleaned, performed maintenance and repairs and looked after the kitchen garden. The men-at-arms undertook escort and guard duty, acted as messengers, and were responsible for the stable and its complement of riding horses. Grim had gone up there to talk to them. I hoped he was having better luck than me.

"I hope that was satisfactory, Mistress Blackthorn," said Senach when the last of the servants had gone back to his duties. We were back in the dining chamber, where a small fire burned, keeping the space just warm enough. It was a house of spacious proportions and, despite its obvious comforts, there was a gloomy feeling to it. That could be put down to the monster's voice, which could still be heard indoors, though faintly. Even in summer the place held a chill. "May I fetch you some ale?" Senach asked. "A small cake or two?"

I was tempted to snarl at him—my mood was not benign after so much wasted time—but I nodded assent. I had eaten almost no breakfast and I was hungry. "And bring some for yourself, Senach. I'd like to speak with you a little more."

He did as he was asked, but after setting the tray down on the table he remained standing, reaching over to pour ale for me with a well-practiced hand.

"Please," I said, "do sit down. I find it awkward being waited on."

"As you wish." He sat down opposite me. "Was there something further you wanted to ask?"

"I was hoping you might unbend sufficiently to sit with me awhile and give me your opinion on a few things. Your fellow serving folk were faultless in their courtesy and told me almost nothing I didn't know already." I filled the second cup and pushed it across to him.

Senach put his fingers around the cup but did not lift it. "They have nothing useful to say. The monster, the tower, the woods . . . Lady Geiléis has already told you everything."

"Forgive me, but you can't know that. You were not present at court when she told us the story. Nor were you on the journey west."

He gave a little smile. "I have served the lady a long time."

"Not so very long, surely. In Prince Oran's household there are servants who have known him since he was a small child. Folk whose mothers and fathers served there before them; folk whose children are growing up at Winterfalls and will no doubt serve Oran's son when he lives there in his turn."

A silence. "I am not certain what it is you want to know," Senach said. "We are loyal to the lady. That is exactly as it should be. It pains us that she is so unhappy. If you can help her, we will be forever grateful."

"Is there anyone still in the district who worked here when Lady Geiléis's father was alive?" I could hardly ask how old the lady was, but I guessed she might be close to my own age, and that meant her father had been gone perhaps twenty years. It was surprising that none of his retainers remained here. Some would still have been young enough to work, and in households like Oran's—and, indeed, his father's—it was customary for serving folk to stay on even when they were fit only to offer an opinion on whether the bread dough was fully risen, or to wander out occasionally and scatter handfuls of grain for the chickens. They were part of a community; part of a family. But not at Bann, it seemed.

"I don't believe so."

"Geiléis said her parents died when she was quite young. Who looked after her until she was old enough to assume control of the holdings? Were there other kinsfolk? An aunt or uncle, a grandparent?"

"Those are questions best put to Lady Geiléis, Mistress Blackthorn. I certainly cannot answer them." He seemed about to say more, but instead lifted his cup and took a mouthful of the ale.

"But?" I ventured.

"Lady Geiléis is a strong-minded woman. I imagine she was strong even as a child. Very possibly, on losing her parents, she assumed control of her household straightaway and proceeded to order it to her own tastes."

Was that a trace of a smile? "You're fond of her," I said.

He closed up into himself like a crab into its shell. "We want the best for her. Lady Geiléis is a good mistress."

I finished my ale in silence, thinking hard. Pushing Senach further would achieve nothing; that one small insight was all he was going to give me, and as soon as he'd let it out he'd regretted it. Perhaps the odd behavior of these folk was a result of living under the curse. Two summers filled with the doleful, dismal voice of that creature in the tower would be enough to turn anyone a little strange. Indeed, the more I thought about it, the more I admired their loyalty to Geiléis. I wondered if any had been driven away by the monster's wailing, but that was not the question I asked. "Why do you think the monster wails all day? Is it angry? Sad? Could it have been put there as a sort of punishment for Geiléis and her family? There are old tales in which something of that kind happens—a curse laid in the form of a beast that lurks in the woods, or a kelpie in the well, setting a blight on all who live close at hand."

"I couldn't say, Mistress Blackthorn. Who would have the power to lay such a curse?"

"In the tales, it's generally one of the fey. A powerful one. But that is only one theory. The creature could be calling for help, as any of us would if we were trapped in the Tower of Thorns. Those wordless cries might be an attempt to say, *Let me out*."

Senach took his time to answer. "Might not those two explanations be one and the same?" he said eventually. "When you see the thorns that encircle the tower, you will realize that the creature's plight can be no accident. If it were, and if we could be sure the monster meant us no harm, then it would be a simple matter to cut a way through and set the tower's tenant free. But the blight its presence casts on the land all around, and the impenetrable nature of the thornbushes, must mean this is indeed a . . . a curse."

"So you do believe the monster may be more victim than evildoer? That it's been imprisoned there as a punishment for someone? Perhaps for the whole district? That raises a whole new set of questions." Had something happened two years ago that had angered the fey? The felling of a special tree, the shedding of blood in a protected place, a blatant flouting of the ways of nature? If that were so, my cleansing ritual might actually have some effect. If I could persuade myself I believed in it.

"The whole matter is riddled with doubt, Mistress Blackthorn. That the fey still walk this land, that they choose to meddle in our lives to such an extent—it is not something folk readily acknowledge, even if they secretly believe it. Father Tomas has never been prepared to accept the idea that a fey curse has caused this. He is more inclined to speak of demons. I am prepared to accept the theory of a curse, though I cannot speculate on who might have pronounced it, or how it might be broken." He rose to his feet.

"You have work to attend to. I understand. Thank you for talking to me, Senach."

"Good luck with your investigations, Mistress Blackthorn."

"Not much help," said Grim. "Had a chat about the horses and suchlike. Admired the fellows' weapons. Got a tour of their quarters, very comfortable. But they don't go drinking with the locals. Keep themselves to themselves. And none of them has family in the district. So no invitations to go home and chat to someone's old granddad. Sorry."

"Not your fault. I didn't do much better. I learned that Geiléis's folk would do anything for her. I could have guessed that. And Senach believes what's happened here is the result of a fey curse. Though he never quite said so. They're very protective of their mistress. What she doesn't want them to say, they don't say."

Under the pretext of changing into outdoor shoes, I was having a private word with Grim in our own quarters. A quick word; a pair of men-at-arms was waiting in the courtyard to escort us to the Tower of Thorns. I gathered Geiléis would not be coming.

"It seems odd that nobody in the household, including the men-at-arms, has family living close by," I said. "In fact none of them wanted to talk about family at all, though Dau did mention a grandmother he hadn't seen for years. I wonder when and where Geiléis hired them, and whether it's of any importance."

"Who'd want to work here?" Grim asked. "With the monster and all? She might have trouble finding folk and keeping them. Might need to look farther afield."

"At least some of these people have been in the household more than two years. Possibly all of them, though I didn't ask that directly."

"There's what she said about folk losing hope and making an end of themselves. Or moving away. They could've had family here and lost them. Didn't Geiléis say the place was sad and strange even before last summer?"

"Mm. If this isn't the first time the monster's come to the tower, the curse might have affected land and people for years and years, even when the tower was empty. That theory is starting to sound almost convincing. These are remarkably loyal folk, Grim. Even if they aren't being particularly helpful."

"Men-at-arms are all right. Helping all they can, just haven't got a lot to say. Best go, hadn't we? They're waiting."

I was still thinking through my conversation with Senach. "Grim, did any of the men mention the little folk? Seeing them in the woods, talking to them?" We had agreed earlier not to say anything that might reveal that Grim had already done both. We would respect the wee man's request to keep their presence secret. But it seemed likely at least one member of the household would have encountered them at some point. Perhaps I should have asked Senach outright.

"Not a word," Grim said. "What I expected, really."

"I didn't ask Senach, but he said, more or less, that folk might believe the fey were real but they wouldn't admit it. That was as far as it went."

"Or they might think it was the curse playing tricks." Grim's tone was flat. "Making folk act strange, do things they shouldn't do."

"Don't waste any effort blaming yourself for what happened yesterday. It wasn't your fault, and if it's done anything, it's given us more of an idea of what we're dealing with. And if the little folk *are* real, you did them a favor. Which could mean they'll be well-disposed toward us from now on. That's a good thing."

"If you say so. Best be moving, hadn't we?"

"Don't forget the wadding, to block your ears."

I'd requested that we walk to the ford rather than ride, so I could take my time looking around. And I'd asked if we could have as small an escort as Geiléis considered safe, hoping for only one man-at-arms. But despite the presence of Grim, whose formidable stature was enough to frighten away any potential attacker, we'd been given an escort of two: Onchú and another man-at-arms, Donncha.

Geiléis was on the steps to see us off. "Do not be tempted to remove the earplugs," she warned. "Onchú will tell you when to put them in; you will not need them for the first part of the walk. Once your ears are blocked, you must keep the others in sight at all times. The monster's call is far more powerful at close quarters. Do not linger on the island long. Do not allow the thorns to pierce your flesh."

"Why not, apart from the fact that it would hurt?"

"Last midsummer, I managed to avoid scratches. My men-at-arms were not so fortunate. Show them, Onchú."

The guard rolled up his sleeve to reveal a network of lumpy, raised welts, stark red against his pale skin.

"Ill humors were quick to enter the wounds," Geiléis said. "He suffered from a fever for many days; we thought he would die of it. Another of my men sustained similar injuries. I think it possible that these thorns contain a poison. Take the utmost care, all of you."

I was still staring at those scars. Had Onchú attempted to fight his way bodily through the thorny hedge? It seemed that he had taken very little care for his own welfare. In my opinion he was extremely fortunate to have survived. Indeed, though they were terrible to see, the wounds had healed remarkably well.

"How was your illness treated, Onchú?" I asked. "Poultices? Lotions? Leeches?"

"The fever abated with time, Mistress Blackthorn. The swelling went down of its own accord, about ten days after midsummer."

"You were badly scarred."

"Every warrior carries scars."

"What Onchú will not tell you," said Geiléis, "is that he incurred these injuries in an attempt to free me from the branches that were whipping back and threatening to encage me. He was a true warrior that day, as was Mechar."

Something in her tone alerted me. "Is Mechar still here?" I asked.

"He died. The fever burned him up. That was almost merciful, as he would have lost his hands."

The two men-at-arms made a gesture, both at the same time; a clenched fist laid over the heart.

"Sad loss," said Grim.

"It was indeed a grievous loss," Geiléis said, "and serves as a warning to all of us. Be cautious. Keep your ears blocked at all times, unless Onchú tells you it is safe. And do not touch the thorns."

I was the one she was looking at; I was the one she thought most likely to disregard sensible advice. I could hardly blame her for that. "We understand," I said.

"Go safely."

It was interesting, how being told to stick to a single path made a person long to explore all the others. But we had no real choice. As Geiléis's guests, we could hardly disregard her precise instructions. So we followed Onchú along what appeared to be the main way through the woods, a track broad enough to accommodate a cart and a pair of horses, though its state of repair suggested it seldom had to carry anything but foot traffic. In days past, when the ford was still in use, this path would have allowed people and supplies to be conveyed to and from the north; it must have formed part of a whole network of tracks between the various settlements on Geiléis's holdings. I did not ask our guards who was responsible for maintaining the area. I would save my questions for the time when I most needed the answers. Thus far, Onchú had not told us to block our ears, so we walked with the monster's cries ringing in our heads. I tried to make words from them—*I'll kill you! Get off my land! Help! Let me out!*—but could not. The creature's voice was odd indeed, like that of someone calling through a strange horn or a restricting mask. What shape was its head? What of its mouth and nose? The cry was not that of a wolf or a horse or a stag. It was not the bellow of a bull or the screech of a bird or the grunting of a wild pig. It was most surely not the voice of a man.

There were many side tracks, most of them half-hidden, for where human foot no longer trod, a small army of shade-loving plants had made itself at home beneath the shelter of ancient oak, venerable ash and guardian holly. The place must be rich with healing herbs and fungi. I longed to explore those byways, to forage and to learn. The forest called me. But no voice was louder than the monster's. My own inner voice suggested I might slip out again later, on my own. If I kept my ears blocked I should not be led astray. And who could object to a wise woman gathering herbs?

The stands of oak and ash gave way to willow, elder and alder. Sunshine streamed down between the leaves, brightening the path. Although the monster's voice was loud, I could also hear running water.

"This river," said Grim. "Deep, is it? How do we get across?"

"We wade," said Onchú. "At this time of year the water is relatively shallow. There's a boat, but it fell out of use long ago. We should block our ears now. If you need to draw my attention or Donncha's, make a gesture or tap us on the shoulder. Your earplugs won't keep out the monster's voice entirely, but they'll mute it so it's bearable."

I could imagine what kind of response there'd be to the sudden hand on the shoulder, when a man could hear nothing and was traversing an island that held some kind of unspeakable creature. I knew enough about fighting men to be fairly sure the first reaction wouldn't be a polite query as to whether anything was wrong.

"Stay well away from the thorns. And keep in sight of us at all times. We won't be on the island for long."

"All right?" asked Grim as we took our supplies of woolen wadding from our pouches.

"Fine." I was sorely tempted to disobey Onchú's instructions; how could we investigate properly if we couldn't hear? But I'd given Geiléis my word, so I blocked my ears. I saw on Grim's face, as he stuffed the wadding in his own ears, that his thoughts were running on the same path. If the tower had nothing to tell us this morning, we might need to come back another time. An unofficial visit, without the escort.

Our track through the woods had taken us down a gentle slope; at no point during our walk had the tower been visible. Now, as we came out from the cover of the trees, the ford lay before us, a broad expanse of rippling water, with the track reappearing on the far side, climbing before it vanished into another tract of woodland. To our right, downstream, was the island, and on it stood the Tower of Thorns.

"Morrigan's curse," I muttered. If you wanted to keep the most savage of enemies, the most cunning and troublesome of adversaries in custody, this would be the place to do it. The circular tower was higher than I had thought when I'd seen it from a distance; it seemed to reach for the sky. It was all of shaped stones, laid cunningly to create the curved walls. Inside, I assumed, there must be a spiral stair leading to the high chamber from which the monster wailed. From this spot by the ford, I could see neither door nor windows. The tangle of thornbushes wreathing the tower must conceal an entry; how else had the creature got in? If it could fly, it would surely have snatched the opportunity to escape, whether to wreak further havoc in the district or to wing its way to freedom.

Onchú was gesturing us down to the water's edge. I began to tuck my skirts into my girdle. I wasn't keen to walk all the way back in a sodden gown. The shore was pebbly; the sunlight made the wet stones shine. Black, white, every shade of gray and green and brown. Some speckled like eggs, some bearing a stripe, some covered with markings resembling spidery writing. If a person could read them, those would be old and strange tales indeed.

Grim was beside me, gesturing in his turn. *Carry you over. If you want.*

Weighing a little awkwardness against the prospect of wet shoes took only a moment. This would be an easy task for Grim, who stood head and shoulders over the tallest of Geiléis's tall retainers, and whose strength I had seen demonstrated over and over since we were first incarcerated together. The exercises he'd performed nightly to keep him from going mad in Mathuin's hellhole had been rigorous almost beyond belief. I'd wondered, often, where the man had acquired such self-discipline. I'd never asked.

He scooped me up in his arms, carrying me like a child, and followed Onchú into the river. Donncha came behind us. Gods, it was frustrating not to be able to hear properly! The monster's voice was still there, muffled but insistent; if I took out the wadding, I imagined it would be deafening. Which meant that even if I did unstop my ears, most likely I would not be able to detect the softer sounds that might tell me something. Were creatures about their daily business in this part of the woods? Squirrels, voles, foxes? Did animals venture to the island, or were those birds that roosted on—or in—the tower by night the only ones bold enough to visit the place? What about the small fey folk Grim might or might not have encountered? Perhaps they too were affected by the curse. Or they might be the ones responsible for the whole thing. Who knew?

Grim moved steadily on the shifting stones; in the ford, the water was quite shallow. But the island did not stand in the ford itself. At a certain point the three men had to turn and wade into deeper water, knee-deep for Grim, deeper for the others, and the current was strong. I'd have had difficulty staying upright here. Onchú gestured to Grim to keep directly behind him; I guessed that the riverbed was uneven. My mind filled with unsettling possibilities. A sudden arrow from the cover of those trees, an eldritch surge of floodwater . . . The creature driving Grim mad, so the two of us were swept away and drowned . . .

Grim was setting me down, and we were on the island. Onchú had his knife ready in his hand; Donncha had taken his bow from his back and an arrow from his quiver. Their bearing suggested high alert. It seemed I was not the only one thinking this was an ideal spot for an attack. But save for the rippling water the place was still. The tower stood at the highest point, in the center of the island. Around it the thornbushes rose tall and dense. The wild hedge stood far above my own height, and was so thick it would surely be impossible to get anywhere near the tower's entry. If there was an entry.

I showed Grim in gestures what I wanted to do. *Walk right around. Him, me, you, and him at the end. Look for a door.* He understood me straightaway, and managed to convey my meaning to the other men. Onchú and Donncha might have argued the point with me; they were less ready to do so with Grim. His very size earned him respect from a certain kind of man.

We circled the Tower of Thorns. Where was the door? The fearsome hedge stretched all the way to the base and enclosed the tower completely. If any entry existed, it was masked by the tangle of branches. What was the point of hacking a way through only to emerge face-to-face with an impenetrable stretch of wall? Maybe Geiléis's theory about Midsummer Eve had some substance to it, but even if the thorns could be cut on that day, how would a person know where to start?

We went around again. The men-at-arms were getting restless. Onchú kept looking over his shoulder, and once or twice I saw Donncha lift his bow, arrow on string, and sight across the ford, back toward the woods we'd come from. Geiléis's house could not be seen from here, but the creature up in the tower must be able to see her at her window, as she could see it at its own. What must be in its mind as it stood there day by day, screaming and screaming and never getting an answer?

At the point directly below the tower window, I halted. I could see the underside of a ledge and a hint of shutters to either side, but I could catch no glimpse of the being within. I wondered if it might be visible from the riverbank, a little farther downstream. What would it do if it spotted a watcher? Shrink back into the darkness within the tower, or only scream the louder?

Onchú had turned, alerted by Grim. I used my hands to convey, *Just a moment. Just let me think for a bit.*

Onchú frowned, pointing toward the ford. *We must go.*

Grim raised a hand, palm out. Then a placatory movement with both hands. *Not long.* He pointed to something on the far bank, diverting Onchú's attention, and engaged him in a conversation made up entirely of gestures.

I didn't have long; these men were highly trained and wouldn't miss much. No time to find the door, but I might snatch a better look at the thorns themselves. I edged a step nearer, and another step. Almost close enough to touch. I had a little knife in my belt, but the memory of those welts on Onchú's arm quashed any desire to experiment. So I only looked. It was not a plant I recognized. Not blackthorn—hah! That would have been almost amusing—not bramble, not briar rose. The stems looked woody and resilient; the snapping branches were studded with barbs. The thorns were monstrous, each as long as my index finger and wickedly curved. Even without the poison, they would inflict bloody damage. The leaves were small, holly-dark and set in pairs. No flowers . . . ah! Wrong. Flowers there were, but small and few. Tight-furled as if in self-protection. White as new-fallen snow. Red as heart's blood. Twined together so close, they might have been growing from the same stem. I felt tears sting my eyes and ordered myself not to be so foolish.

Screaming and screaming and never getting an answer . . . But how could anyone answer? The monster cried so loudly it must drown out the puny sound of a human voice. Meaning the only time to talk to it, to get through to it if such a thing were possible, would be between dusk and dawn. Though it seemed likely its silence at that time meant it was asleep, and would not hear anyway. And what about the ritual? If I performed it at a time when the folk who came could participate without screams deafening them, most likely the monster would not be aware that it was happening. Unless I held it here on the island, and I agreed with Geiléis on the impracticality of that. It would be too hard to bring folk across with any safety, even supposing they were willing to come. So, if the creature could neither hear nor see the ritual, did that mean it would be a waste of time? Or could I, full of anger and bitterness and doubt as I was, still tap into the old magic of this place and make something good happen? Right now, the tower, the island, the woodland felt empty of hope. Surely the sorrow here was so deep my efforts could achieve nothing at all. Why was I wasting my time in this godforsaken corner of Dalriada?

Conmael, I thought, I never imagined I'd ask for your help, but I could do with some advice now.

My fey mentor did not appear in a magical shower of colored sparks; indeed, he did not appear at all, and I had not for a moment expected that he would, since he was very much his own master. "You're an apology for a wise woman, Blackthorn," I muttered. "Stop feeling sorry for yourself and concentrate." And out of the blue a useful thought came to me: when one was dealing with the uncanny, the rules of the human world did not necessarily apply.

I waited until the monster paused in its lament to snatch a wheezing breath, and in that moment of quiet, with my ears still blocked, I whispered, "Tell me what you need. Tell me how I can help."

Did I imagine that the silence stretched just a little longer this time, while the monster filled its lungs? No time to consider, for as the screaming began again something came hurtling past my head, making me duck. The missile landed in front of me with a crash that was clearly audible, blocked ears or no. Then Grim was beside me, grabbing my arms and hauling me away from the tower.

"No!" I protested. "Wait!"

He couldn't hear me, of course. I struggled in his grip, trying to point to the object that had been thrown from the high window. *Just that. Get that, and I'll go.*

Grim kept hold of me with one hand, as if he feared I might rush toward the thornbushes and impale myself or fling myself bodily into the river. He bent down and stretched out to take hold of the object. It was a stone the size of a man's fist. Had it hit me on the head, it might well have been the end of me. Especially as I was the only healer in the district. I'd hoped for a signal, some indication the creature had heard my whispered message and answered. Perhaps it had. Perhaps its answer was, *Get off my island or I'll kill you.*

Grim had the stone on his palm; he was squinting at it the way a scholar might look at a manuscript in an unknown language. Before I could take a closer look, our two minders came up beside us. Onchú had turned pale; I realized, belatedly, that his memory of what had happened to him here must still haunt him, and that setting foot on the island must have required a great deal of courage. Didn't Grim and I dream of Mathuin's lockup every single night?

I motioned to Grim to put the stone in his pouch. As we made our way down to the river, I listened to the rhythm of the creature's voice, and when it paused for breath, I whispered, "I mean you no harm. I'm here to help."

It was only when we had waded back across the river, and walked up through the forest to Geiléis's house, and retreated to our quarters so Grim could change his wet clothing, that he took the stone from his pouch, and we saw that the markings traced on the gray were not the random patterns found on some of the river pebbles, but drawings scratched there with a sharp implement. I sucked in my breath, turning the thing over. Nausea welled in me. In my hand was the rusty nail; in front of me was the filthy wall of my cell, and the rows of lines I'd made there, one for each day, each endless, vile day of my incarceration. A sound burst from me, half sob, half oath.

Then, Grim's hand gentle on my shoulder. "It's all right," he said. "It'll be all right. Deep breath, now."

For once, I did as I was told. "Flea-ridden cesspit," I muttered. "Will it never go away?"

"Can't answer that." Grim was pouring water into a cup. "Drink this. I'll get a brew on." He busied himself while I sat down on the bench and wrestled with my troublesome thoughts. Mathuin. The truth was, that man and what he stood for would not go away until I found the courage to do something about him. And I had the opportunity now. I could head south with Flannan on Midsummer Day. I could make sure the chieftain of Laois got his just deserts at last. I could have vengeance. Then, surely, the evils of the past would start to fade.

Grim went out with a bucket in hand, heading for the pump. He'd left the stone on the table beside me. I could not bring myself to pick it up again, but I looked at it; studied the markings, swallowing bile, forcing my unruly mind to settle to the task in hand. And I realized that this had been no missile intended to kill me, or to force me off the island. It was the answer to my whispered question. The drawings were crude, as if executed by a clumsy child. A circle with lines coming out from it: the sun. A stick figure with something in its hand—was that an ax? Another figure, crouched with its head against a bench or box.

I couldn't make my fingers reach out and touch the thing. Coward. Useless apology for a woman. I got up and paced, arms folded tightly. Four strides across the room one way; four strides back. Ground my teeth until my jaw hurt. Resisted the urge to pick something up and throw it, just to hear it smash. Ordered myself to breathe. I would be calm before Grim got back. I would.

"All right?" He was at the door, full bucket in hand. "What do you think? Like writing, isn't it? A message." He set down the bucket and reached into his pouch again. "Funny. When I got that out, I found this. Under that stuff they gave us to block our ears. Not from Geiléis, though, or anyone here. Can't be. Look at it."

He laid the tiny item on the table beside the stone. It was a whistle like the ones the traveling folk played, only in miniature. The instrument was carved from oak and elaborately decorated with a design of leaves and tendrils and tight-furled, delicate flowers.

"You mean you don't know where this came from?" I asked.

"No idea. But I can guess. Did those wee folk a favor, didn't I?

Thought they'd paid me back by finding my way for me. Thought our exchange was all done. But it looks as if they left me a gift."

I wasn't going to argue with that. The whistle was so small and so finely made that the most doubting of folk would surely have conceded it must be fey. "Be careful," I said. "Blow a tune on that and you might summon something you don't want hanging about."

Grim stowed the whistle back in his pouch. "Or find myself in some other land, where monsters are as common as squirrels, and all the folk walk on their hands."

"You'd do all right there," I said. The urge to hurl heavy objects around was abating. "Listen, don't blow the whistle. I mean it. If the old stories are right, you should use it only as a last resort. And . . ."

"Maybe you should take it." Grim had his back to me; he was ladling water from his bucket to the kettle.

"Me? Hardly." If I obeyed my heart and went south with Flannan, Grim was going to need whatever help came his way. "If they gave it to you, you're the one who's meant to use it."

"It's just, I wouldn't know what was the right time. Might make a mess of things."

"You'll know. When everything else fails. When you have no other solution."

"Like when you ran away and I had to shout for Conmael." He set the kettle on the fire, then began to look for herbs.

There was nothing I could say. I imagined myself leaving with Flannan, fleeing into the night while this household slept. I imagined Grim waking in the dark, finding me gone, blowing his magic whistle to summon fey help. My mind refused to go any further. For the life of me, I could not conjure an image of Flannan and myself apprehended by an army of clurichauns. "The thing to remember," I said, working hard on a calm tone, "is not to use it unless you really have to. These things always come with a catch. If the fey help you, they always want something in return." Like Conmael, who had saved my life only after I'd promised to abide by his ridiculous conditions for a whole seven years. It had never been realistic. That I'd even tried had been stupid. I simply wasn't cut out to do good in the world, no matter what Conmael believed.

"Mm-hm," Grim said. "Don't much care for Conmael. But he did me a favor, that day. And he's never asked me for a thing."

"Maybe he just hasn't got around to it yet. The fey live long lives. They have long memories." Something was teasing at me, something I'd seen or heard long ago. The harder I tried to capture it, the more it eluded me. That trip to the tower, the stone hurled down, the wall of thorns . . . Why had it disturbed me so badly? My hands were shaking. I wrapped my arms around myself so Grim would not see it. What was wrong with me?

"Shawl," Grim said. "Put it on till you've warmed up a bit more. Brew should help."

My anger boiled up again. "What, have you got eyes in the back of your head now?" I snarled. "Stop being so understanding!"

Grim set two cups on the table. Put the honey jar beside them, with a spoon. Went back to the fire to see if the water was hot enough. "Back home," he said in his own time, "I'd say busy yourself with something: cutting herbs, making a potion, scrubbing the floor. Stops your mind turning in circles. Works the anger out of you. Can't do that here." He fetched the meager supply of herbs I had brought home on our first day. He shredded peppermint and chamomile leaves into the cups. "You did good," he said. "Even if you did nearly get yourself killed. That stone, it's a clue. If we can work out what it means."

"The person with the ax is a woman—see, a skirt? It fits with what Geiléis has already told us. The sun might mean midsummer. Or midday. The part I don't understand is this other figure. Is it the monster? What is it doing?"

"Could be two folk up there."

"Who'd want to be shut in with that screaming? But yes, I suppose there could be. If there isn't, the monster must have made this picture and thrown the stone. That doesn't tell me what I'm meant to do when I reach the top of the tower." I pictured myself with ax in hand, hacking a way through the thorns. Climbing the tower. Facing this creature with no idea of what to do next. If I was looking for a good reason to abandon Geiléis's quest before midsummer and slip away south with Flannan, this most certainly was it.

"Creature's fey, isn't it? The fey are full of tricks. Could be this is another one. That picture on the stone might not mean what you think at all." Grim looked at me sideways. "You going to show Lady Geiléis?"

"Not before I have another good look at it. But yes, I suppose I must show her. I expect she'll want a full report." I got up, fetched my shawl from the peg and wrapped it around me. He was right; the simple warmth of it made me feel better. "Grim?"

"Mm?"

"You realize that every time we get angry or muddled or frustrated while we're here, we'll be wondering if it's the monster messing with our thoughts. It's a cruel and devious kind of curse. We won't be able to trust any decision we make. We won't even be able to trust each other." But then, I'd been withholding the truth from him since before we left Cahercorcan. I'd been as good as lying since the day Flannan told me about the plot.

"Rubbish." Grim carried the kettle over and poured hot water into my cup, then his. "Team, aren't we? That means we trust each other, no matter what. Watch each other's back. Keep an eye out for trouble."

A pox on it, I was on the verge of tears again. What in the name of the gods was this? I busied myself with adding honey and stirring it in, hoping he would not notice.

"That's right, isn't it?" A note of uncertainty had crept into Grim's voice.

"That's right." I had never hated myself quite as much as I did in that moment.

19

Late in the afternoon Flannan turns up, looking serious. Here to check on Blackthorn after what happened yesterday. Keeps looking at me, waiting for me to do something crazy. See it all over his face. Senach brings everyone ale and cakes.

Lady Geiléis comes and keeps us company for a bit, and Blackthorn tells her about the trip to the tower, leaving some parts out. Shows her the stone with the drawings scratched on it. Expected the lady to be interested. Thought she might be angry we went close enough for Blackthorn to nearly get herself killed. What she does is cup the stone in her hands. Holds it as if it was some sort of rare treasure, or a baby just born. Tears rolling down her face. Three of us, that's including Flannan, are staring at her. Lady Geiléis is off in her own little world for a bit. I fish out a handkerchief and pass it to her. She takes it without seeing me, dabs her eyes.

"I'll be wanting to keep that for now," says Blackthorn, breaking the spell. "Part of the investigation."

"Yes," says the lady, coming back from wherever she's been. "Yes, of course." But she doesn't hand over the stone.

"What do you think it means?" Blackthorn asks her, not saying what *we* think.

Geiléis clears her throat, wipes her eyes again. Giving herself time before she answers. "It is what I suspected. A woman must cut through the thorns, using an ax. If . . . if it was indeed the creature that threw this down, I believe . . . I believe that may be what is required. On Midsummer Eve. The drawing of a sun . . ." Still struggling to be calm. Haven't seen her so upset since the day she came to court and threw herself at Oran's feet. "This other part, the crouching figure, I cannot interpret. It could be good news—that is, if this is a deliberate attempt to tell us something, and not just . . . accident. There is no sign of a—a confrontation here. No indication that you might need to . . ."

"Fight? You think when I get up there the creature's going to say, 'Thank you very much, I'll be off now'?"

"Believe me," says Geiléis, "if I knew, I would have told you straightaway. It seems unlikely this could be so simple."

"Why would it throw the stone down?" Hoping Geiléis won't object if I say my bit. "Why would it give Blackthorn a clue? Whole thing could be a trick."

"I cannot answer that," Geiléis says. "It is possible that all the creature wants is to be released from the tower. Perhaps Blackthorn need only cut a path through the thorns, at the right time on the right day. But it would be foolish to assume that. The prolonged screaming suggests a certain violence of feeling; that could quickly turn to acts of aggression. We must tread with care."

"Time's a bit short for being careful," says Blackthorn.

Everyone thinks about this for a bit. Then Flannan speaks up. "The situation is more perilous than I'd realized. Blackthorn could get herself killed. How can you expect that of her, Lady Geiléis?" Which is the same thing I'm thinking, more or less. I wait for Blackthorn to tell him to mind his own business, but it's the lady who puts him in his place. She stares at him like a queen telling an underling he's brought her the wrong breakfast.

"Mistress Blackthorn is her own woman and has come here of her own choosing. As for what may lie ahead, we have time to make a plan. To provide whatever protection is necessary."

"What about today?" asks Flannan, sounding angry. "Where was that protection when Blackthorn nearly got hit on the head by this rock?"

That's a bit rough. Onchú and Donncha did their best. Not their fault if Blackthorn doesn't obey orders if they don't happen to suit her.

"Flannan," says Blackthorn in that special soft voice, "this is not your concern."

"It is if—"

"Flannan."

He shuts up after that. If Blackthorn tells you to stop talking, you stop. End of story.

"Will you go ahead with the cleansing ritual, Blackthorn?" Geiléis asks.

"Most certainly," says Blackthorn, "since if it's effective, I may not be required to enter the tower at all. I'll go looking for a suitable spot tomorrow. I need to gather herbs as well."

"Onchú will arrange—" Geiléis starts, but Blackthorn cuts her off.

"The correct practice of a cleansing ritual requires the wise woman to perform various stages of preparation alone. Fail to observe that rule and you risk rendering the ritual completely ineffective. I will take precautions."

Can't say I like the idea of her going off alone any more than Geiléis does, but she's the wise woman and I'm just the hanger-on, so I keep quiet. If I say what I think, she'll only bite my head off.

Senach speaks up. "Rain is expected, Mistress Blackthorn. You may have noticed the clouds building. When wet weather comes to Bann, it tends to linger. The next few days may not be ideal for walking in the forest."

"I'm used to getting wet," says Blackthorn. "But thank you for the warning. We'll need to wait for fair weather before we hold the ritual. The local folk won't want to stand about getting soaked."

"You'd best be on your way soon, Master Flannan," says Geiléis, "if you want to stay dry. I hope Father Tomas and the brethren are treating you well. They must be pleased to have a scholarly guest at last. It's been some time."

"I've been well received, yes. And comfortably accommodated, by monastic standards. The place is at sixes and sevens right now. They know rain's coming, and there's a problem with leaking roofs. Damp weather and precious manuscripts are not a good combination."

"What sort of roofs?" asks Blackthorn, though why she'd want to know this I can't think.

"Thatch," says Geiléis. "Reed thatch. There's nobody in the district who can repair it properly. Folk fiddle about with it themselves, patch it up as best they can. But St. Olcan's needs the thatching done again, on the scriptorium in particular. Father Tomas says the roof needs to be completely replaced."

My belly churns; I feel sick again, like this morning. No prizes for guessing what Blackthorn'll say now. She looks at me. I look down at my hands. Can't warn her not to say it. Never did tell her my story, never told anyone, and now it's too late.

"Grim is a thatcher."

"This requires an expert," Geiléis says. "Perhaps more than one."

She doubts I'm good enough. No surprise there. Doesn't bother me. I'm feeling too sick to care.

"Grim is an expert," says Blackthorn. "If the monks have the materials, he can mend the roof. He'll do a good job."

That's it. No room for argument. No room for much at all. Never mind that Midsummer Eve's just around the corner. Never mind that I'm supposed to be helping Blackthorn deal with the monster and keeping her safe. Just got myself a job that's going to mean I hardly see her from now till midsummer. It'll mean I have to walk up to St. Olcan's. All the way there. Go in the gate, talk to the monks, hear the singing . . .

"Grim?" Blackthorn's just asked me something, could have been anything.

"Sorry, what?"

"You'll do it, won't you?"

Looking at her, looking at Flannan, it comes to me all of a sudden. Why she'd want me to go, I mean. She wants me away so she can spend time with *him*. She likes him. Likes him more than anyone. He makes her happy. Angry too, sometimes. But they've got that closeness, like Prince Oran and Lady Flidais. Always know what the other one's thinking. Understand each other without needing to talk.

"Grim?"

"Can't thatch in the wet." Comes out as a grumble. Can't help that. "Rain could last for days. Whole roof—that sounds like a big job. Take a while."

"But afterward, when the weather clears. Considering everything that has happened here, these folk deserve some help."

Can't speak. Help? From me? If this Father Tomas and the rest of them knew my story, I'd be the last person they'd want inside their walls. Not to mention that I can't get anywhere near the place without going half-crazy. I manage a sort of grunt. Which Lady Geiléis takes as a yes.

"Thank you," she says, talking to Blackthorn, as if I was too much of a bonehead to understand anything. "Grim's help would be most welcome, I'm sure. I believe the brothers have the necessary materials in storage— there was a thatcher here some time ago, but he left the district. Of course we would wait for fair weather." She gives me a glance that says, *That numbskull, an expert?* "Master Flannan, you might let Father Tomas know about Grim. Best head off now or you'll surely be caught in the rain."

"A little rain won't do me any harm," Flannan says, but he gets up all the same. "Private word with you?" Meaning Blackthorn.

The two of them go off outside. I'm not keen to sit here on my own with Lady Geiléis, so I make my excuses and go to our quarters. Tidy the place up, not that there's much to tidy. Bring in some water, boil the kettle, wash out the cups. Sweep the floor. Doesn't take long. Hands are itching for work to do, anything to slow down the rushing things in my head. Can't do what I'd do at home, chop wood, bake bread, dig the garden, fix something that needs fixing. I sit down on my bed and think how funny it is—the thing I could be doing, and doing well, is rethatching that roof up at St. Olcan's, making it nice and watertight, like new, finishing it off with the creatures on top and all. Making, not breaking. Making folk glad, not sad. And that's the thing I can't do, because just thinking about it turns my insides to water, brings out a cold sweat, fills me up with black terror. Funny, hah! Funny what's just under the surface, bubbling up when you don't want it. Coward. Failure. Not strong enough. Not brave enough. Not man enough. That's what the voices say, over and over in my head. Not enough. You were not enough. Another thing that's funny. All those voices are my voice, all of them. I know that. But it doesn't make me feel any better.

She doesn't come back. Still talking to Flannan. Master Flannan. He's right for her. Well made, even handsome, not that she'd care about that. Makes me wonder if Cass was a good-looking fellow too or a weedy scholarly kind. Not something I can ask. Flannan's clever. Book-learned. Could find work anywhere. Could make a good home for her. Would she want that, if he offered? Does she like him enough? Can't see it really, him and her in a cozy little house, perhaps with a child or two. But that might be because I don't *want* to see it.

I stand on my hands, count up to fifty. Come down, take a breath, do it again. Sixty. Jump up and catch onto a roof beam, pull myself up a few times. Twenty. Thirty. Heart's not in it. What I want to do is run. Run away quick, hide down deep.

She still doesn't come. I chop herbs for a brew, leave them tidy on the board, wash the knife, dry it, put it away. Say the words under my breath. How long before I forget? How long before I jumble them up and don't even know? *Scuto circo . . . circum . . . circumdabit te . . . veritas eius non timebis a timore nocturne.* Scuto, that's a shield. Something about truth making a shield all around a man. A shield against the dark things that creep into his head in the night. It's a lie. Truth can be the worst thing of all. Dark enough to blot out everything good. Funny, though; the words do help, a bit. It's like if I pretend to believe, pretend hard enough, I can almost think that shield might be a real thing.

20

Dusk was near. Rain was falling steadily now, a soft blanket over the darkening forest. Not like that day of long ago, when it had come down as harsh as a flail. Nearly time to begin. The voice from the tower was cracked and broken, worn-out by exhaustion and despair. She wondered, often, if he knew how faithful she was; how hard she worked to keep her promise, to hold firm. "Not long until Midsummer Eve," Geiléis whispered. "This time . . . oh, this time . . ."

It might fall into place. It might just work. If his skills as a thatcher were as good as Blackthorn seemed to believe, the man, Grim, would be easily got out of the way. Fixing the roof at St. Olcan's would keep him busy until midsummer. Beyond midsummer, in fact, though he'd likely need silencing once the thing was done. Fortunate indeed that Blackthorn had failed to interpret fully the scratchings on the stone. She pictured him hurling it down. How desperate he must be growing, to try that! He could have killed Blackthorn, and with her another precious chance.

Gods, could she let herself believe this might at last be possible? Blackthorn was a strong individual. Clever. Sure of herself. Prepared to take risks. A better candidate than any who had come before. "Hope," murmured Geiléis. "You must hold on to hope, or this cannot happen. Let hope go, and your battle is lost."

She had thought Grim would be the problem when the day came. But the other fellow, the scholar, seemed altogether too interested in Blackthorn's welfare. The two of them had spent a long time in intense conversation earlier, standing in the hallway together with heads bowed and voices lowered. Between the drumming rain and the monster's cries, nobody would have heard a word. Still, she did not want the scholar interfering. With luck he would become absorbed in his studies and lose interest. If not, she would have to take steps.

It was time for the story. And, as if someone out there knew it, the rain slowed and ceased, and behind it came a chill breeze from the north. Geiléis drew a deep breath. *Hope*, she thought. *How fragile hope can be. Short-lived as a March fly . . .*

Despondent, soaked through and trembling with cold, Lily arrived home just as her father was riding out of the courtyard with an escort of men-at-arms. Between her stumbling explanations and the summoning of serving folk to prepare a hot bath, dry clothing and nourishing food, Lily learned that her father was not looking for her, but heading out to help search for a missing man. A young man. And as she stripped off her wet clothing, then lowered her shivering body into the bath, she discovered from Muiríol that the young man was named Brión, that he was the son of a chieftain from the south who had been visiting a neighboring holding to hunt, and that he had been gone two days and two nights. The dogs had picked up his scent once or twice but kept losing it. Brión, thought Lily, trying it out. Brión. Fate must surely be on her side, to deliver this answer without her needing to ask a single question.

An inquisition followed the bath, though at least her mother waited until Lily was dry, dressed and seated in comfort in her bedchamber eating her meal—broth, fresh-baked bannocks, soft cheese—from a tray. By then Lily had her story all ready. She had been at her window, watching the storm approach. She'd spotted a light in the old tower; at least, that was where she'd guessed it was. But nobody ever went to the island; the old tower was empty. She'd been about to call Muiríol when she'd seen something else, something small and pale running off under the trees. She knew now that she'd been foolish, she told her mother, but she'd thought it might be one of the lapdogs, Pearl, known to have a great terror of thunderstorms. No time to tell anyone where she was going; no time to fetch help. If Pearl ran off into the forest she would be lost forever. That was what Lily had thought. She'd slipped out the little side door.

Her mother was not entirely satisfied with this neat explanation. How was it that Lily had run all the way from her bedchamber to the little door in the wall without anyone seeing her? How was it that the shutters of her chamber had been left open?

"I was watching the storm," said Lily sweetly, hoping the trembling of her hands was not too visible. Hoping her desperate need to hear more about the missing man was not too obvious on her face. "I did tell you."

"Hmmm," said her mother, but asked no more. Lily had always been a good girl, a biddable girl, and her mother had no wish to punish her if that could be avoided. She decided to overlook the small inconsistencies in the story. "If it ever happens again, don't give in to your instincts. Come straight to me and ask for help. Or to anyone close at hand. This was ill-considered behavior, Lily. As it happens, Pearl is with Poppy in my quarters. They're both tucked up safely in their basket."

"Oh, good," said Lily, feeling herself blush. "I'm so relieved."

"Just as well you are home safely, since your father has had to ride out into the storm in search of this boy," her mother said, unwittingly helpful.

"I'm sorry to have caused any worry, Mother. How long has this boy been missing? Not a child, but a young man, Muiríol said?"

"Eighteen. Old enough to know better," said Lily's mother. "His friends' behavior also leaves a great deal to be desired. The lad might

have encountered a wild boar and been terribly injured. He might have fallen and broken his neck. Yet they waited days before telling the truth about where they had been and how they lost sight of him. His father is almost out of his wits with worry, so I hear."

"Oh, but—" Lily stopped herself. Not yet; best if her mother made the connection herself. Provided she did not take too long. "Who is the young man? You know the family?"

"From Ulaid. A good family. I believe we met them once at court." Her mother's tone dismissed any place beyond Dalriada as unworthy of interest. "A pigeon came in, carrying an urgent message. One might think a personal visit would be more appropriate, especially since the offense seems to have occurred on our land. Apparently these lads took it upon themselves to venture farther north than they had authority to do. Your father decided to be magnanimous about the hunting— he doubts they had much success—and to offer his assistance with the search. If the boy has survived he'll be wet and cold. Your father hopes to find him before nightfall."

"My lady?" Muiríol spoke up from the corner where she was folding garments into a chest. "Might not that light in the tower have been the young man signaling for help? I mean, nobody else goes there. Nobody would dare. But, being a southerner, he might not know the tales folk tell about that place."

Lily resolved to give her maid a very special gift of some kind in the near future.

"You're sure you did see a light, Lily?" her mother asked, frowning. "The old tower is nothing but a ruin. Who would be there? And if it was the young man, why would he be on the island in the first place? Why not take the obvious path up to the house?"

"I can't answer all those questions," Lily said. "I don't know about any of it. Only that I saw a light, and I can't think what else it would be. Someone should go and look. Think how we would feel if we sent nobody tonight, and tomorrow we found the young man in the tower, dead of cold."

"Very well," her mother said. "I will arrange for someone to search, though I doubt there will be much enthusiasm for the task. If you are wrong about this, Lily, your father will be somewhat displeased; as it is, we have half the menfolk of the household gone."

"I'm sorry, Mother. And grateful. I have a feeling I'm right."

A small contingent of men-at-arms had been left behind to keep the household safe while Lily's father was away searching. Three of these men now headed out toward the tower, accompanied by the household steward and a couple of brawny grooms. Lily watched without comment as they assembled. What did they think Ash—Brión, she had to start calling him Brión—was, some kind of fearsome monster? Or maybe they were afraid of the uncanny creatures some folk thought lived in and around the old tower, those mysterious beings that had kept the island untrodden by human foot for years and years. Until Brión dared venture there, and after him Lily herself. Chances were that cold and hunger and exhaustion had driven the young man temporarily out of his wits. Perhaps he had endured disturbing dreams in the tower, dreams so real-seeming that he had come to believe he was beset by danger. Now they would bring him out, and he could get warm and dry and receive the services of healers. He could be reunited with his family, and all would be well. And if he was the son of a chieftain, he would be an entirely suitable candidate for her hand. Even if he had gone hunting where he should not. No need to tell anyone that they had already met, and under the oddest of circumstances. They could let their friendship develop quite naturally.

After that, everything started to move quickly; almost too quickly for Lily. She had longed for Ash—Brión—to be found and freed. She had wished for him to come home with her, to find his people, to be rid of whatever burden he was carrying. Most of all, she'd wanted a future in *which they could be together. Where they could in time become husband and wife. But even with the youthful hope of her sixteen years, she had not expected so much so soon.*

Brión came back from the tower. The four men carried him on a board, covered by a cloak. He was so white he looked dead. Lily exercised all her will not to shriek and run to him; her whole body was filled with terror. "Still breathing," said the head man-at-arms. "But only just, my lady."

Lily's mother bustled about, commanding her serving people as a leader might order an army. A warm bath, a warm bed, a quiet chamber, gentle hands. One message to be sent urgently to Lily's father, and another dispatched to the distant home of the young man's family, though birds could not be sent out with that before morning. Brión's father was close at hand, conducting his own search; a runner would be sent to find him at first light.

There was nothing at all for Lily to do. She had no reason to be in the chamber where Brión was being nursed, and if she hung about the doorway, her mother might get suspicious. He was alive; that must be enough, for now. So she went to her own chamber and opened the shutters a chink, wondering if she might catch a glimpse of her father's party riding back in.

That was odd. Even now the men had brought Brión back, there was a light in the old tower. It glowed and moved as if someone was walking about in that high chamber with a candle or lamp in their hand. The view was impeded by the branches of the great oak. She could climb out, go higher, see more clearly. But after what had occurred earlier, she'd better not try that particular trick for a while. Might the ferryman or others of his folk have gone up there for some reason? Lily thought of the stairs winding around the tower's interior; remembered how climbing had hurt her legs and made it hard to breathe. Such small folk surely could not manage that. Unless they could fly. She had seen no hint of wings. Could the search party have left a lamp or candle behind? It was possible. But not likely.

Should she alert someone? Her mother? The steward? As Lily stood there hesitating, the light blinked out, and the old tower fell back into darkness.

She did not see the light again that night. In the morning Brión was awake and talking sense, though much weakened by his ordeal. Or so Lily's mother told her; their unexpected guest needed nursing back to health, and a young man's bedchamber was no place for a well-brought-up young lady.

But then, Lily was not entirely what she seemed. Beneath the good manners and ladylike presence was a person of strength, a person who knew her own mind and was prepared to fight for what she believed in. She did not understand, then, how monstrous a fight it would prove to be.

21

BLACKTHORN

It rained for seven days straight. It was too wet to ride out to the settlement. Besides, I could not fix a day for the ritual until we were fairly sure of a dry spell, so there was no point in issuing invitations. It was too wet to gather herbs. It was too wet to do much at all. Cooped up indoors and unable to achieve anything, I came so close to boiling point I suspected folk might see the steam rising. The temptation to leave was strong; the more so because, even in such inclement weather, Flannan came down almost every day to talk with me in private. His argument was simple and convincing: the task Geiléis had given me sounded dangerous to the point of stupidity, and the fact that nobody really knew what was expected when, or if, I entered the tower, made it even more so. If we were talking of foolish risks, he said, which sounded more perilous—going south and working with a known group of trusted allies to bring down Mathuin of Laois or hacking through a hedge of poison thorn and climbing an old tower to confront a screaming monster? The likelihood of suffering an unpleasant death seemed significantly higher here at Bann than it would be in the south, and a great deal more immediate. Flannan reminded me that the plan was to go

only as far as Mide to start with. We'd be protected there. When I
pointed out that I'd need to go on to Laois if I were to find witnesses
and persuade them to talk, Flannan said arrangements would be made
to ensure my safety at every stage. This time around, it seemed the plot
had been worked out in meticulous detail. After his visits I found it
impossible to talk naturally with Grim. Most nights the two of us went
to bed in uneasy silence.

Late one afternoon the weather did clear briefly, and Onchú and
Donncha took me and Grim up the hill to watch the birds fly in to the
tower at dusk. If nothing else, this outing gave me a better feel for the
lie of the land. As the sun set, the birds winged their way to the tower,
settling on every ledge, in every nook and cranny. The shutters were
closed and the tower's inmate fell silent. I suspected it would be the
same every day. There was a pattern to the creature's existence. If not
for the abandoned nature of the screaming, one might have imagined it
as a being of orderly habits.

Grim suggested maybe the monster could not tolerate light; he'd
wondered if the brightness hurt its eyes, even on an overcast day or a
rainy one. Hence its quietening down during the hours of darkness. But
then, why did it open the shutters in the mornings? I, in my turn, had
wondered if there was some compulsion over its behavior. Could there
be a charm or spell in place that forced it to scream during the daylight
hours?

Or, Grim said, it might be enduring a routine of strict discipline, as a
prisoner would in a place of incarceration, for instance. Or a monk in a
monastery. Or a man-at-arms in a school for warcraft. But if that were
the case, who had instituted that discipline? Save for the birds, the monster seemed to be all alone in the tower. But perhaps there was someone
else there, invisible, silent. The crouched figure of the drawing. A captor?
A torturer?

After the brief dry spell, the rain set in again. The enforced inactivity
made Grim morose and restless. He needed something to keep him occupied, but it was too wet for the thatching. He did not seem enthusiastic

about that job anyway. He could have gone over to St. Olcan's to take a look at the roof—if Flannan could walk in the rain, Grim surely could— but he hadn't so much as suggested the idea, and that wasn't like him at all. At Winterfalls he was always out helping one person or another with some job. Long days and hard labor suited him. Sitting around idle in a lady's house surely did not.

Eventually I suggested it myself. "You could chat to the monks while you're there," I told him as we sat over our breakfast on yet another wet morning. "You might meet other folk too—they may have lay brothers or locals who go to help with the stock and the garden. You could start a conversation about the monster. Subtly, of course. You never know what might come out."

"Mm-hm."

"Grim. Remember that time after we escaped from the lockup, when you followed me for miles and miles and got soaked to the skin? You can't be putting this off just because of the rain. What is the problem?"

"Nothing."

That was quite plainly untrue, but anytime I raised the subject of the monastery he went silent, so I stopped asking. And there was another problem: Flannan. I'd expected him to be quickly caught up in his work, as scholars tend to be—I knew all about that; I'd been married to one. But that hadn't happened, or he wouldn't be finding the time to come down here so often. I was fond of the man; always had been. But I was starting to find his frequent visits unsettling, and his constant pressing of the case to head south even more so. I wanted to make the decision on my own, without him filling my mind up with his plans. The choice had to be mine alone. That way, if things went disastrously wrong, I could only blame myself.

But he gave me no respite. After I had expressed doubt about sur-viving long enough to see Mathuin brought to justice, should we make the decision to try, he told me more about the monastery in Mide where we could be offered a safe place to stay—as there were religious sisters in a separate part of that establishment, I would be welcome, he said, though I might have to keep quiet about being a wise woman. Flannan was using the pigeons at St. Olcan's to keep in contact with that very monastery, where one of the brothers was an ally. He gave me more names; explained where they were all located and their parts in the plan. He reminded me of how much I had to offer. He assured me that this time it would work. He came close to criticizing me for getting too caught up with Geiléis and her monster.

After four visits of this kind, I snapped. He had brought up that most hurtful argument again, the one about Cass, and I turned on him. "Stop it! Don't say another word! I'm starting to wonder if you really know me, Flannan. I'm starting to wonder if you're still the man you were. In case you've forgotten, we did discuss how Geiléis and her creature could provide us with the perfect cover for slipping away from Dalriada more or less unnoticed. That was the idea, wasn't it—that we'd leave quietly once I've done whatever I need to do at the tower? I'm more than capable of making up my own mind without constant pushing. I'm surprised and disappointed that I need to tell you that. Now I'll bid you farewell, and I don't want to see you again until the day of the cleansing ritual. That's if you plan to be present; I doubt Father Tomas would approve."

He gathered his cloak and staff in silence. He'd left Ripple behind this time, because of the rain. "If that's what you want," he muttered. "I thought it was important to you. The most important thing in the world."

"It is," I said. "So important that I need no reminding. It's in my thoughts every moment, even when I'm asleep. Now go. We'll talk about this another time. A time of my choosing."

He put his cloak on and headed for the door without another word.

The weather cleared at last, the sun shone, and Grim could no longer use the rain as an excuse for delaying his walk to St. Olcan's.

"You could go up this morning," I said as we sat at breakfast, just the two of us, since I had told Senach we were happy to serve ourselves. "Talk to the brothers, have a look at the building that's worst affected, this scriptorium, and see if they really do have all the materials you'll need."

"Mm-hm." Grim chewed on his bread, not looking at me.

"If you're worried about going up on your own after what happened before, then I'm sure Senach can find someone to walk with you. I don't think Flannan will be here today."

A long silence. Then, "Be a good day to ride out and visit the locals," Grim said. "Sun shining and all. Might be more forthcoming than these monks."

"They might and they might not. It's too soon to go to the settlements; we haven't decided when to hold the ritual yet, or where. And I do need time to prepare myself. You walk up and have a look at what needs doing at St. Olcan's first. If the job turns out to be too much for one man, or too much to do by midsummer, then tell them so."

"If that's what you want."

My sigh was no doubt audible to him. "It would be useful. In several ways. You're a good listener, and there may be someone up there who can give us some insights. St. Olcan's has a famous collection of books and manuscripts. It's full of scholars. And people trust monks; they confide in them. If there's a written version of the tale about the monster in the tower, it may be in their library somewhere. Or one of the monks may remember it. One of us needs to go in there, make some friends and get chatting, and if anything's certain, it's that it won't be me."

Grim looked up at last. His expression could only be described as shuttered: the look of a man who does not want you to know what he's thinking. "Thing is," he said, "Flannan's clever. A scholar. Writing a book about old tales, isn't he? And he's staying at St. Olcan's. What's certain is you're asking the wrong man."

"Morrigan's britches, Grim, what's got into you? Flannan is nothing to do with this. He just happens to be here at the same time we are. Geiléis didn't ask him to solve her problem; she asked us." Not quite accurate, and certainly not fair. I *had* asked Flannan to talk to the monks; I had told him what it was I needed to know. He just hadn't brought me any answers, or shown much interest in finding them. "I'm asking you because I trust you to do the job and do it well," I said. "And I'm not talking about the thatching. I know, and you know, that you could do that standing on your head."

His mouth twitched in the ghost of a smile. "That'd be a sight to see," he said.

"So, will you go? Today?"

Another weighty pause. He had stopped eating. "Got to, don't I?"

"In fact, no. I don't give you orders; I ask for your help." This must be the result of that strange episode on the day we arrived; he was afraid the monster's voice would play havoc with his mind and drive him off the path. And he was too proud to say so. Men could be infuriating. "You should take someone with you."

"Or I'll go crazy, even with my ears blocked," Grim said. "That's what you think."

"Lady Geiléis did warn us. On the other hand, we've been out and about since then, including our trip to the island, and you've shown no signs of losing your mind."

"Only thing is, those little folk. You know how they came out, that day. Might want to talk again. Won't make an appearance if I've got a guard with me. Or your scholar friend."

"Never mind that. Just go to St. Olcan's and have a look. And get someone to walk back with you. Not Flannan. He and I have had a falling-out. Ask Brother Dufach or one of the others. Nobody will think badly of you for that. It's just common sense."

"What'll you be doing?"

"Talking to Geiléis, choosing a day for the ritual. Going out to gather herbs. Spending time in the forest on my own. Part of the preparation, as I said."

"Senach won't want you going out without a guard and for once I agree with him."

"Don't concern yourself. I'll persuade Geiléis. She only needs to hear that without the proper preparation the cleansing ritual has no hope at all of banishing the monster." Even if I did fit in the hours of meditation and fasting, the solitary vigils, the prayers that were supposed to be offered in the days leading up to the ritual itself, I doubted my efforts would achieve anything. But I did not say so.

"Be careful," Grim said.

"You too."

I returned from the privy to find our quarters empty. Grim's cloak was gone and with it his water skin and his weapons. It seemed not quite right to visit a monastery armed to the teeth, but the forest of Bann was a tricky, mysterious place, so maybe it was common sense.

Geiléis always took breakfast in her private quarters. Sometimes she did not emerge until well into the morning. I wondered what she did with her time. I had seen no sign of loom, of distaff and spindle, or indeed of musical instruments or writing materials in her bedchamber. No little dogs; no husband or children to keep her occupied. It was a solitary life, which in itself was no bad thing—there had been times when I had longed for nothing more than to be all alone, with no need to bother about anyone. I'd imagined a little house in the forest where I might live without human companionship and be as ill-tempered and unsociable as I pleased. But that house had always contained implements of work: quills, parchment and inks; herbs and fungi drying; knives and boards, stoppered jars, jugs and vessels for the making of remedies. There'd always been a dog too, a big ugly one to keep folk away. The idea of living alone pleased me. But living alone with nothing to do was quite a different matter. Geiléis was not alone, of course; she had her servants and her men-at-arms. But she kept them at arm's length. She was, in effect, without family or friends. Despite myself, I felt sorry for her. Who would want to come and visit her, with the monster's voice ringing in their ears and casting a blight over the whole place? I did wonder why she didn't ride out and call upon the folk of the district, the way Oran did at Winterfalls. All the local people there knew the prince and respected him as their leader and guardian, young as he was. Perhaps Geiléis was unwelcome at the local farms and settlements. Perhaps folk believed she had somehow brought the curse down on them.

Time passed and she did not appear. So I took my basket and my knife and headed out into the forest, not bothering with an escort. My mood was snappish. If I was to conduct a public ritual within a few days, I'd need to stop my mind from going around in circles and at least pretend to be calm. Gathering the appropriate herbs for the rite, in my own company and at my own pace, would be a good start.

It was a fair day. The forest was refreshed by the rain, the sun shone and the trees were alive with birds. But there was no escaping the sorrowful voice from the tower. I thought I could reach the spot I remembered without needing to block my ears. A little side path, off to the left. I'd seen it when we went to the tower. It had looked full of useful herbs and fungi, and there would be no need to go too far from the main track, the one deemed safe. When I went back to the house I would beg a corner of the kitchen and make up a few handy remedies—the kinds of salves and lotions that were a little too complex to be produced by a village wife, but were nonetheless in frequent demand. I already had herbs drying in our quarters, gathered from Geiléis's kitchen garden. When we rode out to invite the local folk to the ritual, I would also offer my services as a healer.

It was good to be on my own. It wasn't as if Geiléis's household was noisy. Her servants went about their business with soft-footed efficiency, not speaking unless it was necessary in the course of their duties: *More soup, Mistress Blackthorn?* But they were always *there*. If not quite in our bedchamber, then somewhere very near, bringing in water from the well or sweeping the hallway. And Geiléis herself, though often closeted away, had a habit of appearing unexpectedly.

I walked farther down the main track, wondering if Geiléis would send someone running after me as soon as she learned I had left the house on my own. I tried to imagine what it would be like here once the monster was gone. Its voice rang constantly in my ears; I had seldom been without a headache since we arrived here. Ah. A headache potion. That would go down well among the locals.

I reached a little side path. I was fairly sure it was the one I'd noticed before, all grown over with ferns and low, creeping plants. I wrapped my shawl more tightly around me and ventured forward, moving slowly lest I crush some delicate stem making its way up to the light, or some small creature crawling at its own short-legged pace across the pathway. A little farther, and a little farther again. A few leaves taken from one plant, a few from another, with a murmured apology and thanks. I should have prayed as I gathered; it was part of the ritual preparation. But I found I couldn't. I couldn't lie to the wild world around me. I no longer believed there were any gods worth praying to, since if they existed they allowed the innocent to die in agony and evildoers like Mathuin of Laois to treat folk as if they were less than the dirt under his boot soles. What god could stand back and let that happen without moving so much as a finger to stop it? The words I spoke as I harvested were as much habit as anything. I'd been taught well, and early; along with the names of herbs and their medicinal uses, I had learned never to harvest without giving thanks, and never to cut so much from a plant that it could not recover itself.

I'd wandered farther than I'd intended. The path, if path it was, wound between the mossy trunks of the trees and over small streams. It climbed steps formed by the roots of a venerable oak and narrowed in one spot to cross a dip by means of a plank less than a hand span wide. I paused, not sure I wanted to venture over, and that was when I saw her, coming the other way with a wee basket over her arm and her shawl drawn tight around her shoulders. I froze, not quite believing my eyes. A little figure hardly as high as my knee, clad in a gown and apron and shawl as I was, with her dark hair sticking up as if she had walked through a prickle bush without noticing. She had a basket over her arm and a good knife in her belt. Her errand was the same as mine.

So Grim's wee folk were not a product of the curse addling his wits after all. They were real. Unless my mind too had been turned inside out by the screaming.

The little woman must have had her thoughts on something else; she didn't see me until she was halfway across the plank bridge and looked up suddenly. There I was, a healer like herself, but giant-sized. No wonder she turned pale. No wonder she wobbled on her narrow purchase.

"It's all right," I said, as she regained her balance and stood glaring at me from the middle of the bridge. "I'm out gathering herbs, the same as you. Maybe you can tell me where I might find druid's balm. It may have another name in these parts. It has leaves somewhat like peppermint, but red-tipped. Useful for warding off headaches. Do you know it?" I was babbling now, desperate to get her talking before she took it into her head to flee. "I wouldn't need much, only a leaf or two." I gathered my wits; reminded myself that there were rules for dealing with the fey. An exchange was easier to negotiate than a gift, always. "I managed to find some of these beetle-foot toadstools; I've found they work well in a poultice to draw out ill humors from a wound. If you could use some, I have enough to share. Or I can show you where they grow, back along this path." When I turned to indicate the path behind me, I was disturbed to notice that it now looked rather different. Surely I had not come down a hill as steep as that, or walked between those massive oaks. I turned hurriedly back to find that the miniature healer had advanced over the bridge and was standing right in front of me. It seemed she was not afraid of the giant after all; not now she had taken my measure.

The creature in the tower screamed on. This little person might not have heard a word I'd said. On the other hand, when I'd whispered my offer of help, on the island, the creature had responded, if in a less than civil way. And Grim said he'd had a conversation with his wee man. So maybe she could hear me. And maybe she knew the old story.

Best not tell her why I had come to Bann. What Geiléis wanted might not be what the fey folk of the forest wanted. I set down my basket. "My name is Blackthorn. I'm visiting Lady Geiléis, with my friend. May I talk with you awhile?"

The wee woman put her own basket on the ground. Shook her head; laid a finger across her lips.

"You can't talk?"

She rolled her eyes at me and clapped her hand over her mouth.

"You're forbidden to talk to me?"

The little woman nodded, then pointed into the woods. She mimed picking something and putting it in her basket. Indicated me, then herself.

"I can come with you, yes. But not far; I'm not familiar with the forest, and if I'm gone too long Lady Geiléis may send folk out looking for me."

She made a complicated face, then took up her basket and headed off. I followed.

We did not go far; only to a clearing where the rain and sunshine had coaxed up an exuberant growth of plant life. It was a healer's dream. She and I worked side by side, filling our baskets. She could talk all right; I saw her lips moving each time she cut, no doubt giving thanks as I was. But she would not talk to me.

She found a patch of druid's balm and tugged at my cloak to draw it to my attention. I plucked sufficient to make a healing draft; I would give it to Grim to take to the settlement. I passed her a share of the toad-stools. As soon as she had put them in her basket she tugged at my cloak again, pointing toward the other side of the clearing, where a fallen tree sheltered a prolific growth of small-leaved herbs. She led me there; squatted down, indicated that I should do the same.

I did not see it immediately, and she did not point it out, simply waited, her eyes on my face. What was it she wanted me to notice? A clump of the tiny herb known as true love's tears, with its cream-hued florets and feathery leaves? A growth of fungi like elaborate tiny palaces? A shiny green beetle?

Still she waited, and at last I saw it: markings made by a knife on the trunk of the fallen giant. Markings so small that a human eye would most likely not notice them unless directed there. I glanced at the little healer, and she lifted her brows as if to say, *Well?*

Ogham. It was so long since I'd last used the tree alphabet that I doubted I remembered how to read the script. On the other hand, what you learn as a child stays deep in you, and can usually be found when needed. "I'm not sure I can read this right now," I said.

My companion indicated with grimaces and gestures that this was not good enough, and that if I did not at least try to read the script, I was not much of a wise woman.

"All right, I will try." Ogham was not like, say, Irish or Latin. The letters could be used to spell words, but each had a range of other meanings too, according to the nature of that particular tree. A person did not write in ogham something like, *Good morning, my friend! How are you, and what did you have for breakfast?* It was more of a code; a language that gave you the essentials but left you to work out the bits in between. I recognized the last sign here: *straif.* Blackthorn. Some of the others too. But all the letters together did not spell out any word known to me.

The little healer reached out a bony finger to touch the double line of the first letter. Perhaps this had to be read for its deeper meaning. "*Duir,*" I said. "Oak."

She nodded encouragement, gestured to indicate more was needed. "Leader? Druid?"

She shook her head, then reached up as if to put on a hat. Or a crown. "Queen?"

An encouraging wave of the hands suggesting I was almost there. "King."

A vigorous nod. And was that the very faintest trace of a smile? Morrigan's curse, this wise woman bestowed her smiles no more readily than I did mine.

The little woman skipped to the end, pointing to *straif*—four diagonal strokes across the center line.

"Thorn," I said.

Before I could start on the magical interpretations of the tree, she signaled yes. Thorn was all she wanted. And now, with first and last letters accounted for, I understood the word between.

"Imprisoned, shut in, captive. The king is captive in the thorn?"

That sent a shiver through me. "Does this refer to the creature in the tower?"

She rolled her eyes again. *No, stupid.* She pointed to *duir,* then indicated a height somewhat similar to her own.

"*Your* king? The king of the . . . small folk?"

Her nod said I was right. The curl of her lip suggested my choice of words could have been better. It was perhaps just as well I had not mentioned clurichauns. I was working out what question to ask next when someone shouted my name, not far away.

"Mistress Blackthorn! Where are you?"

In a trice, my companion was gone into the depths of the forest. And only just in time, for here was Onchú, striding toward me between the trees.

"I'm here, quite safe, gathering herbs for the cleansing ritual." I picked up my laden basket, making sure my skirt screened the ogham inscription. "Did Lady Geiléis send you? I did explain that I need to make most of my preparations alone."

"She was concerned, Mistress Blackthorn. Let me escort you back to the house now."

"Very well. Thank you." I had what I needed, for the time being. And the little woman was not going to reappear while this formidable man-at-arms was with me; of that I was quite sure. His voice had made her blanch with fear.

"Onchú?" I ventured.

"Yes, Mistress Blackthorn? Careful, don't slip." He reached out a hand to steady me as I came down a bank.

"Have you ever seen fey folk in these woods? Small ones, about this high?"

"Why do you ask?"

"I spotted something in the distance." I wasn't going to talk about what had just happened. I would tell Grim, of course, but nobody else. If the small fey folk were afraid of Geiléis's guards, I'd best not reveal the fact that I had just met one of them. If the little woman was sworn to silence, at least where talking to me was concerned, I'd best not make it known that she had communicated in another way, a way known only to druids and wise women. It was hard to believe Geiléis's household did not know of their existence already. Surely everyone in the district must know. Why had nobody mentioned them? "It looked like a very small person in a cloak, running through the woods. But I might have been wrong; it could have been a—a squirrel. Or a bird."

"The woods play tricks," Onchú said. "They make folk see things that aren't there. Or turn things into what they're not. That's why you shouldn't come out on your own. Especially when you're not used to the place."

"How can you know if what you see is real or not?"

For the first time, Geiléis's head guard looked uncomfortable. "Father Tomas would say such manifestations are the work of the devil, and should be shunned."

"But what would you say?"

We had walked some considerable distance back toward the house before he replied. "Too many good people have wandered from the path in pursuit of strange visions, and have come to grief as a result of it. I do not believe it matters what they are, real or false, human, animal or fey. A person should turn his gaze away and walk on by. Unless he cares nothing for his survival."

"You've known people who saw and followed these small fey folk, and were lost or hurt?"

"I cannot say what they saw, Mistress Blackthorn. Only they could do that, and of those I know, two are dead and the other out of his wits. We found him floundering in the shallows of the river one winter morning, close to the shore but unable to take those few steps required to reach the safety of the bank. A local lad, a swineherd who had taken his animals to forage for acorns in the wood. Almost dead from cold, and completely mad. He could not tell us what had happened."

This alarming tale was consistent with what Geiléis had told us about the curse. "But," I said, "that story might have nothing to do with the fey, real or imagined. The swineherd might simply have slipped and fallen into the river." But, of course, that was not the whole story. The cold does not drive people mad. And if he had fallen in by accident, why hadn't he simply waded to the bank? "Was the man injured? Did he suffer physical damage? Where is he now?"

"With his family, in one of the settlements. He had no visible wounds; the hurt was within. He requires constant care. Without that he would do harm to himself or to others."

After that, I could find nothing else to say until the two of us were back in the courtyard. My services as a wise woman, useful as they might be for dressing wounds and setting broken bones and lancing boils, would be next to useless in such a case. I might perhaps offer tonics or sleeping drafts for the other family members, but the victim himself would likely be beyond any healer's help. Did those wee folk really possess the ability to lead folk astray to the point of driving them permanently crazy? I recalled various old tales in which that was exactly what happened. *She left her home behind and went dancing off over the hills, and if she hasn't come home yet she's dancing still.* Yet that little woman had seemed full of common sense.

"Thank you for walking back with me, Onchú," I said. "I'm sorry if I haven't seemed to take due heed of the warnings. I do weigh the odds up carefully. Always." That was perhaps not entirely true; where Mathuin of Laois was concerned, I had more than once let my desire for justice outweigh my common sense. "I will have to take some risks if I'm to find a solution to this. Midsummer Eve is getting closer all the time."

"We are always happy to accompany you, Mistress Blackthorn. Our duties here are hardly onerous; the men are glad of something to occupy their time."

"Thank you, Onchú. Some things, a wise woman must do alone."

Geiléis was up and waiting for me in the dining chamber. That did not surprise me. Nor did the displeased expression on her face.

"You went out on your own," she said.

"And here I am, back again." I would not allow her to conduct an interrogation as if I were a wrongdoer. I'd had enough of that to last me a lifetime.

"If Onchú had not gone to fetch you, you might be wandering in the forest still, unable to find your way. Or drowning in the Bann. Do you think yourself indestructible?"

That made me smile. "I am not so much of a fool. But I know how to calculate risks. If you want the ritual to have some chance of working, you must let me do it in the way most likely to achieve that." I sat down at the table. Senach appeared from nowhere with a tray of refreshments, which he set down noiselessly before departing. "Now," I said briskly, "we should set a day and time for this observance. Far enough ahead for word to go out to the settlements and for folk to make their way here. But not too far ahead." Gathering folk together was important. It would give me the opportunity to talk to them. I could not believe that none of them knew the story of the monster in the tower. "Five days? Six?"

"Six," Geiléis said. "Some folk have a long way to travel."

"Dawn or dusk?"

"Ah," said Geiléis. "I understand your argument on that point, but it can be neither. Both dawn and dusk would require me to accommodate everyone here for a night. People simply would not come. So close to the tower, right in the woods . . . They might be prepared to tolerate that for the duration of the ritual, but not in the dark, even if they were housed in the barn. This place terrifies them. Your ritual would be attended only by the members of my household."

A pox on it! I wondered sometimes if she had any belief in me at all. "You're telling me I need to do it by day, with the screaming drowning out every word I say."

"Why not conduct the ritual farther from the tower, where the sound is not so overwhelming? In a grazing field, perhaps, beyond the forest's edge? A place from which the tower is visible; somewhere with sufficient space for a large number of folk to gather. I'm sure the men could help you find a suitable spot. If you are not too tired, you could ride out this afternoon to do so." When I did not reply, she added, "I am quite sure the local people would prefer that. If you want them to attend in numbers, offering a spot closer to home and farther from the tower will help."

I could hardly object to this; it made sense. Since I did not think the ritual would work anyway, I could not argue that it was best conducted a stone's throw from the tower, though my instincts told me that was where it should be performed. I was hardly prepared to admit, even to myself, that I wanted to do it down in the woods, where the little folk could see and hear. Where the creature in the tower might catch a consoling word or two, a scent of healing herbs, a glimpse of sacred fire, even as it wailed its despair over the forest. "Very well," I said. "Let's hope the weather stays dry for six days. Maybe there will be time this afternoon, after we've found this spot, to ride on to the nearest settlement and start spreading the word."

"You must not exhaust yourself, Blackthorn." She was all smiles now. "Let me pour you some ale."

"Thank you. I'm not exhausted. Just keen to get on with what has to be done. At this rate, Midsummer Eve will be here before we know it."

"Believe me, I understand the urgency all too well. It would save time, you realize, if my men took the message of invitation out to the community, leaving you to get on with your preparations?" Geiléis glanced at my herb-filled basket, which I had set on a chest, and I remembered belatedly that I'd intended to spend the day making salves, lotions and other cures to take with me when I visited the local folk. I frowned, eyeing the basket. Was that a tiny bunch of true love's tears tucked in the corner next to the sage? Whoever had picked that, it certainly hadn't been me.

"Mm," I said absently, wondering what it was the little folk of Bann were trying to tell Grim and me. *Our king is captive in the thorn.* So, they wanted me to free him? "You're right," I said. "Today all I need to do is ride to see this field and decide if it's suitable. I will ask Onchú to arrange an escort. But not right now—I have some work to do first."

Back in my quarters I changed my shoes, hung up my cloak and unpacked the basket. And yes—among the contents was a neat bunch of true love's tears, tied up with a green thread. Another message, no doubt. It might as well have been a letter written in Armorican, for all the sense I could make of it.

22

G ot to do it. Can't put it off any longer. Got to be a man; got to be the man I should be. Funny thing is, if I told her the story, she'd say, *It's all right, Grim; you needn't go.* She'd understand. I know that. But I can't tell her. Can't tell anyone. It's my worst thing, my dark thing, like hers is Cass and Brennan burning and her not being able to reach them. If I told the story out loud, I'd break into so many bits even Blackthorn wouldn't be able to put me together again.

Best not think too much. Shove my feet into my boots, grab my weapons, out the door and off up the hill. Don't want an escort. Don't want anyone seeing me like this. Cold and shaky, bringing up my breakfast under a bush, then bringing up bile and water, then retching on an empty stomach like my whole guts are going to burst out. As if I had poison in me. Which in a way I do. Made my own poison, haven't I?

I reach the spot where I turned back last time. Still can't remember much of the story Blackthorn was telling, the clurichaun story. From what she said, I spoiled that tale for her, turned it dark and bloody. Clurichauns with axes chopping at each other. Folk screaming in terror. Folk running, running. Only they weren't quick enough, and they died. All dead. Even Brother Galen. And all he wanted was to save his book . . .

Can't make my feet move forward. Can't take that one step farther. St. Olcan's is up ahead somewhere, not far at all. Wouldn't take much effort to get there. No need to tell them about any of it. Just walk in and say, *Come to do the thatching.* Pity I can't get in there while they're all out, finish the job, go away before they come back. But they're monks. Monks live by a pattern. Know that pattern like the back of my hand. Over the monster's miserable voice I hear a bell now, and I know it's the bell for Terce. Don't need to be there to see them, in my mind, walking along the path to the chapel, two and two, faces all peaceful in the morning sun. Just think about that. Don't think about what came after. Take another step, you coward. Take another step, you failure. Take another step, Bonehead. Take a step for every one of them that fell in his blood because you couldn't save him, because you weren't strong enough, weren't brave enough, weren't good enough. Because you weren't enough, never were, never will be. Wretched apology for a man. Mathuin was right to lock you away. What good did you ever do in your life? What good could you ever be to anyone?

I collapse under a tree. Not being sick now. Just sobbing like a child in trouble. Big lump of a man, all tears. What a sight. No wee fellow popping out to help me this time. No Blackthorn making a brew, then sitting down to drink it with me, and not saying a thing until I'm ready to hear it. Nobody but the big man and the woods and, not so far away, the bell that's stopped ringing. And the monster; it's always there. That creature's even sorrier and sadder than me. Stuck in there, it can't do what I'm doing, which is not a lot when you think about it. Go to St. Olcan's, fix a roof, do the brothers a good turn. Folk in these parts could do with a bit of help. Should be easy. Would be easy, if the past wasn't on my shoulders, weighing me down. Would be easy if I wasn't near shitting myself in terror.

They're singing now. Wonder if the monster can hear it? My bet is, all it can hear is its own wretched voice. Morrigan's curse, what a life!

I try to hear words in that noise. Keep thinking maybe it can talk, or could, but something's getting in the way. There was a fellow like that in Mathuin's hellhole for a while. A short while. They burned him, trying to get something out of him. Burned his face half off. Stupid way to try to make someone talk. After they did it, all that came out was a horrible sort of gargling noise. Crazy thing was, he'd have wanted to talk then. He'd have told them whatever it was just to make the pain stop. But he couldn't. Not anymore. Died the next day. They never got a healer for him. Blackthorn—Lady, she was back then—begged them to let her out for a bit so she could tend to him, ease the pain. Guards just laughed at her. We listened to him dying, all that night and into the morning. Said a few prayers, this and that, though none of us was godly folk. Blackthorn told a story. We sang for a while, until the guards shut us up with buckets of water. Thing is, this monster's voice sounds a bit like that dying man's did. Like its mouth's injured, or its throat. Not burned, like him, or it'd be dead. But damaged, or odd-shaped, or covered up with something. Teeth knocked out, tongue sliced off. Doesn't bear thinking about. But I do. Think about it, I mean. Wondering, like I did before, if the groans and howls and wails and sobs add up to, *Save me!* Or, *Make it stop!* Or even, *Kill me!* That's what the fellow with the burned face was trying to say. We all thought the same. That's how it goes when they torture you. First you're quiet. You're strong. You keep your promises to yourself: I will be a man. I will not scream. I will not tell my secrets. Then the pain gets too much, and you can't keep quiet anymore, so you scream and curse and shout. But you still don't tell them what they want to know, so they throw you back in your cell to wait for next time. So it goes on. When they're done, when you're lying there with smashed knees and broken fingers and bruises all over or worse, there's one thing you want. For the pain to stop. After the second time or the third, it hurts so much you want to die. Once you're dead the pain stops and never comes back. No words, but we all knew the burned man was calling out, *Kill me! For god's sake kill me!* Would have, if I could have. Poor bastard.

"You poor bastard," I mutter, in the silence while the monster grabs a breath. "You poor, poor bastard." Wonder if I'm right? Wonder if the creature in the tower would yell out words if it could? Crazy idea, now I think about it. What would I know about anything anyway?

Make myself get up. Stand on the path. Feet, go. Go that way. Ahead for St. Olcan's, you win the battle. Back for Geiléis's house, you lose. You fail. I think about the burned man screaming. I think about the monster, and how lonely it must be up there, shut in with its hurts. How does it keep going? How does it stay alive? I think how lucky I am not to be them; how lucky I am that in the stink and filth and misery of Mathuin's lockup I found Blackthorn. Why am I feeling sorry for myself? She asked me to do this, and I'm going to do it.

The feet walk on. I make myself take slow, deep breaths. Don't want to turn up on these monks' doorstep a weeping wreck. Need to tell them who I am, why I've come. Through another patch of woodland, pretty in the sun though I hardly see it. Keep going. Keep walking.

The monastery's in sight; wattle and mud buildings with thatched roofs, all of it showing wear and tear. Straw dark with mold. Wind damage. Looks as if they need a man to lay drystone as well as a man who can thatch. I come closer. There's a stone tower with a bell; there's a pigeon loft near what looks like a barn. A yard with chickens scratching about. Hen coop down the end. Big vegetable garden, all very tidy. Looks as if the brothers work hard in it. Feel bile rising in my throat. Push back the memories, down deep into the dark. Got to keep walking on. Blackthorn. Doing this for Blackthorn.

I'm at the garden wall. Nobody about. All in the chapel. Singing coming from over at the far side, where the bell tower stands. Haven't set foot in a chapel since the day it happened. What god would want me?

Walk on. Down the path. Hands itching for a spade or fork; nose twitching with all the smells: lavender, rosemary, mint, parsley, basil, the rich scent of compost that's ready to go in the ground. I could do it. I could help them. I could give them more time for their praying and singing, their reading and writing, their bright paintings of creatures

and saints and strange beings. I could do that. I've done it before.
Wouldn't ask, though. Couldn't. What happened then might happen
all over again. Could be I bring my own curse with me.

Want to turn back. Want to run away. Walk on. Try to unclench my
teeth. Try to slow the galloping warhorse in my chest. Try to breathe.
Here for the thatching, that's all. Go and look at the roof. And wait.

Easy to spot the scriptorium. Roof's a sorry sight, holes here and
there with rough patching that won't keep out more than a light shower.
Thatching's been done well but it's old. Too old to do its job anymore.
Long past the time for replacing. Not a high building; ordinary ladder
will do. And not so big either. At a pinch, if it stays fine, I could do it on
my own by midsummer, even with the creatures on top. Always do
those. Maybe it keeps a place safe and maybe that's only a fancy. Always
do them anyway. Looking up at the old roof, I can see them now in my
mind: dove at this end, salmon at the far end, and in the middle maybe
raven and cat. In that old story of the flood, Noah sent a raven and then
a dove. Fish, that's a sign for Christians. Cat because monks like cats.
And I'm back there straightaway, seeing Brother Galen with Bathsheba
on his knee, an old scholar with snow-white hair, a cat with fur as dark
as night. Brother Galen telling a story, me listening, as still as a stone so
I don't miss a word. Bathsheba purring like a small thunderstorm. On
the day, when it happened, when I came to myself and stumbled around
looking, looking to see if any of them had got away, if any of them were
still alive, the last one I found was Bathsheba. Even she was dead. When
I stopped howling, when I was able to think again, the first thing I
thought was that the man who took her on would have walked away
with scratches all over. He'd crushed her head with his boot. He'd stolen
Brother Galen's book for its jeweled covers. I thought of that man by his
campfire, tearing up the pages and feeding them into the flames. One by
one, the stories, the lovely little pictures. A cat with wings, gone. An owl
riding a dragon, gone. Men with the faces of foxes and badgers, all in a
line, dancing. Gone. I thought of that warrior, a Norseman, and knew
he wouldn't remember killing an old man and a cat. For him, for all of

them, it was just another raid. They wouldn't remember me, fighting them off until someone knocked me out cold and I couldn't fight anymore. They wouldn't carry it with them the way I do. If they did, how could they go on?

Curses! The bell's ringing again, and they're coming out. Got tears all down my face, can't help myself. One of the brothers spots me and walks over. Tall fellow, dark hair. He's going to ask what I thought I was doing, walking right in without a by-your-leave, and I'll have no words. Only sobs, like the monster in the tower.

"Come," the monk says, pointing to a bench. It's in a nice spot, under the shade of a plum tree that'll have a good crop in autumn. "Sit with me awhile. You look disturbed. If you wish, tell me what is troubling you." Then, as we sit down, "I am Brother Fergal. I look after the garden. And if I may hazard a guess, you are the man with a talent for thatching. Staying in the household of the Lady of Bann."

I fish out a handkerchief and dry my eyes. "How did you know?" My voice is a bit of a croak, but not too bad.

Brother Fergal smiles. A good smile, warms up his face, no tricks in it. I try not to see him with his head cloven in two, blood and brains spattered everywhere. "There are no other men in this district of quite your size," he says. "And I noticed you were studying our scriptorium roof. We would be most grateful if you could help us. You'd be well paid for your labors."

I find my voice again. "Big job. I can do it. Only got until midsummer, though. Be quicker if someone can help. Need not be a skilled thatcher. A lad with good balance, to hold things and hand me things. I can show him what to do. They said you've got the materials." Then, because now I've started I can't keep my big gob shut, I say, "Walls could do with a few repairs while I'm at it. Maybe re-lay that whole stretch at the foot of the garden. If you want. That'd be a better spot for your compost. I could set that up for you. Double enclosure built against the wall. Fork new stuff in one side, your animal droppings, your kitchen scraps. Fill it up, then leave it to rot down and start again on the other side. Keep it going, you know? Easier to get that organized before I redo the wall, not after."

Brother Fergal gives me a good long look. "Excellent," he says in a voice that sweeps away the blood and the brains and the burning pages, for now at least. "I'm sure Father Tomas will want the thatching done first. Our most precious books have been stored away in the building that houses our infirmary, where they can be kept safe and dry. Over there." He points. "But our scholarly brethren want things back the way they were. They prefer to work in the scriptorium, which they tell me is the only place with adequate light, and which in addition feels like home to them, since it has always housed St. Olcan's scribes and illuminators. If you can render the place weatherproof again, you will be every scholar's friend."

"Might make a start today," I say, thinking I'd be no friend to them if they knew my story. "Clear out what's in there. Then strip off the old thatch—looks too moldy to leave underneath. Start straightaway, better chance of finishing in time. That's if the weather stays dry. If it does rain, I could work on the wall. Only if you want."

He smiles again. "I feel certain Father Tomas will say yes to the wall. But I should ask him. Thank you, Grim. Do I have your name correct?"

I nod, *yes*.

"I will not pry. But if you want to talk, to lay your burdens down for a while, please seek me out. I and my two helpers—novices of this order—are often in the garden. I could at the very least provide a listening ear. Are you of the Christian faith?"

No good answer to that. Not one I can give to a nice fellow like this and still be truthful. "These days, I've got no faith," I say. Which is true, as far as it goes.

"God forgives sinners," Brother Fergal says quietly. "Our Lord Jesus Christ embraces all humankind—the weak, the strong, the bad, the good, the sheep that stay with the flock and those who wander and lose themselves. Those who know their path, and those who are yet to find it. You might give some thought to that." He gets up. "Now," he says, brisker, "if you'll come with me, I will introduce you to a few of my brethren, and you can cast an expert eye over the thatching materials. I'm sure we can find you a tall novice as an assistant. Someone eager to learn." He pauses. "We can accommodate you here while you're doing the work. That would save you the daily walk. And the meals are very good."

It comes to me that I've just promised, more or less, to be here all day, every day, from now until midsummer. Do that and I can't look after Blackthorn properly. But I've given my word. "Suits me better to stay at Lady Geiléis's," I tell him. "I'll come up early. Put in a good day's work, don't worry. Only I have to be there. For a bit each day, at least." I shut my mouth. Already said more than I meant to.

Brother Fergal has a little frown on his face, but he doesn't ask awkward questions. "If that suits you, Grim," is all he says.

Lot of good things about monks. They don't pry; they don't hammer their beliefs into you. They listen. They have answers when you want them. They tell fine stories. Of course they want you to become a Christian. Only natural. For most folk that come to a monastery, that's what it's all about. Even for me, the first time. Breaks my heart, remembering that. Such hope. A new dawn, that's what I thought. And for a while, that's what I got. Never been so happy. Then, in an eyeblink, or that's how it felt, it was all gone. They gave me something precious: open arms, a safe home, work for my hands, learning. Brothers. Family. And I failed them. I lost them. I lost everything.

"Right, then," I say, swallowing tears. "Show us these reeds."

23

GEILÉIS

At last Grim was out of the way, and likely to stay so. The job at St. Olcan's would keep him so busy he'd have no time to poke his nose into anything. A man like him wouldn't try to winkle out secrets. He'd do his job and keep himself to himself, and even if he did discover anything, he'd lack the wits to understand its importance. Besides, he'd be on the roof all day. Up there, a man was unlikely to get into conversation with scholars.

As for Blackthorn, she'd be busy enough for the next six days, with her ritual preparations. If she did insist on riding out to see the local folk herself, there would be no harm in it. Nobody would talk. The curse ensured that none of them remembered.

The healer was an odd creature. Angry, prickly, full of a crackling energy that was almost frightening. Stubborn. Disrespectful of authority. There was no doubt Blackthorn considered herself Geiléis's equal, even perhaps her superior. It was hard not to find that offensive. It was a struggle to swallow her first response, hold her tongue, exercise patience.

Geiléis paced her bedchamber, mulling it over. The fact was, the very qualities of Blackthorn's that so annoyed her—notably, sheer bloody-mindedness—might be what fitted the woman for this task. She really might be the right one. The one who would not decide, on Midsummer Eve, that she'd changed her mind about going through with it. The one who would wield her ax like a warrior and cut through the thorns, not looking back. The one who would climb the tower out of a fierce will to get the task done. The one who, on reaching the chamber at the top, would perform the deed, unflinching. Who would not be too frightened to act. Not be too weak. Not be overcome by pangs of conscience. Not enrage him, get herself hurt and become incapable of action. Not run screaming back down the steps and have to be dealt with. Blackthorn had qualities none of the others had had. If there had been a woman like her the first time, they might have been spared the years of torment, the years of weeping, the long years of telling the story over and over.

"But she's here now," Geiléis muttered to herself. "She's here and she'll do it and this will all be over." How things would be afterward, she could not quite imagine. In truth, she did not want to think beyond the morning of Midsummer Eve, when the thorns would part to let the healer through. In this tale, happy endings seemed impossible.

Why weren't Blackthorn and Onchú back yet? Dusk was close and still they had not returned from their expedition to the ritual ground. The delay could mean nothing good. Had they been led astray riding through the forest? Would they be found at dawn, sodden and lifeless on the river-bank? Could the little folk have broken the rules and made themselves known to Blackthorn? Surely not. The price of disobedience was too high.

There was nothing she could do but wait, and go on with the story. Tell of the time when they were happy. It was so hard to believe those long-ago lovers had ever been happy. Geiléis lit her candle and climbed the stairs. The creature's voice was quieter now; he knew the approach of dusk heralded a respite. She told herself that hush meant he was eagerly awaiting the tale. Perhaps, against the odds, he really could hear it. Perhaps it kept him going from one day of agony to the next. He had heard it more times than anyone could count. She had told it in as many different forms as she could devise. She had told it so often that one telling blurred into another, and sometimes the story made little sense. But the rudiments were always there: the girl wandering in the woods, the man in the tower, the rescue, the days of happiness. Then the cost of that brief happiness, a higher cost than anyone could have believed possible. A cruel price to pay. A punishment so long that its end often seemed beyond her reach. Had that brief time of joy really been worth so many years of sorrow?

"Of course it was," Geiléis murmured with her gaze fixed on the Tower of Thorns, where someone would soon reach out to close the shutters. The setting sun touched the tower gently, turning it gold as a ring, rose-pink as a young girl's blush, blue as the wing of a butterfly. "If not, why would I still be here? Let me tell you how fine that time was. It was like the first blossoming of spring flowers; it was like sweet honey from the hive; it was as precious as the first whispered words of love. Oh, that time was as wonderful as all those things and more . . ."

Brión's recovery was slow. The physician recommended that he not be moved until he was fully restored to health, and neither the young man nor his kinsfolk raised any objection. He stayed on at the home of Lily's parents, where folk fed him a special diet and fussed over him, while the physician tried bloodletting and the application of leeches. Brión's illness, declared this learned man, was an ague brought on by his two days and two nights wandering lost in the chill and damp of the forest. They gave him possets and wrapped him in warmed cloths.

Lily behaved impeccably, though she longed to see the man she had first known as Ash. She yearned to hold his hand, to comfort him and whisper tender words. But she held back, hoping her mother might start to forget her foolish escapade in the woods. In time, her patience bore fruit. Brión told Lily's mother that what he wanted most was someone to tell him stories or read to him; lying in bed all day was difficult for a young man who loved riding and hunting. Was there perhaps someone of his own age, or near his age, in the house who might be prepared to visit him and perform this service?

Lily was the only highborn and well-educated person in the house-hold who was anywhere near Brión's age. When asked if she would help, she managed to conceal her delight. "Very well, if you wish," was her response to her mother, who had suggested Lily might sit with the invalid twice daily for an hour, always in the presence of Muiríol or one of the other handmaids.

Now Muiríol, having received a gift from her mistress so generous that very soon she and her young man could be wed, was happy to do whatever Lily asked of her. She was ready to slip out of the sickroom for at least half of the appointed time. She waited within sight of the closed door. Should anyone happen to come by, she would say she was fetching a draft for Brión or a warm shawl for Lily. Who would challenge that?

Those snatched hours, or half hours, became the most precious time in the world. Young as they were, the lovers behaved as nobly born folk are supposed to behave; their passion was balanced by restraint. So there were soft kisses; tender touches; sweet whispered words. There were blushes; there was stammering; there was poetry. And if, after many days had passed, the passion threatened to out-weigh the restraint, time always intervened. Half an hour was not very long at all; not with one's mother in the same house with an ear out for trouble.

Besides, though Lily was certain Brión loved her—he had not only told her so, but demonstrated it with his eyes, his lips, his hands—she found him oddly reluctant to talk about the future. And although she had been bold in going to the tower, and bold in arranging the cap-tive's rescue, she was not sure she was bold enough to ask a man to marry her. Should not Brión be doing the asking? He must soon be well enough to go home. What if he went, and that was the last she ever saw of him? What if the caresses and words of love were only some kind of game? But then, if she spoke to him of these doubts and it turned out he'd been planning to propose marriage that very day, or the next day, or the day he was due to leave, she would hurt his feel-

ings terribly. She might never win back his trust. She knew nothing of young men; she had no idea if they thought the way young women did or quite differently. She could hardly ask her mother for advice. And though she was close to Muiríol, it did not seem right to burden a maidservant with such questions. Besides, Muiríol had an easy confidence with young men—not only her sweetheart, but any man she spoke to—that Lily knew she herself would never develop.

After one-and-twenty days of lying in bed or sitting on a padded bench in his quarters, Brión was declared well enough to venture outdoors as far as the kitchen garden. He was not especially keen to go, but allowed himself to be helped along the hallway, through the garden door and out to a bench in the sun. Here, Lily was to do her customary reading. Muiríol came as chaperone, and a gardener, forking dung in a corner, made an uninvited fourth. A little way into the reading, Muiríol wandered over to have a word with the gardener, and Brión addressed Lily in an urgent whisper.

"I need to ask you something, Lily. It's important."

"Mm?" Was she naïve to expect a proposal of marriage? Or was that reasonable enough under the circumstances?

"Will you run away with me?" Brión whispered. "Far from here. And soon, before they make me go home. Will you?"

Lily was too shocked to say yes or no. His words had made her insides churn with unease. And perhaps just a little disappointment. When she found her voice again, she said, "Run away? But why? And where?"

"Anywhere that isn't here." Brión had dropped his gaze; he appeared to be studying his hands, clenched together in his lap. "I can't stay here."

"You'll go home, of course," Lily said, confused. "As soon as you are well enough. That's what everyone expects."

"You don't understand." Still he would not meet her eyes. "You can't understand."

"Ash," she said, using the sweet name, the name that was just between the two of them. "Tell me. Tell me what this is. If you love me,

you should trust me, even if it's something terrible." She could not imagine what it might be. He was betrothed already? Married? He had some vile illness nobody had thought to tell her about? None seemed at all likely. "Please," she added in a whisper. "And if you can't tell me, you should tell someone else, someone who can help."

"You're saying you won't go with me." Now Brión looked up at her, and his eyes were bleak. "You don't love me enough to go."

"That's not fair!" Was this to be their first argument? "You must know that! You ask me to leave everything behind, to leave my family without a word of farewell, to travel away when I don't even know where I'm going, and you expect me to do it without any idea why? I've always thought that if you love someone, you trust them with the truth. If you can't do that, then perhaps . . ." *Then perhaps we should not be together. Perhaps we are not right for each other after all.* She could not say it. She loved him with all her heart; she knew he was the only one.

"I should go," Brión said. "I should go away and leave you to get on with your life. I am no good for you, Lily."

"No," said Lily. "You should be brave. Running away isn't brave. The brave thing, the hard thing is to tell the truth. To face up to whatever it is."

Brión glanced across the garden to where Muiríol and the gardener were still engaged in conversation. He looked back toward the house, then over to the outer gate, as if there might be listening ears everywhere. "Not here," he said. "I can't risk anyone overhearing."

"Then we'll walk a little way. You're supposed to be walking to get your strength back." It had surprised her that he had not wanted to exercise much; indeed, he had seemed reluctant to venture far at all. Now he got to his feet and they walked together, down to the far end of the garden, farther away from the others. The little gate in the outer wall stood open; that would earn the kennel lads a reprimand. "Why don't we go out toward the forest, just for a short while?" Lily suggested, at the same time gesturing to Muiríol across the garden to indicate what she intended. Muiríol was sympathetic; she would turn a *blind eye unless there was a real risk involved. "We'll stay close to the gate, of course. But out there, we can talk in private."*

It was most improper, and perhaps unwise as well. Lily slipped her hand through Brión's arm and felt him shivering, deep within. Probably she should send for someone to take him inside, and straight back to bed. But Lily had a greater fear—that the mystery would never be properly explained, and that the man she loved would head off home or, worse still, run away to an unknown destination on his own, and that she would never see him again. That fear was enough to draw her out through the gate, leading her sweetheart with her. And now they were on the greensward, between the outer wall of her father's stronghold and the edge of the forest. The day was fine; the birds were singing; a light breeze tossed little clouds about in the sky. Here and there flowers bloomed in the long grass. Not far away, a stream gurgled into a small pool; frogs sang a croaking chorus. From this spot only the very highest point of the tower could be seen above the dark blanket of the trees. Lily screwed up her eyes, trying to see the window. Were the shutters open or closed?

She had learned nothing new from Brión about the night he was rescued. They had spoken of a hundred other things, a thousand, but on that matter, as on the future, he'd had nothing to say.

"You're afraid," Lily said now. "Afraid to tell me." She expected him to deny it; if she'd observed anything about boys, it was that they did not like to be thought cowards. "I love you. If you're in some kind of trouble, I want to help you."

"If you knew the truth," Brión said, "you too would be afraid. And I don't want to draw you into that. How can I put you at even more risk? I shouldn't have stayed so long here. It was selfish. I wanted to be with you, to be close to you, but . . ."

"Brión," said Lily, gritting her teeth, "just say it. Just tell me. It's to do with what happened that night, isn't it? Before I found you?"

He muttered something.

"What did you say?" Suddenly she was shivering too. Wishing she had not pushed this; wishing she had waited for him to be ready to tell.

"*You will despise me," said Brión.*

Lily could think of nothing to say.

"*There was a woman," Brión said in a whisper, glancing this way, that way. A little cold breeze came up out of nowhere, ruffling the grasses. "A beautiful woman. On a white mare, with silver jingling on the harness. We were out hunting, and I saw her, and . . . I followed her. Rode after her. Left my companions behind. I was dazzled, Lily. Out of my wits. I did not consider that she might be fey."*

In Lily's shocked mind, everything began to make a terrible kind of sense. "Go on," she said, keeping her voice calm.

"*I rode deeper and deeper into the woods. I could see her ahead, the white shadow that was the horse, the tall figure riding, with her fair hair all twisted and twined with jewels and her silken gown in more colors than anyone could find names for, flowing around her with a life of its own. The paths grew narrower; I had to get down and lead my horse. And still she went on, just too far ahead for me to reach her, but close enough for me to catch glimpses of her now and then. I followed her all the way to the Bann, and when she rode into the ford, I did the same."*

"*But . . . your horse . . ."*

"*He shied and threw me into the water. He bolted. I hardly noticed. The woman was on the island, standing motionless by her own horse, waiting for me. The moonlight shone down on her; she looked like a goddess. Lily, I am ashamed to tell you this story. So ashamed of my weakness."*

Lily said nothing, simply waited.

"*My thoughts had room for nothing but her. So I waded over to the island. Wet, disheveled, with any dignity I'd had completely gone, I walked up to the lovely woman and stammered a few words. My name. My admiration. Something foolish."*

"*She had you under a spell," Lily breathed. This was like something from an ancient tale, not real life. Innocent though she was, she had no difficulty in imagining the missing part of the tale, from Brión's first dazzled greeting to the woman to the moment she had found him next day, lying exhausted in the tower, his body all over bruises and scratches. She tried not to judge him; she tried hard. "Tell me the rest, Ash."*

He flushed scarlet. "I . . . She and I . . . It was as if I was in a different world, and the rules of this world were forgotten. I wish I had not done it. I could blame her. I could say she made me do the things I did, lured me, worked her magic on me. But the blame is mine. I should not have followed her. I should have said no to her. I should have been brave enough to refuse. And I should have been brave enough to tell you the truth from the start." His voice was stronger now, and the blush had faded somewhat. He fixed his eyes on hers, and the look in them was clear and honest. "I'm sorry. From the bottom of my heart, I'm sorry. I hope you can forgive me, Lily. What I have to offer you . . . as a husband, I mean . . . is spoiled. Tainted. I should not have let this happen."

"She ensorcelled you," Lily said. "That's why you're still afraid."

"If we went away, we could be free of it. Far away, where she could not find us."

The idea seemed to Lily no more reasonable than it had been before she knew the truth. "No," she said firmly. "We should stand up to her. We should be brave. Running away never solved anything." Oh, the naïveté! Oh, the youthful confidence! Oh, the stupidity!

"I can't go on," Geiléis whispered. "I can't go past that moment, I can't. Not again. Please don't make me tell it again." But there was nobody to hear. She clutched her shawl around her, staring out into the gathering dark. She'd been a fool to believe for a moment that he could hear the story as she told it, night after night. The curse was cruel in its every careful particular. There was nothing soft about it. There was nothing in it to her own advantage, no kindness, no concession, no provision to make the long penance easier to endure. *Tell it. Tell it until you understand what you have done. Tell it over and over until this all comes to an end.*

"All we wanted was to be happy," she said to the empty air. "That, surely, did not merit such suffering." The cruelest part was this: she who had worked the curse had not been seen from that day on, but still the spell endured. A powerful magic indeed. That boy who had followed a beautiful woman into the forest could have had no idea what he would unleash.

The quiet of the woodland below her window was broken by the sound of horses' hooves on paving stones, and of voices. That was Onchú speaking. And now a woman's voice—Blackthorn. They were back, and if her ears did not deceive her, so was Grim; nobody else had such a deep voice. She would go down soon and greet them; she would express polite interest in what they had been doing. The ritual preparations; the roof of the scriptorium. But her mind would be full of one thing only. She wondered, sometimes, whether she should have told Blackthorn the truth from the start—not the full truth, but almost all. The woman was open to the strange and uncanny. She might have been prepared to accept it, saving Geiléis and her household the need for lies. It was too late now. Once she'd told that story at court, with Blackthorn and Grim present, there'd been no choice but to stick to it. Gods! It was almost midsummer. Let Blackthorn not find out she'd been lied to all along. If she learned of that betrayal—she'd see it as that—she'd surely walk away. Or try to. And Geiléis would have to silence her. The true story, the full story could not be allowed to go beyond these four walls. If it did, there might never be an end to this.

"Stop it!" she muttered. "Get ahold of yourself!" Less than a turning of the moon remained until Midsummer Eve. After so long, she must not stumble at the very end. She must walk on steadily, one step at a time. While her guests were tidying themselves up for supper, she would tell the next part of the tale—the part she feared and loathed, but must revisit over and over because the curse bound her to do so. If she told it now, tomorrow would be easier.

Geiléis drew a deep, steadying breath and took up her story once more.

Not long after this, Muiríol appeared at the gate, making urgent gestures, and Lily and Brión were obliged to return within the walls. He was

whisked back off to bed, and she went to her chamber to think in soli-
tude. What he had told her was terrible. To meddle with the fey . . . to lie
with one of them . . . that had been beyond foolish. Had he never lis-
tened when his mother told him the old tales?

But they could not run away. She hoped that in the morning he
would see how ridiculous that idea was. What did he think they would
live on? Did he imagine their families would not move heaven and
earth to find them? Each was an only child; each was of noble birth.
They could not simply turn their backs on one life and start another
with no resources save their love for each other. Of course, in the old
tales, such things did happen. He might find work as a swineherd or a
gardener, and she as a rather inept seamstress or washerwoman. And
eventually, years later when they had a child of their own, they might
be rediscovered by their families and brought home to a welcome
attended by tears and joy. In those tales, anything could happen. And
this felt just like such an ancient story, so unlikely it could hardly be
believed. But it was real. She had seen the dazed expression in Brión's
eyes when she found him in the tower. She had seen the torn clothing
and the injuries to his body. And she had seen, late at night after he
had been rescued, a light in that high window, as if someone was walk-
ing around the tower room with a candle in her hand. As if someone
was sad. Or angry. As if someone did indeed still have her eye on him.

"He's mine," she whispered. "You can't have him. You're no good
for him. You can't frighten me; I will hold on with everything I have."
Fine words; fine and strong. But she was cold, all the same. She felt the
shadow of approaching danger.

That night, Brión had supper alone in his bedchamber, and when
Lily asked if she could go in and speak to him before she retired for the
night, her mother said no, that would be entirely inappropriate.
Besides, Brión had a severe headache and needed to rest.

Later, when the household was abed, a strange wind blew up. It
whispered through the treetops and whined across the garden; it insin-
uated itself between the shutters, blowing out late candles; it whooshed

down chimneys and stirred up the embers of fires. Lily stood by her window looking out over the forest, and the wind wrapped itself around her in an icy embrace, making her heart shrink. Were there words in that stirring of the air, harsh words meant only for her ears? She could not understand them, but she felt the hatred.

"You can't frighten me," she said again. But that was a lie. A terror gripped her beyond anything she had felt before. "I will hold on," she said. "I will. I love him. You can't have him." And she thought she heard an answer in the wind: Oh, foolish human girl. If you want him, come and fetch him! He's of no more use to me. The wind swirled around Lily, teasing at her hair, tugging at her shawl, dancing in and out the open window.

"What do you mean?" Lily fought for composure. Was the fey woman giving up just like that? Passing Brión back to her as if he were of no more consequence than a loaf of bread gone stale or an apple turned too soft for eating? "What do you mean, fetch him?"

From the tower. He's in the tower. The wind rattled the shutters and was gone, leaving the chamber in stillness. Her heart cold, Lily gazed out toward the tower. The moon was dark; the forest lay hidden. But she could see a light. A faint, faltering light, as of a candle struggling to hold its flame against an eldritch draft. Now her heart was pounding. The fey woman was giving up. She was releasing Brión from the spell. But only if Lily was brave enough to go out in the night and bring him home. A quest. The old tales were full of quests. And she'd have to do it alone. If she woke her father and arranged an expedition with men-at-arms and horses and iron weapons, chances were they'd get to the tower to find it empty.

Lily flung on her warm cloak, searched for her outdoor shoes, tried to calm her racing thoughts. She was about to climb out the window into the dark embrace of the oak tree when common sense prevailed. This could be a trick. The fey loved tricks. What if Brión was tucked up asleep in his quarters, and what the fey woman really wanted was to lure Lily out into the forest so she could work some fell charm on her? It would be foolish indeed to rush out there without at least checking whether Brión was still safe in the house. But she mustn't be seen by anyone. It wasn't so much the impropriety of being spotted slipping into a young man's bedchamber at dead of night; it was that once seen, she would likely be questioned. When folk discovered that Brión was gone, that mounted search party would go out whether she liked it or not.

She carried her candle in one hand and her shoes in the other, making her way as softly as she could to the door of Brión's quarters. There were no guards in the hallway; she breathed a prayer of thanks and pushed the door ajar. The bedchamber was in darkness. All was silent. Lily lifted the candle, peering in, not quite prepared to walk right up to his bed.

The covers were on the floor. The pillows had been torn open; feathers drifted uneasily in the draft, an eerie summer snow. The chamber was littered with clothing, most of it shredded. It was as if some monster had run riot here. There was no sign of Brión.

"Go," whispered Lily to herself as her gorge rose and her mind filled with unspeakable images. "Go now and don't look back." No creeping out the front door. No slipping out the kitchen door. There would be guards outside; her father was careful. She must go back to her own chamber and out the window, the same as last time. And hope nobody saw her before she reached the little side door. Hope that door was open. She suspected it would be; the uncanny wind would have seen to that. Her adversary had challenged her. Lily had promised herself she would be brave, and she would meet the challenge. Ash, she thought, making his name a talisman to keep her safe. I'm doing it for you, Ash. I'll fetch you home and make an end to this.

A sudden tap at the door.

Geiléis started, nausea rising in her at the wrenching interruption. She had been deep in the tale. She ran down the steps, strode to the door and flung it open. Senach cringed visibly, as if he expected her to strike him. She had never hit him; he was a good servant. "What?" she demanded.

"I'm sorry for the intrusion, my lady. This is something you will want to hear."

At her gesture, the steward entered her quarters, closing the door noiselessly behind him.

"Very well. Tell me."

"The scholar, Master Flannan, has come down from St. Olcan's, and he has brought some news that may be unwelcome to you."

"What news? Should I be speaking to Master Flannan in person?"

"You are the best judge of that, my lady. Master Flannan is talking to Mistress Blackthorn. Telling her and Grim of a secret store of manuscripts that was uncovered when the contents of the scriptorium were removed in preparation for the roof repairs. They thought they'd got everything out, but these were cunningly concealed, and were only discovered today. Master Flannan believes one of the documents may concern the . . . the history of the Tower of Thorns."

She was as cold as ice. It was that night all over again, and the chill embrace of a fey wind. *Oh, foolish human girl!*

"I suppose it's too much to hope that Master Flannan has brought this document with him," she said. She would burn it. Tear it in small pieces and scatter it to the winds. Drown it deep.

"I did ask, my lady. He said it's locked in a chest at St. Olcan's, along with all the most precious manuscripts in the collection. This particular document is written in a strange tongue and will be difficult to translate. Master Flannan is not sure of the meaning. But he said it does seem to relate to the tower."

What could she say? Senach knew her mind. If she ordered Master Flannan's immediate removal from Bann, he would ensure it happened, one way or another. If she required that the removal be permanent, that too would be attended to without question. She could not ask her folk to steal and destroy the document; it was in the possession of the monastery. Young Lily, Lily-before, might have believed the Christian God stretched a hand over the brethren, shielding them from harm. Geiléis put no credence in gods of any kind. But Father Tomas had been kind to her. He had been generous, and she had come to rely on him, as she had on his predecessors. If not for their protection, she'd likely have been thrown off her land long ago, one way or another. It would make choice pickings for the Tirconnell chieftains.

And it wasn't only that. Blackthorn was astute. If Blackthorn got suspicious—and what more likely to arouse suspicion than a raid on the monastery and the disappearance of the very document they all wanted to know about?—then Geiléis might lose her chance to break the curse. Likewise, Blackthorn would most certainly ask questions if her friend the scholar suddenly vanished on the brink of sharing his great find.

"I'll come and speak to them," she said. "I'll need you to be present, Senach. Watch them closely. I cannot imagine what this document is. Perhaps it is harmless. Perhaps Master Flannan is wrong about its contents. I do not see how a written record could exist. Nobody knows. Except for us, and the little folk . . . Could they have told? Would they dare?"

"That seems unlikely, my lady. They are bound by the curse, as we are."

"Even so . . . it may be necessary to remind them. I will speak to Onchú. In the unlikely event that Master Flannan is right about the document, we must keep its contents from Blackthorn. Should she learn the full story before midsummer, our precious chance is lost. That cannot be allowed to happen."

"I understand, my lady."

24

Dusk had fallen before we got back to Geiléis's house. Overall, the outing had been a success. Onchú and Rian had escorted me to a spot that was just as Geiléis had described it: level, grassy and well sheltered yet allowing a good view of the tower. It might not be perfect for a ritual, but it would serve well enough. The two guards had offered to take me out to the nearest settlement tomorrow to spread the word, if I was up to another ride. Between the throbbing headache and the aching back I suspected I'd be fit for nothing but lying in bed feeling sorry for myself, but I said yes anyway. If these folk had anything useful to say, I needed to hear it as soon as possible.

We rode into the courtyard just as Grim arrived back from St. Olcan's in the company of Flannan, with Ripple following like a gray shadow. It was almost dark. Unless Geiléis had invited Flannan to supper, he must have something particular to tell us. Hadn't I ordered him to stay away until the ritual?

Grim was unusually quiet, even by his standards. He looked wrung out, exhausted. And sick, the same as this morning. Seemed a day of work at the monastery had not settled his stomach.

"You all right?" I asked while Flannan was speaking to Senach, who had come to the door to welcome us.

Grim answered with a grunt that might have meant yes or no. Not sick, I thought; or not in the ordinary meaning of the word. Something different. Something I should have recognized earlier.

"We can talk if you want," I said under my breath. "When you're ready."

"Nothing to tell." Grim rolled his shoulders, eased his back. "You?"

"Found a spot for the ritual. And . . ." Morrigan save me, had that encounter with the tiny woman been only this morning? "Something else too. I'll tell you later." Flannan was coming over. He wore a broad smile. "I didn't expect to see you so soon," I said to him.

"I found something." Flannan's eyes were alight with excitement. "A document—it could be exactly what you're looking for. I'm almost sure what's set down there is the story of this monster and the Tower of Thorns. I found it in the—"

"Supper is almost ready." Senach was courteous, as always. I was in no doubt, however, that he had interrupted the conversation on purpose. "There's hot water available in your quarters, Mistress Blackthorn; you might like to refresh yourselves before we gather for the meal. Master Flannan, I'm sure Lady Geiléis will want to be present when you share the news of this discovery. Meanwhile you may also wish to avail yourself of our home comforts. I don't imagine they provide hot baths at St. Olcan's."

We were neatly separated. Dau took Flannan off to the men's quarters while Grim and I went to our own chamber. There was a screen now, of Grim's making; it had a spray of flowers painted on one side and a fearsome hound on the other. The artwork lacked the refinement of, say, an illuminated capital. But there was pleasing life in the images. Another of Grim's surprising talents. I wondered often what he had been before; what manner of life he had led. Being stuck with me was a waste of what he had to give, even if it was his choice. If I chose to go south with Flannan, I'd be setting Grim free. When I thought of it that way, it felt like less of a betrayal.

I had first bath. Scrubbed off the sweat and grime of the ride; tried to scrub away my misgivings along with them. On the other side of the screen, there was a heavy silence.

"I met one of them this morning," I said as I dried myself off and got back into my clothes. "The wee folk. A healer, out gathering herbs just like me. When I tried to talk to her she wouldn't answer. Seemed to be telling me she was forbidden to speak to me. But she gave me a message anyway." I told him about the ogham letters and what I'd guessed they meant. "When she heard Onchú coming she ran away. She was scared of him."

"But not scared of you," Grim said. "Stopped to listen, didn't she? And to give you a clue."

"A clue to what? That's what I can't work out."

"*Our king is captive in the thorn.* If it's the king of the wee folk, who'd want to lock him up? Could it be like that story with the clurichauns, two tribes of them at war? Maybe there's a whole other part to this. Something Geiléis doesn't know anything about."

The silence drew out as we considered this possibility. We changed places; he bathed, I got everything ready for a brew, though I would not make it until after supper.

"Grim, what was Flannan talking about? What is this manuscript?"

For a while I heard only splashing sounds. "Scholars' business," he said eventually, and there was a darkness in his voice.

When it became obvious that he was not going to elaborate, I said, "It sounds as if it may be our business too. And Geiléis's. That's if Flannan is right about what the manuscript contains. Who knows? It might even tell us about the wee folk and this captive king of theirs. Were you there when they found it? How is it that nobody knows what's in it?"

"Not for me to say. Only . . ."

"Only what?"

"Meddling. Not right, is it? Some of these old fellows, the old monks, their books are like their children, the ones they never had. Not right to mess around, just take things when you want."

"What are you talking about? Did Flannan take something he wasn't supposed to? Has he brought the manuscript here to show us?"

"Wanted to. Brothers wouldn't let him. Only found those old documents today, when we were clearing out the far end of the scriptorium. All hidden away. In a secret part of the wall. Brothers were as surprised as I was." I heard him stepping out of the small bath; saw him stand to dry himself. The screen was not tall enough to conceal fully a man of his height.

"*You* found it?"

"Mm-hm. Old oak box with a heavy lock. They got me to open it up. Lot of excitement. Not just the manuscript your friend was talking about, but quite a few others too. They called him—Flannan—to ask him what he thought they were. Written in some odd tongue, that's what they were saying. Flannan had a look, started reading the one he was talking about, but it was hard even for a scholar. Told them he wanted to show it to Lady Geiléis right away. They said no, the documents were too old and precious. They had to go back in the box. Locked up again, taken over to the infirmary." He moved the screen away. He was fully dressed, with his damp hair sticking up on end. It had grown since we left court. Time was passing all too quickly.

"The infirmary? Why?"

"Scriptorium's been damp, with the roof and all. Most stuff was already over in the infirmary. Now it's all there. Right conditions for the manuscripts, that's what they said. Not in with the sick folk, of course. Out the back, in an old part. Space for the writing tables and suchlike. But the scholars want their scriptorium back. Better light. Roof's going to keep me busy till midsummer. Hope that's all right with you."

I looked at him closely. "You don't really want to do it, do you? This thatching job?"

"They need it done. I know how to do it. Told them I'd help. Rather be here, true. But not up to me, is it?"

"You don't have to do what I tell you, Grim. There's no doubt it will be useful to have you at St. Olcan's, especially if you get close to some of the monks and they decide to confide in you. But you look . . . you look unwell. Disturbed. I wish you'd tell me what's wrong."

"Head hurts a bit, that's all. No surprises there. Thing in the tower must have a monster headache from its own screaming." He waited for the space of a breath. "Tip out this water in the yard?"

"Leave it for Senach's people to deal with. We're guests here, and we're both tired. We'd better make an appearance for supper and find out what's in this mysterious manuscript. I hope it is the story of the monster. That would mean we could stop looking for answers that don't want to be found, and get on with doing whatever has to be done."

"Mm-hm."

At supper, Flannan was aglow with scholarly excitement. It reminded me of old times, when he and Cass would get into fierce debate over some obscure point of scholarship, often late into the night. For all my reservations, it was hard not to be caught up in his enthusiasm. We heard the tale of how the old box had been discovered within the wall— somewhat belatedly, he acknowledged Grim's part in that—and how the monks had asked him, Flannan, to take a look at one document in particular.

"Brother Ríordán is the head archivist," he told us. "He's a respected scholar, and most particular about the preservation of the collection, which contains many rare items. The moment he set eyes on this document he was intrigued; firstly because it was extremely old, and secondly because it was in a tongue unknown to him. He thought I might recognize the language. I'm familiar with many, but I had never seen this one before. It seemed somewhere between Latin and Gaulish—Armorican, perhaps?—but scrambled in some way, almost as if the writer had applied a code. The title of the document included the word *Bann*, and another word I interpreted as *tower*."

Was I the only one who heard Geiléis suck in a shocked breath when he said *Armorican*? What did that mean to her? Two spots of red had appeared on her cheeks; she put a hand up to her face, as if to shield her expression.

"That's not much." I regretted this as soon as I'd said it; Flannan was so proud of the discovery. "It's interesting, of course, especially when we have so little to go on. But it might be a discussion of local landmarks, or a guide for finding the way between monasteries, perhaps intended for wandering scholars to copy and take away with them."

"Nah," put in Grim. "Code, isn't it? Why would you bother with a code for something like that?"

"I believe I can decipher and translate the document, given time," said Flannan, as if we had not spoken. "Brother Ríordán is zealous in his desire to protect his treasures at all costs; I am not sure he will be happy about my working from the original. The script is very small and rather untidy, but the document is not especially long. I'm hoping he'll allow me to make a quick copy, verbatim, then work from that, so he can keep the old document in safe storage."

"How long will this copying take?" asked Geiléis. "And the translation? The information will be useless to us after Midsummer Eve."

I glanced at her. Her cheeks were still flushed. "There's always next midsummer," I said. "If the creature is still in the tower then, I imagine you'd want to try again."

Geiléis made a gesture, a quick, dismissive sweep of the hand. Then she seemed to think better of it. "Of course, Mistress Blackthorn." The tone was placatory. "Master Flannan, how long before you can bring us a full translation?"

"One day for the copying. I'll do it in wax, not with pen and ink. The translation—it depends how quickly I can work out the code. Once that's done, I'll render the text into its plain form and then attempt to translate it. The result may be as much informed guesswork as anything. I'll do the best I can. There don't seem to be any Armorican brethren at St. Olcan's. If indeed that is what the tongue is. I assume this was written by a monk in times long ago."

"Written and set away in secret," I said. "Extremely secret. First the coding, then sealing it in a box and hiding it in the wall. I wonder why anyone would do that? It seems rather excessive."

"Raids." Grim's tone was like the brush of a cold hand. All eyes turned toward him. "Norsemen," he said. "Common target, houses of prayer like St. Olcan's. Silverware to steal. And books."

"Books? What, the Norsemen like to have a good read between their acts of violence?"

"For the covers," Grim said flatly. "Set with a fortune in jewels, some of them. Rip the boards off, prize out the stones, throw the pages on the fire." He seemed about to say more, but fell abruptly silent, staring into his ale cup. His hands were clenched around it; the knuckles showed white. This had brought back the past; that was written all over him. This manuscript, or perhaps the monastery in general, had awoken something deeply painful. And I wouldn't be able to ask him about it later, not straight-out. The unspoken agreement between us would forbid it. I willed him to stay strong, even as my heart bled for him. I knew how he felt: as if the layer of protection he had set around his memory had been flayed off, exposing the wound beneath.

"There were no jeweled covers in the box," said Flannan. "Only the sheets of parchment. A few scraps of gold leaf on some of the others, but nothing worth stealing."

"Thing is," said Grim, "some fellows, some monks, they mightn't see it that way. This hidey-hole, it could be for one man's precious things. Precious just to him, I mean. He might have done the writing or the pictures. Set the story down, whatever it is. Could be the work that earned a scribe his job. The picture that showed what was in his heart, hidden away. The story everyone loved to hear, back when he was young."

There was a silence.

"But what would I know?" he muttered, looking down at his hands.

"Master Flannan," said Geiléis, "you said this document was old. How old?" There was an edge to her voice; she was desperate, I imagined, for this parchment to contain what she needed: a step-by-step guide to getting the monster out of the tower. Unlikely, in my opinion. But if it was the original tale, it would at least explain why the creature was there in the first place. I had always believed that was the key to driving it away.

"It's difficult to judge," Flannan said, "but the state of the parchment, the fading of the ink and, above all, the style of script suggest more than a hundred years. It may be closer to two hundred. Its very age makes this a valuable piece, even before we start to consider the contents. It was no wonder Brother Ríordán was reluctant to let it out of his sight. If you want to see it in person, Lady Geiléis, I believe you'll need to come up to St. Olcan's. And even then, it might not be possible. Ríordán might refuse to let the document leave the temporary scriptorium."

Which, of course, would be out-of-bounds to women. "Since it's in code, there's no value in any of us seeing the original," I said. "What we need is your deciphered, translated version, as soon as possible. But there is something you could do to help, Geiléis."

She looked at me, brows lifted. A little muscle twitched in her jaw.

"You have some influence with Father Tomas, I think? You could pay him a visit and mention how useful it would be for Flannan to have access to this particular document for a few days so he can make a copy. I imagine Father Tomas can overrule the head archivist. You might remind him of the favor you're doing St. Olcan's by letting them have Grim's services while he is a guest in your household. Rethatching a roof is no small task."

Geiléis narrowed her eyes at me. I stared straight back. "You are a devious woman, Blackthorn," she said.

"I prefer the term strategic thinker. We're running out of time. We all need to work together. If you imagine I'll be happy to hack my way through the thorn hedge that killed one of your men and wounded another, then climb the tower on my own not knowing what sort of creature I'll find when I reach the top or exactly what I'm supposed to do with it, you most certainly underestimate my good judgment. Let's find out what's in this document, and do so quickly. And while Flannan's deciphering it, and Grim's continuing his very generous work for the monks, I . . ." *I'll be going out into the forest on my own to seek out the little folk and hunt for ogham messages.* "I'll go out as planned to invite the community to the cleansing ritual. We must go ahead with that regardless of this new discovery. After all, the document may prove to be no help at all. Or Flannan may fail to decipher it in time."

"I'll do my best," he said with a smile. "I'm confident that I can make some sense of it."

"Come and tell us the moment you've worked it out," I said. "I'd like to see your transcription of the original as well as the translation, if you can manage that." Not that I knew more than a smidgen of Gaulish, but I might spot something he would miss; I'd helped Cass more with his work than anyone knew. "Were there illustrated capitals? Any other decoration?"

"A border. Faded almost to nothing. I'll have a good look tomorrow. I hope I'm right about what this is."

"Indeed," said Geiléis. Her voice sounded odd. I glanced at her and was struck by the tight set of her shoulders and the way her fingers were knotted together. Worried, perhaps, that Flannan could not do it by midsummer. Horrified at the thought of having to wait another whole year. Senach moved to pour a cup of ale and set it beside her. She gathered herself visibly. "Thank you, Senach. We're not doing justice to this fine meal; we should eat. Master Flannan, you'd best stay here tonight. It is too late for a walk back up to St. Olcan's. You'll want to make an early start on the manuscript, of course. But I imagine that will depend on persuading Brother Ríordán to give you the key."

Flannan grinned. "It will."

"You can walk up with Grim in the morning," I suggested. "That would be early enough for anyone."

"And I will make my own visit later," said Geiléis, eyeing me. "To have a word with Father Tomas. Not to make bargains or interfere in any way with the workings of the monastery. Simply to point out that this document may be the key to ridding the district of the creature. Which would, of course, open St. Olcan's once more to scholarly visits year-round."

"Good strategic thinking," I said. Which was as close as I was prepared to go toward a thank-you. "Flannan, did you tell the brothers where you were going?"

"I did, so nobody will be sending out search parties. I just hope Ríordán hasn't hidden the document away in some spot known only to himself."

"Grim?"

"Mm?"

"I can tell something's wrong. Badly wrong, I mean, not only an upset stomach and a headache and being tired out. If you want to talk about it, I promise I'll shut up and just listen. And don't say it's nothing and you're fine, because I can see it's not and you're anything but."

I waited in the darkness awhile, lying still under my blankets. Wondering about a lot of things. Hoping he would be ready to talk. I hated to see that wounded look on his face.

"Thanks. But no. Sometime, maybe. Not now."

"If you're sure."

The only response I got was a grunt as he turned over to face the wall.

"Just don't wait as long as I did," I said, more to myself than to him.

This time there was only silence.

25

GRIM

Manage not to bring up my breakfast. An effort. Could have done without Flannan's company—nothing against the fellow, but it's hard enough to make myself go up there at all, without having to pretend nothing's wrong. No easier than yesterday. Makes no difference that I know I can do it now, go to that place and put in a day's work without losing control of myself. Makes no difference that Brother Fergal's been kind to me. Makes it worse, in a way. Brings back the past, sharp as a knife. Hard to look at him without seeing that day all over again, only it's not St. Erc's I see, but St. Olcan's with blood and brains spattered everywhere, and a cat with its head crushed to nothing. Fergal and his helpers sprawled dead between the bean rows. The chapel silent, the bells still. Broken men everywhere. Bits of men. I can still feel them in my arms, feel the weight of them, smell the blood. Trying to put them together as best I could. Face running with snot and tears. Howling like a whipped dog. Howling like that thing in the tower's doing. Flannan's trying to talk to me, over the noise it makes. I'm answering in grunts, when I answer at all. Man must think I'm an oaf. Nothing new in that.

Halfway there, sunk in my thoughts, I nearly miss it. Moves again, quick as quick, and I spot it. Ripple halts, ears pricked, whole body quivering. All set to give chase, only Flannan says, *Ripple, wait,* and she holds still by his side, whining under her breath.

"What was that?" Flannan stares into the shadows under the trees. "Look, there it is again! Under the oak, there!"

"Shh!" I hiss. Want to say I've seen nothing, but too late now. Anyway, he's Blackthorn's friend. No reason to lie. "Don't point—you'll scare him away. And hold on to the dog."

"Scare *him*? Who?"

"Shh." I squat down closer to the wee man's level, though still a bit too high up, and call out to him, not too loud. "Greetings to you! Fine morning." Wouldn't show himself if he didn't want to talk to me, I'm guessing. Must've taken courage, with Ripple there.

Little fellow doesn't come any closer. Stands right by the tree, like he's pretending to be part of it.

"Greetings, Grim," he says. "Friend all mended. We thank you again."

"Friend—you mean the fellow that was trapped? All better? Glad to hear that. You must have good healers."

"Crafty folk. Wood-crafty. Message for you. For your friend."

I look sideways at Flannan, who's standing there with his mouth open, staring. But the wee fellow doesn't mean him.

"For your healer. Midsummer Eve soon. Tell her, true love's tears. Do not forget."

"True love's tears." Odd sort of message. "Is that an herb?" Got a feeling I've heard of it somewhere. Blackthorn'll know.

"Remember," says the small one. "Important."

"I will. Thanks."

And he's gone, just like that. Quick as a snap of the fingers, before I remember the whistle they gave me. Would have liked to ask about that, what it's for, what rules there might be about using it. Too late now.

"Best walk on," I say. "Want to make an early start. Keep hold of Ripple's collar for a bit."

Flannan's just staring at me. Dumbstruck, that's the word.

"Fey folk," I say. "In the woods around here. Seen them a couple of times. Harmless." How much should I tell? Not too much, that's for certain. "Blackthorn knows. But not Lady Geiléis. Blackthorn said not to tell her, or anyone."

"Astonishing." He shakes his head. Looks as if he's testing to see if he's lost his wits. "Incredible. I have never seen . . . I did not imagine . . ."

"That they're real? Might not be. Might be the curse putting ideas in our heads. Making us see what isn't there." Making us doubt our own minds. Making us lose our good judgment. Seems best to keep this bit to myself. "Don't know why you're so surprised. Scholar and all. You must know hundreds of tales. And the tales are full of wee folk."

"The work I do doesn't require belief," says Flannan, "only accuracy and a capable hand with the pen. I did not expect beings from ancient lore to step out of the woods and engage me in conversation. Allow me to be a little surprised, Grim."

"Not up to me, is it?"

"Did you hear what he said? Midsummer Eve. So they know Lady Geiléis wants Blackthorn to do something that day. Did Blackthorn tell them? Did you?"

Trying to remember if I was like that, first time I saw the fey. So excited I was near jumping out of my skin. Don't think so. With me, it was more of a slow wonder. Like a warmth spreading through. "The fey know all sorts of things," I say. "Chances are they know the old story, the one that's in your document. But they don't always tell."

"Couldn't they be made to tell?"

I give him a straight look. "If that's the way you like going about things, then maybe."

"Why hasn't Lady Geiléis asked them? She must know about them."

"We should be getting on."

"Why, Grim?" Flannan was insistent.

"You'd need to ask her. Lady Geiléis. Thing is, though, if you do that, she'll know we've seen the wee folk. Talked to them. We promised them we wouldn't tell."

"But—"

"Speak to Lady Geiléis about this and you'll make Blackthorn very, very angry. You wouldn't want that, would you?"

He runs out of words, which suits me perfectly. We walk on together, and the only sound is the sad voice of the monster. Didn't have my ears stopped before, but I get the plugs out now and stuff them in; Flannan does the same. Damps the sound quite a bit. Helps, too, if I try to think about something good, block out the bad stuff. So, no thinking about what happened at St. Erc's. Nor in Mathuin's lockup. Nor early on, before St. Erc's. No thinking of the red coming down and making me do bad things. No remembering the names folk have called me. Names don't matter. Instead, I think about Blackthorn strapping up a farmer's leg; I think of her by the fire, her hair as red as the crackling flames, her hands stretched out for warmth. She's telling a story; it turns her face soft. I think about the night I was in the woods, all wet and shivering and hating myself, and how she yelled at me to stop being stupid and come up to dry off. How she let me come with her all the way to Winterfalls. How she stopped me from making an end of things, that night at Dreamer's Pool when I thought she'd lied about being my friend. I think about her standing in a mess of broken crockery, beside herself with fury, and me talking quiet to her, calming her down. And the time she tried to run away south on her own, back to Laois to have it out with Mathuin, and how she listened when I told her she was wrong. How she came home. Think about the name that does matter: *friend.*

And before I know it, we're at St. Olcan's, where the bells are ringing for Prime.

"I'll leave you now," Flannan says once we're in the gate. Ripple's off across the garden already, and for once he doesn't call her back. "I will observe the Hour with the others before I start the day's work."

"Fine with me," I say, though he's telling me, not asking. I'd like him to come and let me know if he finds out anything. Don't ask, though. Chances are I'll be up on the roof, and he's hardly going to shout the news out so I can hear. "Good luck."

"It might be more a matter of skill," Flannan says, more or less to himself, then heads off toward the chapel. Don't expect to see any more of him, at least until my working day's over and I head back to Geiléis's place. And from what he said, he won't have anything to tell until tomorrow or the next day, and only then if he can work out first the code, then the translation from a language he doesn't even know. Way I see it, luck's going to play a big part.

Weather stays fair. Me and the lad they've given me to help, Tadhg, his name is, get on with the job, which today is mostly stripping off the last of the moldy old thatch and cleaning things up, ready for the new. We get sweaty and filthy, and we sneeze a lot, but he's strong and willing and I'm glad to have work for my hands. Manage not to think too hard. Manage not to look at one thing and see another.

Middle of the day, they feed us. Glad nobody makes us go inside and sit down with the monks. That would be too much; couldn't do it. Couple of fellows bring out a tray with bowls of broth, hunks of bread and wedges of cheese, and there's a flask of good ale with it. Goes down a treat. While we eat and drink, I run through the next part with Tadhg, tell him the stages of getting the fresh thatch ready and putting it up. What he'll be doing and what I'll be doing. He's a clever lad, listens well, asks good questions. Wonder if I was ever like that, eyes bright, mind clean and fresh, ready to take on the world? Or did that get beaten out of me before I even knew it was there?

Good view from up on the roof. Down over the forest one way; glimpse of Lady Geiléis's house between the treetops. Farther off, the Tower of Thorns, though I can't see much of it, only the top with the open window. Howling's not so loud up here; don't need the earplugs. I can almost forget the monster, listen to the bells and the singing and the quiet footsteps instead. The brothers have a bit of a farm, not far off. Cows. Chickens. Couple of sheep, for wool, not for the pot. Good place. I'm all wrong here. Bad luck. Bringer of trouble. Feel as if I should tell them the story, tell them the truth, so they can throw me out if they want. But here I am teaching the lad to thatch a roof, making myself useful, and I can't tell.

Forest spreading out to the west, and a strip of road going through it; that's the Tirconnell side of the river. Road they can't use because the ford's not safe. Farmhouses dotted here and there, patches of cleared ground, a few cattle. Closer at hand there's St. Olcan's own bell tower, and a barn, and at one end of the barn the pigeon loft. They had one at St. Erc's too. My mind shows me broken bodies, feathers everywhere, smears of blood on the stone floor, injured birds thrashing about. I had to pick the poor sods up and wring their necks, one after another. Said a prayer for each one, same as I did for the men. Would have been a miracle if God picked up the meaning, I was crying so hard. *Fly safe to heaven. Sing with the angels.* Only birds. Still. Brother Galen used to say, *God knows what is in your heart.* That day, my heart was saying, *There is no God.* Said the prayers anyway. Felt like the proper thing.

"You all right?" Tadhg's looking at me, a bite of bread and cheese halfway to his mouth.

"Fine. Thanks." I apply myself to my own meal. "Thinking of something sad, that's all. Who looks after the pigeons here?"

"Brother Eoan. Only they don't fly out much, not now. Not since we stopped using the ford. See, pigeons always fly back to their home loft. So if you want to exchange messages with, say, a monastery in Tirconnell, you have to get some pigeons that were bred there, and move them here. And they take some of yours in return. Then you can send as many messages as you've got birds, until they've all gone home. Then you start again."

"Is that so?" I don't tell him I know quite a bit about pigeons, from St. Erc's. "Where did they send them before? Only to Tirconnell?"

"All over. It's a good way for scholars to share their discoveries, or for a monastery to invite visitors. They keep the birds in marked cages, so they know where each one's from and where it will fly when it's set free."

"Be safe to send them south," I say. "No need to cross the ford, so you could still bring birds in from there, couldn't you?"

"That's right," says Tadhg. "There's a few birds from Dalriada in the loft, and some from Ulaid. Farther away, even. Long way to fly, but they can do it. Brother Eoan could tell you all about it. Knows everything about pigeons, that man. Ask him a question and he'll still be talking when the sun's down and everyone else is at supper."

Tadhg is a talker too. I don't mention that. He's good at his work, doesn't waste time, and he's ready to learn. Don't mind listening. He might even say something useful.

"Finished? We should get back to work."

He doesn't answer, because there's a sound of raised voices from somewhere near the gate, and one of them's a woman's. Geiléis. I can tell even from over here that she's angry. Seems wrong to listen in. But Blackthorn and me are at Bann to solve a mystery. That means doing some things we wouldn't naturally do. So I'm listening hard and remembering so I can tell Blackthorn later, but at the same time I'm putting cups and bowls back on the tray and moving the ladder round so we can get to the next bit of roof. Old thatch should be all stripped away and the beams cleaned up today. Brothers have got the reeds tied in bundles, so they're all ready to go up. The spars from the old roof are oak, and mostly good to use again. And there's a fellow here, one of the monks, who's said he'll make replacements for the worn-out ones. Means I don't have to carve them myself, which is good. Would have taken time we don't have.

"I need to see it!" Think that's what Geiléis is shouting. Whoever she's talking to—Father Tomas, must be—answers in a deep, quiet voice. Could be saying anything. Monks don't shout. Only when . . . No, won't think about that.

"Careful!" I say, keeping a close eye on Tadhg. "Remember what I said—move slow, two hands and two feet on the beams whenever you can. Not a job you can rush. Unless you want a fast trip down and a few broken bones. Move like a spider."

He's more careful, then. A quick learner. Pity I can't stay after midsummer, in a way. If I had longer, I could teach him to do the job properly. Other things I could do here too. The walls. The garden. The pigeons. But no. First there's Blackthorn. Second there's the past. Third there's God. Don't believe in him anymore, and if I did I'd hate him for letting bad things happen and not stopping them. Meaning there's no place for me here, or in any house of prayer. All very well for Brother Fergal to say God forgives sinners, and Our Lord embraces those who have lost their way, by which he means me, plain as plain. But who could forgive him, God I mean, for standing by watching while Norsemen hacked a bunch of monks to death? Boys, old men, scholars, gardeners, peaceable folk? Not content with that, they butchered the livestock too. Not for the pot. Just for the pleasure of killing. If God's so all-powerful, why would he just look on?

Worst thing is, in a way I understand why they did it. The red. Those fighters, those raiders, I saw their faces. Saw their crazy eyes. They didn't see me, they didn't see an old white-haired scholar and a cat, they didn't see a sacristan and an infirmarian and a scribe; they had the red filling up their heads and coursing through their veins and pumping in their hearts, and it didn't go away until they'd killed or maimed every living thing in the place. Except me. And they must have thought I was dead, or they'd have stuck an ax in my head as a parting gift.

"This is quite unsatisfactory!" shouts Lady Geiléis, not sounding much like a lady. "All I am asking of you . . ." Her voice goes quieter, so I can't hear the rest. Sounds as if she didn't stick to what Blackthorn told her to say last night. And sounds as if Father Tomas isn't afraid to say no to her. Don't know why she'd push to see this document, if she can't read it. Could be I'm wrong. Could be she's upset about something different.

Tadhg is perched on the beams with a hard brush in his hand, looking at me. "Lady sounds cross," he says.

"None of our business. Right, we'll clean off this end; then we'll go down and give the inside a good sweeping. I don't leave a mess behind for other folk to clean up. Weather seems set fair for a bit. But what if rain came? What would you do?"

"Me?"

"What would a fellow do if he was halfway through a thatching job?"

"Oh. If it's reeds, you'd want to get something up over the work you'd done, keep it dry before you put on the next layer. And maybe cover up the rest of the roof too."

"What with?"

"Hempen cloth? Maybe oiled?"

"Good. Might need to ask the brothers about that. Doubt if they'd have an old sail. But maybe they've got something we can use. Be a miracle if it doesn't rain from now till midsummer."

"Why midsummer?" Tadhg asks.

Ah. Walked right into that. "That's when Blackthorn and me have to go back home. So unless you fancy finishing the job on your own, that's when we need to get it done by."

Can't hear Geiléis anymore, only the monster, and birds singing, and Brother Fergal and his helpers talking down in the garden. The two novices are crouched down weeding, and Fergal's harvesting runner beans and explaining something to the others as he moves along the row. Quiet spot, this. Good place. This'd be the sort of place where you could start thinking God was real. You could believe he did open his arms to everyone, like Fergal said.

"Grim?"

"What?"

"This is a lot of roof. And you said three layers."

"All the more reason to work harder. Not just you—both of us. And yes, it'll be three layers. At least. If the old thatch hadn't been so moldy, we could have just put the new on top. But that wouldn't have been a proper job."

Not long after, from my high perch, I see Flannan walking across to the infirmary. A bit later I catch sight of Geiléis with Donncha, going down the track home. Can't see her face. From the way she's walking I'd guess she's angry, upset. Seems Father Tomas didn't say yes to what she wanted—maybe to see the manuscript herself. Which is a surprise. Would've thought a lady like her could twist men around her little finger. Even monks.

26

GEILÉIS

Armorica. Brother Gwenneg. She had all but forgotten him. He was long dead by now, along with the brethren whose number he had traveled so far to join. Brother Gwenneg had been kind to her that night, when she'd returned, weeping, to find all the doors to her home wide-open and banging in the wind. When, soon after, she'd discovered her family, their servants and retainers, all wrapped in a sleep like death, as if this were some ancient tale. She had run all the way to St. Olcan's for help, with only the moonlight to guide her steps. Gwenneg and three other monks had come back with her, bearing lanterns. That was when she'd discovered this was no magical trance. All those she had loved, all those who had loved her, were stone dead. All but one, and he was beyond her reach. Lily's punishment, the long ordeal set down in the curse, was just beginning.

The monks of St. Olcan's had become her friends. They'd provided for her until she'd been able to claw together a household—she'd been determined to stay at Bann, in her own house. Ten of her father's men-at-arms, under the leadership of Onchú, had been over the border in Tirconnell the night it had happened. On return, all had chosen to stay on at Bann. Seven of the household servants had been given leave to attend a wedding in the south—the bride was Senach's sister—and to stay overnight for the celebrations. They too had chosen loyalty over freedom, even knowing the truth.

The brothers had suggested it might be more appropriate for her, young as she was and all alone, to live with kinsmen or in the household of a neighboring chieftain. She'd been firm in her refusal. She hadn't told them about the curse. She hadn't offered any theories about what had happened. Everyone had understood, without quite saying so, that only the fey could wreak such a catastrophe. When, in early summer of that year, it had become evident that there was someone in the tower, and that the someone or something liked to scream from dawn until dusk, folk had not said much at all. The curse had been powerful indeed. Strong enough to last as long as it took. Clever enough to ensure nobody noticed that the Lady of Bann still walked the forest paths twenty years later, and fifty years later, and eighty years later and a hundred. That she was still young and lovely, with golden hair streaming down her back and a complexion like peaches and cream. That over all that time she had aged no more than another sixteen years. Her name varied with the generations, of course. She referred to her mother, her grandmother, her forebears, her ancestors. And if her household servants, too, did not seem to grow old, nobody made comment.

The presence in the tower screamed through all the days of that first summer, and through all the days of the second, the summer in which he might be released, if only she could meet the terms of the curse. But Lily found nobody to attempt the task; she could not imagine that any woman would agree to do it. There was only one she could ask, one of her own. But that, in the end, was to no avail. So, on the second Midsummer Eve of the curse, Lily found herself on the island, attempting to hack a way through the bristling barrier, although the terms of the curse were clear: this was not a task for her to undertake. Her two guards were terribly wounded saving her from the thorns; one later died from his injuries. A hideous day, still vivid in the survivors' minds. The scars had not faded, even after so long.

When autumn came, Bann fell quiet; folk thought the creature was gone. Around the tower, the thorns grew taller and taller, forming a guardian hedge only a fool would dare approach. Even when all was silent, folk stayed away.

She did not make the story known, save to the trusted folk who served her. Only at dusk did she tell the tale, in a whisper, to fulfill the requirement set out in the curse. If the truth had become known in the community, she would never have found a woman prepared to attempt the task. Only . . . only she *had* told, just once, in those early days when she'd been young and terrified and full of a sadness that had threatened to break her. She'd told her confidant, her kind friend of the merry eyes and charming Armorican accent: Brother Gwenneg. Made him swear never to tell anyone. Had he sworn? It was so long ago. Surely he had given his word. Yet the wretch had written it down, or so it seemed. Written it and hidden it away, to be unearthed at the worst time, just when at last, at last she had found someone who might perform the task in a willing spirit, unafraid. On Midsummer Eve, two hundred years would have passed since the curse was pronounced. Four times she'd tried and failed; four times the district of Bann had endured two summers of screaming, for the curse offered a chance only once in fifty years. One summer to prepare; the next summer to try her luck. It was remarkable how the magic endured; astonishing how the local folk forgot so quickly, over and over. This time she must succeed. But how? How could she make sure Blackthorn did not learn the contents of Brother Gwenneg's wretched manuscript? How could she silence Flannan without making Blackthorn suspicious? How, how . . .

"Perhaps this document is not what you imagine, my lady," said Donncha, who had accompanied her to St. Olcan's and now walked beside her on the homeward journey. "It may be something quite harmless. Or Master Flannan may fail in the translation."

"Maybe, maybe. And maybe not. I cannot believe I was such a fool as to confide the whole story."

"You were young, my lady."

"Yes, young and stupid. I should not have relied on a promise. It seems even monks break their word. I don't know what to do, Donncha. We are so close to success. A hair's breadth away from it. I need the right woman to win the day. But the right woman is observant. She sees beyond the obvious. That sort of person is very hard to trick. I do not believe she has any weak point."

Donncha said nothing. They walked on.

"There's Grim, of course. She's fonder of him than she knows. Grim might fall ill or meet with an accident. Nothing too serious, but serious enough to distract her for a while. Perhaps to keep her busy nursing him, so her attention will be divided."

"Yes, my lady. But Master Flannan—"

"Will still come straight here as soon as he manages to decode the manuscript, yes. Senach will intercept him. He will be directed to speak to me first. At which point I will find out what the manuscript contains and, if necessary, take immediate steps to silence him. He might be bought off; every man has his price."

"Yes, my lady." A pause. "You wish Grim to be incapacitated? A broken leg? That might be hard to do discreetly. He's a big man."

"Nothing so drastic, or Blackthorn will suspect foul play. Let us leave Grim for now. The job at St. Olcan's keeps him conveniently out of the way. But you should have a plan in place for later. Grim might well insist on being close to Blackthorn on Midsummer Eve, even if this job at the monastery isn't finished. We'll need a reliable means of ensuring he is not present when she goes to the tower. Talk to Onchú and work something out."

"Yes, my lady."

They walked on a distance in silence. "My lady?"

"What is it, Donncha?"

"If it works . . . if Mistress Blackthorn succeeds in the task . . . what will become of us? The rest of us?"

She had considered this, of course. Over and over she had tried to think it through. But there was no good answer. "I suppose, in one way or another, we will all be set free," she told him.

27

BLACKThORN

Two days until the ritual. As midsummer neared, I felt as if time was slipping past ever more quickly. I wished I'd never said I would conduct the cleansing ceremony—it was pointless. A complete waste of time. After my visit to the settlement it was obvious nobody was going to tell me anything about the monster in the tower. They'd been welcoming enough, accepting the potions and salves I had brought with gratitude and seeking my advice on a range of ailments from aching joints to the ever-present headaches. For those, I gave them a tincture of true love's tears, and showed some of the women how to make more. Which had perhaps suggested a lack of confidence in the ritual, since if it worked the creature would leave and the headaches would leave with it, but never mind that. Grim's little man had popped up again, showing himself to both Grim and Flannan, and had mentioned the herb. A pity the wee folk hadn't bothered to explain why it was important and what I was supposed to do with it—use it as a cure, find a message where it grew, something else entirely. Tending to the local people's sore heads was at least a start.

Geiléis still wasn't happy to let me go out alone. My arguments about the proper way to prepare for a ritual had not convinced her. She seemed to think I'd tolerate the presence of a man-at-arms provided he tailed me at a distance, waiting discreetly just within sight while I gathered herbs or sat in meditation or practiced the words and movements I would need on the day. There was no doubt I needed the practice. It was a long time since I had done this, so long I could hardly remember the last time. If the druid, Master Oisín, had come here, perhaps his ritual would have silenced the creature in the tower. Mine surely would not. Some wise woman I was, when I couldn't even make up my mind about where I was going after midsummer, let alone work out the answer to Geiléis's problem. I was failing in another way too: Grim was still walking about with a dark cloud over him, and making it clear he didn't want to talk about whatever was wrong.

Now Grim was gone up to St. Olcan's for another day's work, and Geiléis was still in her chamber, and if I didn't get out of here, on my own, I was going to start screaming and throwing things. There was no leaving the house without being stopped by Senach or Dau or one of the guards who might happen to be in the courtyard—I was beginning to suspect Geiléis had set a watch on me. But what Geiléis did not know was that I had my own means of evading notice. I'd been a wise woman for quite a while, even if you didn't count the lost years in the middle. I was good at what I did, the healing and herbalism part of it, though being kind to folk had never come easily to me. But there was another part of being a wise woman, and that was hearth magic. I knew a few tricks that went beyond the skills of an ordinary woman, though I seldom used them. The night we'd solved Prince Oran's mystery, I'd managed to make the rain hold off until we had achieved our aim. Not easy.

I wished I could make myself invisible, the way Conmael did when he'd had enough of talking to me. He would simply wink or fade out of sight. That was beyond any human woman's abilities. But I could cloak myself in a lesser form of the fey glamour, making myself blend into my surroundings. I thought—I hoped—I could keep it up for long enough to get me out of the circle of watchful minders. And if I couldn't, I could pretend I was heading to the guards' quarters to find an escort.

I chose a moment when Dau was drawing water from the well, and slipped out behind him, holding the glamour around me. I walked as softly as I could, though the monster's voice would have drowned out all but the heaviest tread. I whisked around a corner and out of Dau's sight only to find that the kitchen door was wide-open, and another of the serving men, Cronan, was standing at the table packing items into a willow basket. *Don't see me*, I willed him, and passed like a shadow, holding my breath. The spell took great concentration; my teeth were gritted so hard my jaws ached, and my skin was all cold sweat. Later there would be a headache of monstrous proportions. Never mind that. I was out the gate; I had reached the trees; I was gone.

What to do first? Simply walk and enjoy the solitude? Rehearse the ritual prayers? Take the path to the log bridge and look for another message?

I found a spot under the oaks, out of sight of the house. There I stood quite still, closed my eyes, shed the glamour, and breathed in slow patterns to clear my mind. Made myself calm. Listened to the screaming, much louder here than in Geiléis's house. Heard the wrenching gasp as the creature sucked in a breath, and the pitiful wail that followed. Remembered the stone with its crude drawing. Thought about Grim's tight mouth and shadowed eyes. Thought about the boiling rage that gripped me sometimes and turned me into a madwoman. Remembered all those poor sods who suffered alongside us in that hellhole of Mathuin's. Angry men. Crazy men. Wounded men. They'd screamed too. We all had. We'd screamed and raged and beaten our heads against the wall, we'd hurt ourselves and each other, we'd acted like wild beasts, because being locked up does strange things to you. Turns you inside out. Puts a mark on you that never goes away, even if you get the chance to be free and move on with your life. You're never quite free. You take the dark and the terror and the pain with you. Inside your head, the screaming keeps on.

Morrigan's curse, I was crying now. I fished out a handkerchief and scrubbed my face. Just as well there was no guard; I'd have yelled at him to mind his own business and thrown in a few oaths for good measure. And it wasn't Onchú's fault, or Donncha's, or the fault of any of those men that they guarded me so efficiently. They were only doing their job, and doing it well.

I knew now where I would go: the island. Perhaps on the way back I would visit the log bridge. I headed down the path toward the ford, leaving my ears unblocked. As I walked, I imagined Grim on the roof at St. Olcan's, and thought of the work he had done back at Winterfalls: the meticulous thatching, each layer placed just so; the little creatures on top to finish it. I wished he would talk to me. I wished he would let me help him. I thought of Flannan, busy with quill and parchment, another worker who set high standards for himself. I thought of how many different ways there were to tell a story. Even those roof animals were a kind of story, chosen carefully to fit the building's occupants, its purpose or its setting, and to keep all within safe. The monster's story would be a strange one indeed. Interesting how Flannan, a scholar, a doubter, a man who needed things proved, now seemed so excited by this manuscript's possibilities. He'd spotted Grim's little man on the way down from St. Olcan's, of course. Maybe that had been enough to convince him such a tale could be true.

The river was almost in view, a glimmer between the trees. Maybe the creature would throw another stone and kill me this time. Or deliver a new set of drawings, with instructions on what to do once I came face-to-face with it at midsummer. The first stone had been short on detail, and Geiléis clearly didn't know. No wonder Grim wasn't happy about me going ahead with this. A monster was a monster, after all—big, strong, unpredictable. Most likely furious or crazed from being locked up so long. I was quite strong for my size, but I was no fighter.

Chances were I'd be dead the moment I stepped over the threshold. A sacrifice. That was how most folk would see it. But a person with an extensive knowledge of lore—I was one such, Flannan another—understood the inevitability of a magical curse, and how it allowed the weak to overcome the strong. In an old tale, the prey could turn on the predator. The youngest son, the one everyone believed worthless, could win a kingdom. And a woman like me might just possibly battle a monster and prevail.

I stumbled over a tree root and halted abruptly. Something odd had happened. While I was mulling it all over, I had wandered off the path without realizing it, and now here I was in among the oaks, with no sign of any track, only a maze of old roots clawing at the earth and clumps of fungi sprouting here and there. In here, the creature's voice seemed less insistent. I could hear the whirr of dragonflies in the air, the high peeping sound of a bird up in the branches, and from St. Olcan's came the distant sound of bells. And I felt the tingle of magic; there were fey folk nearby, though I could not see them.

"Anyone there?" I called softly. "It's Blackthorn, the healer. May I speak with you?"

No reply. But there was someone close; I was sure of it. "I mean you no harm. And I'm here on my own."

Nothing. But wait—were those lights, deep in the shadow under the trees? I walked forward, stepping carefully over the tangle of oak roots, making sure I did not crush the tiny mushrooms. Who knew what small creatures might live in such a place? The very air breathed magic.

The lights faded and were gone, leaving me in a darkness too profound to be anything but uncanny. Cold sweat broke out on my body; my heart pounded. I could hear Geiléis's voice saying, *I told you so.* This would be the time I went out too far on my own and ended up drowned or mad or worse. Just like the others, the ones the villagers had told me about—sons, cousins, friends, lost in the forest or dead by their own hands, driven to despair by the screaming. A curse that lay over every last one of them.

Deep breath, Blackthorn. You are a wise woman. If you're going to die, make sure it doesn't happen because of your own miscalculation. That would hardly be better than succumbing to Mathuin's torturers. Use your wits. Use your training.

"I give thanks for this good earth beneath my feet," I murmured. "I give thanks for the sun that warms it and brings forth the new shoots. I give thanks for the rain that nourishes great oak and creeping moss, filling the flowing river and the tranquil pond. I give thanks for the clear air I breathe. I give thanks for the gift of life."

A shaft of sunlight pierced the canopy. Not, I was quite sure, in response to my prayer, but remarkably well-timed all the same. It illuminated a patch of open ground. On first glance, what lay there seemed like a jumble of sticks, as if a very small person, gathering firewood, had taken fright and dropped its load. But no; there was a pattern here. A long stick in the center, and beside or across it shorter twigs placed to make ogham letters. I'd been left another message. Let a cloud not obscure the sun before I'd managed to read it. Willow—a strongly feminine tree. Holly—something to do with battle, defending oneself. Elder—the end and the beginning. Birth, death, rebirth. This was full of insight. As I examined the other letters, I saw that there were two layers of meaning. At least two. For there was a simple message too, spelled out by the letters: *Strike hard. Strike true. Free us.*

The sunlight stayed just long enough for me to memorize the letters. Then the clouds came in, and there was no reading them. I made my way back to the main track without difficulty—the confusion that had gripped me before was gone—and down to the ford. Odd: the position of the sun told me it was close to midday. How could it be so late already? Had I been taken into some other place, some other time, so I could read and understand that message? Had I stood there for hours in contemplation of its meaning?

Now here I was on the riverbank, with the ford before me. I'd misremembered how far out the island was, and the difficulty of wading in those deeper waters. The fact was, it would be stupid to attempt it on

my own. All very well when Grim had been there to carry me over.
Today, if I slipped on the way, I might drown. Then the curse would
not be broken, and Grim would carry a new weight of guilt to add to
those he already had on his shoulders. Not that it was his fault he was
not with me, but he would see it as his failure. That was the way his
mind worked.

I'd have to turn and go back. If it really was so late, it was remarkable that Geiléis didn't have a search party out looking for me. "Sorry,"
I whispered, looking across to the tower. "Not much closer to finding
the answer." Strike hard, strike true, free us. Strike what? The thorns,
to hack a path through? Or was this after all to be some kind of battle?
I'd chopped a lot of wood in my time, but using an ax in combat was
not quite the same. And free us? Not only the king in the thorn, but all
the small folk? Weren't they already free, out in the forest?

Danu save me! Something was moving on the island. Not the monster; its voice still rang forth from the high tower window. But something smaller, at the foot of the tower. A cloaked figure: one of *them*. I
edged into the concealment of the trees, watching. The small one took
something from its shoulder—a coil of rope—and weighed it in one
hand, evidently preparing to throw. A sharp whistle pierced the air,
and the monster fell quiet. Then, with a strength and accuracy that
would have done a man of Grim's size proud, the small one tossed up
the end of the rope, and someone reached out from the high window
and caught it. I had to remind myself to breathe. *Show yourself*, I willed
the creature in the tower. *Let me see what you are.*

The small fey person, whose hood had come off to reveal a head of
raven-dark curls, was doing something with its end of the rope. Ah. It
was tying on a basket. Not a tiny basket like the one the small healer had
carried, but a basket the size of mine. Supplies. But how could it be pulled
up? It would be quickly snagged on the impenetrable barrier of thorns.

The small one was ready, the basket in its hands, the rope stretched
taut all the way to the window. There was a creaking, a groaning, a
shifting sound that rattled my bones, a sound that was nothing but

magical. I did not see the thorns part; I was too far away, and the gap
they made too narrow. But the small one seemed to step within the
hedge, basket and all, and the rope became a near-vertical line up to
the window. Someone hauled; the basket rose; at the window, someone
took hold of it and lifted it in. A moment later the rope was released at
the top and came falling down. The fey personage stepped out from the
hedge, coiling up the rope as it came. There was that eldritch sound
again—the hedge was mending itself. Startled as I was, I made sure I
noted where the gap had been. In that precise spot I would make my
own attempt to cut through the thorns. Despite the message to strike
hard and strike true, I suspected my ax would play very little part in
doing that job. If the conditions for breaking the curse were met, the
hedge would open up and let me in.

Beneath my wonder at what I had seen, something was nagging at
me, some detail. I pondered this while I watched the small person walk
to the shore of the island, step into a tiny boat and pole the craft back to
the riverbank. It climbed out and stood a moment on the shore, turning
its head to look directly at me. I'd thought I was well concealed, but the
fey have their own ways of seeing. *Secret*, someone whispered in my ear,
but when I started and turned, nobody was there. And when I turned
back, the figure on the bank was gone. *Keep the secret.*

Only it wasn't so very secret, I thought, as I remembered myself
slipping past the kitchen door earlier, using a glamour so that Cronan
would not see me—Cronan who had been packing a willow basket just
like the one the monster had hauled up into the tower. Exactly like,
down to the pattern of ivy woven along the side.

It might have been coincidence. Baskets did have a certain similar-
ity. This one had been big enough to hold a flask of mead and sufficient
food for a long day and night. Big enough to take a warm blanket,
folded tightly, or a change of clothing and a full water skin. Could
Geiléis's retainers be feeding the monster without her knowledge? Why
in the name of all the gods would they do that? To keep the thing alive
was to let the curse drag on and on. If there was one thing I knew

about Senach and the rest of them, it was that they loved Geiléis and wanted to serve her well. But the alternative was even odder: that Geiléis knew what they were doing; that she had sanctioned it. If that was true, she had been lying to us from the start.

The wailing had started again. The fey folk's gift had not kept the creature quiet for long. A pox on this! Wretched secrets! I needed to ask Geiléis straight-out about this. Tell her what I'd seen, what Grim had seen, demand a full explanation. But I couldn't. Wouldn't. At every point the small folk had asked us to keep our conversations secret. They had trusted us. Gods help me, what a tangle! I could only hope Flannan's manuscript was exactly what he hoped it was: a clear and complete account of the whole story, monster, curse, tower, fey helpers and all. Then Geiléis would have no choice but to tell the truth.

As I walked into the courtyard I clothed myself in the glamour again. I'd planned to use the door that led from the yard to my quarters. But there in the yard was Caisín, filling a bucket at the well. Her hair was caught back in a scarf; her sleeves were rolled up. I froze. On the seamstress's bare arms were scars twin to Onchú's, raised, livid. This young woman, too, had been marked by the thorns.

I made the decision almost without thinking. I dropped the glamour, then cleared my throat. "Good morning, Caisín."

She spun around, tugging down her sleeves. "Oh! Mistress Blackthorn, you startled me! Have you been out walking?" Her voice was shaking.

"Down to the river and back. Caisín, may I ask you a personal question?"

It felt cruel; the look in her eyes was that of a rabbit facing a hunting dog. She made a little sound, neither yes nor no.

"I couldn't help noticing the marks on your arms," I said. "Might I have a closer look? I can see they distress you, but I am a healer, and such things interest me."

"They're nothing," she said in a mumble. "They're healed now. I need to get on with my work, Mistress Blackthorn."

"Caisín, were you there last Midsummer Eve when Lady Geiléis tried to cut a way through the thorns? Is that how you hurt your arms?"

"I . . ."

"Tell me." I moved closer, speaking as I would to someone sick and frightened, though the brief glimpse I'd got of her scars had suggested that, like Onchú's, they were well healed. "Did you help Lady Geiléis that day? Or . . ." Gods, I hoped I was wrong. "Did she ask you to do it? To cut a path and go up the tower at midsummer?" The only woman in the household, apart from Geiléis herself. And loyal, like the rest of them.

"I did try." Caisín's voice was a whisper. I imagined her up in the tower, confronting the monster. She was even less of a warrior than I was. How could Geiléis have asked that of her? "But I couldn't cut the thorns. My arms weren't strong enough." She sucked in a breath. "It's best that you ask Lady Geiléis. I don't like talking about it."

"You're alive," I said. "Your wounds have healed. That is something to be grateful for, under the circumstances. I think you should be glad you failed to get through the hedge, Caisín."

She gave a curt nod, then went back to drawing water as if our conversation had not happened.

Behind the closed door of our quarters, I made a brew and drank it. Plain peppermint, without any sweetening; I felt the opposite of sweet today. My mind was full of questions. The ogham message: *Strike hard, strike true, free us.* There was most certainly a task ahead of me, and it would involve some work with an ax. The fey folk providing the tower's inmate with supplies, possibly helped by Geiléis's own household with or without her approval. And now this: a young woman disfigured by those thorns in an attempt to break the curse. Why had Geiléis not mentioned Caisín when she told us of the terrible toll taken by last midsummer's attempt: one man dead, another gravely wounded? Did she think it would frighten me off? I shivered, wrapping my fingers more tightly around the warm cup. I'd be stupid if I wasn't scared: scared of the thorns, scared of the monster, scared of failing. Scared, above all, of my own indecision. "Hurry up, Flannan," I muttered to myself. "Get that thing translated, and let it have all the answers in it." And I felt, for the first time, a longing to be back at Winterfalls, in the cottage, just Grim and me with the woods close by and the settlement a safe distance away across the fields—close enough so folk could reach us if they needed to, far enough so they did not often disturb our peace. "A pox on it, Grim," I said to my absent friend. "I'm turning soft. I'm becoming an old woman."

28

GEILÉIS

he mirror taunted her. She despised the woman there, a youthful vision in gold and white, staring back at her with defeated eyes. The look in those eyes said, *You can't do it. This will be just like the other times: first plans, then that terrified mixture of hope and dread, and then, once again, bitter defeat. She never intended you to break the curse. She meant it to go on forever. You will be older than the most ancient of tales, and I will still be in this mirror every time you look: the foolish young girl who ran through the woods at midnight to save her sweetheart. The girl who was stupid enough to think she could challenge the fey.*

"It's not true." She turned her back on the mirror. "This time will be different." Because Blackthorn was not Caisín, who had attempted the task the very first time and failed to make the slightest impression on the thorns, seeming to prove the curse a lie. It had been after that vain effort that Geiléis herself had tried, thinking that if one part of the curse was wrong, perhaps another part, the part that said she could not complete the task, might also be incorrect. She'd wondered, afterward, if Caisín had been less willing in her heart than in her words, and if the thorns had sensed that. But she'd kept the girl on. She could hardly ask

Caisín's husband and his fellow guards to make her disappear, and she knew Caisín would keep her mouth shut.

Blackthorn was not the village woman who had tried the second time, at fifty years; tried and balked at the threshold of the tower room, running back down the stair and out the door only to be caught up on the thorns, which had closed behind her after she cut her way through. As she'd screamed, they had shouted instructions from beyond the hedge: *Use the knife to cut your clothing away from the thorns! Go back up! Finish the job!* But the woman had been out of her mind with terror; she'd been beyond understanding the simplest command. Unable to get through the hedge themselves, unable to make her listen, they had left her there. By Midsummer Day she was dead, hanging limp and bloody among the thorns.

By the next opportunity, at a hundred years, that woman's bones lay deep in the earth below the tower, entwined with the strong roots of the hedge. The Lady of Bann had paid a visit to the king of Tirconnell, begging for help, telling the tale of a monster come to terrorize the district and turn folk half-crazy with its wailing. The king had laughed at her. Mocked her. Humiliated her. She had wished, then, that *she* had the power to pronounce a curse. That summer she had used a young girl, a simpleton who did not fully understand the task. They promised her a new gown, a puppy and a bag of sweetmeats. She cut through the thorns and went up the tower. Not long after, they heard her falling down the stair. Perhaps she broke her neck and died straightaway; perhaps not. There was no way to tell.

Another followed, fifty years later. This woman woke on the morning of Midsummer Eve and decided she would not, after all, go through with it. There could be no forcing a person to act; the terms of the curse required that the task be undertaken willingly. Geiléis had wondered whether, if she let this woman go home after her failure, the magic would conveniently erase the memory from her mind, the way it made the local folk forget that the wailing monster came regularly every fifty years to bring two summers of sick animals, poor crops and deep, debilitating sadness. The way it caused them to forget that, while the rest of them aged and died, making way for their children and their children's children, the Lady of Bann and her household grew only a little older year by year. Fear that it might not be so, that the woman who had failed the task might go home and spread the word of what had occurred, meant Geiléis did not put this to the test. One still lived in her own household, loyal and discreet. One lay in the tower, broken. One lay in the ground beneath the hedge. The last was buried in the woods; buried deep. Geiléis's folk were thorough.

If Blackthorn failed, both she and Grim would have to disappear. Perhaps Master Flannan as well—he seemed fond of Blackthorn, though she hardly saw it. What was it about the healer? She was hardly the most comely of women, and her manner was the opposite of tender. Yet there she was with the two of them hovering around her. And she was completely blind to it. Not that it mattered. Whatever happened, Blackthorn would be out of the way by Midsummer Day. If she failed, Onchú and the others would ensure neither she nor her companions lived to tell the tale. If she succeeded, this would all be over. Then Grim and Flannan could take whatever action they pleased; tell the tale to the whole world if they wanted to. Chances were nobody would believe them anyway.

There was a flaw, of course. This was the first time she'd used a woman from beyond the district. The curse had seen to it that those others were soon forgotten; that their kinsfolk did not come asking awkward questions. It would not be like that with Blackthorn. She'd been resident at the Dalriadan court; the prince and his lady were expecting her back. They wouldn't let her and her companions simply vanish without explanation. And hadn't someone said she had a whole community depending on her back home? It would be necessary to invent a story, a convincing one. The three of them might have headed off somewhere together, somewhere as far away from Dalriada as possible. No need to say why; only that they had packed up and left suddenly. Prince Oran would not send folk out searching for a village healer. And Flannan was a traveler anyway, not the prince's concern.

But she would not need the story, because this time would be different. It had to be. Another failure simply could not be endured. What had they done to deserve this wretched penance, this endless suffering? Fallen in love, that was all. Young folk did that. It was natural. The one who had cursed them, the fey woman—Geiléis would not use her name, could not bear to speak it—could have had any man she wanted. She was the loveliest creature in all Erin. Even in her terror, even in the dark, even as she knew she had encountered a power so far beyond her own that she could never prevail, Geiléis had recognized the other's remarkable allure. Why had the fey woman claimed Ash as hers? Why couldn't she let him go? Why couldn't she find someone else, someone who did not have a human girl who loved him with all her heart and would do anything, anything to keep him safe?

She lay down on her bed and closed her eyes. That night, the night of the curse, was as clear in her memory as if it had been yesterday. The tower was in darkness, save for that one lonely light flickering in the high chamber. The wind howled; the trees bowed down before its chill breath. It was like winter in summertime. Clouds fled across the moon's face; lightning split the sky and thunder growled deep. She ran, heedless of peril, ran with her heart leaping about in her chest, ran until her sides ached, ran with tears of hope and terror running down her cheeks. *Ash. He's in the tower. Find Ash.* What would happen when she reached the tower, how she would rescue him, she hardly thought; only that he was there, and that if she had got him out once before, she could do it again.

"Gods," Geiléis muttered, "I was a child. I knew nothing. Nothing."

And then the river, and the dark swirling water, and the recognition that there was no way she could get across on her own. Was that a sound of laughter from the high chamber? Gritting her teeth. Tucking up her skirt. Trusting in the power of true love to get her over. One step, and her shoes filled with water so cold it turned her feet numb. Another step, and suddenly she was in to her knees, and the river was pulling at her, insistent, perilous. "Ash!" she shouted. "Ash, are you there? I've come to bring you home!"

Then the little voice in the darkness. "Try it on your own and you'll be swallowed up as quick as the snap of a hawk's beak. I'll take you over. If you're sure that's what you want."

The ferryman. He was right beside her, holding his wee boat steady in the swirling waters, the pole dug deep. "I'm sure," she said, and he said, "Climb in."

The swift, uneasy passage to the island. She gasped a thank-you as she ran for the tower. Up the spiral stair, not thinking what would happen if she fell. No waiting to catch her breath. Forward. Forward into the high chamber.

The fey woman stood waiting, a shielded candle in her hand. Tall. Beautiful. Terrifying. Behind her was Ash. A cruel gag cut into the corners of his mouth. He was chained tight against the wall. When he saw Lily he made a terrible sound of anguish. A monstrous sound. That sound said, *Lily!* It said, *You shouldn't have come.*

"Ah. The foolish human girl has come to your rescue." The woman took a step toward Lily. "Or so she believes. What is your name, young woman?"

She swallowed. Found in her quaking heart a kernel of pride. "I am the only daughter of the chieftain of Bann. They call me Lily." Another breath. A step of her own, forward. Tonight she was a warrior. "You said I could come and get him. Ash. Brión. So I'm here. Unchain him. I'm taking him home."

The woman's lustrous eyes widened. She threw back her head and let fly a peal of mocking laughter. "Oh, I don't think so. I really don't think so. Are you truly so lacking in understanding that you imagine you can stand up to me? Don't you know who I am, *Lily*?" She made the pet name sound like something she might toss on the midden.

"I love him." Lily kept her voice steady, though her whole body was trembling. She kept her back straight and her head high. "True love is the most powerful thing of all. It doesn't matter who you are: noble lady, enchantress, great queen of the fey. If you believe in love, you will let him go." Still thinking, at that moment, that she could do it. Still hoping, for all her terror.

"Oh, Lily," the woman said. "There is no such thing as love. Passion, yes. Possession, most certainly. But love? It exists only in the soft minds of human men and women. Love will not save your young man. Nor will it save you from your due punishment. You think he's suffering now?" She gestured toward Ash, who was writhing in his chains, moaning animal sounds through the tight gag. "You understand nothing of pain. But you will. Believe me, you will."

Every instinct told Lily to flee while it was still possible, down the stair, over the river, back home through the forest before the fey woman cast a spell. But there was Ash, captive, chained, hurt. She could not leave him.

The fey woman spread out her arms. She became even taller, far, far beyond the height of the tallest human woman. The tower room darkened; the candle glowed an eerie blue. "Hear now my curse!"

Someone coughed behind Lily, making her jump.

"No, you don't," said the ferryman. "Leave the girl alone; she's only trying to help her young fellow there."

The fey woman's face became a mask of anger; it was terrible to behold. The air seemed to crackle with her fury. Outside, lightning flashed white.

"Go," whispered Lily to the wee man. "Run, go!"

But it was too late; both he and she found themselves unable to move, frozen in place as the words of the curse rang out. Ash would be changed. He would be condemned to suffer in the tower until Lily could rescue him. The ferryman and his folk would be bound to serve and to hold their silence.

It had seemed important, Geiléis remembered, to ask questions while she still could. How might the curse be broken? How long would it take? Why could she not do what was required herself? The fey woman set out the details, complete in every particular. It must be done on Midsummer Eve, soon after dawn. The chosen woman must act willingly. Lily could not come with her; if she attempted the task herself she would fail. One chance every fiftieth year; only then would the thorns permit a woman through. Yes, there would be thorns—a hedge impassable save by magic. One warning summer beforehand, giving Lily time to prepare—see how kind she was being?

"Once every fifty years?" Lily echoed, shocked, disbelieving. "But—that's impossible! By the second time I would be old. By the third time I would be dead." Ash's eyes were agonized; through the gag he roared a protest.

"Oh, you will live to see him freed." The fey woman was calm now, calm and cold. "In time. The tale must have its ending."

"What about Ash's family? They'll be searching for him. What do I tell them? What about my family?" Suddenly there were more questions than she could imagine.

"You speak so readily of love, you human folk," the fey woman said. "How long will your love endure when you must witness this man's suffering day and night? How long will love last when your only companions are heartbreak and loneliness? You vowed to save your sweetheart. How long will that vow last, I wonder? A year? Fifty years? A hundred, two hundred? How well will you love your handsome young man when he becomes a monster?"

The air seemed to tremble; a shadow passed across the tower room. Ash's stifled groans became something far more terrible, a primal howling that set an icy hand around Lily's heart. The fey woman lifted her candle higher. "How do you like him now?" she asked in honeyed tones.

The fetters had fallen away, and Ash had collapsed to the floor. The candlelight threw his shadow onto the wall, an odd shape, curiously hunched, like that of a creature from an old tale, something that lurked in dark corners and came out at night to frighten passersby. The howling filled Lily's ears; it made her head ring like a high bell; it brought tears to her eyes, whether of sorrow or pain, there was no telling.

"What have you done?" she breathed. "What have you done to him?"

"Make your farewells. Then leave the tower and take that little wretch with you." A contemptuous glance at the ferryman, who was muttering something to himself, perhaps a prayer. "He'll see you home. The curse binds his folk to help; they'll see your precious Ash fed and watered when he's awake. Fifty years is a long time. I'll be kind; the boy did give me some satisfaction. He can sleep away the years between. He'll bother you and your neighbors only for the fiftieth summer, and the one before, so you can make your preparations. A reminder, in case you ever think of forgetting the curse and moving on. There might be other young men, after all; other opportunities. Don't think of marrying and going away. That will only lead to disaster."

Lily crouched down beside Ash. Or what had a few moments ago been Ash. She could not see him clearly in the fitful light, but what she did see was ... cruel. Monstrous. Vile. His mouth ... his hands ... She swallowed acid bile. She made herself reach out and touch, with the same gentleness she had used when he was a man, and as handsome as a prince in a tale. "I love you," she whispered, stroking his hideous face. "Remember that, Ash. I will always love you. I will save you. I promise."

"One thing more," said the fell voice from behind her. "He'll get lonely in here. He's young. He'll get bored."

A reprieve, oh gods! She would be able to visit, to bring him what he needed, to read to him, sing to him, help him endure.

"You'll tell him the story of how this happened," the fey woman said. "At dusk each night, over the seasons when he is awake, you will tell it one part at a time. That way you'll be in no danger of forgetting the price of your offense. He was mine. My plaything. You took him. You should not have done that."

"Are you saying—do you mean I can come here to the tower and see him every day?" Ash had quieted under the touch of her hand; he had lifted one great scaly paw to rest it against her cheek.

The woman laughed again, her scorn echoing through the stone chamber. "Did you not hear me mention a hedge of thorn? You will not come to the tower; no one will come save the small folk, to bring him food and water. You will tell the tale wherever you are. You will tell it whether he can hear you or not. But do not forget. If you miss a day, he will believe you faithless. He will lose hope. And you wouldn't want that, would you, since his predicament is entirely of your own making? Go now. Who knows? If you prove resourceful, you may free him next summer and walk hand in hand into the life you hoped for. I said go!"

That last touch, thought Geiléis, that very last touch of his misshapen hand had broken her heart. He'd tried to say something, *Lily*, perhaps, though the odd shape of his mouth turned the word into an agonized grunt. No gag could have disabled his speech more effectively than that vile distortion of lips and teeth. She'd bent to kiss his poor face; his skin was as rough as pine bark against her lips. "Good-bye, Ash," she'd whispered. "Wait for me."

Then down the stair, across the island, into the boat, back to shore, home through the woods. To find that the nightmare was there before her.

29

GRIM

Days go by, and Flannan still doesn't work out the code for this document of his, the one he said he'd start on straightaway. Took a while for the archivist to say yes to him making a copy. But he did in the end. Don't know much about these things, but you'd think by now Flannan would have the job half done, at least. Time's passing quick as quick and nothing at all from him. Not even a visit to tell us how far he's got. Haven't seen hide nor hair of him, and I'm at St. Olcan's all day. Seen Brother Ríordán a few times—that's the archivist. Tall fellow, pale and a bit bent over, though he's not an old man. Comes out of the infirmary sometimes, stands in the garden looking at us, goes back in. Doesn't walk over and say, *Good morning. How's the work going?* the way some of the others do. Just stares. Likes books more than folk; that'd be my guess.

Back at Geiléis's, Blackthorn's on edge. Stamping around the place, chopping herbs like she wants to kill them, cursing under her breath. Upset because there are too many secrets in this place—the wee folk taking food to the tower, Geiléis's people maybe helping them, the messages they're leaving. And Blackthorn can't ask about any of that because she's promised the wee folk not to. Then there's Caisín and those scars that nobody said anything about, not even when Geiléis was telling the story about what happened last midsummer. Blackthorn did ask Geiléis about that, and Geiléis said she was sure she'd mentioned it, hadn't she? The curse must be making Blackthorn forget, she said. Hah! Not likely. My guess is, Geiléis left that bit out so Blackthorn wouldn't get cold feet about the whole thing. One look at those scars and any woman in her right mind would be saying no thanks, I'm not doing it.

Geiléis is even worse, nervous as a caged ferret. Easy to understand. This bit of writing could be the end of all her worries with the monster. That's if Flannan's right and it does say how to drive the creature away. Me, I'm not so keen to hear the translation. Suit me if Flannan never did translate the thing, if it meant we could just go home instead. Thing is, though, that's hard on the monster. Sad old life, up there on its own. If we can help it, we should.

At least I've got something to keep me busy. There's the roof to get finished, and only me and Tadhg to do it. Pity I can't make myself stay up here, work at night too. But I can't. Like walking right into your worst nightmare, that'd be. Turn me into a gibbering wreck, not fit to do up my own shoes, let alone thatch a roof.

When Blackthorn does the ritual, I take the day off thatching. We all go to this spot she's chosen, big open field with a nice view of the river. Long walk up there; Onchú did ask if we should ride, and Blackthorn said no, walking would give us time to put our thoughts in order. And not set us above the local folk. Quite a few of them are there waiting when we arrive, some with horses or donkeys. There's a dog or two. More folk than she expected. No monks, of course. And no Flannan.

Opens my eyes, watching her do this. Shows a whole new side of her. Makes me wish I'd known her when we were younger. She's borrowed a gown from Caisín, color of a stormy sky, looks nice. Fancy shawl around her shoulders, green like shadows under trees. Her hair's long enough now to make a little plait at the back. She looks solemn. She looks beautiful. Not that she needs borrowed clothes and done-up hair for that.

She calls all the people in. Tells them what we're going to do. Four folk are helping her, one of which is me. She gets everyone lined up and leads us into a circle. Big iron pot in the middle. We've carried that all the way from Geiléis's house, hanging from a pole, man at each end. Small fire burning in the pot, meaning it's not only heavy and awkward but baking hot too.

The four helpers stand at north, south, east and west. I'm north. Geiléis is east, looking a picture with the sun on her fair hair. Took a bit of persuading, Blackthorn said, to get her joining in and not just look-ing on. A local farmer's in the west. Big burly fellow, frowning a bit like he's thinking hard, wanting to get it right. Onchú's in the south. When we're all in place Blackthorn walks around the circle on her own, stop-ping next to each of the helpers and calling the spirits. Sort of greeting, welcome and thank-you all in one. I've got a little basket of soil from down by the river, and when she stops by me I do what she's asked me to do, take a handful and cast it out like I was sowing seed. Geiléis is holding white feathers, long ones, maybe from a goose or swan, and when it's east's turn, she moves them in a sort of dancing pattern.

Onchú's got a bundle of sticks that Blackthorn bound together and soaked in some mixture or other, then hung up to dry. When it's his turn he dips the bundle into the fire pot until it catches alight, then blows it out. Smoke coils and twists everywhere. When Blackthorn calls the west, the farmer sprinkles water from the bowl he's holding.

Through all this the thing in the tower's screaming, the way it does. We're far enough away so I can hear Blackthorn, though. She steps into the center. Talks about cleansing and what it means. Talks about what a sad place Bann is, with the shadow of the curse over it. Says it was once like other places, healthy and happy and hardworking, a place where children could grow up without being frightened, and folk could go about their daily business without that sound hurting their ears and filling up their heads with nightmare thoughts. Says it will be like that again, and that even in the darkest times there's hope. The way she puts it, it's like poetry, something deep and lovely and powerful. And her face—it's all lit up with her words, like the spirits she's talking about are in her, shining out. Hard to believe, looking at her, that she doesn't believe in gods and spirits anymore after what happened to her family. Hard to believe she thinks she's useless as a wise woman, though that's what she's told me more than once. If she could see herself now she'd know how wrong that was. That look on her face is holding everyone in wonder. Even Geiléis. And me? I'm remembering Brother Fergal saying, *God forgives sinners*. Funny old world it is.

Blackthorn walks around the circle again. "May all-powerful fire warm all who dwell here; may its light banish the shadows," she says. "May the sorrows of this place be cleansed by the purity of water. May the peaceful heart of this place be nourished by the good earth. And may the clear air raise us up, as it does the lark and swallow, the dove and raven, and send us forth on strong wings of hope."

She stands quiet a bit. The rest of us do likewise. And there's a small miracle. The screaming stops. The monster falls silent too.

Blackthorn hasn't been expecting it. Nor has Geiléis, who's gone white as milk. All around the circle folk look startled, almost afraid. Me, I'm holding my breath, wondering how long the silence will last. Not that I doubt Blackthorn. Just got a feeling, that's all. My feeling is this isn't going to be done with until Midsummer Eve.

Turns out I'm right. We're following Blackthorn out of the circle when it starts up again, as mournful as ever. Geiléis puts her hand up to her face. Doesn't want folk to see she's crying. Blackthorn's not crying. Only sad.

Geiléis pulls herself together. Thanks everyone for coming and thanks Blackthorn for the ritual. Senach and the others have carried food and drink up from the house. But folk don't stay long. Quick bite to eat, then away off home, even though it's a long ride or walk for most of them. If they're disappointed, they're good at not showing it. Maybe they've had so many disappointments they've forgotten how to hope. Know how that feels. So it's over, and we go back home, and my belly starts to churn because tomorrow it's back to St. Olcan's for me.

It rains again. Not just one wet day, a whole run of them. The brothers find us a couple of big lengths of oiled cloth to get up over the rafters, keep things dry underneath. I do some repairs on the wall and make the double compost enclosure for the garden, jobs I can get done in the wet. Weather clears, but we've lost a lot of time. Starts to feel as if we mightn't get the job finished by midsummer. I say so to Tadhg while we're eating our midday meal, and Brother Fergal, who's in the garden nearby, hears me. Doesn't say anything. But that afternoon, later on, suddenly we've got six monks carrying bundled reeds over from the barn in relays, and one of Fergal's garden helpers doing Tadhg's job of carrying the bundles up the ladder, and Tadhg, so pleased with himself he's pink in the face, helping me put on the next layer and peg the bundles in place. At the end of the day there's only one end to finish before I do the ridging and make the creatures for the top. Which is just as well, because there are only five days left until Midsummer Eve. Only five, and still nothing from Flannan.

We're done for the day. I climb down and say thank you to the helpers. Hard to find the words. Feels wrong, them helping me. Feels like I should tell them who I am and where I came from. The truth. Then they'd throw me out and the roof wouldn't get finished after all.

"Good job," I say. "Don't suppose we could have help again tomorrow? One morning's work, then I can finish up on my own." A bit awkward, asking. The monks look worn-out. But pleased with the day's work too.

"I think we can manage that," says Brother Fergal. "We've watched you work on this with something approaching awe, Grim; it feels as if you've become part of this community. Why don't you join us for a meal this evening? You'd be welcome to attend the service first."

Know what they mean when they say your blood turns cold. Feels like mine's draining away. I shake my head. "Thank you, but no, I'd best get back to Lady Geiléis's place. Haven't seen Flannan around, have you?"

"He'll be in the infirmary," says someone. "Wrestling with his translation."

"Or with Brother Eoan," says someone else. "He was waiting for a bird to come in. I'll take you over there if you like."

Thing about thatching is, it's messy. End of the day, you're filthy from head to toe. "I'd better have a wash first," I say. "Don't worry. I know where the pigeons are." Back at Geiléis's, I'll have a bath, change my clothes, get properly clean. But I'll put my head under the pump and wash my hands before I go looking for Flannan.

The bells start ringing. My helpers head off to the chapel, grubby as they are. Come to think of it, God most likely wouldn't care if a man was clean or dirty, as long as his heart was in the right place.

"Be doing it on your own soon," I tell Tadhg as we splash under the pump. "You learn quick."

He blushes again, a surprise. "Thank you, Grim." After a bit he adds, "You're a good teacher."

Got nothing to say to this. It makes me feel happy. And it makes me feel sad. Makes me think of the life I could have had. The man I could have been.

"There's Flannan now," Tadhg says, looking across the garden.

Flannan's coming out of the pigeon loft. Got something in his hands; looks like he's reading, though it's too small for a book. Little scroll of parchment, I'm guessing. Must have got that message he wanted. Wonder what it says. Must be interesting. He stumbles over a rock and just keeps on walking. Then I think, ah! Maybe he's got a friend somewhere who speaks Armorican. Or who knows codes. Maybe he's got the answer.

He's a couple of strides away before he sees us. Almost walks into us.

"Grim! Brother Tadhg." He's lost for words. For him, that's unusual.

"Got your message, then?" I try to be friendly. Fact is, I'm worried.

Not just about Midsummer Eve, but what comes after too. Him and her. Flannan and Blackthorn. Got a feeling he's not going to say good-bye, nice to see you again, and head off on his travels.

"Who told you about that?" He just about snaps my head off. I give him a bit of a look, wondering what it is I've said—thought I was being polite—and Tadhg mutters something and makes himself scarce.

"One of the brothers." I keep my voice easy. Seems Flannan's as jumpy as the others about Midsummer Eve. "Mentioned you were wait-ing for a bird to come in. Hope it's helpful." I nod toward the little scroll.

"Helpful," he says, sounding as if he doesn't understand the word.

"With the translating. Thought you might have been waiting for expert help." The man keeps staring at the parchment, almost as if he's lost his wits. "Getting anxious, down at the house. Blackthorn and Lady Geiléis both. Only five days to go."

"Yes." He slips the parchment into his pouch. "Yes, it will be very helpful. I hope to have the translation finished by tomorrow evening, all being well. Please tell Lady Geiléis that."

Am I imagining things? I'm tired, no doubt of that. And strung-up about Blackthorn and the monster, and not knowing what's coming. Could be it's all in my head. But Flannan's not his friendly self. Some-thing odd about him today. Funny look in his eye; can't read it.

"And Blackthorn," I say.

"What?" He's been miles away. "What's that?"

"I'll tell Blackthorn too. That you'll be down with the translation tomorrow."

Flannan smiles. He doesn't look happy, though. He looks like a man who's standing on the edge of a cliff, deciding whether to jump. "Thank you, Grim," he says. "I think I owe Blackthorn an apology. It's been some time . . . lack of news . . ."

"She's been worried, yes." I keep it light. Something's bothering him; can't guess what. None of my business anyway. "Good luck."

"Luck? With what?"

"Ah," I say, can't help myself. "More a matter of skill, isn't it? Never mind the luck, then."

He opens his mouth to say something, but thinks better of it. He goes off toward the infirmary building, and I finish washing, shake myself dry-ish and set out back to Geiléis's, not sure if I've got good news or not. News, at least. That should be welcome.

30

BLACKTHORN

News at last! By evening we would know the contents of Flannan's mysterious document. I'd been thinking I would have to go up the tower blind, so to speak, trusting in my instincts or in the nature of curses to ensure I would know what to do when I reached the top. That might still happen, of course. But if Flannan's hunch about the manuscript was right, I would climb the tower armed not only with a weapon but also with knowledge, which I'd long considered the sharpest of knives.

The house was quiet. Grim was long gone up to St. Olcan's, ready to tackle the last section of his roofing. Not happy, exactly—he'd been looking gloomy and distant ever since he'd started the work—but pleased the job was nearly finished. Pleased we would soon be going home. Only I wouldn't be going. The knowledge of that, the immensity of it, was a cold weight in my stomach. I knew I should be honest with him. I should tell him straight-out what I was intending to do. But then he'd insist on coming with me, and something bad would happen to him, and . . . that would be a waste. A waste of a man who, whatever he might think, was good through and through. A man who, someday, might make some woman a fine husband, strong and gentle, faithful and generous, and in his own way wise. A man who would be a loving, patient father. I wasn't going to let that man fall victim to Mathuin's thugs again, not when he'd got me out of that foul place and stood by me ever since, even when I'd told him to go away and leave me alone. No, he would go back to court, and then to Winterfalls, and I would go south to face Mathuin. That was how it would be.

The ritual had made up my mind for me at last. Curious; while it had unfolded I'd almost felt I was outside it, looking down at myself, watching myself go through the invocations, the prayers, the blessings, as if I had the power to make the rite real, potent, full of meaning and power. My own duplicity had sickened me. Who was I to call upon the spirits? Who was I to ask them for help when I didn't even believe anymore? Who was I to stand in front of a community and pretend I had any kind of spiritual authority? A liar, that was what I was. A liar in every corner of my being, for conducting this ritual when I did not believe for a moment that it would achieve its purpose. A bitter, angry woman with no room in her for the little flame my mentor had spoken of, the flame of spirit we all had within us, the light that never truly went out, even in our times of deepest despair. So I'd been taught. So I'd once believed. But my light had been snuffed out years ago. The last of it had died with Cass and Brennan. All that was left was anger and bitterness. Wise woman? Hah!

Yet I'd finished the cleansing ritual. I'd spoken nicely to people, and smiled, and thanked them for taking the trouble to be there. I'd held myself together, and all the time a tide of loathing had been rising in me, a wave of disgust at the worthless creature I'd become. So I'd made my decision. I would go to Laois. I would see Mathuin brought to justice or die in the attempt. Because, deep down, I knew that unless I did that, unless I stood up to him, I would stay wretched and furious and bitter for the rest of my life.

Four days left until I dealt with the thing in the tower. It had been awkward talking to Geiléis about Grim. Of course I'd said nothing to her about what I planned for afterward. I only told her, on the quiet, that it would be better if Grim were not present when I went to the tower on Midsummer Eve, since he would be anxious, maybe angry, and that would be a distraction I'd do better without. She had understood immediately and suggested, with a sympathetic smile, that I should tell Grim I intended to make the attempt in the late afternoon. He should be happy enough to go up to St. Olcan's as usual, for the morning at least. By the time he got back it would all be over. *One way or the other*, I thought, but did not say it. I didn't like the lie, but there seemed no choice about it.

I couldn't pack for the journey south, though I planned that Flannan and I would leave that same day, before Grim returned from the monastery. As soon as the creature was gone, or dead, or whatever had to happen, I could gather my belongings and we'd head off. I would tell Flannan tonight, when he came with his translation. He would be pleased with me. Proud of me for being the woman who always spoke out against injustice. The one who always stood up to be counted, even if it got her in trouble. Funny. I didn't feel proud myself. I felt sad. Sad that I had to do this at the cost of Grim's friendship. I felt like a traitor. And it didn't help to repeat the familiar arguments to myself, about how people liked him and he had a house and work and so on. Because I knew, deep inside, that if I asked him to come with me, the big fool would throw all that away in a heartbeat.

I could not settle to anything. I wanted it to be evening now, and Flannan here telling us what he had discovered. I wanted to run up to St. Olcan's so I could sit right beside him while he completed the translation. I wanted . . . I wanted to be free of lies. To start telling the truth. Often, since we came to Bann, I had wondered if I was surrounded by lies. The bland-faced servants, so courteous and efficient, so guarded in their responses. Geiléis, with her odd defensiveness and her reluctance to let me investigate properly. The local folk, those few I had managed to meet, with their strangely vague memories. But then, the curse itself might be deadening their minds. Making them forget. It might have been making people forget since the time of Geiléis's ancestors. The monster could have come back over and over with nobody remembering long enough to pass the tale on. It could have been going on since that document of Flannan's was set down. Before, even. Which would explain why nobody at court had known anything about Geiléis or her situation, even though Bann was within Dalriada's borders and right next to St. Olcan's, which was famous everywhere for its scholarship and had the means to send messages out and in. Even the monks might be caught in a web of forgetting.

I took this theory to Geiléis, who had arisen late as usual and was talking to Senach in the dining chamber. "It's possible, don't you think? Something as big as this doesn't simply vanish from the tales. Even if it's a long time since the creature was last in the tower—a hundred years, say, or longer. The tower is right next to what used to be a busy river crossing, only two years ago. It's not the sort of place you forget seeing. And the monks are not so very far away. You'd think every scholar who visited St. Olcan's would take the story with him when he left. You'd think it would have spread not only throughout Dalriada, but right across the north. Perhaps even more widely. Grim said those pigeons fly as far south as Mide, or even farther. What about those young men you said have moved out of the district because they can't bear the effects of the curse? Don't they talk about this once they're settled somewhere else? It seems not. I thought maybe folk did know the story and for some reason weren't telling. But maybe they're silent because they can't tell. Because something has made them forget."

Geiléis and Senach had listened in silence while I expounded this theory. Now Geiléis said, "You seem strung tight today, Blackthorn. Are you having second thoughts?"

"Of course not!" I snapped. I'd expected an informed opinion on my theory, not a comment on my demeanor, which had nothing to do with the matter in hand. "I said I'd attempt this for you and I will. But it's stupid to go into it without learning everything I can beforehand. To be quite honest with you, I've sometimes felt as if I'm being prevented from doing that, and that this household is part of it. But that's nonsense. You're asking me to risk my life on your behalf. Why wouldn't you do everything in your power to help me succeed?"

A pause, during which I wondered whether I had gone too far; let my frustration get the better of me. After all, Flannan was coming with his translation today, and that might answer all the questions. I could have waited for that before offending my hostess. Besides, I had hardly been open with information myself; I had not asked her about the small folk. Even now, so close to midsummer, my instincts told me I must keep their secret.

"Forgive me," Geiléis said, "but I do not understand how your theory about forgetting relates in any way to my willingness or unwillingness to help you. I have provided shelter, food, all the comforts you need. We have not prevented you from carrying out your investigation; all we have done is insist you do not attempt these activities without suitable protection. We have told you everything we know." She was a model of calm.

"So you've said, several times. But you can't tell me what you've forgotten."

Did I imagine the shadow that crossed her features, a look of terrible pain? For a moment I was at Cahercorcan again, in Prince Oran's council chamber, and she was telling us the tale for the first time, in such despair that even my hard heart was touched. Then she gathered herself, drawing a deep breath, making her face calm. But when she spoke, her voice cracked with emotion. "I have forgotten nothing!" She rose to her feet, graceful as always. "Excuse me." And she was gone from the room.

I looked at Senach; he gazed back at me.

"I've upset her," I said. "I didn't intend to."

"Lady Geiléis understands that, Mistress Blackthorn. With Midsummer Eve so close, we are all on edge. Hoping that Master Flannan's document will provide some enlightenment." He hesitated. "If you still wish to pursue other possibilities, one of the men could ride out with you to a more distant group of farms today. I cannot promise you will have any more luck there, but if you want to try . . ."

"How distant?" One thing I did know, and that was that I wanted to hear Flannan's news as soon as he arrived.

"I understand it's about an hour's ride each way. Donncha visits the place from time to time. If you left straight after the midday meal you would be home in plenty of time for supper."

He was astute. "It might be better to leave earlier. I don't want to miss Flannan."

"The weather is fair," Senach said. "Folk will be busy with their work until later in the day. You wouldn't want to ride all that way and find there was nobody to talk to."

It was exactly the kind of response I'd been speaking of when I'd accused Geiléis of obstructing my investigation. I refrained from telling him so. After all, he was only doing his job. "Provided we're back in time, it sounds a good plan," I said. It would at least give me something to do other than pacing up and down and wrestling with my troublesome thoughts. "I wonder . . . might I take a gift? Not only headache potions and the like but something more immediate. Fresh-baked bread, maybe?" An offering of some kind, however simple, was a good way of loosening folk's tongues. "It smells as if Dau has been baking this morning."

Senach came as close to a smile as he ever did. "Yes, Dau has been plying his skills, and there are fresh loaves in the house. If you wish, take one or two with you."

I trailed after him into the kitchen, where Dau was packing a small bag with various foodstuffs. I could not help noticing a willow basket on the bench, with a pattern of ivy leaves woven into the side. "Do the men ever take food out to folk who need it?" I asked. "Isolated cottages? Sick or old people?"

Senach tensed beside me; I did not think I imagined it. But Dau went on fitting items neatly into the bag, unruffled. "Not often, Mistress Blackthorn. The brothers go out sometimes. From St. Olcan's. They're better placed to offer fresh food than we are here."

"Oh," I said. "I did wonder . . . This will seem an odd question, maybe . . . But what about the creature in the tower? It must eat and drink to survive. Where does it get its food from? How could anything be taken up to that high chamber when the whole tower is surrounded by thorns?"

Dau looked at me calmly. "Birds?"

"It would need to be rather a large bird," I said, eyeing the willow basket. Would Dau be filling that next? "And who would be sending them?"

"I can't think, Mistress Blackthorn. If the creature's fey, maybe it doesn't need to eat."

I had the sense of being toyed with, and I did not like it. "It's just . . . I thought I saw someone walking in the woods near the river. With a basket. It was very like that one."

"When was this?" asked Senach from behind me.

Curse it, I'd made a trap for myself. "A few days before the ritual. I went out by myself for a little. I'm not accustomed to all these restrictions; they make me restless."

"Was this someone a man or a woman? One of the monks? A farmworker?"

I regretted my half-lie already; nobody here was going to tell me what I needed to know. They were a practiced team of players in a game whose rules I did not understand. "A man. I didn't see him clearly—he was too far away."

"It was probably Cronan," said Senach. "He sometimes takes supplies to an old fellow who lives over the far side of the river. A hermit, more or less. On baking day we send fresh bread, if the water's low enough."

I tried to remember if that had been a baking day. "An old fellow," I echoed. "Maybe I should be going to talk to him, not to these folk who live an hour's ride away."

"There would be no point," Senach said. "The hermit is stone deaf and ill-tempered to boot. He wouldn't give you the time of day. Besides, with Midsummer Eve so close, I am certain Lady Geiléis would not want you to risk the ford. Now, if you'll excuse me, I'll go and speak to Donncha . . ."

I returned to my own quarters. No sign of Geiléis; my idea about the curse making folk forget had upset her more than I'd expected, though it had seemed plausible to me. This entire household was deeply strange. Everyone behaved as if they had rehearsed their responses. There were only two exceptions I could think of—that brief episode with Caisín, when I'd caught her off guard, and the times when Geiléis lost control of her feelings, whether in anger, sorrow or frustration. At those times, and they were rare enough, I thought I got a glimpse of the woman she was underneath. A woman of passions and conflicts. A woman I thought I would like better than the Lady of Bann with her cool composure. That other woman felt far more real.

31

GRIM

It's enough to start a man thinking of magic, and not a good kind of magic. Last bundle of reeds goes up, I knock in the last spar, and the next moment the weather starts playing tricks. Could've sworn it would stay dry. Know the signs like I know my right hand. But clouds come over, quick as quick, and rain starts falling, so it's up with the cover again, and no more work for us today.

Pretty soon it's bucketing down, soaking the garden. Paths turn to squelching mud. Still, job's more or less done. Only the ridge left to finish off, and the animals for on top. Don't need Tadhg anymore. All he'd be doing is passing things up to me. Those last jobs, they're fiddly. Take a while to learn.

One dry day, that's all I need. Maybe two, to be quite sure of finishing. If the rain stops for a bit I can take a bundle of reeds back down to Geiléis's now and start on the creatures there. Bring them back up after I do the ridge. Tie them on safe—that's the last job of all.

Tadhg goes off to the refectory for a meal. Says why don't I go too, and I say no thanks. I shelter in a dryish spot, where the new thatch sticks out above the door. Thinking that if it stops I'll go and get that bundle of reeds right away. If I work tonight too I can maybe get the creatures all done. Be fiddly by lamplight, though. Still, time's short and even if I never see it again, I want the roof looking the way it should, with a proper finish.

Rain's coming sideways now, sharp sort of wind behind it. Winter in summer. I hold an old sack up over my head. Doesn't keep much off. Think of those little folk in the woods, so finely made, like something in a dream. Sheltering where they can. Wonder where they live. Down under the oak roots? In hollow trees, like squirrels? Or are there wee houses hidden all through the forest? Maybe they can make things invisible to our kind. Themselves, even. Gives me a funny feeling, that. Means they could be watching us anytime they wanted, and we wouldn't know. Easy enough to believe. That little man knew things about Blackthorn and me that nobody could have told him. The one Blackthorn met, the healer, she knew things too. Something about true love's tears, that herb with the funny little flowers. The small folk are all tangled up in this, same as Geiléis and her servants. Can't make sense of it, though. Even Blackthorn can't.

I'm looking across at the infirmary, thinking of Flannan in there reading that manuscript. Maybe finding the answers to the puzzle right now. If I was a different man I'd go and knock on the door, ask to have a look, ask to hear the news right away so I could run back and tell Blackthorn. If I was a different man I'd be sitting in the refectory enjoying a hot brew instead of shivering out here. Wind's howling now, odd sound, like voices. Loud enough to drown out the monster. If I was a different man I'd maybe have a corner of my own here.

It comes crowding back, catching me by surprise. The blood, the screams, the suddenness of it, no time to make a plan, nothing. Heart beating like a big drum. Men coming from everywhere, men with axes and clubs and knives. Yelling, shouting, can't understand the words but no need for that; they're saying, *Death!* Monks running, trying to get away, trying to protect each other, falling. Can't be everywhere. Mochta falls, Padraic falls, Ronchu's head goes flying, blood spurts from what's left of him. A weapon, need a weapon—Ah! The iron bar from the scriptorium door. Wrench it off. Want to rush out and fight all of them at once. My brothers are screaming, praying, dying. Go out there and I'm dead too, in an instant. Here, I can do some good.

Stand in the doorway, both hands gripping the iron bar, smashing one way, the other way. I fell one man, two men, three, more, more, and all the time, out in the courtyard, the brothers are falling, falling in their blood. Behind me the scriptorium door. In there the scholars, Brother Galen, the books, the precious books. Someone praying like his chest's on fire, like sobbing, the words over and over, hear them in my head now, *Deus, Deus meus, respice in me: quare me dereliquisti?* But God's not answering. Nobody is. The words break up and fall apart. The sound of men dying. Me shouting in time with the blows, *No! No! No!* Swing the iron bar, break an arm, break a head, put out a fellow's eye, and then I'm hit and I'm down and it all goes to black.

"Brother Conall?"

Christ! I whirl around, thatching knife in my hand, knees bent, ready to strike. There's a heartbeat in it. In front of me, a stride away, two monks with faces the color of fresh cheese and their hands up, palms toward me. One's Brother Fergal. The other one's Brother Ríordán, the head archivist.

I suck in a breath. It hurts. Can't seem to move.

"Grim," says Fergal in a voice like sun on an herb patch. "For the love of God, put the knife away."

I fumble it back into my belt. Can't find words.

"You're safe here," Fergal says. "You're among friends."

"Can't . . ." I gasp. "Tried . . . They wouldn't stop . . ." Take another breath. Make myself straighten up. Aching all over. Then it sinks in; what Brother Ríordán just called me. "Sorry," I mumble. "I'll go now. Take myself off. Sorry the job isn't finished." I turn my back and head for the gate, walking first, then jogging, then running so fast I slip and skid in the puddles, and the rain's all over me, soaking my clothes, dribbling down my face, only that's tears too, tears for what I didn't do, tears for what I lost, tears of guilt for keeping quiet about who I really am, tears because it looks as if these fellows know anyway and that makes me an outcast all over again. Tears for the creatures I was going to put on the roof, dove, salmon, raven, cat, that now won't get made anymore. Means the job's not properly done, and I like it properly done . . .

Make it halfway to the gate, more or less. Someone calling behind me, "Grim! Stop!" I slip and fall, sprawl flat in the mud, rain falling, can't make myself get up. Head on my arms, lying there like a fool, big lump of a man all tears. Sobbing, sobbing, can't seem to stop. Why won't it all go away? Why can't someone take it away?

The two brothers are here, crouching down in the rain, one on each side. Feel a hand on my shoulder. Under the roar of the rain, Brother Fergal's voice. "We've known who you were since early on, Grim. We sent a bird south to confirm it. Come inside; let's get you to shelter."

But I can't move, can't stop crying, like that thing in the tower. Sorrow's rolled on top of me, won't let me up, won't let me out. I try to say something, comes out as just noise.

Then the archivist speaks, Brother Ríordán, the fellow with the cold face. "The lost hero of St. Erc's," he says. "That's what they call you. Nobody knew where you went."

"Until now," puts in Brother Fergal. "Help me here, Grim. You're on the big side to tuck under my arm and carry. The vegetables love this weather. I am not quite so enthusiastic. We have a pot of soup on the boil inside, and dry clothes. Please, come out of the wet."

I'm mumbling about vegetables and compost and when I get up on all fours I try to crawl to the gate in the mud. When Fergal helps me stand up I pull away from him. But I don't run. Feeling wobbly, not right in the head. Don't think I can get far without fainting. Big fellow like me. All I can think now is that I just waved a thatching knife at them, and they stayed with me and helped me. Doing what that fellow in the story did, the Good Samaritan. Doing what Jesus would have done. If he was real.

"Come," says Fergal again. Now I've got one holding my left arm and one holding my right, not like guards, like friends. Leading me toward the refectory.

"Can't." I stop in my tracks like a stubborn donkey. "Can't go in." The blood. The brains. The broken men.

"Then we will sit on the doorstep." Brother Ríordán's got the sort of voice that's good for giving orders. The kind you can't help listening to.

"You'll be wanting me to go," I say, but I'm walking again, between the two of them. Through the rain, the sound of bells. "You'll be wanting to sing Sext." Then something he said sinks in. *The lost hero of St. Erc's.* "Hero," I say. "Someone else. Not me. Didn't save anyone. Not one. Even the cat was dead. Even the pigeons. Nothing left. Like a battlefield. Only not warriors. Men of peace. After that, couldn't believe in God. If God was real, he'd have been there." And we're at the refectory. Covered area outside, benches set along the wall. Nice for the brothers to sit out on sunny days. Today, cold, wet and not where you'd want to be.

I sit down anyway. Legs don't want to carry me one more step. Sit there and watch my clothes dripping onto the paving stones, making a pool around my feet. Think of blood pooling under Brother Galen's head, his snowy hair turned sticky red. Hero, me? Not likely. Anyway, who was there to see anything? Nobody.

The fellows go inside for a bit; then Brother Ríordán's back, standing next to me. "It helps, sometimes, to take things one step at a time," he says. "It's cold, you're wet through and you need to change your clothes. Do it out here and you'll get even colder. Or take one step inside and you'll be in a small chamber where you can put on these dry garments and wrap a blanket around your shoulders." When I start to say I can't, he goes on. "I don't suppose it will help if I suggest you hand your burden over to God. Not at this moment. But the first step toward lightening the load is to take control. This is your first step."

"Why would you want me here?" I say, not understanding. "Why don't you throw me out, after what happened?"

"Come in," he says, as if I haven't said a word. "Come and warm yourself. Time for talk when you've got dry and had a bite to eat. There's nobody else in the refectory; they've all gone to the chapel. Just me and Brother Fergal, and he is the gentlest of souls."

I take the step. Shivering, and not only from cold. I'm inside. Fergal helps me take off my wet things, put on a shirt and trousers, bit small but not bad. Blanket on top. Feels good. I was colder than I knew. Remember Blackthorn suddenly. What about her, if I'd wandered off and got led astray and died of cold?

Warm and dry. But trembling head to toe. If I can take the first step, the second might not be so hard. Into the refectory. Fire burning on a hearth. Long tables with benches. Clanking and clinking next door, that'll be the kitchen. I sit down. Ríordán sits next to me. Fergal's taking my wet things out, talking to someone, but nobody else comes in.

I'm thinking, what can I say? I'm thinking, what's he going to say? Holding myself together by a thread, but I'm here; I'm inside; I'm working hard not to see them lying in their blood, and everything ruined.

"Brother Galen was my mentor," says Ríordán. "He taught me everything I know. I completed my novitiate at St. Erc's. Before your time, Brother Conall."

Stray tear dribbles down. Can't speak for a bit. Then I ask, "How . . . ?" All I can get out.

"After I came to St. Olcan's, he and I corresponded for some years. Galen always loved to write. You'd know that. To write and to draw. He was fond of you. Said you had a great deal to give."

Now I'm crying again. Different sort of tears. Don't wipe them away. Feels like I should let them fall. "But how . . . ?"

"How did we know who you were? No great mystery. Galen described you, a giant of a man with a gentle manner, who could turn his hand to anything around the place. Building, thatching, painting. A man who loved stories. A man who would listen for hours as he read from the scripture or told tales of magic and wonder. A man who was kind to animals. A man who generally kept himself to himself, until he was sure he could trust. He mentioned the creatures you put up on the roof, after you'd finished thatching. Fergal told me you'd spoken of doing the same here."

Fergal's back with a tray. Cups of mulled ale. Bread, butter. Smells good. Not sure if I can eat, though. "Dove, salmon, raven, cat," I mumble, then clear my throat. They're being kind. They deserve better. "Still do it if you want. Four days left. Got time, if the rain stops."

"Grim," says Ríordán. "Drink." He puts a cup in my hands, like you'd do with a two-year-old. "One sip, come on."

I drink. Had mulled ale before, but nothing like this. Warm, tasty, spices go right to my head. Need to drink slow.

"Eat," says Fergal. He breaks up bread, spreads butter, passes me a platter.

I do as I'm told. Manage to get a bite or two down.

"Tell me why you chose those particular animals," says Ríordán, as if none of the rest of it's happened. "Dove, salmon, raven and cat."

I go through it for him. "In that story, the one about the great flood, Noah sent ravens and then a dove. Raven's for clear eyes; suits a house of scholars. Dove for peace. Salmon for wisdom. Not book learning, but the kind that's in the bones of the land. A fish, that's a Christian thing. A sign."

"And the cat?" asks Ríordán.

Feel my mouth twist. Tears close again. "Bathsheba," I say. "For Brother Galen. He loved her like a child." Manage to say his name. Long breath in; long breath out. Feels like climbing a mountain. "Used to sit right next to him when he was writing. Watching the quill move, one way, the other way. Wanting to stick out a paw and bat at it, but not doing it. Purring deep down."

Nobody says anything for a bit. I eat and drink some more. The two of them do the same. Voices outside but nobody comes in.

"You said you were no hero," Ríordán says after a while. "That's not how other folk understood it. What they saw was a man who fought hard to save his friends. Fought on and on against impossible odds, until he in his turn was cut down. A man who gave everything he had to give."

Something wrong with this tale. "Nobody saw," I tell him, the scene clear in my mind, coming to and finding them all dead. Every single one. The place as still as the grave, but for the scrabbling sounds of those hurt pigeons, poor little sods. "Nobody there, after. Only me."

"Where did you go?"

"Away. Couldn't live with what I'd done. Couldn't face up to it. Got into trouble, on and off. Lost my way. Like that sheep, the one who strayed from the path. Only Jesus didn't find me and lead me back. Why not? Because the day the raiders came, I stopped believing he could."

"And now? Here you are, back among us."

"Only chance. Found Blackthorn. Got a reason to go on now. She needs me. And this, the thatching . . . Hard to come up here. Kept seeing them. All the time. But she wanted me to do it."

Silence again for a while. "You're wrong about that day, Brother Conall," says Ríordán, quiet-like. "Someone did see. One of the lay helpers, hiding up in the tower, knowing if he came out he'd be slaughtered along with the others. He stayed up there a long time, too frightened to come down. It was only after folk from the local village arrived that he emerged to tell the remarkable tale of how you stood up to a band of thirty armed raiders, and kept them out of the scriptorium until, at long last, you were overcome and collapsed. Dead, he thought; but by the time he came down from the tower, you were gone. Gone before anyone could thank you. Gone before anyone could acknowledge your remarkable courage. They found Brother Galen laid out with his hands crossed on his breast, and Bathsheba beside him, wrapped in a man's shirt. A torn fragment of manuscript in his fingers."

"They took his book. His beautiful book with all the little pictures. Not even for reading, only for the cover. I loved that book. He put his soul in it. You know what the Norsemen do? Just toss the pages on the fire."

"His soul is in Heaven now," says Fergal.

I say nothing. I may not believe in God anymore, but I can't believe a good soul like Brother Galen's could go anywhere else, unless it's to be a lark singing high in a perfect sky or something of that kind.

"That's what it is to be a hero," Ríordán says. "It's fighting on even when you're hopelessly outnumbered. It's seeing your friends dying all around you, witnessing the most shocking cruelty you could imagine, and still finding the courage to go on. It's doing the very best you can."

"Didn't feel that way," I say, but his words are some comfort. Someone was there. I wasn't alone, not quite. "Felt like defeat. Felt like failure."

"And you've borne it on your shoulders ever since," says Fergal.

That's the truth. Funny thing, though. The burden feels a bit lighter now.

We finish the bread and butter. Drink a second cup of mulled ale each. I'm warming up at last. Can feel my feet. Outside, it sounds as if the worst of the rain might be over. Be a muddy old walk back.

Still a lot of questions to ask. So many I don't know where to start. Think about Blackthorn, not myself. "Who else knows?" I ask. "Who I am and where I came from, I mean." Even Blackthorn doesn't know that story. Hadn't planned on telling her. Or anyone.

"You mean here at St. Olcan's? Very few. The two of us. Father Tomas. Brother Eoan who looks after the pigeons. I believe that's all." Ríordán looks at Fergal.

"We thought it best kept to a small number," Fergal says, "since it was plain you did not want to share it. We knew the story of St. Erc's, of course; it was one of the cruelest raids."

"Does Flannan know about me?" If he does, then Blackthorn's going to find out soon enough. Don't want anyone else telling her the story. Only me.

"Master Flannan?" Ríordán half smiles. "We would not share your story outside our own brotherhood, Conall. Besides, Flannan has been so absorbed in his work that I doubt he would have taken in the tale even if we had told it. He seems a man on a mission, blind to all else."

Never seemed like that to me. But I'm guessing they mean this translation Flannan's doing. True, I've hardly seen him since he got started on it, so maybe he's putting in long hours. And he was a bit odd when he crossed my path yesterday. "Thank you," I say. "For not spreading it around. I'll tell Blackthorn in my own time. Not anyone else. And best if you don't call me Conall. That name's gone. Done."

They look at each other. Fergal pours more ale. "As to that," says Ríordán, "it might not be gone and done. Not unless that's what you want. You could resume your novitiate here. Father Tomas has said so. Not only because your practical skills would be a great asset to our community, but because we believe you have all the qualities required. We would welcome you as one of us, Grim."

I'm gob-smacked. This is too much. A second chance, a home, a community, the stories, the pictures, the singing . . . All that I lost, given back so easily. "I'd bring down ill luck," I say. "Be a blight on you, like that sad creature in the tower. Soon as you let me in, soon as I get comfortable, something bad will happen. Always does."

"I don't believe that for a moment," Ríordán says. "How could you be in any way responsible for the raid on St. Erc's? Nobody in his right mind would have expected one man, however big and strong, however remarkably brave, to fight off thirty armed Norsemen."

Maybe nobody expected that. Thing is, though, *I* expected it. Or that I'd go on fighting until someone killed me. Should have died protecting them. Then I'd have done my best. But I'm here, and they're dead.

"What would Brother Galen want you to do?" asks Ríordán.

Big question. Too big to answer. To Brother Galen I was good. Whole. No missing parts, no wrong parts, no bad parts. He taught me to love learning. If I told Brother Galen I didn't believe in God anymore, he wouldn't be shocked. He'd talk through it, listen to what I had to say, offer his own ideas. While we talked he'd paint his little pictures, so magical. Something about those pictures . . .

"He'd want me to do what felt right," I say. "Inside, I mean. Deep down. Got a question for you." Man with the head of a bear. Creature like a cat in a snail shell, sticking out its tongue. Row of horses in hats, kicking up their feet. "You know the little pictures scribes put in manuscripts?

Sometimes angels, folk praying, chapel bells. But sometimes odd things. Old things. Strange creatures, maybe fey folk. Brother Galen put lots of those in. Don't know if the fellows here do that too. Just thinking, where do they get the ideas for those?"

They don't laugh at me. "Did you ask Brother Galen that same question?" says Ríordán.

"Didn't think of it then. He was always telling stories, knew hundreds. Some of them from scripture. Some not. Liked to mix them up. But the pictures were so real. Did wonder later if he'd ever seen them. The fey, I mean. Never got around to asking."

For a bit they've got no answer. Then Ríordán says, a bit disapproving, "Father Tomas would tell us such beings are manifestations of the Devil and should be shunned. At the very least, they represent primitive beliefs. Unhealthy beliefs."

Then they go quiet again. Want to ask, *But what do* you *think?* Only that seems rude, so I keep my big mouth shut.

"Brother Galen had a different view," Ríordán says. "He used to say, God is everywhere. In the work of your hands; in the beating of a bird's wings; in the roots of an oak and in the stones of the riverbed. In the rising of the sun. In the heart of a man. In the wonders we know, and those that are beyond our knowing." He sighs. "I cannot tell you if he ever saw beings of the kind he loved to draw, Grim. But if he did, I am quite certain he would say they too were part of God's creation, and should be treated with respect."

"I like that," says Fergal. "God is in the work of your hands. We feel that every day in the garden, in the richness of the soil, the wonder of new growth, the circle of the seasons."

Got no words. Nearly in tears again. All very well, all very comforting. But why would God let them die? Why would he stand by and let Brother Galen be struck down?

"A good teacher lives on in every one of his students," Ríordán says. "In me. In you. In all the others to whom he was mentor and friend. We carry him in our hearts. As we carry God, deep within us."

"Not me," I mutter. "Not after St. Erc's. How could I be a man of God if I don't believe in him?"

"Ah," says Ríordán, and puts a hand on my shoulder. "You may no longer believe in Him, friend. But be certain He believes in you."

We're quiet a long time then. Not sure how it happens, but after a bit I start telling them about that day, the day of blood. Not sobbing and screaming and running away, just saying what happened, what I saw, how it felt. The three of us have some more to eat, and I keep talking and talking until it's all out. They knew the story already, of course. Messages go from one monastery to another all the time. Pigeon if it's urgent and short. For proper letters, folk like Flannan bring them. But they didn't know my side of the story. Good listeners, the two of them. Like Brother Galen.

"That book, he loved it as much as he loved Bathsheba," I say at the end. Feeling wrung out, like an old cloth that's been pounded and pummeled and washed half to shreds. "Makes me sad to think of the little pictures all shriveling up in the fire."

"I understand," says Ríordán. "It is sad. But there are other scribes, those to whom he taught his craft, those who teach others in their turn. And there are other books."

"Maybe," I say, thinking of the odd things he put in his drawings, the magic of them. "But not the same."

Ríordán looks at Fergal. Fergal looks at Ríordán. What I see is, *Do we tell him?*

"What?"

Ríordán clears his throat. "We have one of Brother Galen's books in our collection, Grim. The original, not a copy. A book of saints, which one might expect to be illustrated in quite a conventional manner, but . . . Galen was Galen."

Again, I'm dumbstruck. Not like he was alive again, but . . . feels that way, all the same. Wish I could see it. Love to see it. Can't ask.

"It's locked away, of course," Ríordán says. "We consider it very precious. After the raid on St. Erc's, I made a copy. We sent that south to St. Brigid's in Laois, which as you'll know is the monastic foundation closest to the site of St. Erc's. It will be well looked after there. I lacked the skill to reproduce Galen's paintings perfectly; I did my best." He smiles. "Would you like to see the original?"

"Me?" Can't believe he's offering.

"Provided you do so under my supervision, in the scriptorium, and wear gloves to turn the pages, I don't see why not."

Fergal chuckles. "Now you've really surprised me, Ríordán. I think this may be a first." He turns to me. "Our head archivist here is famous for his reluctance to let anyone near his precious collection. Your friend Flannan only got a look at his mysterious document because nobody else had a word of Armorican, if indeed that's what the language is. Count yourself a scholar for the day."

I say nothing at all. Next to this I'm small. This is so big you can't measure it. If I could write, if I could draw, if I could ever make my own book, I'd have a picture of a monk and a cat, and a story to go with it.

"Now, if you wish."

The two of them are standing, waiting for me, and I've been off in a dream. I get up and follow them out. Still in my borrowed clothes. Then I see where the sun's got to. Shadows creeping; cows coming into the barn. Day's all but gone while I've been talking away.

"Need to get back to Lady Geiléis's house," I say, feeling bad. Want to see the book more than anything. Might be the only chance; they might not ask again. But Flannan was going to finish the translation and come down to tell us the story, and by the looks of it, he'll be doing that soon. Blackthorn will be wanting to hear what this document says straightaway. She'll want me there too, listening. Means I need to go back when Flannan does. "Promised I'd be back to hear the story."

"Story?" asks Fergal.

"Flannan's document. The story of the tower and the monster and all. Said he'd have it translated by tonight. Need to hear it before midsummer."

"Let us walk over to the scriptorium now and see what progress Master Flannan has made." Ríordán sounds calm.

"I'll bid you farewell," says Fergal. "The rain seems to be over; I'd best check what damage the garden has sustained. It looks as if you may be able to finish our roof after all, Grim."

He's right. The rain's eased; the air's fresh. Smells like new beginnings. Garden should be full of things sprouting up, reaching out their leaves. Good feeling. Makes me braver. "Brother Ríordán," I say as we head for the infirmary building, "can I still see the book? Tomorrow, maybe, or the day after?"

"My offer stretches as long as you wish, Grim. Tomorrow, by all means. When your work is finished for the day, or earlier if it suits you. You know where to find me. My opening the collection to you may put some folk's noses out of joint a little. Don't let that trouble you."

"Should say, though . . . never did learn to read. Couldn't get the knack of it. But I'd dearly like to see it. The pictures and all."

"You could learn. Time and patience, that's all it takes. And faith in yourself."

We get to the infirmary. Go round to the back, where they've got the scriptorium set up. He goes in. I wait at the door; can't make myself follow after. Step by step, they said. This is a step I can't take, not yet.

Ríordán's not gone long. What he tells me when he comes out is that Flannan's left already. Finished his work, packed up and headed off early, while the three of us were sitting over our ale. Means he will have got to Geiléis's house long ago. So maybe I've missed the whole thing. Blackthorn won't be pleased with me. I say a quick good-bye, then turn tail and run.

32

GEILÉIS

T he scholar did her a favor. He did not wait until supper time, but arrived in midafternoon, while Blackthorn was away and Grim still occupied at St. Olcan's.

She had spent most of the day pacing up and down, biting her nails to the quick, her body full of a restless anticipation. Onchú, on watch outside, saw Flannan coming and sent Dau in to warn her. By the time the scholar arrived she was ready to receive him, with men-at-arms in place to divert Grim, should he come back too early. Her guards had another purpose: to take action should Flannan prove troublesome. She hoped that would not be necessary. If he suddenly disappeared, questions would be asked that had no easy answers. Blackthorn was not going to believe that on the day he'd planned to share his discovery with them her friend had packed up and left without warning and without explanation.

The dining chamber was unsuitable; too central, too many door-ways. Her own quarters would be inappropriate, though there was no denying they were private. Geiléis settled herself in a small chamber near the main door, a room where visitors had been received in happier days. Her guards could be close at hand but discreetly placed. Better if Master Flannan did not know the potential danger his document represented, and what peril he consequently faced. If the thing turned out to be harmless, he need never know how close he had come to the edge of a sharp blade.

"Master Flannan, welcome." Dau spoke courteously at the front door. "Lady Geiléis wishes to speak with you privately. This way."

She rose; greeted the visitor and invited him to sit down. Dau poured mead, then departed, closing the door behind him. Save for the voice from the tower, muted by distance and the thick stone walls of the house, all was quiet. Geiléis scrutinized the visitor. His demeanor was less than buoyant. It was distinctly lacking in the excitement she had expected. Had he failed? Was this a reprieve? But he did not look despondent either. He seemed, rather, to be holding something in. Over that, a well-practiced air of calm control.

"Have you brought the document?" The question burst out, despite her best intentions.

"I don't have it with me, Lady Geiléis. The senior archivist has very strict rules—"

"Even for a copy on a wax tablet? I cannot believe his authority stretches so far."

"There was no need to bring the original text, in any form. That would be pointless, since no one here would be able to read it."

"But—"

"Fortunately," Flannan said, and she got the odd sense that he was playing with her, as a cat plays with a mouse, "I can remember the translation word for word."

"Ah." So he had done it. He had unlocked the code. "And is it what you believed?"

"It is most certainly a tale about the Tower of Thorns, and the monster within, and how he came to be there, Lady Geiléis. An old tale. A very old tale. It seems this monster has been in the vicinity of your home for far longer than anyone believed. That makes me wonder."

Gods, her heart was going like a blacksmith's hammer. She must appear calm. She must not alert him until he had told her everything he knew. "May I hear the story?"

"Of course. You will be interested to learn that the details you have mentioned are present in it. Midsummer Eve. A woman to cut through the thorns and break the curse."

"Tell it, please. If possible, exactly as it is set out in the document." Oh, gods! Brother Gwenneg had written down the whole story. This man would have to die, and all because he possessed a scholar's natural curiosity. She felt cold sweat break out on her skin.

"Very well. It begins with a young woman named Lily, only child of the chieftain of Bann. Living in this house, in these woods, at a time when the island on which the tower stands was a place of greensward and burgeoning wildflowers. A time when there was no monster, no wailing voice, no hedge of thorns, no magic. Or if there was magic, it was not a curse, but only the presence of the fey . . ."

"Go on," she said, and despite her best efforts her voice cracked.

"Very well." Flannan took a mouthful of the mead; all the time his eyes were on her. "The monk who wrote this document tells how Lily came to St. Olcan's in great distress, at night. How he and some other brethren accompanied her back to her home. There they found her parents, along with those of their retainers who had been home at the time, lying dead in their beds. Lily was distraught; incoherent. But in time she confided in this one monk, recounting a strange sequence of events leading up to that night. She had gone to the old tower . . ."

Geiléis sat silent, her back rigid, her mind working very fast indeed, as he told the tale. Lily and Ash, the tower, the rescue, the sweet time of hope—all too brief—and then the curse. Ash would become a monster; was already becoming one even as the fey woman spoke. Lily would have one chance to save him every fifty years; one chance to see him restored to human form and freed from the tower. She would live long enough to see it happen. She need not be alone—if she could find folk to serve her, they too would live on as long as she needed them.

But Lily herself could not perform the task, the terrible task that would ensure Ash's release. Geiléis winced as Flannan described that task; that she already knew its nature did not make it any easier to hear. The document stated, Flannan said, that this task must be performed by another woman, one who agreed willingly to help. The morning of Midsummer Eve was the only time the thorns would yield. While the curse remained unbroken, the small fey folk of the forest would be bound to tend to the monster, who would sleep the years away, all but the fiftieth summer and the summer before, when he would scream his pain every day from dawn till dusk. Lily must tell the story over and over, so she learned her lesson. The magic would ensure folk forgot. They would not notice that she stayed young. The small folk were bound to secrecy; should they attempt to tell the story to a passing stranger or indeed to someone in the local community, they would bring down a terrible sorrow on all their kind. For when Ash was imprisoned, so was their king; he was condemned to dwell within the thorny hedge until the curse was lifted. Each time they disobeyed the rule of silence, the barbs would pierce him harder.

And? Geiléis waited for the last part, the part that Blackthorn must not learn. The part that nobody else must learn.

"It is a terrible tale," Flannan said. "And strange indeed. This Lily must have been an ancestor of yours."

She could not speak. That was all? Brother Gwenneg had left out the final words of the curse? Could she dare to believe it?

"She must have given up on her sweetheart," he went on. "If she was her parents' only child, and they had been struck dead, she would have been the last of her line and you would not exist."

She never gave up. Never considered it, even for a moment. She kept faith for two hundred years; if she had to, she would keep faith for two hundred more. For Ash. She had promised. Geiléis bit her tongue. Her nails dug into her palms.

"But then," said Flannan quietly, "the woman who cursed Lily told the girl she would live to see her sweetheart freed."

Geiléis was suddenly alert to danger. She made herself unclench her fists, relax her jaw. Her guards were right outside the door. They would act in an instant if she summoned them.

"Perhaps she lives on, even now," she said. "An ancient woman, old almost beyond endurance, clinging to life until the curse is broken at last. Not daring to make herself seen, lest she be cast out. Lest she be taken from him."

"She'd be more than two hundred years old," said Flannan. "It defies logic. Blackthorn might be prepared to believe it. I am more inclined to think that this monk, the man who recorded the tale, was an imaginative soul. But then, there is the tower, and the thorn hedge, and the wailing monster. There is the undeniable effect of the curse. A shadow that lies over you and your people even to this day."

She gathered her wits; spoke calmly. "If your accounting is accurate, Master Flannan, this tale does indeed explain many of the troubles that plague the district. Small fey folk—how odd. I had no idea . . . And it tells us what Mistress Blackthorn must do in order to break the curse." She hesitated. His tale, thus far, had contained nothing that could not be repeated in front of Blackthorn—with less than four days left, it was time the nature of the task was spelled out for her. Grim would raise objections, no doubt, but Geiléis judged it unlikely Blackthorn would change her mind about going through with it. This account might even strengthen her belief in the mission. But Flannan . . . why had he brought this to her first? Why was his manner so odd? What if the document did indeed contain the curse in full, and he was playing a trick? Was he planning to come out with that last part in front of Blackthorn, and doom the venture to failure? But if so, why not wait until she was here?

He had his chin on his steepled hands, and was regarding her gravely. She was going to have to ask him. She could not assume he had told all he knew. She could not afford to let him walk away, not knowing. But no direct question. Do that, and his suspicions would be quickly aroused.

"Give me your opinion, Master Flannan. The terms of the curse make it clear that once Blackthorn does this, the monster will be a monster no longer. If Lily still lived, the lovers would be reunited; all would be well. But . . . I cannot help feeling there might be some . . . aftermath. Some complication. She who pronounced the curse was evidently both cruel and thorough. I cannot imagine her granting a happy ending. What do you think?"

"One would imagine," Flannan said, "that after two hundred years, the lovers might be considered to have paid the price for their offense—surely even the hardest-hearted person would recognize that. Or were you thinking of a different kind of aftermath? One involving someone else?"

Oh, gods. It *was* in the manuscript. What else could he mean? She would have to do it. She would have to call in her guards and give the order.

"The curse is thorough," he said, "is it not? Everything provided for, down to the last detail. The creature shut away where nobody can reach him. The years of howling, a stark reminder of his presence. The chances offered, leaving a slender thread of hope. But only once in fifty years, so that even if the charm of forgetting failed, even if someone lived long enough to recall the last time, what they said would likely be dismissed as an old person's ramblings, or as a fanciful tale. The small folk of the forest—they do indeed sound like something from a tale, but since the creature has not yet died of starvation, I'm inclined to believe them real—to provide for the monster and to keep quiet about its presence. A terrible penalty to be paid if they broke that rule. Lily unable to break the curse herself; that, I take it, applied also to her descendants, if indeed they in their turn attempted it. And . . . an aftermath. A cruel and unnecessary aftermath, which seems entirely characteristic of the fey woman who ruined two young lives all those years ago."

Geiléis could not reply. Rage and grief tore at her. He could not snatch this chance away. She could not let him do it.

"You know, don't you?" he said. "All of it, or most of it. And, of course, although you could have shared this tale with Blackthorn—she is a woman who believes almost as passionately in honesty as she does in justice—there is that one crucial piece of information you can't afford to have her know. Something that would make even the bravest woman in all Erin walk away. Am I right?"

Geiléis rose to her feet. One click of the fingers, and three men-at-arms would be in the chamber. Still she hesitated. There could be another way out. "What is your price?" she asked. "For silence?"

"You ask that, knowing Blackthorn is my childhood friend?"

"I ask it, knowing you have chosen to bring this to me before you took it to her. I'm not sure you understand how important this is to me, Master Flannan. I will take whatever action is necessary to set things right. To undo the curse, to free him . . . *Whatever* action is required. You understand?"

"One thing I do understand: that once Blackthorn hears the terms of the curse in full, she will no longer be a suitable candidate to undertake the task. It specifies that the woman should be willing. Who would be willing, knowing what the document contains?"

"I say again, what is your price?"

"And if I have no price?" asked the scholar.

"Then I will be obliged to take action." Her hand moved to the knife at her belt: an additional precaution, in case the scholar proved to be more warrior than he appeared. "Action I would prefer to avoid."

"At this point I should remind you that I did mention to Brother Ríordán, up at the monastery, that I had managed to work out the code. I have not discussed the contents of the document with him. Not yet, at least. I have left a complete transcription locked away in the scriptorium at St. Olcan's, in my personal box. Should I disappear under odd circumstances, I feel certain the monks would go through all my papers looking for clues. Sooner or later. Possibly before midsummer. But possibly not. That is a risk you would have to take. Then, of course, there's Blackthorn. She would be somewhat surprised if I vanished without explanation. And as you know, she likes to get her teeth into a good mystery."

Geiléis worked on her breathing. So close, oh, so very close! "I very much hope that you will not disappear, Master Flannan. Such a devious mind would be a great loss to the future of scholarship. I do not ask you to tell any lies. By all means share the tale with Blackthorn and Grim tonight, as they expect. I will be present. Both you and I will behave as if this meeting had not happened."

"And?"

"The sad story of Lily and her Ash will surely touch Blackthorn's heart. She may seem hard on the surface, all bitterness and anger. But she is not devoid of compassion, nor of courage. Master Flannan, I do not ask much of you. Only that you omit the last line of the curse. So little; only a few words. Will you do that?"

Flannan gazed at her; he was somber now. "And what of the aftermath?" he asked.

"I can give you silver," she said. "Land, if you wish. Opportunities a man of your background could not dream of."

"You would kill for this," said Flannan. "Without hesitation, without compunction. I suppose there is a man with a weapon waiting just outside that door."

"More than one. I would do anything to break the curse. Anything. If you give me no other choice, I will have you removed, yes. But only if there is no alternative."

"Happily, it will not be necessary to take such drastic action. But do not forget that I possess the ability to spoil your plan with as few as eight or nine words, spoken in the right ear. Remember that if I am harmed, the monks will read my translation and the story will become common knowledge. If that occurs before Midsummer Eve, you will lose this chance. Perhaps you will lose any chance at all."

Folk would forget, of course. In another fifty years, Blackthorn, Grim, Flannan, the brethren of St. Olcan's would all be gone. But she would still be here, and Ash would still be in the tower, screaming his pain. She couldn't fail again. She would break in pieces. "What do you want from me?"

Flannan smiled. "Even less than you want from me, Lady Geiléis. Oddly enough, it seems we have a common purpose. What I require is this: firstly, that you do not divulge the last lines of the curse to anyone. Secondly, that you do not speak of this meeting with a living soul. Blackthorn in particular."

"And?" This could not be all. The man must surely have some devious purpose. Would he dare try to trick her, with armed guards at the door? She found it hard to breathe.

"No more than that. If you can promise me your silence, I will ensure the document is destroyed. But not until Midsummer Day."

"By Midsummer Day," said Geiléis, her mouth twisting, "none of it will matter anymore."

Her men-at-arms did not even need to draw their weapons. Instead, they stood aside to let Dau lead the visitor through to the dining chamber, where Flannan was provided with food and drink while he waited for Blackthorn's return. The remainder of the afternoon passed, and it was nearly dusk. Geiléis called Senach to keep watch outside her bedchamber door, then climbed the steps to the high window. The sky was all clouds; rain had fallen over the forest and the air was cool and damp. She hugged her shawl around her. His cries were dying down now; the long day was almost over. Only three more to endure. Only three, and then . . .

. . . *Midsummer Eve, and the sun rose over the forest of Bann, bright with hope. There had been rain, but this day was clear, a day of promise and of new beginnings. When it was time, the wise woman armed herself with a sharp ax, and for good measure a knife at her belt. She did not go alone to the tower; Lily herself accompanied her, along with two faithful guards.*

The river was low; unusually so, considering the rain. They waded over without difficulty, and halted at the foot of the tower. Blackthorn hacked at the thorns with her ax, and they fell apart under its blade as if they were straw, leaving a pathway straight to the tower door. The woman climbed the steps with courage and purpose. There she was in the high chamber, and there he was. The monster. And then . . .

She could not imagine it; could not see it clear. Her mind shrank from it. But . . . but somehow she would be in the doorway watching. She would witness the breaking of the curse. How could she not?

Then the deed was done, and at last, at long last Ash was restored to himself. Lily ran to him. She wrapped her arms around him—he was so thin, so pale—and whispered his name. His lips moved against her hair; his fingers brushed her cheek, as gentle as a butterfly's wing. "My love," he said, and his voice was no longer a monster's, but a man's. "My faithful love." The long nightmare was over.

"I will give you the best wedding gift anyone could dream of," she said, as the voice from the tower fell silent. "A happy ending."

33

BLACKTHORN

Everything conspired to slow my progress that afternoon. That was how it seemed, anyway. It rained, not a light summer shower but a downpour that came in drenching sheets, turning the tracks to mud and rendering the steeper stretches slippery and perilous. Donncha led me on a winding course that seemed often to loop back on itself. I asked him if he was sure he'd chosen the most efficient route, and he answered that he was following a path that would get us to our destination in the wet without damage either to ourselves or to the horses. The alternative, he pointed out, was to abandon the visit and try again tomorrow. There was no arguing with that.

The tracks were overgrown; there was little sign that horses or men used them. There was no indication that pigs had been brought into the woods to forage, or that local folk came here to gather mushrooms or berries or to fish in the various streams and pools. Fat fungi clustered in the shade of the oaks; medicinal herbs were abundant, but I had no time to gather them. I thought I spotted the elusive true love's tears, a plant of modest proportions, easy to overlook. But useful; especially useful if the local people had an ongoing need for headache remedies. It was almost invisible beneath a tangle of more aggressive growers. Dead trees lay where they had fallen in winter storms, with neither limbs nor bark stripped away. Where did these folk get their firewood? Did the curse prevent them from harvesting anything at all in this abundant woodland? Even here, where distance made the monster's voice less penetrating, did the curse keep them at bay?

No sign of the little folk today, though I kept my eye out for them. Not that I could do anything if I spotted one; Donncha's presence ruled that out. We rode on through the forest, and eventually out of it onto grazing fields tenanted by a few scrawny cattle. The undulations of the land made it difficult to see far ahead, but there was a dwelling or two scattered about, and smoke rising. The ride had taken us quite some distance south. We had bypassed St. Olcan's entirely, though I had heard the bells as we rode.

"How much farther?" I asked. An hour's ride each way, Senach had said. It felt to me as if at least an hour had passed already.

"Not far."

"Show me."

Donncha reined in his horse; I did the same. "The path leads across those hills"—he pointed to the southeast—"and then through a wooded area. There's a stream where we can water the horses. From there it is only a short distance to the place I have in mind."

It seemed too late to complain that the trip was going to take all afternoon; much longer than I'd been told. I could hardly ask to turn around and head back right now. My life being what it was—full of bad surprises—that would probably mean I lost the one real chance I had to gather some useful information. "You do understand that I need to be back when Flannan comes this evening?"

"Senach told me, Mistress Blackthorn. Shall we head on?"

The rain ceased and the sun came out as we rode across the fields. We reached our destination around midafternoon. First impressions of the place were unpromising. The dwelling was so run-down it was hard to believe anyone lived there. I could imagine Grim looking it over and making a long list in his mind of what needed doing: mend the broken shutters, fix the crumbling walls, dig over the neglected vegetable patch. Then he would roll up his sleeves and get on with it. There was a trough half-full of greenish, foul-smelling water, from which we could not let our horses drink. The door was closed.

"Are you sure this is the right place?" I asked my companion as he tethered the horses. "There's no sign of life." Not even a solitary duck or chicken.

Before he could answer, the door crept open an inch, two inches, and in the narrow gap I glimpsed a pale face, a pair of shadowed eyes.

"This is the place," Donncha said. He unfastened his saddlebag and took out the bundle Dau had packed. My saddlebag held the two loaves of fresh bread, wrapped in a cloth.

"This household has suffered more than most from the effects of the curse," said Donncha as I got the bread out. "The folk here may not be able to help you a great deal. But I believe you will be able to help them."

Before I could utter a word, he called out, "Friend, Ana! It's Donncha. I've brought someone to talk to you. A wise woman; a healer." The change in his tone was remarkable. It might have been a different man speaking, no authoritative guard but a far gentler soul.

The door opened just a little wider. I heard a thin wailing from within; the cry of a sick child. Joined, almost immediately, by an old man's voice, calling in querulous tones, "Ana! Where are you?"

The woman retreated into the house, leaving the door open. I followed Donncha as he went in.

Someone had tried to maintain order here; that was plain. An attempt had been made to sweep the hearth, but the fire was down to ashes and the wood basket held only a scattering of twigs and dead leaves. From a sagging length of cord tied between the rafters hung an assortment of worn garments: a woman's, a man's, a child's. Dishes that might have been from breakfast were stacked at one end of the table, still bearing smears of what looked to be porridge. The house was cold. It felt damp, and there was a smell of mold.

The wailing continued; not the distant voice of the monster, but that of a child in the next room. The woman—young, thin, harried—turned from me to Donncha to the inner door as if pulled in all directions at once. "Sorry . . . sorry. The baby's poorly. I've nothing to offer you—"

"Ana!" The old man's voice this time, louder. "I need the privy!"

Donncha was unpacking his bag onto the table. Cheese, honey cake, dried fruits, a little sack that might contain flour, the remains of a leg of mutton. We had had roast mutton for last night's supper. "Go on, Ana," he said. "I'll fetch you in some wood and we'll get the kettle on."

She disappeared into the other room. Donncha took himself outside, and fairly soon there was the sound of an ax splitting wood. I rolled up my sleeves and set to work. There could be no hot water until we got the fire going, but I removed the dishes to a bench, then gave the table a wipe down. Took the drying garments outside and hung them over a bush in the sun, glad that the earlier downpour had ceased. Discovered that there was very little food in the house—no surprise.

Donncha came back with an armful of wood and a bucket of water. The infant was still crying; it seemed the beleaguered Ana had put the old man's needs before her baby's. I was about to knock on the inner door and offer assistance when Donncha said, "Mistress Blackthorn, do your wise woman's skills stretch to lighting a fire very quickly?"

"They do," I said. "But maybe I should . . ." I jerked my head toward the inner door, behind which the baby's wails had become hiccuping gasps. If Ana did not tend to it soon, I would march right in there and do it myself. Not that I could feed the child. Nor had I seen a goat or sheep outside, or any other means of providing fresh milk.

"You look after the fire; I'll deal with that." Donncha surprised me again by walking over to the inner door, tapping gently, then going in. "I'll get your grandfather back into bed," I heard him say. "You look after the boy."

Soon all was quiet. Remarkably quiet. We had come far enough from the ford to render the creature's cries almost inaudible. It was startling what a difference it made, not to have that sound constantly nagging at one's ears. I felt that at long last I could breathe again.

By the time Donncha reemerged, followed by Ana with a baby wrapped in a woolen blanket, the fire was crackling, the kettle was boiling and I had the food we had brought set out on the table. We might have to eat it from the chopping board with our fingers, but I did not think anyone would object. Once I'd made a brew, I'd boil more water for washing up. And while I had not expected to spend my afternoon carrying out domestic duties—I didn't even do a lot of those back at Winterfalls; Grim was the house-proud one—perhaps my contribution would bear fruit in the form of information. Not that Ana looked in any state to talk. If ever I'd seen a person desperate for sleep, she was it.

The first thing was to feed her, to get some color back into that pallid face. The most surprising thing about all this was not that Ana seemed to be looking after an infant and a demanding old man by herself, with few resources—I had visited sadder households by far—but that one of Geiléis's perfect, unreadable retainers had suddenly turned into a real man. Evidently Donncha was a frequent visitor here. And Senach knew about it. Or did he? Nobody had said precisely where we were going today or whom we were to visit. I'd only been told it was farther away than before, and that there might or might not be someone who could tell me something useful. That would have covered a whole host of possibilities in the district. So maybe neither Senach nor Geiléis was aware of this rather different side to Donncha. If that was so, he had placed considerable trust in me.

I didn't ask questions at first. I waited until Ana had eaten a good meal. She was hungry, but still doing her best to keep up appearances; she ate daintily, making the food last. The supplies we'd brought would be enough for several meals for her and her grandfather. Which led me to think that even if Senach was not in on the secret, Dau was. Donncha and I ate a little, to keep Ana company.

"Ana?" came the old man's voice again. "Where are you, girl?" She'd taken him a share of the food before we sat down to our own meal; he had not been forgotten.

"I'll go," said Donncha, getting up.

"Don't trouble yourself—"

"It's no trouble, Ana. You stay there and have a chat with Mistress Blackthorn."

But when he had left the room, Ana did not say anything. She looked down at her baby, who lay in her arms, still awake. I could hear his breathing, and I did not much like the sound of it. Perhaps I had come here only to deliver bad news. It happened that way sometimes, and it never got any easier.

"I don't think the little one's quite right, Mistress," Ana said now, almost apologetic. "It's that wheezy sound, like he can't catch his breath. And he doesn't feed long, though I've got enough milk. It's like he gets tired of trying, but then he cries as if he's still hungry. Maybe there's something you can give him, a tonic? Something to get him strong again." A pause, during which I listened to the rasp of the child's breath, in, out, in, out. In the other room, Donncha was having a muted conversation with the old man. "He's my only one," Ana said. "My man's gone."

I did not ask what that meant. Her man wasn't here to support her; that was all I needed to know. "What is your son's name?" I asked.

"Fursa. Same as his dad. Born on Beltane night. My man never got to see him. They found him hanging from a tree, a few days before the little one was born. Do you want to hold him?"

Finding myself lost for words, I took the baby in my arms. Born at Beltane—so he was not quite two turnings of the moon old. So small. Surely too small. She'd said she had milk, but she looked half-starved. A child that was too weak to suckle for long was in immediate danger.

He's my only one. "A beautiful boy," I said. I could not banish the image of my Brennan at that age, rosy and content. No amount of robust good health could have saved him from Mathuin of Laois. Ana's child would not even live the two years my son had. The blue-gray tinge to his skin was a sure sign of something seriously wrong. Add to that the rasping cry and the small size, and the odds were against him. "I'll just have a listen to his chest, if I may?"

In my bag was a small wooden funnel I used on such occasions. Grim had made it for me, and its mirror-smooth surfaces and rounded edges were a testament to his understanding of the instrument's purpose, not to speak of his woodworking skills. I parted the baby's wrappings and set the narrower end against his scrawny chest, and my ear against the other end. For a while I listened, wondering what to tell Ana. Would I have wanted to know, as a very new mother, that my child would be dead before his second birthday? If I'd known, I could have taken Brennan away, out of harm's reach. I could have saved him. For Ana's child, the harm already lay within his tiny body, and there could be no rescue.

I looked across and met her tired eyes. Perhaps she already knew. Or guessed; a mother often knows these things by instinct. "Fursa's heart is not strong," I said. "I don't have a tonic for a child so young, and I don't think it would help him much anyway. But I do have a tonic for you, that will help you keep up your milk." It was fortunate indeed that I'd brought a small supply of the most commonly sought remedies with me, thinking they might prove useful in unlocking folk's tongues. With Midsummer Eve so close, I would not be coming back here. "Add three drops to your brew, morning and night. It doesn't taste bad." If Ana had been the wife of a well-to-do cottager, with her husband and family close by, I could have told her to eat well and rest well in order to do the best for her baby. But it seemed that when this household had lost its man, it had lost its heart. "Does Donncha bring you supplies often? Is there someone who can gather wood for you? A neighbor, a friend?"

"Donncha does what he can." Ana lifted her chin. "We manage."

"I can't do much for you in a single visit, and I'll be leaving this district in a few days. Ana, I think you need more help. There's an infirmary at St. Olcan's, isn't there? There must be skilled healers there who tend to sick folk in the community."

"A *man*?" It was as if I had suggested she consult a monster. "A *monk*? Such folk know nothing of women and babies and their ailments. How could they?"

It would be a lot better than nothing, I thought, but did not say it. "If your grandfather is unwell, they could at least help him. Take away some of your burden. I realize it's a long way, but if they knew you were in need, they might send someone to visit."

Ana said nothing. She took her son from me and wrapped his shawl back around him, her hands tender.

"As for supplies, and a hand with the heavy work, can't Lady Geiléis arrange that for you?" I thought about the baskets going over to the tower, and wondered again if the lady's loyal retainers were carrying out all manner of activities unnoticed, right under her nose. The fact remained that Geiléis was, in effect, the chieftain of Bann. It was surely her responsibility to ensure that all the folk who lived within her holdings were adequately provided for. Even if her mind was much occupied with other matters.

"We don't see anything of the lady. Or her men, apart from Donncha. Fursa was good with horses. Helped Donncha with a difficult mare, a couple of years ago. Friends ever since, the two of them, though Lady Geiléis wasn't happy with it. Doesn't like her men to be out among folk much. Mostly they keep themselves to themselves. It was different with him and my man."

"Oh?" I busied myself building up the fire, refilling the kettle, looking for herbs to make a brew.

"They were close. Fursa had work back then, helping folk with their stock. We weren't . . ." Ana cast a helpless look around the room. "Things weren't like they are now."

I found a jar of dried peppermint leaves; they were past their best, but better than nothing. "Mm-hm," I murmured in a manner I hoped was encouraging. No awkward questions. I'd wait for her to talk if she wanted to, and accept her silence if she did not.

"There's something wrong in these parts," Ana said. "Since that thing came to the tower, or even before. My man . . . he was all right.

Got sad sometimes, sorry he couldn't provide better for us, but . . . just sad, not . . . And then it was like a dark cloud came down over him. Couldn't turn his hand to anything. Didn't want to talk about it. He'd say he was going off to do a job for someone, and just wander around until it was time to come home. So, no pay."

"That must have been hard for you." I poured hot water over the peppermint; it seemed the herbs were still good, for a wholesome smell spread through the room.

"Oh, that smells nice," Ana said. "Thank you, Mistress Blackthorn."

"No trouble." Exhausted, beaten down, full of sorrow, and yet so grateful for small things. Perhaps it was at just such times of hardship and sadness that folk noticed the little kindnesses; the brief moments of beauty. "If you wish, I'll have a word to Lady Geiléis for you. I may not have much influence, but I can try at least." I would suggest that someone—Donncha, Senach, Geiléis herself—approach the monks on the same issue. Ana might not be prepared to accept the services of monks as healers, but I did not think she would refuse a share of the good food St. Olcan's still seemed to be producing. Hadn't Geiléis said that most of what we were eating in her house came from the monastery farm?

The baby had fallen asleep. It was as we sat quietly over our brew that Ana spoke again. "Fursa was a good man. Don't think he let us down, me and the babe. He wanted to be a father. Wanted it with all his heart. He wanted to be a good provider. Only . . . only he was just sad. Too sad to go on. Nothing helped. Nothing made him better. I tried, I did try—" Her tears flowed freely now, wetting the baby's face as she held him close. "I did my best. But he—he—"

I moved over to sit beside her; put my arm around her. I thought that if she knew what an angry, broken soul I was, she would not have chosen my shoulder to weep on. Anger boiled up in me, that she was reduced to this pitiful state through no fault of her own. I struggled not to blame her husband, who had killed himself when she was close to giving birth to their only child. It seemed the most selfish of acts; a denial of his love for her. But I had seen enough such deaths before to know that when the cloud of sorrow hangs too heavily over a person, nothing helps; no love, no hope, no faith is strong enough to draw them back from the brink. In my mind I saw Grim, standing dark and still on the high bank overlooking Dreamer's Pool. I remembered the chill of utter terror I'd felt when I'd realized I had only a moment to find the words that would stop him from jumping to his death. Because I knew him inside out, I had found them. Because he had not reached the point of complete despair, he had heard them. Not so Fursa. And now here was his wife, with a grievously sick son and a demanding old man to look after, and not even the most basic supplies in the house. With Geiléis's household only an hour's ride away. Without Donncha, who knew what would have happened here?

"Don't ask Lady Geiléis," Ana said, wiping her eyes on a corner of the baby's shawl. "She'd find out about Donncha coming. She might be angry."

And she might stop him from visiting again, which would be a disaster. It was not only the supplies; it was the friendly face. It was knowing that someone cared. "What about your neighbors?" I asked again. "Can't they help you?"

Ana grimaced. "It's a long way to the next house. And they're all struggling, Mistress Blackthorn. It doesn't seem right to ask."

I wanted to promise I would see them looked after. But I couldn't promise. In a few days I'd be gone. I might ask Geiléis for this as a payment or reward, I supposed, after I had banished her monster from the tower. But since I planned to leave with Flannan as soon as I'd done whatever was required on Midsummer Eve, I would have no way of holding her to it. It came to me with uncomfortable clarity that heading south would be a selfish decision. That I would be leaving unfinished business behind me, sorrows I could have eased, good work I could have done. I could only hope that the removal of the creature would restore this entire district to what it had been before. If these people were free from the curse, they might find the will to take control of their lives again. Not overnight, maybe, but in time.

Donncha and I did not ride back for a good while. He bathed the old man, settled him to rest again, then went outdoors to chop more wood. I told Ana I would watch the baby while she snatched some sleep. She looked at me as if I had just offered her riches beyond compare, and went off straightaway, leaving little Fursa asleep in his basket. There was a lot churning around inside me—I felt sad and powerless and angry. I hated the folly of humankind. There was cruelty and injustice everywhere. Deaths that were unnecessary; loneliness and deprivation where all that was needed, really, was for one person to hold out a helping hand. Ana reminded me of Mathuin's victims, the women I had tried to help back in Laois after he had stamped roughshod over their lives and left a broken mess. Still, after everything, she was trying to keep going. Within that frail, tired body there was a spark of will, a flame of hope. Her son's death, when it came, might be the chill wind that finally extinguished that flame. And there was nothing I could do. I knew no way to keep a child alive and well when his heart had most likely been failing from the moment he was born. Nobody could do that; not the most skilled physician in all Erin.

Since I could not rid myself of my furious thoughts by throwing things—in this house every item, however lowly, must be conserved with care—I set to with broom and cloth and bucket, and gave the place a good cleaning. When the woodpile was replenished, Donncha came inside and stopped short when I put a finger to my lips, signaling silence. He took off his boots and made himself useful, doing the jobs I could not reach such as getting the cobwebs out of the rafters. Fursa slept peacefully as we worked around him, a frail waif whose transparent pallor almost suggested fey blood. There'd been a child long ago in a time of my life I preferred to forget, a boy whom the other village children, and some men and women who should have known better, had called *the changeling* for his spindly limbs and white skin and for an invisible difference everybody felt, but nobody could quite put their finger on. He never talked much, so people thought him a dullard, a half-wit. Called him those names to his face. Teased and tormented him. I hadn't thought about him for years. I hadn't wanted to revisit that time. But I thought of it now as I mopped the floor of Ana's cottage, then went outdoors to wash out a heap of soiled cloths in the water Donncha had heated for me. That long-ago boy had also been a son without a father; his mother was a woman who was rumored to be no better than she should be, and was generally shunned in the village. I'd heard folk say that the lad could have been sired by anyone, though at eight or nine I'd hardly understood the implications. One thing I'd had then that I still possessed now, and that was a fierce love of justice. I could see myself standing with legs apart and hands on hips, between the boy—what was his name?—and his tormentors, delivering a withering speech about tolerance while they gaped at me, dropping the stones from their hands as if they'd never had any intention of throwing them. I recalled threatening to set their hair alight, or send bees to torment them while they slept, if they did not cease persecuting my friend forthwith. Not that he was a friend, particularly; our paths had sometimes crossed, and when they had done we'd talked a bit, that was all. Thinking back on it, maybe I was the only person who ever talked to him. In a way we were both outcasts: he because of his odd appearance and his mother and his unwillingness to stand up for himself; I because I had been sent to live with my mentor, and she was the local wise woman. A proper wise woman, the kind with a wrinkled face and long white hair and frightening objects strung around her neck. The difference was that folk found me frightening too. If I told them to stop doing something, they did. Even when I was eight or nine years old. That was probably why my parents sent me away.

The afternoon was passing; the house was clean and tidy, the water barrel had been topped up and enough wood had been brought in and chopped to last the household a good while.

"We should be going," said Donncha in an undertone, glancing toward the inner door.

I was reluctant to wake Ana, who so badly needed rest. But if we didn't leave now, we had no chance of being back in time for Flannan and his news. "All right, I'll—" I began, but Fursa did it for me, waking with a start, opening his little mouth and letting out a cry that sounded too big for his body. I barely had time to gather him up before Ana was there to take him from me. A careful mother and a loving one, despite everything.

The grandfather still slept. We made Ana another brew, leaving a cup to cool for her while she fed her son. She thanked us, sounding rather desperate. We told her it was nothing and made our farewells. Donncha did not make any promises to return, and Ana did not ask. I reminded her that monks were not ogres, and said again that she should consider seeking their help if she needed it.

And then we left. Donncha was wrapped in a somber silence. As for me, all that scrubbing and wringing had done little to quiet the army of furious thoughts that was marching around in my head. We rode on without talking until we were well into the forest. Then Donncha said out of the blue, "Mistress Blackthorn, I have a favor to ask."

I waited. He was full of surprises today.

"Ana and her child . . . I know the boy is sick, perhaps very sick. I have done what I can but . . . I'm not sure what I will be able to manage after Midsummer Eve. None of us can say what will happen when you break the curse."

"*If* I break the curse," I said. "Right now I am so angry with the injustices humankind visits on itself that I feel disinclined to do anything for anyone."

Donncha brought his horse to a sudden halt, forcing me to do the same. "I hope you will try," he said, his voice full of feeling. "For all our sakes. We believe you can do it. We believe this is the time."

Bitter words came to my lips, but I held them back. Donncha had shown exemplary kindness today, and he did not deserve my anger. "When we get home," I said, "Flannan should be there with his translation. I hope that will tell us what it is that I have to do. It might be something impossible, Donncha. Something I'm not capable of. A task requiring the strength of a giant, or the use of advanced magic. There's no point in attempting something I'm sure to fail at."

"I do not believe the task will be impossible," he said, though how he could know was anyone's guess. "The nature of a curse . . . it cannot go on forever. In time there must come an end."

"Who knows? Midsummer Eve is almost here and still I have almost nothing to go on. If this manuscript doesn't yield any clues, I'd be plain stupid to walk into the tower not even knowing what I'm supposed to do when I get there. Get eaten, perhaps. The curse might only be broken if the creature dines on human flesh."

Donncha made no reply, and we rode on. It was almost evening; the distant cries of the creature in the tower were growing fainter. I remembered something.

"You spoke of a favor," I said. "What favor?"

"Two things," said Donncha. "I don't ask that you go ahead with the task on Midsummer Eve, regardless of what is in the manuscript; that is for Lady Geiléis to say. We all want the curse lifted, Mistress Blackthorn. We serve Lady Geiléis and we want her to be happy again. But . . . it's Ana and the child. The old man too. After you've done it, after midsummer, will you go to the monks and ask them to help her? She won't do it herself. But even if the curse changes everything, even if hope is restored to Bann, Ana's going to need looking after. Little Fursa's gravely ill, isn't he?"

"I won't shield you from the truth. He's very ill indeed, and it's not a malady that can be cured, even by the most skilled healers in all Erin. I think Ana knows, or guesses, what lies ahead."

"She'll need friends. Support. Practical help. I can't be sure her neighbors will step in. Will you go to St. Olcan's and ask them, Mistress Blackthorn? Not now, but afterward?"

I could not make sense of this. Nor could I say yes, since I planned to leave Bann straight after the deed—whatever it was—was done. And that was a detail I did not want anyone but Flannan to know, because the more folk were aware of it, the greater the likelihood of Grim finding out. "Why not now? And why me? Why can't you ask them? Besides, you'll be here—you'll still be able to help her. Or are you thinking Lady Geiléis might order you to stop riding over there? If she does, she's not doing a very good job as chieftain." That was too blunt, perhaps; but it was time someone said it.

"My second favor," Donncha said, as if I had not spoken, "is that you do not talk to Lady Geiléis about our visit today. If she asks you, you might tell her we went to see some local folk and that you did not hear anything useful—the truth, as far as it goes. I would ask you not to mention that I have been visiting Ana, or that some members of our household have been providing supplies for her. If you could keep quiet about this, that would be in Ana's best interests."

"And yours."

"Mine don't matter, Mistress Blackthorn. But Fursa was my friend. My only friend in a very long time. I'm honor bound to see his wife and child right. I need to be sure they'll be looked after as they deserve, and I'm not sure I will be able to see to that myself. I've done a pretty poor job thus far. You'll have noticed that."

He meant the run-down house; Ana's exhaustion. But it was a long ride, and Geiléis kept her retainers on a tight rein. "Ana trusts you; she relies on you. That much is plain. If her husband could see what you are doing for her, I'm sure it would make him happy. Donncha, I can't promise to speak to the monks myself—I'm not only a woman, I'm a wise woman, and I don't imagine Father Tomas and the brethren would be inclined to do me any favors. But I can make sure a message reaches them on Midsummer Day or thereabouts, letting them know about Ana." Just how I was going to manage that—ensuring a message was delivered after I had left Bann—I could not think. Maybe a pigeon could carry it. Grim would know. But he was the one person I could not ask.

"Thank you, Mistress Blackthorn."

"You took a risk today. Letting me in on your secret, not knowing if I'd rush straight back and tell Geiléis everything. I'd never dreamed before this afternoon that any of you had a life beyond being her loyal retainers."

"That is our life," said Donncha, and there was a sad acceptance in his voice that jolted my heart.

"But it need not be, surely." I found myself unable to let the argument go. The men-at-arms in the royal household, and those in Prince Oran's establishment at Winterfalls, had their wives and children living with them. They went out into the community, both on and off duty; they were not forbidden to make friends.

Donncha was spared the need to reply, for we turned a corner and found our path blocked by a huge mound of stones and earth. The run-off from the earlier storm had brought down part of the hillside; there was no way around. Some malign spirit had decided I was not going to be present when Flannan divulged the contents of his manuscript.

I uttered a curse foul enough to make Donncha glance at me, brows raised.

"No way forward," he said. "Our best choice will be to go back to the last fork in the path and take a route downhill toward the river. It's easy enough for the horses and not a great deal longer than this one. I'm sorry, Mistress Blackthorn. It does look as if we'll be late. But surely they will wait for you."

Geiléis wouldn't wait, I thought as we turned the horses and headed back the way we had come. Perhaps it was unfair of me, but I was starting to think the Lady of Bann cared only for herself. She had come to Cahercorcan full of tears and woe on behalf of her poor beleaguered people, yet she made no effort to help those very people when they were in need. She didn't like her men going to visit them and she didn't seem to visit them herself. Instead she stayed in her house, often in her chamber, doing nothing much that I could see. She must have resources, or she would not be able to keep her household going—St. Olcan's might be helping with food, but it surely wasn't providing fodder for ten or eleven horses as well. So why didn't she make an effort to do what a leader was supposed to do? Did the curse work on her mind in such a way that she could not act as a chieftain should? Or was the curse just a convenient excuse for being lazy and irresponsible?

We took the route by the river. Dusk had fallen by the time we came in sight of the Tower of Thorns, and the creature was silent. We were tired and so were the horses.

"I'm so sorry, Mistress Blackthorn," Donncha said as we rode up the forest path toward Geiléis's house. "I did not intend this."

"A mudslide could hardly be your fault," I said. "And neither is my ill temper. I have enjoyed your company today. Just when I was starting to believe all people were selfish bastards, you proved me wrong."

"Thank you," he murmured, clearly taken aback.

"I'll honor your two requests. You have my word. As for Midsummer Eve, let's hope Flannan has all the answers we need."

34

GRIM

"*What?*" Head fills up with pictures. Spurting blood, shattered bone. I can hear it. Smell it. Makes my gut churn. Can't have heard
right.

"That's what it says." Flannan sounds calm, like the scholar he is.
He can't keep still, though. Twisting his fingers, folding his arms,
unfolding them, shifting around. Blackthorn's got her fists clenched
and her jaw tight. Look in her eyes tells me she's working herself up to
be brave, to say, *Cut off his head? All right, why not?* As if she did that
sort of thing every day. As if it's easy. Which it isn't. Not without a very
good weapon, a lot of strength and plenty of practice. Geiléis is strung
up tight, has been since I got here. Even Senach's looking nervy, though
his hands are steady on the mead flask.

"Tell us that last part again." Blackthorn sounds stern. She's got a
look about her that scares me. *Don't try to argue with me*, that look
says, plain as plain.

"The woman must cut the thorn hedge," Flannan goes on, "which
will give way to her blade. As soon as she passes through, the thorns
will close behind her. She must enter the tower alone and willingly. If

these conditions are not met, the curse cannot be undone." He pauses. "I suppose the fey woman who pronounced the curse wanted to rule out the possibility of someone taking an army to slay the monster. That would be far too easy."

Blackthorn clears her throat. "If this account is accurate," she says, "it's not a monster. It's a young man ensorcelled into a monstrous shape. I can't decide if that will make it harder or easier to do it."

"The scribe writes that she must climb the steps to the high chamber, and there she will find the monster—Lily's sweetheart, Ash," Flannan says. Which he's told us already, but Blackthorn did say she wanted to hear it again. "She must use her blade to cut off his head. Then the curse will be broken."

For a bit nobody says a word. Then I speak up. "You can't ask Blackthorn to do that. It's a job for a trained warrior. Needs strength and skill with a weapon. Ask any of your men-at-arms, they'll tell you the same. This creature would kill her before she could strike her first blow."

"Grim," says Blackthorn, quiet-like, "if I do it, I do it. If I don't, I don't. The only one who can make that decision is me." She turns to Geiléis, who's hardly said a word since Flannan told us the story. "This tale raises quite a few questions. What happened to the girl, Lily? If the document's so old, she couldn't still be living. But it says she'll live to see her lover freed. And, curses being what they are, unless we get every detail right, our attempt to undo the thing may fail." She's got that look she gets when she's trying to work out a puzzle in her head. Staring at Geiléis, waiting for an answer.

"I don't believe there's a Lily in my ancestry," Geiléis says. "The name seems very unlikely. I cannot check it. This all happened such a long time ago, and there are no family records. If Flannan's rendition of this document is accurate, it does not state that Lily must be present for the spell to be broken. Indeed, it's indicated quite clearly that another woman must perform the deed, and that nobody else can go into the tower with her when she does it. So even if Lily has lingered on far beyond her years—implausible, but maybe possible by magic—she cannot be present when her sweetheart is freed. We should not let thoughts of her distract us from the business in hand. Do you have further questions, Blackthorn?"

"Even if she herself is long gone," says Senach, "Lily would surely have wanted her man released from his suffering. The two were cruelly punished for what was, on her part, a quite innocent action."

"But would she want it at such a cost?" Blackthorn's still thinking hard. "If I cut off his head, he'll be dead."

"Think how you'd feel," I say. I'm remembering that picture scratched on the stone, the one the creature threw down. I'm seeing the stick figure crouched against a box, and the other one with an ax. That's what it means. Head on the block. Ax ready to chop. "Someone you love, turned into a monster and shut up in a tower for two hundred years. Screaming all summer, so you can't forget even for an instant. If you were Lily, wouldn't you decide he might be better off dead than having that go on and on forever?"

Blackthorn nods. She knows what it's like to watch someone suffer and not be able to help, same as I do. "But she was only a young girl," she says. "She might not have thought it through. And since the curse is magical in nature, he might not die. He might spring back to life, head and all, as young and handsome as he was two hundred years ago."

I catch Geiléis's smile, and it's the saddest thing I've seen in a long time. "I had forgotten," she said. "A happy ending. A fairy-tale ending. I asked you once if you believed they were possible, Blackthorn. Your answer, I recall, was 'sometimes yes and sometimes no.' Which is it for Lily and Ash?"

"How would I know?" Blackthorn sounds snappish. Who'd blame her? She's the one who's going to be risking her life, not Geiléis or Flannan or Senach or anyone else. Not even me, though if I could do it for her, I'd put my hand up without a second thought. She knows that.

"I'm sorry." Geiléis is sounding a bit steadier. "This is all quite distressing; I hope only that you will go ahead with this, even knowing the confronting nature of the task. Most women would lack the courage to undertake such a quest. But you, I believe, are brave enough."

"Brave enough," mutters Blackthorn. "Or stupid enough. Maybe both."

"We are fortunate, I think, that you are prepared to believe this tale," Geiléis says. "A person of less imagination would simply dismiss it as impossible, for it is full of oddities. These small folk, whom I have never once set eyes on, apparently living in these woods and bound to serve the creature or see their captive king injured. And such a rare chance; only once in fifty years. How remarkable that this document has come to light just in time. No wonder I made so little impact on the thorns last summer. I knew nothing."

Not quite true. She knew about it having to be a woman, and on Midsummer Eve, and about it happening before. Makes me wonder. If this document's been hidden away for two hundred years, and it's in a foreign tongue and coded as well, who told her those things? How did anyone know anything, when the curse has that bit about people forgetting? I don't say any of that. It'll keep for when Blackthorn and me are on our own. She's holding questions in too. See it on her face.

"I suppose I'll need a weapon," she says. "I'll speak to Onchú in the morning."

She's going ahead with this. Made up her mind. That turns my bones to ice. Can't go with her. Can't stand beside her and protect her. Helpless. Useless. One thing I can do, though. Make sure she's as ready as she can be. Means St. Olcan's will have to do without me for now. Might not get to finish off the creatures for the roof. Might not get a look at Brother Galen's book, not before midsummer, at least. I was looking forward to that. But she comes first, always. "I'll talk to Onchú," I say. "You don't just need the right weapon; you need training."

"Training?" Blackthorn makes a face at me.

"Not like cutting bread," I say. "If you're going to do it, you've got to do it right. Three days isn't long. Start tomorrow, mm?"

"If you say so. I suspect all the training in the world won't make any difference. If the curse is meant to be broken, it will be broken. And if not, not."

"Still," I tell her, "makes sense not to go in unprepared. Practice your skills; sharpen your tools; do the best job you can."

Blackthorn smiles, a good smile that lights up her face. I think of her in the tower, facing the monster all on her own, and it twists the heart in my chest. I give her a smile back. For a bit, it feels like just the two of us in the room.

Then she says, "Flannan, I'd like a private word, if you have time. Will you be staying here tonight?"

"Since it's so late, I must request Lady Geiléis's hospitality again, I fear."

"But of course. You've done us such an immense favor, Master Flannan, with this discovery . . . Senach has sleeping quarters prepared for you already, in anticipation of this."

"Thank you. Blackthorn, perhaps we might walk around the court-yard?"

They get up and go out, the two of them. Leaving me with Senach and Geiléis, and the whole heavy weight of what Flannan's told us, an odd tale indeed. Something about it doesn't add up. Hope Blackthorn's not long; I want to hear what she thinks.

"I'll take my leave," I say. "Might stroll over to the stables and have a word with Onchú tonight, see about a weapon for Blackthorn. Sooner the better."

"Take a lantern," says Senach. "Dau will have one in the kitchen. We don't want you tripping and breaking a leg, so close to midsummer."

Funny how that sounds more like a threat than a warning. Got too much on my mind, not thinking straight. Tired too. Long day. Telling my story up at St. Olcan's, that's the part that wore me out, not climbing around on the roof. Felt good when I'd got it all out, cried some tears that have been a long time coming. Felt almost peaceful. Didn't last long. She's going to do it. She's really going to do it. Hack through the thorns, rush up the tower, chop off the monster's head. All by herself. Crazy. What if that thing Flannan translated is only a made-up story? What if it's all a trick?

Shut it, Grim. Get your big self over to the guards' quarters and do the stuff you can do. And if Blackthorn's out there having a heart-to-heart talk with Flannan, be glad she's got a friend, a proper one who's book-learned and clever. A man she's known since she was young. A man who's not carrying a burden on his back, a man who won't lose himself in his own troubles. A man she can trust. What you think of him doesn't matter. It doesn't matter one little bit.

35

BLACKTHORN

"Don't tell me you're having second thoughts," Flannan said. "Lady Geiléis will be devastated."

"I'm not. Not now I've heard the story. But you can't deny the risk. Even if this creature was once a man, the curse transformed it. It could be all teeth and claws, and strong enough to snap me in two. But then, you probably don't believe any of it. You always said the old tales were too fanciful to contain any grain of truth. So why aren't you simply dismissing this whole thing? What do you care about Lady Geiléis's feelings? It would make more sense for us to forget her and her monster and slip away south while everyone else is planning for Midsummer Eve. Wouldn't it? We could do it as soon as Grim goes back up to St. Olcan's."

We kept our voices to an undertone. Although the courtyard was deserted, Geiléis's retainers had a habit of appearing without warning. Then there was Grim. If there was anyone I didn't want to hear this conversation it was him.

"I thought you wanted to do it," Flannan said. "I thought you wanted to help her. Another day or two, it's not long."

"I do. I did. Only . . . I think I'm missing something. It feels a bit too clear-cut, the appearance of this manuscript too timely, everything a little too neat. And . . ."

"And what?"

"I went out to visit some local people earlier today. That visit made me sad. Disillusioned. I never had a lot of faith in folk's natural goodness, not even when I was young. Didn't have much cause to. But this . . . Since we came here, I've started thinking we're all selfish bastards, every last one of us. Don't care about anything but our own interests."

"That's pretty harsh."

"There might be a handful of exceptions." Prince Oran and Lady Flidais. Donncha, when he wasn't under Geiléis's thumb. Emer, the young woman I was training back at Winterfalls. Grim. "But they're not enough to balance up the hate and selfishness and distrust. And I'm sick of dealing with it." My promise to Conmael meant I must use my gifts only for good. It bound me to say yes to anyone who asked for my help. And it forbade me from leaving Dalriada or seeking revenge against my old enemy. Within days I would break that third part and head south with Flannan. As for the second part, I was having difficulty finding the will to help anyone. I wondered if it was really worth the effort. Especially when I might get myself killed trying.

"Blackthorn," said Flannan softly. He stopped walking and took my hands in his. "That doesn't matter. None of it matters. You and I have a mission, and it's far bigger than Geiléis and her monster in the tower. But you need to think this through. The time for us to leave is Midsummer Eve, as we planned. After you break the curse, everything will be confusion for a while. It's the ideal time to slip away unnoticed. Provided Grim's not around, that is."

"You can leave Grim to me. Just don't say anything in front of him about what time on Midsummer Eve we'll be attempting this. His work at St. Olcan's isn't finished yet, and if he plans to spend tomorrow teaching me how to chop off a man's head, it most likely won't be finished by Midsummer Eve. I'll tell him he can fit in a half day's work and still be back in time." Now I was sounding as selfish and untrustworthy as the rest of humankind. And who, after all, was I to judge anyone? A worn-out, angry apology for a wise woman, who only did good deeds because Conmael's agreement bound me to it. That solitary cottage deep in the woods, the one I sometimes imagined for myself, was sounding very appealing: a bolt-hole where I could live out my life and be as bitter and cantankerous as I wanted. "Only . . . I have a strange feeling about this. About Geiléis and the whole thing with the tower. As if there's something more, something I need to know or it will all be a disaster." Not to speak of having to lie to Grim and get away with it.

"You can do it," Flannan said. "Trust yourself, and it will work out for the best, I'm sure. Of course I don't like to see you walking into danger; it's a daunting task. But you'll succeed. I'm absolutely sure of that, and I know Cass would be too."

A pox on the man; now he was making me cry. I needed to stay strong, whatever happened. Strong enough to face what waited for me in Laois; strong enough to stand up in front of Mathuin and speak coherently even if anger and terror were ripping me apart. Maybe the monster in the tower would be good practice.

I scrubbed a hand over my cheeks. "Cass would think I was crazy even to consider tackling Geiléis's monster," I said.

"But that was one of the things he loved about you. The way you never trod the common path. And that's been in you since the first; since long before you ever met Cass. Remember that strange little boy back in Brocc's Wood, the one everyone called the changeling? What was his name—Cully? That day when you stood up for him, I remember wishing I could be brave like you. You didn't care a bit what anyone thought. You weren't afraid of anything; you just went ahead and said what needed to be said. You're still that same person, Saorla."

A strange bell sounded in my mind. Cully. How odd that Flannan had mentioned that outcast boy from our childhood, when I had been thinking of him not long ago, for the first time in many years. An odd coincidence. "Don't call me Saorla," I muttered.

"Blackthorn, then. You can do this. I'm sure of it. If you break this curse you won't just be doing Geiléis a favor, you'll be changing many folk's lives for the better. Isn't that what we were trying to do in Laois?"

"Still are, from what you've told me." I was only half listening now; in my mind I was sitting under the trees in a faraway forest, watching in silence as Cully coaxed a squirrel to take a nut from his hand. The scene was clear in every detail: an awkward, spindly boy with hair so dark it was more black than brown, eyes of midnight blue, skin unnaturally pale even in summer. Features that were somehow not quite right for a human child. Those who had called him changeling had not really believed he was one—what they'd meant by the word was different, out-side, someone who did not fit. Like me. Only nobody had dared to call me names.

"Blackthorn?"

Flannan had been saying something and I'd missed it completely.

"Sorry," I said. "I don't want to talk about this anymore, not tonight. If you're not prepared to leave before Midsummer Eve, then I suppose we won't. You're the one who knows the way. You're the one who knows the people involved."

"So you'll go through with it?"

"It seems so, though I can't quite believe I'm saying that. Flannan, I really don't want to talk about it. I'm going inside now."

"I'll see you in the morning."

"In the morning I think I'm going to be learning how to cut off a man's head. I doubt very much that I'll want an audience."

I'd been planning to talk a few things over with Grim. The odd neat-ness of the old tale. The fact that it had been uncovered at the only time any of us would have a chance to break the curse. The visit to Ana's cottage and the way it had disturbed me. The question of Lily, who was supposed to live long enough to see her lover freed. That one was tug-ging at my mind. I couldn't discuss it with anyone but Grim.

But when I got to our chamber Grim wasn't there. He'd gone over to the guards' quarters, to talk weapons with Onchú and the others, I assumed. I made a brew—usually a reliable method of bringing back whichever of us was missing—but he did not make an appearance. I sat over the fire awhile, thinking. The tower . . . the creature that was really a young man, a very young man named Ash . . . the unfortunate Lily, who must have given up on her sweetheart and married someone else, or that family line would have died out and Geiléis would not be here . . . The nature of happy endings, and whether such a phenomenon truly existed . . . The small fey king trapped within the thorny hedge, and his folk bound to serve and hold their tongues . . . One, at least, had broken that vow to seek Grim's aid and to provide help in his turn. And while the little healer had not spoken to me, she had most certainly conveyed a message. They were brave folk, those small ones; brave and patient. How odd that Geiléis had known nothing at all of them.

I was falling asleep where I sat, and there was still no sign of Grim. Perhaps they'd given him a bed over in the guards' quarters; it was a fair walk back. Though he found it hard to sleep unless I was close by. Well, he'd have to deal with that particular problem, because pretty soon I wouldn't be here any longer. He must have managed somehow in the time before he found himself in Mathuin's lockup. He would manage again.

I went to bed and fell asleep almost instantly. I did not wake until the sun rose and the voice of the sad being in the tower made slumber no longer possible. Grim's bed had not been slept in, but as I went outside to the privy he came into the yard, looking wide-awake and very serious. "Make sure you have a good breakfast," he said. "Going to be a busy day." I saw, then, the ax in his hand, a weapon that to my inexpert eye looked rather on the small side for the intended purpose. The blade glinted in the morning light; I guessed the cutting edges were lethally sharp. There was some kind of carving on the handle. My appetite for breakfast vanished.

"A warrior needs to practice and practice," Grim said. "So that when the time comes his body just does what has to be done. In a battle you don't have time to work out right and wrong. All you've got time for is making sure the other fellow doesn't kill you before you kill him. A couple of days, that's not very long. But it's long enough."

"A pox on it all," I muttered, finding my eyes drawn to that shining blade, that elegant handle. "Why in the name of the gods did I ever agree to this?"

"You're the only one can answer that," said Grim. "Come on, breakfast."

"Did you sleep in the guards' quarters?"

"Didn't do much sleeping. Talked about the job you have to do, worked out what weapon was best. This one's the right weight for you. They've got a supply of seasoned wood there. Made a new handle, did some work on the blade. Better balanced now. Want to hold it?"

"No, thanks. I'll wait until later. To tell you the truth, the very idea makes me feel sick."

"Doesn't get any easier." Grim ran a thoughtful finger along the ax's cutting edge, somehow managing not to draw blood. "You never get used to killing. You just get better at making yourself do it."

If I hadn't known already how patient he was, I'd have learned it that day. We worked from breakfast time until midmorning before he let me try the ax. It was all foot positions, balance, turns. Practicing slowly so everything was correct, then speeding up. Going through the movements and then having to tell him what I'd seen around me while I was doing it. In case, Grim explained, there was something unexpected up in the tower, apart from a monster, of course. You couldn't leave anything to chance, he said.

We worked in a small yard next to the guards' quarters, a place designed for just such a purpose. I was pleased to be without an audience for my fumbling attempts to make myself into a warrior. In particular I didn't want Geiléis watching. I'd been thinking about her a lot since Flannan had told us the old story, and those thoughts set me on edge.

The ax was perfect for me. Holding it, lifting it, swinging it, I understood what Grim had meant a little earlier when he'd talked about balance and trajectory and using the strength you had to best advantage. The handle was of ash wood and there was a spray of blackthorn carved along it—thorns, flowers, berries, similar to the one he'd done along my bed back at Winterfalls. This decorative carving had been carefully placed so it would not affect the grip. I wondered if its purpose was the same as that of the creatures he'd made to decorate the roof of our cottage. To ward off danger. To keep the user as safe as he possibly could.

The men-at-arms came out to watch us as the morning went on, one or two of them at a time, so I had an audience whether I liked it or not. There was encouragement—"Good strike, Mistress Blackthorn!" "Well blocked!"—and advice—"Bend your knees!" "Go for his privates!" And this from the usually aloof Onchú, toward the end: "Morrigan's curse, Mistress Blackthorn, you're a real fighter!"

At around midday Grim called a halt. My arms felt like jelly, my back ached and I was all over sweat. "Enough for now," he said. "Food, rest." And, after a pause, "You did good."

I didn't ask him if he'd ever been a fighting man, though it seemed more than likely. If he wanted to tell me, he'd tell me. Not that there was much time left to tell anything.

Strange, how time seems to speed up when you most want it to slow down. The closer we got to that moment when I'd have to go up the tower, the less prepared I felt. Even with Grim drilling me in warcraft. Even with Geiléis telling me, often, that she truly believed I could do it. She praised my courage until I was sick of hearing it, and on one occasion she offered a generous payment in silver. I wanted to refuse. I wanted to say she should use her funds to help the struggling folk who had the misfortune to live within her borders. But Geiléis was hardly going to do what I told her, and besides, it would be useful for Grim to have something to keep him going when I left. I told her she could pay me—or him—when I'd actually broken the curse.

"Grim," I said, after a second long day of training. "There's something I want to ask you. Or get your opinion on."

"Mm-hm?"

We were lying on our beds, ready for sleep. Grim had banked up the fire for the night; in the faint glow from its embers he loomed against the wall, a big dark shadow. A watchdog to keep enemies at bay. A guardian spirit to ward off evil. A listening ear. A shoulder to cry on. The voice of common sense. As familiar as a comfortable old cloak, which was not at all the way I'd intended it to be when I'd first encountered him on the road and agreed to let him walk on with me. It had just happened. A big nuisance, because all that was going to make it so much harder to walk away and leave him behind.

"What?" he asked, and I realized I had drifted off into my own thoughts.

"The story. The curse only giving Lily one chance every fifty years, and that part about her living to see Ash freed. Or to see the curse broken. Which was it?"

"To see him freed. That's the way he told it. Flannan." A pause. "You thinking it might be her? Geiléis?"

I sat up, surprised. Not that I should have been. Grim was quick at working things out. "So you thought of that too?"

"Did wonder. Only, if it's her, Lily, why didn't she say so from the start? When she came to court? Why tell all those lies?"

"She did say that she'd gone to a chieftain for help and that he'd thought she was crazy. She probably thought that if she said she was over two hundred years old, Oran would just laugh at her."

"But she could have told you," Grim said. "You're a wise woman. Strange things don't scare you."

"She might have reasoned that the more of the truth she told, the less likely I was to agree to do this for her. If it is the truth. It's a bit hard to swallow. If she's Lily, she's known how to break the curse all along. And what would it say about her retainers, Senach and the others? Are they all more than two hundred years old as well? Bound to secrecy? What happens to them when the curse is broken?"

"Nothing in the manuscript about after," said Grim. "Not the way Flannan told it."

"Mm." For me, what happened afterward wouldn't matter. Flannan and I would be gone as soon as I'd completed the task. If Geiléis remembered to give me the bag of silver first, I'd leave it with Grim's belongings. The weakest element of this plan was Grim's dogged capacity for tracking me. In my heart, I knew he wasn't simply going to let me vanish. I could fool myself all I wanted with the notion that he would go home and settle down and meet some nice woman; I could reassure myself with the established fact that he could find work wherever he wanted, and friends, and a home. But he wouldn't. That was just the way it was.

"What?"

"I didn't say anything."

"You sighed, like you were fed up with it all. Had enough. Wanting to go home."

"Not yet. I came here to do a job and I'll see it through. Can't put all that training to waste, can I? But yes, I'll be happy to be gone." After a bit I added, "You?"

"You want an honest answer?"

"What sort of stupid question is that?" I blinked back sudden tears, furious with myself for losing control. Just as well it was dark. "When have I ever wanted you to tell a lie?"

"All right, then. I'd like us to be back home right now, and all this to be a bad dream. Same time, there's been a good part about coming here. Two good parts. First, those little folk. Seeing them, real as the thumb on your hand. Talking to them. That was magic. Second, St. Olcan's. The garden. The roof. The work, the brothers, teaching the young fellow. Hard for me to make myself do it. Tell you why another time. Thing is, it felt like I walked out into the light for a bit. Went somewhere I never thought I'd be again. Can't say I'm sorry about that.

Only thing is, the roof's not finished. Still got the ridge to do, and the creatures. And Midsummer Eve's the day after tomorrow."

I wished I had not asked him the question. I wished Midsummer Eve was right now and I could just get this over with.

"You all right?" His deep voice in the shadows.

"Fine. Well, not exactly fine, but I'll do. You never said. About St. Olcan's."

"You had other things on your mind. No need to dump more on."

Another silence. Then I said, "About Geiléis. Lily, if it's her. I'm not going to ask her. It can't make any difference now."

"Mm-hm."

"You know," I said, "there is time for you to finish the thatching. I'm not going to be able to practice with the ax for another whole day, and even if I was, Onchú or one of the others could help me tomorrow. They all seem to be getting friendlier the closer we get to Midsummer Eve; have you noticed? Even Senach has unbent slightly."

"No lies, right? Not even the kind that make folk feel better. Give me the choice, I'd leave the roof the way it is and be here keeping an eye on you. Hurts that I can't go up the tower with you. Hurts that I can't do my job."

"The best thing," I said carefully, "will be for you to keep busy. There's nothing to be gained from dwelling on what might go wrong. Work for your hands, that's the best cure. No reason why you shouldn't do a full day tomorrow, or if you're concerned I won't be ready, work a half day, then come back and put me through my paces. And you could work on the morning of Midsummer Eve. You'd be back well before I went to the tower; I think around dusk would be the right time, when the creature's growing quiet. Would that be long enough to get the roof done?"

"If it's dry. And if I make the creatures tomorrow night." He yawned.

"Another night without sleep."

"Not as if I'm not used to it."

"So will you do that?"

"I'll think about it."

"Good night, Grim. Sweet dreams."

"Night." He rolled over; became just one shadow among many. I wiped the tears from my cheeks and lay down again. Beside this, chopping off a monster's head was starting to look like child's play.

"Lady?"

I did not respond. He wasn't supposed to call me that anymore.

"Not crying, are you?"

"Of course not!"

"Just asking."

36

GRIM

Up on the roof again. Mind's full of Blackthorn and the monster and Midsummer Eve. Hands working more or less on their own, finishing off the ridging. Plan is to bring home a bundle of reeds, make the creatures tonight, put them up tomorrow first thing. Then straight back to Geiléis's place so I'm ready when Blackthorn heads out. Ready to run up the tower behind her, soon as the thorns let me through. Not sure how we'll all get over to the island. For me that doesn't matter. Unless there's a flood, I can wade. Maybe carry her over, like I did last time. Save her getting her feet wet.

"Grim!"

I look down and there's Brother Ríordán looking back up at me, shading his eyes against the sun. "Fine day," I say.

"It is. When you're finished, why not come and take a look at that book I mentioned? You know where we are."

I think about how filthy I am. I think about Blackthorn, and Midsummer Eve being tomorrow, and how we'll be heading home after. I think about Brother Galen and his little pictures curling up and going to ashes in the Norseman's campfire. The ridging's more or less done. I can wash under the pump. And the sun tells me there's still a bit of time to go until midday. Only one problem. That book's in the scriptorium. Stupid. She's ready to go up the tower and kill a monster, and I can't bring myself to step inside a room full of monks and books, not even to see something Brother Galen's made with his own hands. Something that's like a part of him still alive.

"Thanks," I call back down. "Won't be long."

I finish the job neat as I can. Check all along the ridge to be sure it's perfect. Then climb down and have a good wash. The scriptorium. I see it in my mind, only it's not this one at St. Olcan's, it's the one at St. Erc's, and the lovely books are torn and broken and all over blood. Monks lying where they've fallen, arms and legs askew, eyes staring at nothing, faces like tortured ghosts. Brother Galen. Bathsheba. Don't think I can do it. Got to try.

I stop to have a word with Brother Fergal in the garden. Know I'm putting off what I have to do. "Won't be here this afternoon," I say. "Need to be back at Lady Geiléis's. Things to get done."

"Midsummer," says Brother Fergal, looking solemn. "Yes, I have heard that Mistress Blackthorn will be making an attempt to silence the creature in the tower. Father Tomas is somewhat uncomfortable about the whole matter, and prefers that we don't discuss it. But please wish your friend our very best in her endeavor."

"Thanks." Not sure how much I should say, how much they know. "Wish she wasn't doing it, to tell the truth. Worried about her. But there it is. I'll pass on the good wishes. A few prayers wouldn't go astray. But then, she's a wise woman, so maybe not."

Brother Fergal smiles. "God stretches His merciful hand over all of us. The righteous man and the sinner, the faithful and those who have lost their faith."

"Those who know their path and those who are yet to find it."

"Ah. You remembered."

"Liked the sound of that. Only, Blackthorn knows her path. Always did. Straight and true."

"I will have a word with Him on her behalf. You might consider doing the same. God hears your prayers, Grim. Farewell, now."

Head for the scriptorium. Halfway there I remember the reeds I'll need to make the creatures. A few bundles left, stored in the barn. Get them first, makes sense. I turn back across the garden. There's Ripple waiting outside the pigeon loft, and there's Flannan coming out the door. Sends a lot of messages, that man. Always in and out of there. I give him a nod. He nods back. Looks as if his mind's on other things. Same could be said for me.

"Heading back early," I tell him. "Job's finished on the roof. For now."

"Finished." He's seeing me now. Question in his eyes.

"That's right. Planning to help Blackthorn with some moves this afternoon. So she's as ready as she can be tomorrow." Shut it, Grim, I tell myself. Babbling on, trying to put off the time when I open the scriptorium door, because my stupid mind's telling me what I'll see inside is a pile of dead men. "I'll be off, then. Just got to pick up a bundle of reeds. Make the creatures for the top, you know?"

"So it's not finished," says Flannan, though why he'd care one way or the other I can't think.

"All but. Make the creatures tonight, put them on in the morning, early. Then it's done. Back down to the tower in time to keep an eye on her." Can't seem to stop talking.

"I see. Please wish Blackthorn the best of luck from me," says Flannan. "I don't suppose I will see her now until it's all over."

What? He won't even come down to see her tonight and wish her well? Her old friend that she relies on?

He turns his back and walks away, with Ripple alongside. Just as well, since I was about to say something God wouldn't like me to say in a monastery.

I fetch the bundle of reeds. Good thing these fellows had the supply all gathered and sorted and stored; made the job a whole lot easier. A thing I like about the life in a monastery. Well organized. Tidy. You always know where you are. Until something goes so wrong there's no putting it right. Not ever.

Pretty soon I'm on the path back down to Geiléis's house, bundle on my shoulder, heart down in my boots somewhere. Just couldn't do it. Just couldn't make myself go in there, even though I know it'd only be monks writing. Even though Brother Ríordán's invited me to see Brother Galen's book. Even though I want to see that book so much it's like a pain in my insides. Fact is, alongside Blackthorn I'm a craven coward. Look what she's gone through. Husband and son burned to death before her eyes. A whole year in that cesspit of Mathuin's. There'll be other stuff too that she hasn't told me about. Thing is, every foul name she's been called, every hurt, every blow has made her that bit stronger. Strong like one of those winds that comes up and sweeps everything clean. Or a fire. A hot, angry fire roaring, *Get out of my way!*

This is how it is. Big fierce warrior with a weapon doesn't scare me. What scares me is the things in my head. Things that come out of the blue. I can be walking along and suddenly it's my worst day ever all over again and I'm seeing what I never wanted to see for the rest of my life. If Blackthorn could make a cure for that I'd thank her till my dying day. I know potions can't fix it. Not unless they're the kind that kill a man. Something I have to sort out myself. Thought I was going to do it today. Nearly sure of it. Failed again.

Forget that for now. Got to get a grip on myself. Don't want to walk into Geiléis's house with my face all sad. Set aside my worries; they're nothing beside what Blackthorn has to do tomorrow. So, leave the reeds for later. Take her through a training drill again, not as hard as yesterday—don't want her tired out. Go through the possibilities once or twice more. Tall monster, short monster, big monster, skinny monster. Sharp claws, maybe. Lots of teeth. Tail he can use as a weapon. She'll need to be quick. She'll need to be really quick. Well, she's light on her feet—that's something. Might ask the fellows if anyone's got a leather tunic small enough for her. A helmet too. Should ask her about magic, whether she can use it in a fight. You never know with a wise woman. Especially her.

Thinking all that through gets me back to Geiléis's. I put my bundle of reeds away. Blackthorn's not in our quarters. Can't find her anywhere. Feel my heart drop, which is stupid. Midsummer Eve's not until tomorrow. And she wouldn't go off to do it on her own anyway; that would be stupid. I go and ask Senach. He tells me she's over at the practice yard already. Which is good. Means Onchú and the others are helping her. I head off to join them. One more day. Morrigan's britches.

37

GEILÉIS

One more day. Less than a full day, since they would make the attempt in the morning. She would have preferred dawn, but they must wait until Grim was out of the house, or he would insist on following Blackthorn like a big clumsy shadow. She could not risk the possibility that he would get in the way somehow, stop the wise woman before she finished it. Who knew what would happen with the thorns, once she cut her way through? Besides, Blackthorn herself did not want her so-called companion there. She'd told him that the attempt would be made just before dusk. He would be out of the way, at St. Olcan's, until the deed was done.

As for the scholar, who knew what game he was playing? A man who would turn his back on an old friend could not be trusted. He too must be kept at a distance until it was all over.

All over. At last, the end of this. Could it be? There had been so many times of hope before, and so many bitter disappointments. She moved to her mirror and drew away the cloth that veiled it. The woman who gazed back at her seemed calm; there was no sign of the anticipation that gripped her body from head to toe. *Tomorrow. Oh, gods, let tomorrow be the end.*

A tap at her door. "Come in, Senach," she said without turning.

"It's Onchú, my lady." His broad-shouldered figure appeared in the mirror behind her.

"Ah." She turned. "How is Mistress Blackthorn progressing with her training?" The lengthy rehearsal was pointless; if the curse could be broken, it would be broken no matter how inept the woman was with her ax. She needed only to go up there and do it. Something her predecessors had not managed. But at least Blackthorn's activities in the practice yard were keeping her busy. If she was occupied in swinging her weapon, she might not spend too much time thinking. Questioning. Reaching conclusions.

"She's being fitted out with some protective garments, my lady, at Grim's request. We saw no harm in doing that."

"Perhaps it's a wise precaution. None of us can anticipate exactly how this will unfold. Onchú, Grim will be here this afternoon. Make sure the others are careful with their words."

"Yes, my lady."

"Another thing. Tomorrow, when we go to the island, I want a presence of guards at the house, watching out for Master Flannan. Should he come down from the monastery while the attempt is under way, he must be stopped. He must not reach the island. I don't want him speaking to Mistress Blackthorn again."

"Stopped?"

"By whatever means are required. Including lethal force."

"Yes, my lady. And if Grim should return early?"

"The same would apply."

There was a silence; then Onchú said, "Stopping Master Flannan would take, at most, two men. Grim would be another matter."

"I'm sure it is not beyond your capabilities, Onchú."

He bowed his head. "Yes, my lady. Lady Geiléis?"

"What is it?" There was a new note in his voice, one that unsettled her. They all knew what might be coming. They all wanted this brought to an end.

"I will obey your orders, of course. If you wish me to remain at the house myself, I will do so. But . . . I ask that you allow me to accompany you to the island. Myself and Donncha. The men are all expert. We have sufficient guards to watch the track and to deal with anyone who might happen to arrive."

"You've given me loyal service, Onchú. I wish I could reward it with something better than this. I will leave the deployment of guards to your expertise. Just make quite sure that neither Flannan nor Grim can reach Blackthorn before this comes to its conclusion."

"I will, my lady," Onchú said, somber-faced. "Thank you."

"It is hardly worthy of thanks. But I am glad you will be there. You and Donncha. Tell him I said so."

"Yes, my lady."

He left, closing the door behind him. Geiléis threw the cloth back over the mirror. How was she to spend this day, this last full day of the curse? Odd that now, after the years of waiting, on the brink of success time seemed to have slowed; it was as if the day were a year long. She moved to her storage chest and opened it. There had never been a maid-servant, only Senach and his faithful men, tending to everything. And Caisín, of course. Caisín was clever with the needle and kept Geiléis's clothing in excellent condition. But she did not like having Caisín too close; the girl made her feel guilty, even after so long. Geiléis had learned to dress herself. To look after her own hair. She was no longer the privileged child she had been when she first saw a light in the Tower of Thorns and climbed out her window to investigate.

Tomorrow she would see him again. Tomorrow she would climb the tower stair and he would be there waiting, a monster no longer. She had changed over the years, though in that respect the curse had been kind—she looked perhaps two-and-thirty, no more. Her skin still pale and fresh; her hair still glossy. But what of Ash? The long punishment must surely have taken a toll on him. He had been forced to endure the unendurable.

"It doesn't matter," she murmured, lifting one gown after another from the chest. They were layered with lavender sprigs; the smell was wholesome and sweet. "It doesn't matter how you look. Only that you will be free. Only that I can put my arms around you at last, at long last. Only that I can say *I love you* face-to-face."

Ah! Here it was. The gown Caisín had made at her special request: a simple style, fashioned in finespun wool dyed willow green, edged with darker ribbon. It was twin to the one young Lily had worn on the day she tried to wade to the island and nearly drowned, and Ash ran down from the tower to save her. The day she first felt his arms around her. In her memory, that day shone bright. It was innocence and first love and summertime. It was joy and awakening. She was not that bright-eyed sixteen-year-old anymore. But she would wear the gown, in honor of that girl and her long-ago dreams.

She draped the garment over the chest, ready for the morning. It was not yet time for the story. Still day, still the endless day. But she climbed to her high window anyway, to gaze out over the trees and listen to the sad voice from the tower. To shape in her mind the words she would speak to him later, as dusk fell on his last day in the Tower of Thorns.

Once upon a time there was a girl named Lily, who was the apple of her father's eye . . .

38

BLACKTHORN

Neither of us slept much that night. Grim's big, clever hands were busy with his bundle of reeds and his sharp knife, working minor miracles. As for me, my body was protesting after the day's unusual activity, and my mind was teeming with misgivings, unanswered questions, and—though I didn't like to admit it even to myself—hideous visions of how this whole thing might go wrong. I must have been crazy ever to agree to it. Two days of training were hardly going to equip me to defeat a monster, even if that monster had once been a man. Any one of Geiléis's guards would have beaten me in a fight within the count of ten. Five, most likely. And they were men.

We didn't talk. Not much. I kept the fire going and made a brew or two. Grim sat in the light of two lanterns, narrowing his eyes over the intricate work. Raven, dove, cat, fish, that was what he'd planned. Only when the night had worn on until it was nearly dawn, and I lay on my bed watching him through half-closed eyes, I saw that the last creature was not going to be a fish after all. Unless he was so tired that he had forgotten a fish does not have four legs.

"What's that one?"

My question made him start. "Thought you were asleep," he said.

"I can't sleep. There's too much going on in my mind. What is that, Grim? It looks like no fish I've ever seen."

"Changed my mind." He used his knife to feather the reeds that formed the tail, making it into a brush. "Red fox. This one's for you."

"Me? Why would St. Olcan's want a symbol of an unbeliever, and a woman at that?" I could understand why he'd chosen a fox. Apart from the obvious—red hair—a fox was wary, aloof, inclined to snap. Fiercely protective of her own. Cunning, folk said. I didn't feel very cunning right now.

"Maybe they wouldn't," said Grim, forming the fox's ears into a more pointed shape with a quick twist of the fingers. "But I'm the one making the roof. Fox'll remind them of what you did. Not just for them, for the whole district. Breaking this curse, that's no small thing."

"I haven't done anything yet. But thanks. You've earned a fresh brew. I'll get up and make it. I might even creep out to the kitchen and find you some food. That was a long night's work. You'll need to catch some sleep later."

"Nah. Want to get these up on the scriptorium roof and be back as quick as I can. Make sure I'm here when you need me. Time enough to sleep after. When it's all over." He glanced across at me. "Unless you were planning to pack up and leave straightaway."

I froze, thinking that he had somehow guessed what Flannan and I planned. But no, of course not. He meant himself and me. The two of us going back to court. Answering would require me to tell another lie. I got up, found the ladle, refilled the kettle from the bucket of clean water, making sure my back was turned to him. "Not today. It'll be too late. And we'll all be tired out, no matter what happens. I imagine Geiléis will be happy to house us for another night, especially if I really do manage to break the curse. She offered me silver; did I tell you? We should take it, when this is over. It would be useful back home."

"Lady," said Grim, which was a sure sign he was heading into deeper waters, somewhere I did not want to follow, since my self-control was not at its best right now.

"Don't call me that. I don't want to think about that time. There's enough churning around in my head already."

"You don't have to do this," said Grim. "She never asked you, did she? Not straight-out. So you're not bound to it." A weighty pause, during which I said nothing at all. "Thing is," he went on, "no matter how brave you are, no matter how much you practice, you could . . . you could come to grief. It's not just cutting off this thing's head. It's a curse. Magic involved. Anything could happen."

"What are you suggesting? That I tell Geiléis, *I'm sorry; I've changed my mind*, and head off home? She's counting on this. They all are. Even the creature in the tower. This is his only chance in fifty years to become a man again. And the little folk—I'll be setting them free, letting their king out of the thorns. They helped me. I should do it even if it's just for them." The idea of turning tail and fleeing back to Cahercorcan was all too appealing right now, not only because of the thing in the tower, but also because of Mathuin of Laois, and the perilous mission that would take me south tomorrow, far away from all this. Far from Dalriada, and from Lady Flidais, who was expecting me back. Far from the cottage at Winterfalls and young Emer who was such a good learner. Far from Grim.

"Thing is," he said, using his knife to trim a few stray ends of reed from the little fox, "what the wee folk said to *me* was go home. Both of us go home."

I stared at him. "They did? When was this? Why didn't you tell me?"

"Back a while. That day when you told the clurichaun story. Thought it might be all in my head. The curse, you know, making me crazy."

For a while we didn't talk. I made a brew; he set his handiwork aside and cleared up, sweeping the remnant reeds into a neat pile and tipping them into the kindling basket. He wiped down the table, then went outside to wash his hands. I caught a glimpse of the sky when he came back in. I didn't think I was imagining the first faint traces of day.

"Too late now," Grim said, sitting down on the bench. "To ask the wee folk about it. I know that. One says go. One says stay. Could be they're like clurichauns, can't agree about anything."

"Or one choice might be better for us, and the other one better for them. Grim, I don't want to talk about this anymore. By the end of today it'll be all over, one way or another."

"Be a lot happier if I could come up the tower with you."

"We know you can't, so there's no point worrying about it."

Interesting, how silence can sometimes say so much more than words. He sat there with his elbows on his knees, looking at the floor. I tried not to think about the fact that after today's breakfast I would never see him again. Ordered myself sharply not to let tears fall.

"I'll go and find us some food," I said. "Where's that candle?"

But when I tiptoed through the house and gently pushed open the kitchen door, it was to find the room lit by lamps and all the household serving folk gathered there, sitting or standing with cups of mead in their hands. The remains of a modest meal were on the table, with a neat stack of used platters. They'd been talking in hushed voices, but the conversation ceased as I went in.

"You're up early," I said, noting the pale faces, the tight lips. "I was just looking for something for Grim to eat—he's been up all night making the finishing touches for his roof."

"Let me find you something, Mistress Blackthorn." Senach moved with his usual smooth competence to the larder, picking up a tray as he went. "I hope you got some rest."

"I haven't slept. But thanks."

Nobody commented, but I guessed it had been the same for all of them. They had spent the last night of the curse together, in what I imagined must be a mixture of hope and doubt. I suspected that Geiléis would be awake in her quarters, as tight with anticipation as I was. Perhaps she was up at her high window, waiting for the dawn. Thinking that this might be the last day that voice rang out to play with folk's minds and to turn all within her holdings sour and sad.

"I hope I can do it," I said quietly. "I can't promise I'll succeed. But I can promise to do my best for you all."

"Let me carry this through for you, Mistress Blackthorn." Senach was by my side, the tray in his hands laden with sufficient food to make breakfast unnecessary.

"Best if I take it myself. But thank you." I set my candle on the only free corner of the tray and headed back.

We ate the food, though neither of us had any appetite. We tidied up and got dressed. Dau came to the door and asked if we wanted breakfast and we said no. Grim packed his reed creations carefully into two bags. Raven and dove, cat and fox. I watched him. He suggested we might pack up the rest of our things, since we'd most likely be leaving tomorrow morning, and I said no need, there would be plenty of time in the evening. Then we waited. All too soon the sun came up, the creature in the tower began its daily lament, and it was time for Grim to head for St. Olcan's where, according to him, they would be singing Prime and after that sitting down to breakfast. The pattern of daily prayers meant monks were up before first cockcrow.

"I'll walk out to the courtyard with you," I said.

"If you want."

He didn't know this was good-bye forever. And if I had any wits at all, I'd make sure I did nothing to put that idea into his mind. We walked out side by side, he with his two bags and his knife in his belt, I in my ordinary clothes. The leather breastplate and cap the guards had fashioned for me were in the bedchamber. I was not quite sure yet if I would wear them; it felt like pretending to be something I was not.

At the small gate in the wall Grim halted. "See you later, then. Be a good idea to catch some sleep this morning, if you can."

"I'll try." I ached to stand on tiptoes and kiss his cheek, to give him a hug, to tell him without words that I was sorry. To say that if I did one worthwhile thing in my life, it would be going to Laois and seeing Mathuin brought to justice, and that I had to take the chance Flannan had offered. And that I was leaving him behind, not because I did not want him, but because, in the long run, he would be so much better off without me. But if I touched him I would cry, and he would decide he couldn't go to St. Olcan's after all, and I wouldn't be able to get away without him. "I hope the monks like your creatures. They don't know how fortunate they are to have such fine work for their roof."

Grim smiled. "Should be good luck for the place. For everyone who works in there. Scribes, scholars, folk that love books and learning. I'll be getting on. Sooner I finish the work, sooner I'll be back. You all right?"

"Fine," I said. "Or as fine as I can be with this thing to do. See you later, then."

He walked out the gate and was gone. Just like that. I pressed my lips tight together. *You're a warrior. Be strong. You managed just fine without him before, and you can now.* I turned and walked back to the house. We would wait just a little, to be quite sure he was gone. Then we would head for the tower.

39

GRIM

Shouldn't take long. Want to do a proper job, not rush things, but all the same. Should be back at Geiléis's by midday at the latest. Plenty of time. That's what I'm thinking, walking up through the woods. Hear the bell ringing for Prime. Hear the thing in the tower wailing. Wonder if it knows today's the day. If *he* knows. Poor fellow. Poxy life that must be. Two hundred years of it. Doesn't bear thinking of. Not the best for her either. Lily. Geiléis, if it's really her. Like being stuck in your worst nightmare forever, or what feels like forever. Having to listen to him and not being able to do a thing. The woman that thought up that spell was a nasty piece of work.

Been hoping I might catch sight of the wee folk, maybe have a word about what's going to happen. But no; no sign of them today. They know, of course. That today's Midsummer Eve. That Blackthorn's going to give this a try. I talk to them anyway, going past the spot where I turned back once before.

"If you're there, today's the day. Hope it turns out well. Hope everything's better for you, afterward. Hope you get your king back safe and sound. Kind folk, you are. Glad you showed yourselves to me. I'll never forget that, not till the day I die."

Nothing comes back to me, but that doesn't mean they're not there, looking and listening. I get an idea, something that would be good to do. There's bread and cheese in my bag, in case I get peckish on the job. I get it out, break it up, lay a good share on a flat stone by the path. "For you," I say to the empty air, feeling a bit stupid. "Thanks for what you've done. Can't have been easy." Blackthorn's told me about the basket going up the tower and the wee man she saw on the island. If Flannan's document is right, they've been looking after that fellow, Ash, ever since he first got trapped up there. All these years.

Enough of that; need to get on. I'm shouldering the one bag and bending to pick up the other when I spot something on the path up ahead. Not one of *them*; something smaller. Something hurt. A bird, lying on its side, fluttering a wing, trying to get on its feet. A pigeon.

I go close, kneel down, take a good look. Bird's terrified. Eyes wild. Struggling and struggling, can't get up. I push down memories, move slow, take my time. Little leather tube fastened to its leg. One of Brother Eoan's messenger birds. That leg looks all right; other leg looks all right. Could be the bird's fallen foul of a hawk or owl. Been dropped for some reason, still alive. Can't see any blood. I reach down, gentle as I can, and slip one hand underneath. Other hand on top, lift nice and slow. Looks like it's the wing. Broken feathers. Handled the birds often enough at St. Erc's. Not the kind of hurt where the only thing to do is wring the creature's neck and end the pain. This one could be patched up. Might only need some peace and quiet, a bit of a rest. Brother Eoan will know what to do with the wing.

"Come on, then," I say. "Let's get you home."

Can't carry everything with the bird in my hands, so I leave the bag with fox and cat by the side of the track. Plan is, take the pigeon to St. Olcan's, then run back down and fetch the bag. Won't take long.

. . .

I'm in luck. Brother Eoan's not in the chapel; he's in the pigeon loft filling up the containers with water and seed. Birds are clustering around, wanting their food, making those little soft sounds they do. Wonder what they're saying to each other?

"Found this one in the woods," I tell him. "Broken wing, I think."

He comes to take the bird quick, carries it through to a smaller room with pegs to hang things from and shelves to store things on. Everything to look after the birds, and stuff for the messages too, those leather carriers, so small and neat, just room enough to fit a scrap of parchment rolled tight as tight. First thing Eoan does is lay the bird on a table, on a cloth, while he has a good look at it.

"Unfasten the cord, will you, Grim?"

While he holds the bird still, I fiddle with the fine cord that holds the letter carrier in place. Manage to get it off the leg, but I've undone the wrong bit so the message falls out. "Sorry," I say, picking up the scrap of parchment. All covered over with tiny little writing, a wonder anyone can read the thing.

"That message will need to go back to Master Flannan," says Brother Eoan. He's checking the flight feathers on the damaged wing, running his fingers along each one in turn. "This is one of the Laois birds. He's the only one who's been using them."

All of a sudden I'm cold. "Laois?"

"From the foundation at St. Brigid's."

Something not right about this. Seems all right on the surface but it's not; I just know. "Long way for a pigeon to fly," I say. "You'd need to be in a rush to hear someone's Latin translation, to send it with a bird."

Brother Eoan is smiling. "This one is doubly fortunate. Whatever caught her let her go before too much damage was done. And the next person to walk by knew exactly the right thing to do. She'll be fine. I can repair the wing. She'll need rest. No more long flights for quite some time. As for St. Brigid's, as well as their scholarly correspondence the brethren there send and receive messages on behalf of their local chieftain. I believe they're located quite close to his stronghold. Muadan, Maolan, something like that."

"Mathuin," I say. Something sinks its talons into my belly and squeezes tight. "Mathuin of Laois."

40

BLACKTHORN

"Are you ready, Mistress Blackthorn?"

Geiléis herself was at my door, come to remind me of my mission in the tower. Hah! As if I needed any reminding that today was the day of reckoning. Here I was in my leather breast-piece, with the ax on my back—my aching shoulders told me how many times I had practiced getting the wretched thing quickly into my hand—and my knife in my belt. Ready? Hardly. Who could ever be ready for this? But I was doing it, ready or not.

That reminded me. True love's tears. I'd picked a small supply of the leaves and dried them; they were wrapped in a handkerchief. "I'll just be a moment more," I said as I put the little bundle away in my pouch. What possible use the herb might be I did not know, but if I was heading out to break a fey curse, taking the little folk's advice seemed a good idea. I cast a glance around the chamber. Anything I'd forgotten? A mage's staff would be handy, or a cloak of invisibility.

"Mistress Blackthorn?"

I snatched one last item for luck, then followed her out. Stuffed the red scarf into the pouch as I went, on top of the herbs. That scarf had its own story. Grim had bought it for me at a fair, coming north last summer. I'd thought that inappropriate and had probably made my feelings obvious. The scarf had been a key clue in solving the mystery of Branoc the baker, who had abducted and hurt a young woman. It had served as a good-bye and as a call to action. The scarf wasn't going to scare off enemies or behead the monster for me, but I took it anyway.

The entire household was assembled in the courtyard to watch us go. Nobody said, *Good luck*, or, *You can do it*. Nobody clapped me on the shoulder or offered a reassuring smile.

Senach was pale and shaky, quite unlike his usual self. When he spoke, his voice was choked with emotion. "Farewell, Lady Geiléis. Our hearts go with you."

There was a murmur from the others, serving folk and guards alike. The men-at-arms made a gesture I had seen before, laying a clenched fist over the heart.

"Come, then," said Geiléis. "Onchú, lead the way. Do you wish to block your ears, Mistress Blackthorn?"

I shook my head. I would need all my senses alert.

The forest felt different this morning. The day was clear and bright, but everything was somehow . . . veiled. Uncertain. It seemed to me that pathways might shift, trees switch places, sun abruptly turn to storm. The magic was stronger, as if the land knew this was a time of change. I wondered if the little folk were watching as we passed, thinking this might be the end of their long servitude. Remembering the ferryman, I asked, "How do we get across to the island? I'll do better in the tower with dry shoes." It was hard to keep my voice steady; already, my heart was going like a war drum.

"We have a boat, Mistress Blackthorn," said Donncha. "It's been long out of use, but the men have made it watertight. It will take all of us at once."

"I see."

We reached the ford. Today, the water looked shallow enough for a person to wade safely all the way over. But it was deeper around the island, and with so much at stake it would be foolish to take unnecessary risks. Onchú led us downstream to the point where the distance to the island was least, and there indeed was a boat, no tiny fey craft this time but a sturdy rowing boat drawn up on the bank in readiness. I stepped in; Geiléis did the same. The men pushed the vessel into the shallows, then climbed aboard. Donncha rowed. Onchú was alert to danger, scanning the woods all around as we crossed the narrow channel. The creature's voice was piercing, painful to the ears. Could he see us coming?

The boat scraped onto the other shore, and we were on the island. I accepted Donncha's help to get out with my feet dry; beside me, Geiléis had allowed Onchú to assist her. Now he offered her a handkerchief, and I saw that she was weeping. She turned away to wipe her eyes, then reached to untie her cloak and toss it into the boat. There was I in my uncouth garb of working gown under leather fighting garments, my hair covered by the cap the men had made for me, the ax on my back. And there was she in a gown befitting a princess from an ancient tale. It was simple and flowing, its hue a delicate green, its decoration a border of darker ribbon. The garment fitted her perfectly, subtly showing the curves of her body. Now, with one impatient hand, she untied the fastening that held her hair in a single plait, and shook the long fair tresses out over her shoulders. If I had doubted up until this moment that she was Lily, I doubted it no longer.

She looked up toward the high window. She said something, but the voice from the tower drowned it. He was not so much wailing now as shouting. Trying to say something, trying to form words we could understand. But all I could hear was pain, grief, longing.

Geiléis turned toward me. Pointed, gestured. *This way.* I did not say I knew already where the door was, or that the unerring path she took to that spot told me more than she realized. It was too late for doubts. Too late for accusations. Too late for anything but getting on with the job. Here I was, just below the high window; this was where the little man had sent up the basket. Geiléis stepped away, leaving me on my own. Now it really was time.

My palms were too sweaty to hold anything steady. As for my heartbeat, if I'd been tending to anyone with such a fast rate I'd have thought them about to expire on the spot. *Slow your breathing*, I told myself. *Concentrate. Call upon your training. It may have been long ago, but a wise woman never forgets. This is a good thing you're doing. A good thing. And when it's done, you're going on your true mission, the one you've been waiting for. Breathe deep. Strike hard. Strike true.*

I faced the hedge of thorns. I had thought perhaps the creature might fall silent. But his strangled attempts to speak continued as I drew my knife. I shut out the memory of Onchú's scars, and Caisín's, and of the man who had died from his wounds. I gritted my teeth and cut into a branch.

There was a groaning sound, then a cracking and splitting; pieces of wood flew through the air all around me, making me duck. I shut my eyes.

The noise ended; the creature in the tower fell silent. Now there was a pathway before me, arched with thorns and just wide enough for one woman to walk along without being damaged. At its other end, the door to the tower stood ajar. The hedge had opened to let me through.

No matter how many old stories a person knows, there is no preparation for finding yourself right in the middle of one. I drew a breath and moved forward. One step. Another step. The pathway ahead remained open. But behind me I heard the thorny branches snapping back into place, barring the way to anyone who wanted to follow.

Red flowers and white bloomed side by side on the bushes; underfoot the earth was broken and uneven, as if the hedge had pulled back its roots to make the path. Deeper in, I thought I saw a scatter of bones where some poor creature had crept in long ago and been trapped. What if—no, I would not consider the possibility that the thorns would bar my way out. If I completed the task, the curse would be broken. I just had to cut off someone's head. I just had to get my mind into the fighting mode Grim had spoken of, where all you thought of was killing the other fellow before he killed you.

I was at the door. A glance over my shoulder showed the hedge unbroken. I could not see Geiléis and the guards. From the tower, silence.

I stepped inside. The light from the open door illuminated the lower part of the spiral stair; I could not see any light from above, though the high window had been open. And I hadn't brought a lantern. I'd have to feel my way up. *Deep breath.* I tucked my skirt into my belt and headed for the steps, only to trip over more bones—a jumble of bigger ones this time. Was that a human skull? *Don't think about it, Blackthorn.* Two twists of the stair and I was in total darkness. I imagined the creature listening as I approached. Standing at the top, waiting. This was crazy. I needed both hands to feel my way; I could not unsheathe the ax until I reached the top. Gods, it was dark!

But no. There was a light now, like a tiny lantern a pace or two ahead of me, bobbing from step to step, leading me. Someone was showing me the way. Someone small, in a hooded cape. I could have wept with the relief of not being alone in here. But I gritted my teeth, reminded myself that I was a warrior, and made a steady way upward.

Just as I reached the high chamber, the little light blinked out and the small personage was gone. But there was light here, from the window that opened onto the forest. And against that light stood a figure. I could not see him clearly, but it was evident that this monster was roughly of human size and shape. Morrigan's curse. I unsheathed the ax; weighed it in my hand. The chamber was coming into better view as my eyes adjusted to the light. A bed, a water bucket, a flask and cup, a platter. A basket with a familiar pattern along the side. A neatly folded blanket. The place was orderly.

The creature stepped forward. A man; or surely something that had once been a man. My fear vanished. I bled for him. His face was indeed monstrous, the jaws crammed with crooked teeth, the skin as rough and scaly as tree bark, the features . . . It was as if he had been beaten so hard everything was askew. No wonder he could not form words. I could not imagine how he could eat and drink. He was clad in a loose shirt that came to his knees. Every part of his exposed skin was covered with those harsh scales; his fingers were like stiff claws.

"Ash," I said. "I am Blackthorn. I've come to help you." Not knowing how this would fall out. Knowing only that it was a magical curse, and that magic was full of surprises.

He moved toward me; my grip tightened on the ax. There was a bench two strides away from me. When he reached it he knelt. Put his misshapen hands up awkwardly, as if his whole body was stiff and slow, to push his long dark hair away from his neck. Bowed his head onto the bench and closed his eyes, ready for the blow.

Strike hard. Strike true. "I'm sorry," I whispered. "Lily is waiting for you." Then I lifted the ax, my eyes full of tears, and struck the merciful blow.

Everything shimmered and shifted. I could not hold my balance and fell sprawling onto the floor; the ax dropped from my hands. Outside, the birds screamed. My breathing came in gasps. My vision was so blurred I saw only a fuzz of shifting shapes. But I could hear. I heard a man's voice, hoarse and shaky, saying, "Thank you. Oh, gods. Oh, gods, at last."

With an effort I sat up. I rubbed my eyes. Things settled and came clear. I made my myself look at what I had wrought. There was no gore, no severed head, no body pumping lifeblood. Only a dark-haired man of around five-and-thirty, gaunt and pale, clad in a long loose shirt. It was Ash, and the curse was broken.

He reached out a hand to help me up. "I'm sorry," he said. "I'm so sorry."

I had no time to ask what he meant, for there was a sound of footsteps from the stair, and in ran Geiléis in her lovely green gown, with her golden hair shimmering around her like an enchanted cloak. For a moment I saw them as they had been, young and in love and full of desperate hope. Then Lily reached Ash, and they threw their arms around each other and clung tight, like an image of lovers from an old tale of magic and wonder. Which, in a way, they were.

There was someone else there too. A little man in a hooded cape, standing up on a stool to reach the tabletop, pouring something from the flask to the cup. For Ash had not been quite alone during his long, long imprisonment.

It was over. No further need for me here. I would leave the tower, return to the house, find Flannan and head south. South for Laois and Mathuin. I just had to get up and walk down the stair. But my body was curiously unwilling to obey me. I felt weary beyond measure, as stiff in my joints as if I had spent a whole day in the saddle. I reached up a hand to brush stray hair from my face and saw a shadow creeping over my skin, like a scaly, hideous garment. My fingers were curling into gnarled claws. I tried to speak, but my lips and tongue would not form the words. Could not.

I'm sorry, Ash had said. *I'm so sorry.* Because he had known. And she had known. She'd known all the time. The curse was not broken after all. I sank to my knees, put my disfigured face in my ruined hands and wailed.

41

GRIM

"I'll find him," I say. Take the message from Brother Eoan. Red fury's rising in me, can't let it get a grip, got to stay calm, think things through. Might be a false alarm. Might be harmless. The claws in my gut are telling me it's not. Why would that fellow be sending messages to Mathuin of Laois? Only one reason I can think of.

I run. See the brothers coming out of the chapel, can't see Flannan, head straight for the scriptorium. Message feels like it's burning my hand. *Stupid Bonehead, why couldn't you learn to read?* I'm there. Hammer on the door. Yell, "Flannan! You in there?" Tell myself not to kill the bastard until he's had a chance to speak. Can't help Blackthorn if I don't know what's going on.

Door opens. One of the brothers, Ríordán's assistant. Turns a bit white when he sees me. I look in past him. No Flannan. Only Brother Ríordán, working on a manuscript. He puts down his quill and stands up. "Flannan is not here," he says. "Grim, what has happened?"

Before I can think, I'm in there and spilling out what I know. Words falling over each other. That someone wants to harm Blackthorn and that I think Flannan's up to no good. That I need to find the truth fast, because today's the day she's going up the tower, and I know deep in my bones that it's all linked up somehow.

"Dathal," says Ríordán to his assistant, calm as calm, "go and find Flannan, will you? Bring him straight here."

Dathal heads off, and it's just the two of us.

"Now," says Ríordán, "take a deep breath and tell me again, slowly."

"But—"

"I know it's urgent. But it can be wise to allow yourself time to breathe. When was Mistress Blackthorn going to the tower?"

"Later. Dusk. Have to tell her—have to warn her—"

"And we will," says Ríordán.

That "we" calms me a bit. I go through the story again. Leave out some things, like Blackthorn and me being locked up together. Have to say Mathuin's name or it wouldn't make sense. That feels risky. But the thing is, I trust Ríordán. Not just because he's a monk, but because he was kind to me when a lot of folk wouldn't be. By the time I get through it all, Dathal's back.

"Flannan's gone," he says. "Packed up his things and left, sometime between last night's supper and this morning. Nobody saw him go."

Shit. Now I'll never catch up with the bastard. Gone where?

Ríordán's looking over at the shelves, where there's a row of little chests like the one I found in the wall. "He hasn't taken his documents. This place was locked all night, and I have the key." He's got a thinking look.

"What would be in his box?" I ask.

"Anything he was working on: transcriptions, letters, notes. Possibly correspondence he had received. You want to look?"

"Thing is, I can't read. You know that." Now he's going to say it's private property and he can't show me.

"I will read this one," Ríordán says, looking at the message that bird was carrying. "And then make a decision." One thing he's not, and that's hasty. But he can help me, so I keep quiet, just bite my nails and try to stop shaking. I'm scared—that's the truth. Scared and angry. Like something's ripping me up inside.

He reads it out. "To Mathuin of Laois: for his eyes only. My lord, it appears the target will be eliminated by midsummer, without the need for any further action on my part. Should the event I anticipate not occur, I will revert to the previous plan and bring her to Laois. She has already taken the bait. Your servant, Flannan."

What in the name of all that's holy is this? The lying bastard! The vile two-faced traitor! She trusted him. He was her friend. I get to my feet, fists clenched, ready to kill someone.

"Brother Conall," says Ríordán, quite sharp. "Sit down. Whatever this is, you will not solve the problem by giving way to your anger. Dathal, will you leave us for a while? Please do not speak of this matter outside these four walls."

"Are you sure?" says Dathal, giving me a nervous look.

"I am. Grim and I are friends. Go now."

When he's gone, Ríordán says, "Tell me what you think this means."

"He wants to kill her. Blackthorn. She's the threat. Because wherever she goes, she'll speak up for truth and justice, and Mathuin's her main target. She got away from him once before. He's sent Flannan to hunt her down. Someone she trusts. An old friend. Someone she'd never suspect."

"You shock me. If Flannan has such evil intent, why has he not done Mistress Blackthorn some mischief before now? There must have been opportunities—you've all been at Bann some time."

Opportunities. Yes, there have been, all those times when the two of them went off for their private talks. But always at Geiléis's house. He might have been able to do it, but he'd never have got away with it. Not with me around. I explain this to Ríordán.

"Eliminated," he says. "That seems clear enough, though I find it hard to . . . What is this talk of taking the bait?"

"Don't know about that part." Think I can guess, and if I'm right that man's the worst kind of scum on earth. But that doesn't matter for now. "The rest of it, it says midsummer; it has to be about the tower and what she's going to do there. He knows something he hasn't told us. She's in danger. Deadly danger. Will you open the box? Could be that document, the one with the curse, is in there."

"The document you found is locked away with the other most precious manuscripts."

"No, the translation, the copy he made. We never saw it; he just told us what was in it. Could you read it to me?" Time's passing, more and more time. Can't stop shivering. Won't be much use to her if I don't get a grip on myself. "Please. I beg you."

He stands there a moment, thinking in that scholarly way, and I try hard not to leap up again and shake him into action. Not his fault, any of it. I think about Brother Galen and how kind he was to me. Take a deep breath. Who'd have thought keeping still could be so hard?

"Very well," says Ríordán, and goes to take the box from the shelf. "Locked, of course; but I imagine you will be able to open it for me."

Something to do; that's better. He finds me some tools, things they use for binding books—seen them before. Try not to damage the box, nice piece in walnut. My hands are steady enough now. A tap here, a tap there and it's done. Not a scratch.

Ríordán opens the box. Takes his time over sorting out what's in there. I can see there aren't any pigeon messages. Nothing from Mathuin. But he lifts out a bigger piece of parchment, rolled neatly and tied with a red cord. "This may be the one you're interested in," he says. "Let me see . . . Ah yes, I believe this is his translation of the old document. Shall I read you the entire contents?"

"Please. He didn't show you before?"

"He told me the gist of it, when I pressed him. About the curse. About the fifty years. That a woman could break it."

He doesn't even know as much as I do. But how much of what Flannan told us was lies anyway? "Read it. Please."

He does. It's the story I know already, Lily and Ash and the fey curse. The Tower of Thorns, the little folk, the darkness come over the whole place. Midsummer Eve. Only it's in fancy language, like poetry; like a grand old tale. He gets to the end. A willing woman has to hack a way through the thorns and go up the tower. When she gets there she has to cut off the creature's head. Then Ash will be restored to himself and the lovers will be reunited.

Brother Ríordán reads that bit—no surprises yet—and I think we're going to get nowhere. Then he says, still bending over the box, "Oh. Wait."

He takes out another sheet of parchment. Only a few words on it. "A second page," he says. "*When this is done, the doom will fall upon the assailant.*"

Takes a while for it to sink in. I look at him; he looks at me.

"Doom," he says. "What doom?"

But I'm already out the door and running.

Pelting along, trees whirling round me. Breath coming hard. I trip over something, nearly fall, kick it away, keep running. The bag with the creatures. Cat and fox. Why did I waste time fiddling with that rubbish when I should have had my eyes and ears open for danger? Why didn't I see what that man was from the start?

Running on, keeping on, got to find her, warn her before it's too late. Make sure he doesn't get to her first. Slipped away, has he? Don't think so. He'll be around somewhere, watching and waiting. Can't leave till he's seen if it's worked, whatever it is. Can't leave before he knows if he's done the job. That bastard! He's probably been Mathuin's tool ever since Cass died, and that whole story about escaping is one big lie. How dare he do that to her? How dare he?

Halfway down to Geiléis's house and something happens. It's like the air shivers and everything changes, faster than the blink of an eye. And the thing in the tower goes silent. That's when I know she's told me the wrong time of day. She's not waiting for dusk; she's there now, hacking through that hedge, climbing those steps, walking into that room ready to cut off its head. With wretched Flannan in Mathuin's pay, grabbing some kind of chance to finish her off. Can't move for a moment. Eyes all tears, stupid fool, what help's that going to be? Might not be too late. Might not be. Let it not be.

Faster, faster. Wish I could fly. Why can't I fly? Why can't I be there now, now, when she needs me? Run right past Geiléis's house, don't bother to stop, run all the way to the river. Water's low. Can't see anyone on the island. No noise from the tower, but the thorns—there's a gap in the thorns, a big one. She's gone up. She's gone up, and now the wailing starts again. Only it's different. It's someone else's voice. It's—no. Oh, no.

I shout the foulest oath I can think of. Plunge straight into the river. Who cares how deep it is? If my hunch is right, pretty soon drowning's going to look like a good choice. Wet up to the chest. Haul myself out on the island, run for the tower. But the thorns are closing—they're creaking and clinging like claws, and the gap's too narrow now to let a man through. I want to hurl myself at them, bite and rip and fight them. How dare they, how dare they! Something stops me. Could be Brother Galen, smiling over his little pictures, stroking Bathsheba on his knee. Could be that I've remembered something important. I reach into my pouch— sodden from the dunking—and fish out the whistle the wee folk gave me. Lift it to my lips and blow as hard as I can. If this isn't the last resort, I don't know what is.

"Ah," says a wee gray prickly man by my knee. Wasn't there a moment earlier. Looks like he stepped out of the thorns. "Needing a bit of help, were you?"

"Please! Let me through! Quick, quick, before it's too late!"

The wee man clicks his fingers, and the thorns part again, slowly. Like they don't really want to. Like they might snap together at any moment if they don't fancy the look of me.

"Go," says the little one, though the gap still looks too narrow, only big enough for an ordinary-sized man. "Quick."

I do as I'm told. Charge through, snagging my tunic, ripping my trousers, scratching my hands. My hair catches and I just keep on. Leave a clump of it behind on the thorns. And I'm at the door, and running up the stairs, hearing those cries all the way. And I'm in the high chamber at the top. Not knowing what I'll see. Not knowing what I'll do. Full of fear and fury and a sadness that goes so deep it's got no bottom to it. Because I do know. I knew the moment I heard that voice. The curse has come round in a circle, only this time it's not Lily and Ash; it's us. It's me and Blackthorn.

This is what I see. The ax lying on the floor. Light coming in from the open window. A green gown. Something white near it, maybe a shirt. Next to them, more old bones and rubbish. A skull. Two skulls. Little men and women in cloaks, kneeling in a circle.

And over the other side of the room, crouching in the shadows, something else. Someone else, crying. Someone with bright red hair and a leather cap, and the face of a monster. Someone in a gown and a breast-piece, with a body all twisted with pain, someone with hands like claws. It's her. It's the worst thing come true.

For a bit I can't move. My heart's all knotted up, so tight I can't breathe. Maybe it's a nightmare and I'll wake up soon. But it's not. I know it's not.

She must see it in my face. What I'm feeling. No hiding it. I walk over, crouch down beside her, and she pushes me away with those ghastly hands, making sounds like a creature in its death throes. Her mouth's got too many teeth, her jaw's all out to the side, there's no way she can speak, but she's trying to tell me something; she's struggling to get the words out. Pointing, gesturing, only the claws won't do what she wants.

"Gently, gently," I say. I sit on the floor and gather her into my arms. "Take your time. It's all right. I'm here." As if I could fix her trouble. The old Blackthorn, the one she was before, would be laughing at that.

She tries again. Puts a hand on the pouch at her belt. Says something with *oo* and *ee* in it, but there's no making it out. The wee folk are up out of their circle. They're lifting the bones and laying them down again in some kind of pattern. Dear God . . .

"Oo! Uh! Ee!" growls Blackthorn, hammering a hand against my chest. Only, not a hand; a poor misshapen thing. But Bonehead can't work out what she's saying. The pouch? Something in the pouch?

I spot a scrap of red; reach in and pull out the red kerchief, the one she left for me once as a way of saying good-bye. That's the last straw. I hold her close and cry my heart out. Rock her to and fro. Tell her I'll be here, I won't leave her, I'll look after her even if it takes two hundred years. Got my eyes shut, but I hear the soft sounds of those wee folk doing what they're doing, which I can guess is laying out what's left of Geiléis and her man. Wouldn't be much after two hundred years. Bones and dust. Memories.

Her hands are sharp against me. Shocking, hideous hands. I think of those hands stitching a wound. Laying flat stones on a dead man's eyes. Making a rude sign when Slammer called her names. Gripping an ax like she meant business. Holding a sick babe. Making a brew. Reaching out to pull me back from the brink, the night I lost hope. I sob and sob until it's a wonder there's any more tears in me. Wipe my face with the red kerchief.

She's crying too. Not wailing like she was before, more of a rasping, hurting sound.

"There, now," I say. "There, now," and I wipe her tears as well. Kerchief snags on her scaly skin and rips a bit. Across the chamber, the wee folk are in the circle again, standing up, holding hands. One of them steps forward, lays something small and gold on what might be the chest of the dead man, only there's not enough of him left to be sure. They start a chant, slow and solemn.

"Grim," someone says.

My heart jolts. I shut my eyes. Don't dare open them.

"Grim." Her hand moves against me, warm, human, and her body on my knees is a human body again, a woman's body, slight and wiry and struggling hard to get up.

I open my eyes and she's back. She's herself. Or maybe not quite, because when she does get up she's pale and wobbly and I have to catch her before she falls straight back on the floor. A miracle. Don't know what's done it. Don't know how it can be. But it's happened. A warm, good feeling fills me up. Must be what they mean by joy. Maybe I do believe in God after all.

"Morrigan's curse!" Blackthorn mutters. "That was vile! That was disgusting!"

Me, I've got no words at all. I mop my face again. Pass her the kerchief.

"Dagda's bollocks!" she says. "That was . . . Grim, did you break the spell? How? If you did it, I owe you a debt I'll be a lifetime repaying."

"Didn't do anything," I mumble. "Wish I could've."

"Out," says Blackthorn, sounding more like herself. "Now. You might need to help me. Lot of steps . . ."

I pick her up in my arms.

"You're all wet," she says, noticing now.

"Happens when you wade across a river."

"Be careful," she says. "If you fall, we'll both be dead and that would be a waste."

"I won't fall. Though if you're worried I can put you over my shoulder. That way, I get an arm free." Brings back a horrible memory from that day we got out of Mathuin's lockup. Saved a man, lost him not long after. Strangler. Poor sod. He just wanted the pain to end.

We stop a moment next to the chanting wee folk and the sad remains of Lily and Ash. Geiléis and whatever-his-name-was. Mind's full of questions. How much did Geiléis know? How could she ask Blackthorn to do it, if she knew what was going to happen to her? And what did Blackthorn just see in this chamber?

"Talk later, mm?" I say, and head for the stair. One thing's certain: can't get out of this place soon enough. Thought I'd already had the worst day of my life. Might have been wrong. And there's still Flannan.

42

BLACKTHORN

I was blundering through a fog, arms outstretched, feet stumbling, not knowing left from right or up from down. My head swam. Everything was dark. Where was I? What had happened? Had I gone blind?

"It's all right. You're all right. Take it slowly." Grim's familiar voice, and now Grim's arm lifting me to sit, and someone putting a cup in my hand. "Take a sip of water, here."

There was light after all; a lamp in a corner, and the glow of a fire. I was in bed, with Grim sitting on a stool beside me. There was someone else in the room too. A monk.

"Wha . . . ?"

"Drink the water, Blackthorn."

The water was cold. It brought me out of the fog. I was in our quarters at Lady Geiléis's house, and it was getting dark outside. I started to remember. Oh, gods . . . When Grim had carried me out of the tower, we hadn't found Onchú and Donncha waiting on the island. Only two heaps of ancient bones. Two piles of clothing. Two pairs of boots. A scatter of weapons. Those things were of our own time; there was no magic in them. But the men had been old. Old beyond old.

"They guessed," I whispered now. "Her men. They had an idea of what would happen to them when the curse was broken. Donncha . . . There was a woman he was looking after, when he could, on one of the farms. The way he spoke about her, he didn't think he'd be coming back."

I sipped the water, remembering. We'd arrived at the house, Grim still carrying me, and all the rest of them had been here. One in the kitchen: Dau, I guessed. One at the high window in Geiléis's quarters: Senach, without a doubt. The other household servants in the dining chamber, all together, with one extra: that must have been Caisín's husband, Rian, for the bones of those two lay entwined where they had fallen. A fresh jug of ale and part-full cups on the table. Every person in the house had been not only dead, but reduced to bones and dust. All gone.

What had happened in the tower had left me weak. Not just fuzzy in the head, not just sad and confused and angry, but tired to the bone. So Grim had put me to bed, saying he'd bolt the door from the outside, and that I should yell if I needed him. I'd fallen into a sleep so profound I was still finding it hard to wake up properly.

"The guards?" I asked. "The rest of them?"

"Up in their quarters," said Grim. "Gone, like the others. Horses were loose in the field. Water trough filled, fodder provided. Fellows from St. Olcan's will look after the animals, see they go somewhere safe."

"Mistress Blackthorn." It was the monk, a small man with cropped white hair and a practical manner. "I am Brother Marcán. I look after our sick and injured at St. Olcan's. Sadly, Father Tomas will not allow us to house you in our infirmary, but I'm here to help. To provide any assistance you require. This has been a difficult time. I hardly understand what has occurred, but at the very least, you have suffered a grave shock."

I passed the cup back to Grim. I tried moving my head from side to side as an experiment. I flexed my fingers and found myself staring with new fascination at the way they worked.

The others seemed to be waiting. "Oh," I said. "Thank you." It was good that this monk was here, even though I could tend to myself perfectly well. Good that someone had been here with Grim; that he hadn't been alone in the middle of all this. "I have a bit of a headache, yes. But as it turns out, I have all the ingredients for a draft to cure it." Even the true love's tears, which Grim never used because I couldn't get the wretched words out. And yet the curse had still been broken.

I'd frozen up again in the middle of saying something.

"I can make the brew," Grim said. "Just tell me what to put in it."

"Let me," said Brother Marcán quietly. The way he spoke to Grim surprised me. It was like brother to brother. Full of respect and understanding.

"All right. Thanks," said Grim. "Think you could eat something?" He was talking to me now. "Brother Fergal—he was here before—sent a lad down with some food for us. Not that there's a lack of it here. Couple of the lay brothers are coming down to sleep in the house with us tonight. Just in case."

"Just in case what?" Grim wasn't making sense. And there was a piece of this puzzle missing. Why wasn't he here? He should have been here. He'd been supposed to wait for me. "Where's Flannan?" I asked.

A terrible look came over Grim's face. A truly frightening look. It was just as well Brother Marcán was putting the kettle on the fire and had his back to us.

"Grim. What? Tell me!" Flannan couldn't be dead too. That wouldn't make sense.

Grim glanced over at Marcán. Looked back at me and shook his head a bit.

I wasn't waiting for this, whatever it was. "I need the privy," I announced, attempting to get up. It was the same as before, in the tower; I couldn't stand upright. Not even after all that sleep. Spots were dancing before my eyes. "Grim, you'll have to take me."

"Tell me the ingredients," said Brother Marcán, not sounding shocked at all, "and I'll get on with making your remedy."

"A good pinch of woodruff. A generous pinch of lavender. Some peppermint. That's only to make it taste better. Druid's balm. And an herb called true love's tears—there's some in a cloth in that pouch over there. Just a sprinkling of that. Pour over hot water, not boiling, enough to fill one cup, and let it steep a good while. And I'd better be the one to test it out."

"Impressive, Mistress Blackthorn," the monk said. "You look ready to swoon, but you can still give me precise instructions in a flash."

"You'd be the same, I expect."

"Well, yes, but . . ." He shrugged and turned away. "I'll go ahead, shall I?"

I wondered whether he'd meant *but men don't swoon* or *but women are fuzzy-headed at the best of times*. Provided the good brother had learned some kind of lesson, it didn't matter greatly which one it was.

Outside, I said to Grim, "I really do need the privy. And you'd better stand right by the door in case I faint. But when I'm done, you're going to tell me what's going on with Flannan." The plan to flee south in secret lay like a stone in my belly, along with the way I'd lied to Grim. I knew, suddenly and surely, that I couldn't go. Knew I'd been a deluded fool ever to consider Flannan's scheme. I had a place at Winterfalls; I had work; I had a purpose. And I had Grim. The truth had been creeping up on me for some time, not altogether welcome: I needed him as much as he needed me. Now I would have to confess everything, and that would hurt both of us. But there could be no more lies.

Grim supported me as I hobbled to the privy. Sitting inside with the door ajar, I realized it wasn't as late as I'd thought; only dusk. The forest was all lavender and purple and gray, and birds were still awake, exchanging occasional remarks as they found their roosting places. Behind those cheeps and chirrups lay a deep and blissful quiet. Lighted torches had been placed by the house doors. And I could hear someone moving around inside, perhaps in the kitchen. "Who's that?"

"Nothing to worry about," says Grim from outside the privy. "There's a few of the monks here. Didn't want us to be on our own. Not after everything."

"When did you organize all that? You went up there while I was asleep?"

"Didn't need to. They came down. Knew we were in trouble, after this morning. And they heard the creature go quiet. Felt that—whatever it was."

"The start of the end. When I cut into the hedge. Only I didn't need to cut; it just opened up. And closed behind me, so Geiléis and the men couldn't come through." Tidy again, I came out and pointed to a bench in the yard, by the well. "I'm going to sit down there. And you're going to tell me where Flannan is."

He told me. Not where Flannan was, since he didn't know. But a story that suggested a depth of treachery I found hard to comprehend. When he was done, Grim said, "You don't believe me."

"But he told me . . ." Oh, gods. The whole thing, the whole story of a plot, the intricate web of informants who were ready to step forward and raise their voices, the safe places where I could lodge with Christian sisters, the folk who would protect me until it was time . . . If what Grim said was true, then all of that must have been lies. An elaborate web of lies carefully woven to trap me. Why go to so much trouble making it all up? Why not kill me when he had the chance? Wasn't that what Mathuin wanted?

There was a look on Grim's face that told me he was edging toward a clifftop. "That message," he said. "The one the pigeon had. There was a part about taking the bait. What was the bait?"

Shame filled my heart. Not something I was used to. Not a good feeling at all. "Promise you'll listen and not interrupt until I'm finished."

"All right."

At this point the door to our quarters opened, light spilled out and Brother Marcán called, "Is all well?"

"We're fine, just talking. Be in soon."

The door closed gently.

I told him. How Flannan had offered me the chance, the rare and precious chance to do the thing properly, not on my own this time, but backed up by all those other folk who wanted Mathuin brought to justice for his crimes and his cruelty. How it had all seemed to fall into place so neatly, the trip west to help Geiléis, the quick flight south on Midsummer Eve—today, still today—to reach Mide and then Laois by a route Flannan said Mathuin would not be watching. The allies, the plan, the witnesses. Foolproof, almost. How, when later on I had begun to doubt, he'd used all the weapons he had at his disposal, suggesting that I would be betraying Cass if I did not agree; that I would be confirming I was not the brave woman I had once been; that the longer I stayed away from Laois, the more new victims Mathuin would find to prey on. I told Grim how I'd got sick of the pressure and ordered Flannan to stay away while I made up my mind. And how, after the ritual, I had been so disgusted by the bitter, useless person I had become that I'd decided the best thing was to do what Flannan wanted. To turn my back and go south. At least then there would be some point in my existence.

Grim spoke not a word. He didn't need to.

"And yes, I didn't tell you. I knew if I did you would come with me, or come after me, and I wanted you to be safe. I didn't want you drawn into it all and hurt or killed because of my wretched cause. You have a good life at Winterfalls. Work. Friends. Perhaps a family at some time in the future. Folk trust you. They like you. You would be so much better off without me. That was my reasoning."

He looked at me. Sad eyes in the torchlight. "Don't know me as well as you think you do, mm?"

I thought of him charging up the tower to find me. Holding me in his arms, a monstrous thing all teeth and scales and claws, and telling me he'd stay by me two hundred years if that was what it took. As steadfast as Geiléis had been for her young man, Ash. Though it was not like that with him and me. Of course it wasn't. "Only," I said, "after what happened in the tower, I realized I couldn't do it. I just want to go back to Winterfalls. I was going to tell Flannan tonight. I hope you believe that, Grim. You'd have every reason not to. But it's the truth."

"You know I'd have come after you anyway," Grim said. "I'd have found you. Even in the middle of a war. Even if you were back in Mathuin's lockup. If you ever decide to get rid of me again, you'll need to try harder. I know you're telling the truth. And so am I, about Flannan. You want to check, there's two monks can back me up. Fellow that looks after the birds, Eoan. He knows how many messages Flannan sent to Mathuin and how many came back. Head archivist, Ríordán. He's seen that translation, with the second page and all. In Flannan's own hand. And there's the message the bird never delivered. *It appears the target will be eliminated by midsummer.* And the bit about the bait. He was planning to take you to Laois, all right. Take you there and hand you straight over. But when he found the document, he got a better idea. Way of getting rid of you with a lot less trouble."

"He could have just killed me."

"Nah. Hasn't got the guts for that. Childhood friend and all. I bet he caved in early after that first challenge failed, the one your man was part of. Found a soft spot betraying his comrades, nice little purse of silver in exchange."

"Now you're making things up."

"Could be true, though."

"I think I'm going to be sick."

"Here—" He was beside me in a moment, supporting me as I leaned over and retched helplessly. There wasn't a lot to bring up. I was done soon enough. Now we were both quiet. I leaned on Grim, despising my weakness.

"He's still out there somewhere," I said, wishing my voice was steadier. "On the way south, maybe. He'll tell Mathuin everything. What we're doing, where we're living . . ." I felt a pang of longing for our little house, our garden, our daily existence at Dreamer's Wood. I even missed wretched interfering Conmael. We wouldn't be able to go back there. If Mathuin feared my influence enough to send Flannan out to hunt me down, he wasn't going to let this go.

"Not if we find him first," said Grim in a voice no less deadly for being soft. "Flannan, I mean. But now's not the time to talk about that. Something you might think about, though. How much of that, after the ritual, was the curse playing with your head. Making you sad, stopping you from seeing the good things. The good in yourself. Easy enough to lose sight of it, sometimes."

He helped me indoors, where I got back into bed. I sat there sipping Brother Marcán's brew and wishing the monk would go away so I could have a bath and change my clothes.

The brew was all right. True love's tears had a bitter aftertaste—appropriate, when you thought about it—but Marcán had countered that with a few drops of honey. Not bad. For a monk.

I rested my head against the piled-up pillows. My heart felt bruised. My mind felt hollow. A blow from an enemy was something you could deal with. It was what you expected. But being betrayed by someone who had once been a trusted friend . . . That was hard to bear. Almost as hard to bear as the knowledge that I had let myself be duped. I should have known. I should have worked it out. I'd had my suspicions about Flannan. The man he'd once been, my friend and Cass's, would not have used those cruel arguments to persuade me. But folk do change over the years. Perhaps I hadn't put it all together because I didn't want to. Friends were few and far between. Most of Cass's and mine were dead. That made anyone who was left doubly precious.

I considered Grim's theory about the curse turning my thoughts upside down. I hoped it was true; I thought it might be. Right now, tired as I was, I felt more clear-headed than I had been for a long time. I still felt bitter, but only toward Flannan, and through him Mathuin. Not toward the whole world. Not toward myself.

Enough thinking about that; I'd soon be tying my own head in knots with no need for the curse's help. I thought instead how soothing the smell of peppermint was, and how comforting the feeling of a warm cup between chilled hands. How pleasing the dance of the flames on the hearth. Peace, I thought. For now, peace.

I had not expected to sleep again so soon, but I did, to be woken much later by Grim saying there was warm water ready for bathing and all monks were forbidden entry until I was finished. He had put up the screen and readied soft soap, a brush, a cloth for drying and a change of clothing for me.

"Be careful," I said. "You'll be turning into Senach soon." But neither of us laughed. What an existence for those men, condemned to live on with Geiléis until the spell was broken, steadfast in their loyalty to the very end. I wondered if they had feared that end at first, and then, as chance after chance passed them by, had begun to long for it? Some, maybe. But I thought Donncha, at least, had caught sight of the life he might have had. I could not imagine him going willingly into death.

The bath was bliss. I soaked and scrubbed, trying to erase the sensation of being scaly and scabby and wretched all over.

"Saved those battle garments for you," said Grim from the other side of the screen. "The ax too. Might come in useful sometime."

"For what?"

"You never know."

"If nothing else, they'd remind me of the peril of trying to be something I'm clearly not cut out to be," I said. "When I got up there, he just knelt down and let me do it. Pushed his hair out of the way and offered his neck. He was desperate for it to be over, poor man."

"Blackthorn?"

"Mm?" He'd put a scattering of dried lavender in the water; the smell was sweet.

"What did you see, after that? Before I got there?"

I swallowed, remembering. "When I'd done it, he was himself again straightaway, head and all. A man of around Geiléis's age with long dark hair, wearing a white shirt. He looked at me and said, *I'm sorry*, and, more fool me, I had no idea what he was talking about.

Then Geiléis was there—the thorns must have opened up again as soon
as I'd struck off his head—and she ran into his arms and they clung to
each other. They didn't speak much, only *I love you*, and *Oh gods, at
last*, and each other's names: *Lily, Ash*. He stroked her hair. She laid
her head against his chest. Smiling and weeping, the two of them. It
was like the happy ending of a tale, only . . . only then I started to
change, and so did they."

I stared up at the rafters, wondering if the memory would ever go
away, or if it would add itself to the nightly parade that visited my
sleep.

"Might help to get it out," came Grim's deep voice. "But only if you
want to."

"The gray began to show in his hair, then hers. Their faces got
wrinkled and wizened, and their bodies bent and shriveled, and still
they held on to each other. Near the end, Geiléis's hair was as white as
snow. Still beautiful, a shining cape over her shoulders. Then . . . he
fell, and she couldn't hold on anymore. She got onto her knees beside
him—oh, Grim, she was so, so old—and lay down with her head
against his heart, and died. And they . . . they crumpled and dried out
and fell to bones and dust. It was so quick. So quick. By then I was . . .
not myself. Only I saw. I couldn't drag my eyes away."

A pause. Then, "You all right?"

"I will be. Only I don't think I'll be up to a long ride tomorrow.
There's nothing I want more than to get out of this place. But I'm weak.
Weak beyond what a day or two's battle training and a climb up a
tower could do. I'm sorry." Telling the story had brought everything
back, stark and clear. I felt a sudden need to be dry, clothed and able to
see my companion when I talked to him. "Getting out now. Thank you
for the bath. I feel much better."

"Mm-hm." Another silence, in which it was quite plain he did not
believe I was better any more than I did. "No need to be sorry. Suits me
to take a day or two. Roof's not done yet. Got to put the creatures on.

I was going to leave it, but Father Tomas wants me to go up and finish off. Think it might be better for the ones who've helped us, Ríordán and Fergal and Marcán, if I do that. Sounds like Father Tomas isn't well pleased with everything that's been going on. Though if you ask me, he should be happy the curse is broken. *Ah, the blessed quiet*, that's what Brother Marcán said."

Ríordán—was that the archivist Flannan had spoken of? I didn't ask who Fergal was. I didn't question how oddly Grim's ease of talk about them sat with his earlier reluctance to visit St. Olcan's at all. There was a tale there. I hoped he'd tell me sometime. "They're being remarkably helpful, aren't they? Christian monks generally have a low opinion of my kind."

"They've been living next to Geiléis and her household," Grim said. "And the monster in the tower. Not to speak of those little folk in the woods. They've had time to get used to the strange and troubling."

"The little folk—I hope their king is safe. I hope this did free him from the hedge."

"There was a wee fellow in there. Might've been him. Might've been a minder. I was in too much of a rush to ask."

Dry now, I got into the fresh shift and gown he had laid on my bed.

"You dressed?" asked Grim after a while.

"Fully enough for even a monk not to be shocked. You can take away the screen." Something occurred to me. "Grim."

"What?" He folded the screen and set it against the wall.

"The little folk should all be free now. Not bound to serve the requirements of the curse anymore. Free to talk."

"That's the way it was in the tale. Not that he told us the whole tale, the lying bastard."

"So if we asked them for a favor, they might say yes?"

"Don't know about that. You know that whistle they gave me? That was a favor. And I used it. Used it to get through the thorns. When I blew it, the little prickly fellow popped out and made a path for me. Strangest thing I ever saw. One of the strangest. Wonder if he was the king." He gives me a crooked smile. "Why? What were you thinking?"

"I have to ask you something first. If we found Flannan, what would you want to do?"

"What do you think?"

"Kill him, no questions asked. Right?"

"Why would you bother with questions? He's only going to give you more lies. Don't tell me you think he's a fine man underneath and we should say, *Just be good from now on and all's forgiven.* I know the fellow's your old friend, but—"

"I'm not stupid! Right now there's nothing I'd like to do more than pick up that ax and bring it down on his poxy lying head. But . . . in the morning I might think differently. And so might you."

He stares at me. "You mean you think this could have a happy ending, like in a tale?"

"What are you talking about?"

"You and him. Your childhood friend. Always off having your private chats. Thought you might have . . . well, feelings for each other." Grim was blushing; it was a strange sight.

I was glad I couldn't see my own expression; it must have been laughable. "Me and Flannan? Settling down in domestic bliss? You must be crazy." How could he ever have imagined such a thing? "I'm never going to settle, Grim. Not like that, with a family. Losing Cass and Brennan . . . Once was enough for a lifetime." I sat down by the fire, suddenly cold despite the bath. "How soon is supper?"

"Whenever you want." He sat down opposite, elbows on knees, very serious. "So what *do* we do when we find Flannan, if we're not stringing him up from the nearest tree? And how do we find him, seeing it's just you and me going back?"

"What do we do? I don't know. But he should be given a chance to explain himself. He should face up to us. We could make him tell us how much Mathuin knows. As for how we find him, I thought we could ask the little folk to look out for him."

"As a plan, it's not the best you've ever thought up."

"I know that! I know he's probably on the way back to Laois and out of our reach already!" I hammered my clenched fist on the table for emphasis. It hurt. Gods, I hated being weak.

"Supper," said Grim. "Now."

43

Midsummer Day and no proper plan worked out yet. Only me doing the roof this morning, and her coming with me and talking nicely to Father Tomas while I'm working. Means I'll know she's safe. Won't hurt to sweeten Father Tomas a bit either. The lay brothers stay at Geiléis's house, in case Flannan comes back, though what I've told them is, in case anyone calls by and needs telling what's happened. And that if he makes an appearance one of them should come straight up and fetch me.

Blackthorn's a lot better today. Not herself yet, but stronger. Manages the walk pretty well. Brother Fergal comes to the gate and lets her into the guest area, which is the only spot where women are allowed. I fetch my bits and pieces and go off to finish the roof.

Thought I'd have to make cat and fox all over again, but no. When I go for my things, there's not just the one bag, there's two. First one, raven and dove. Second one, not a mess of broken reed but cat and fox, perfect. Know I fell over them running down to warn Blackthorn. Felt them break. Someone's fetched them back and fixed them. Fixed them with little weavings and knots and twisty bits. Other things too, row of white stones threaded in, and hairs, long ones, white, gray, golden, black. Scraps of green ribbon. Work's too fine for human hands. What I'm thinking is, better get these up quick before the good brothers know they're getting fey work on their roof.

I don't say anything to Tadhg or Fergal or Ríordán, though they're all there when I get the creatures out of the bags. Don't feel like saying much at all, just doing the job the best I can.

Fergal holds the ladder steady. Tadhg is at the top handing things up to me. I'm on the ridge tying the creatures down, doing the knots right, making sure they'll hold fast in winter gales. Look down once or twice and see a lot of monks out in the garden, or on the paths, watching me. Part of me wishes I could stay here. Another part can't wait to go home. Funny old time it's been.

Midmorning and we're done. Climb down, thank the fellows for helping, pack everything away. No sign of Blackthorn. She can't still be talking to Father Tomas. But she promised not to go back without me. Maybe she's tearing strips off him for not doing more to help.

Brother Ríordán says to wash my hands and come with him. And here we are at the scriptorium door again. Like yesterday when I came barging in not even thinking about being scared. Only not like that, because now I tell them I'm sorry I did that, and then I say maybe I should be making sure Blackthorn's all right.

Ríordán gives a funny sort of smile and says Brother Marcán's just been over to check. Things were a bit frosty to start with. Then Father Tomas found out she knew about mead. So they're sampling his brews and exchanging secrets. There's also been some discussion of other matters. "We knew you'd be worried," Ríordán says. "But we didn't want you to leave without seeing the book."

They've got it ready for me. Brother Galen's little book, laid out on a lectern. Open at a page with an owl. There's an ache in my belly, and that ache is me wanting to understand not just the pictures but the words too. To be able to read. Magic, that'd be, to know just what his hand set down there. Sometime. Maybe. Never been much good at that sort of thing.

I know how to turn the pages without hurting them. Brother Galen showed me, at St. Erc's. There's hare and salmon and prickly hedgehog. There's sleek otter and secret badger and a moth all swirly patterns, flying across the full moon. A long-tailed mouse. A shrew, a salamander, a dragonfly. Pretty colors. Little touches of gold. Like an old tale with a surprise at every turn.

Thought I might be crying by the time I got to the last picture, but no. I'm smiling, not on my face, but deep down. Learned something this summer. When I leave here, when I give back the book and Ríordán locks it away for safekeeping, I'll still have those pictures. I'll still have Brother Galen with his fluffy white hair and his gentle eyes and his scholar's cat. Just like I'll always have what these fellows have given me. Kindness. Forgiveness. The hand of friendship. Faith in God, not so much. A bit more faith in myself, though.

I close the covers and get to my feet. I want to say thank you. I want to say I'm different because of them. But the words won't come out. I dip my head a bit, that's all. Sometimes what a man's thinking is too big to put in words.

Blackthorn's quiet on the way down to Geiléis's. So quiet I ask her if she's all right.

"Mm," she says, not hearing me. Something's got her thinking. After a while she asks, "Who's Brother Conall?"

Shocks me a bit. "Why do you ask?" Didn't think they'd tell her. Didn't think they'd tell anyone.

"Just once, Father Tomas used that name, and it sounded as if he meant you. Marcán corrected him. Hard to believe there's any monk who looks like you."

"Long story. Some other time."

"Mm-hm."

She won't ask again. She'll wait till I'm ready to tell. That's the way we do it, her and me. "Did he say anything about Flannan? Where they think he might have gone?"

"Not much. They were surprised he left his documents behind. I think they were taken aback that he left so abruptly, without thanks or explanation. He's not on horseback, unless he got a mount from somewhere else. Either he was so sure of himself that he saw no reason to wait out Midsummer Eve, or something bothered him and he bolted."

"Attack of guilt, maybe."

"Grim."

"Mm?"

"I'll be able to ride by tomorrow. We should just go. There's nothing more to do here. And the longer we leave it, the farther ahead he'll be. Especially if he's riding. He could have got a horse from one of the farms."

"Might be waiting to ambush us along the way."

"Ambush? Flannan? He's not exactly a fighter."

"All the same. Be happier if we had a couple of guards with us. Even a couple of monks would be better than nothing."

"Well, we don't," she says. "It's just you and me and whatever tricks we can put together between us. Always seemed to be enough in the past."

Couple of last things to do before we leave. We bury Geiléis's guards up near the stables. I do most of the digging. One of the lay brothers says a prayer. Pretty sure Onchú and the others weren't Christians, but never mind. Blackthorn and me say some words too, how loyal the fellows were to Geiléis and how they did their job well right to the end. Then we do it all over again in the kitchen garden, for Senach and Dau and the others.

We don't go back to the Tower of Thorns. Seems right to leave Lily and Ash up there, where the little folk laid them out. Brother Galen would have made a lovely picture of that. The two of them lying there side by side, just bones, watching the sun and the moon go past that high window.

We get the horses ready. There's the three we brought from court, and we take a fourth, a big bay. Ride one, lead one. Next day, switch them over. That way they get a rest from carrying a rider.

We pack up. The monks give us a lot of food. Should last the whole way. Saves us needing to fish and forage, though we still will, most likely. Spare horses can carry the supplies. Bags of fodder for them too. Blackthorn's got a flask of special mead, gift from Father Tomas. Bit of a surprise. She says it's because she gave him some sort of brewers' secret. Passed down through her family. That's what she told him, anyway.

We sleep one more night in Lady Geiléis's house. Don't know what'll happen to the place now. She was the last one in her family. That's if the old tale's all true. Who'd want to live there? House full of sad ghosts.

It's morning again, the day after Midsummer Day. Lovely weather, fine and sunny. And quiet. Hard to get used to the quiet. I saddle the horses and load the baggage on the two we're not riding. We thank the fellows who've been helping us. I bet they'll be glad to get back to St. Olcan's. Then the two of us ride for home.

44

BLACKTHORN

On the third day out from Bann, a westerly blew up and the weather turned cold and wet. We rode on through it, getting crosser and chillier by the moment. Just as the light was fading, we found a sheltered camping spot near a stand of old trees. By then the worst of the rain was over; it had been a passing storm. But we were wet, the horses were wet, and all of us were perilously cold.

Without any need for talk, Grim and I set to work. He unloaded the baggage while I gathered firewood from under the trees, where it was passably dry. He tethered the horses, rubbed them down, got them food and water. I made a fire. It was necessary to use a couple of what might be called wise woman tricks to get it burning well; with everything damp, flint and tinder went only so far. I investigated the bag that contained our foodstuffs, found it had withstood the deluge fairly well, and prepared a rather eccentric porridge using everything I thought needed finishing up. The main thing was to get a hot, nourishing meal into our bellies before nightfall. With the horses taken care of, Grim sorted out our bedding and performed a swift patrol of the whole area. We had seen nothing of Flannan since we'd left Bann. We'd been avoiding encounters with other folk on the roads, thinking he might be about and asking people if they'd seen us. Or, more precisely, seen me. I was starting to believe he'd gone south by that other route, through Tirconnell, if it really existed and wasn't just one more of his lies. If he'd done that, there was no way we could stop him from reaching Mathuin and telling what he knew.

But then, I thought as I stirred the strange-looking mixture, what could he tell? If he'd left Bann before I went up the tower, he'd be going back to Laois in the belief that I was dead. Or turned into a monster. *The doom will fall upon the assailant*, those were the final words of the curse, according to Grim. If that was what Flannan was rushing to impart to Mathuin, perhaps hoping for praise or reward, his departure was good news. If Mathuin believed me dead, I'd be safe for now. I could stay in Winterfalls, keep my promise to Conmael, and wait for the day when I'd finally make Mathuin face up to justice, in my own way, on my own terms. So why did I still have a tight knot in my belly? Why did I feel uneasy every time Grim went out of sight?

"Smells good," he said, coming to sit opposite me and warm his hands. "What is it?"

"Travelers' Surprise. You'll have tasted better. And worse." The swill in Mathuin's lockup had been repulsive. And yet we prisoners had licked our bowls clean, every time. You do that when you're starving. I'd drawn the line at the rats, but most of my cellmates had crunched them up raw, bones and all. "We've been through some odd times, Grim," I said.

"Mm."

"I'm sorry," I said, handing him a filled bowl.

"Sorry about the food, or . . . ?"

"My cooking's not that bad. I mean sorry for lying to you. Again."

"Way I see it," said Grim, blowing on a steaming spoonful, "it's better to care too much, like you do, and make mistakes, than shut your ears and eyes and pretend the bad things in the world aren't there. Big job, though. Bigger than I thought."

"What is?"

"Keeping you safe."

We ate in silence for a while. The supper was a little odd, but we were hungry and cold enough to eat every last spoonful.

"Good meal," said Grim, wiping out his bowl with his finger. "About St. Olcan's. Was that to get me out of your way? Wondered why you were so keen to help them. Monks and all."

Only the truth would do, though it shamed me to say it. "I did plan things hoping you'd be busy up there when I went to the tower, because I thought I might have to do something you wouldn't want me to do. And yes, I intended that Flannan and I would be gone before you got back on Midsummer Eve. A big strategic error. No need to point that out."

"Funny part is," he said, "it turned out to be a good thing. Me going up to St. Olcan's. A really good thing. And not just me fixing their roof for them. Even though I was so scared of going in, the first time, that it made me sick. Learned a bit up there. Wasn't expecting that."

I didn't ask about the mysterious Brother Conall, and he didn't offer the story.

"Question for you," Grim said.

"Mm?"

"Can anyone learn their letters? Reading and writing?"

This was a surprise. "Someone like you, you mean?" I ventured.

"Mm-hm." He was staring into the fire, avoiding my eye.

"That depends on who's doing the teaching," I said. "I was planning on starting some work with Emer when we get home. If she's going to be a healer she'll need to be able to keep her own notebook, at the very least. Read labels, make her own labels. I don't see why you shouldn't learn with her. That's if we do stay in Winterfalls."

He looked up then. Nodded. Gave me the sweetest of smiles. "Good," he said. "Should get these clothes dried out, hmm?"

We built the fire up, draped various items around it and settled again. It was nearly dark, or as dark as it got so close to midsummer.

And beyond the glow of the flames, as cold as the grave. Grim checked the horses again. When he got back I handed him the flask of Father Tomas's special mead.

"I was going to save it until we got home. But I think tonight calls for it. It will put some warmth in the bones."

The mead was indeed very fine; far better than anything I'd ever brewed. We passed the flask from one to the other until a goodly amount of it was gone. Then we settled to sleep. All being well, by the day after tomorrow we would be back at Cahercorcan. It felt as if we'd been in another world.

"Good night, Grim."

"Sweet dreams."

I woke suddenly and fully, my heart hammering, my skin prickling with the awareness of danger. On the far side of the fire, Grim lay as if dead, a motionless dark form. Someone was kneeling over him. The firelight caught the glint of a knife, the red stain on the blade.

In a breath I was up, ax in hand. "*What are you doing?*" I yelled, striding forward. Flannan whipped around, rose to a crouch, the knife pointed toward me. His white face. His wide eyes. A traitor. My friend. My own voice sounded in my mind: *He should face up to us.*

I hit him with the haft, hard. But he was moving and the blow missed his head, glancing instead across his neck and cheek. Flannan let out an oath and staggered to his feet, still clutching the bloody knife. Now he took a lurching step toward me, moving past Grim. Oh, gods, Grim. Grim dead or dying.

I stepped back, tripped over my hem, struggled to keep my balance. Dropped the ax. I fought to find words. Time. I needed time. I would not turn and run. How could I leave Grim? "You don't have to do this, Flannan." I put my hands up, palms forward, in a gesture of surrender. "You didn't have to do any of it. You were a good man once."

"Do what? What are you talking about? Your man here just tried to kill me. Went for me without even asking what my business was. I defended myself as a man does."

"Bollocks!" The lying swine! He thought I would swallow that? "You, beat Grim in a fight?"

"You're angry. I understand that. Just—just be calm and listen. I'm sorry I didn't wait for you the way we planned. There was a—a distraction. But I've found you now, and we can go south. Do everything we were going to do. Just the two of us. You wanted him out of the way, didn't you? We can head off for Mide exactly as we planned."

"So why are you still pointing that knife at me?" A knife that was less than steady. He was pale, sweating, shaking. He looked as if he might do anything. "You're a liar. A liar and a traitor. There never was any plot, was there? There never were any witnesses waiting to speak out; there never was any network of like minds in the south. Just you, a godforsaken coward, doing Mathuin's dirty business." I was damned if I was going to die without telling the bastard what I thought of him.

Flannan opened his mouth, no doubt to deny it all, then swallowed and spoke again. "I had no choice." He shifted the knife from one hand to the other. "If anyone should understand, it's you."

How dared he? I was on the brink of hurling myself forward and attacking the rotten mongrel with my bare hands, knife or no knife. I made myself breathe.

"You mean because I know what Mathuin's capable of? That's rubbish. Cass would never have done what you've done. Not in a thousand years. You were going to hand me over, weren't you? If the curse didn't finish me off, you were going to take me all the way to Mathuin's doorstep on the strength of those cruel lies. That's unforgivable." Could I snatch that knife? Stab him before he wrestled it from me and killed me? He was far taller, but my blow had dazed him. I tried not to look at the weapon.

"You can't know that." Flannan's voice had a wild edge. "How can you?"

"You forget the scribe's habit of setting things down in writing.

Messages to Mathuin, carried by birds. A translation set away under lock and key. And a friend of mine who's been spending a lot of time at St. Olcan's."

"Grim?" Flannan was incredulous. "Don't tell me that dunderhead could read. That, I'll never believe."

"He didn't need to be able to read." I blinked back furious tears. "He just needed an observant eye and a gift for making friends. We know exactly what you've been doing."

"I did what I had to."

"Rubbish! Nobody has to lie and cheat and kill. Nobody has to obey a wretch like Mathuin. How long have you been doing his foul work, Flannan? And why, in the name of all the gods, why?"

"Why did I agree to find you and bring you back? Why did I do Mathuin's bidding? I wanted to live. I wanted my wife and children to live. Is that enough for you?"

My jaw dropped. Another lie? "What wife and children? Traveling scholars don't have wives and children." *Keep him talking, Blackthorn. Wait for an opportunity.*

"I've been wed only five years; my daughters are young. I thought I was safe, Saorla. Far enough away to be out of his reach. What I told you—the first part—that was mostly true. Getting away after the plot failed. Staying away, sheltered in the monasteries for years and years. But I met Banba. Met and fell in love. Wed and moved into the nearby village, in Mide. And Mathuin found me. Found me and gave me a mission: track you down and bring you back. If I didn't succeed, my wife and daughters would be killed. He . . . he described what he would do. In detail. You know Mathuin; you can imagine. There was no choice."

I thought of my baby in the fire. To save him, I would have been prepared to offer up my own life, my freedom, all my worldly goods. But track down an old and trusted friend and deliver her up to gods knew what vile fate? Tell lie after lie to make it happen? Not care who else got killed or hurt along the way? I hoped I would have had the strength to spit in Mathuin's poxy face.

"There's always a choice," I said. "Getting it right can be the hardest thing of all. I wrestled with the choice you gave me. Changed my mind over and over, until I knew what I must do." I drew a breath, glancing at the fire. Could I snatch a burning brand, somehow use that to make him drop the weapon?

"Listen," Flannan said, dropping his tone to a conspiratorial murmur. "I don't have to use this knife. Not if you're sensible and cooperate. You could still come with me. Face up to him. Isn't that what you want, to speak your piece in public?" He took a quick step forward, feinted with the knife. I took another step back.

"Look at it another way." I was all cold sweat, my heart fighting to escape my chest. "This is your second chance. Make the right choice this time. No more killing, no more lies. Be the man you were before, the good man. Renounce Mathuin and his evil. Make that story you told me reality. I will help you." I wasn't so bad at lies myself. "There must be a way to get your family to safety."

"There is no way. It's too late. Mathuin's got eyes and ears everywhere. How can you ask me to stand up against him when it means my little girls will suffer?"

"How can I ask? Because that's just what Cass did. Remember him? Cass, your dearest friend. Cass who died with our son in his arms." I met his gaze steadily, my head held high. And if my voice was like iron, my heart was full of tears.

"That's not fair!" Flannan said on a furious sob. "Don't make me do this, Saorla! Give yourself up. Come on, now—" He made a sudden lunge, shot out his free hand and grabbed my wrist. I saw him draw in a deep breath, as if to steady himself for what must be done. His eyes like death. The knife in his other hand, ready to strike. *Cass. Brennan. Grim.*

Something huge and dark loomed behind him. A pair of large hands closed around his neck. There was an unpleasant crunching sound, the grip on my wrist was released, and Flannan fell limp to the ground, leaving me staring into the eyes of a very unwell-looking Grim.

"You're alive," I said, stupidly. *Don't burst into tears, Blackthorn. Keep control of yourself.* A pox on it, I was trembling as if I had a palsy.

"Seems that way." Grim crumpled suddenly to his knees, his hand against his left shoulder. "Think I might be bleeding a bit."

I stepped over the lifeless body of my childhood friend. The man who would have killed me. Suddenly I was not weak and shaky, but so angry I wanted to scream. The bastard! The godforsaken poxy apology for a man! I should have sunk the ax in his head when I had the chance.

"Let me look," I said to Grim. "What happened? He said you attacked him."

"Hah! If I'd attacked him, he'd be dead. I woke up sudden. Head foggy after the mead. He was right there, leaning over me, knife in his hand. Didn't know if you were dead or alive. I rolled out of the way just as he struck. He got me in the shoulder, just here."

I knelt beside him. "Take off your shirt," I said.

He winced as he did so; the garment was sticky with blood. "Just a flesh wound," he said. "Messy, though."

From what I could see, he was right; he'd been lucky. "Looks as if you'll survive," I said, feeling sick at the thought of what might have been. "For now I'll just clean this up and put on a bandage. I can have a better look by daylight." He looked as sick as I felt. But I had to ask. "What happened then? When I woke up I thought he'd killed you."

"Stupid. Got on my feet, charged toward the bastard, tripped on something and over I went like a felled tree. Hit my head, hard. Knocked myself out cold."

"Dagda's bollocks! I woke up just as he was about to finish you off. Yelled at the top of my voice. Used the ax. Only not the blade, the haft. A big mistake."

"Saved my life," Grim said.

"You saved mine."

"Good team, then."

I nodded, momentarily lost for words.

"You must've done all right for yourself," he said, "or he'd have killed you before I came to."

"I managed to drop the ax. But I did keep him talking. The bastard tried to make out we were still friends. Seemed to think I'd understand why he did what he did, because of . . . Enough of this for now; let's get this wound cleaned up."

"Going to have to make him disappear," Grim said, glancing at Flannan.

"Forget that until daylight." Suddenly I didn't want to think about any of it. I wanted to be back at Winterfalls with the sun shining and the kettle boiling on the hearth fire.

"Got a lump on my head the size of a goose egg," muttered Grim. "Frigging mead. Should've known better."

"Ah—mead. Good idea."

He must have come down hard; there was indeed a huge lump on his head. With luck that blow had not done any serious damage. His eyes looked all right, and he was talking sense. I fetched my healer's supplies. Used the pot of cooling water from our brew to wash the shoulder wound. Dried it with a kerchief.

"I'm going to splash on some mead before I bandage this. It helps keep out ill humors. It'll sting."

Grim attempted a laugh and winced with pain. "Father Tomas's special brew," he said. "Love to see the look on his face."

"I'll write and tell him all about it." I began to bandage the wound.

"Him. Flannan. Need . . . dig a grave."

"Forget him. You won't be digging anything. And you'd be better not riding tomorrow."

"I can ride, Lady. Be fine in the morning. Listen. Should say I'm sorry. Killed your friend. But I'd be lying, and that's the truth."

"Hush, now." He sounded like a shadow of his real self; I suspected a monster headache, not to speak of shock. I was not exactly at my best either.

When the bandage was done to my satisfaction I draped my blanket around his shoulders. Used the rest of the hot water to make a brew. Splashed a generous amount of mead into his cup and handed it to him. "Now Father Tomas would really be offended," I said, sitting down beside him and realizing, now that I had done what had to be done, that the night was still freezing cold. The fire's warmth was a blessing; its light in the darkness was indeed good.

"Nah," Grim said. "He'd understand." There was a pause; then he said, "Thanks for the brew."

"You lie down. I'll keep watch. I know I won't be able to sleep. In the morning we can work out what to do next."

"If you say so." He lay down, failing to conceal how painful the process was. "Still got your blanket." It was wrapped around him. "You'll be needing it."

"Keep it. If I get cold I'll put your cloak on."

"It's wet."

"Stop talking, shut your eyes and go to sleep, big man."

"If you say so . . ." He was dropping off even as he spoke.

For a long while I simply sat there with my empty cup in my hands, listening to the sounds of the woodland at night and looking at the flames. What had happened felt too big to take in. It was a tale of cowardice and courage, intrigue and simple goodness, choices that were complicated mixtures of right and wrong. It wasn't just us—Grim and me and Flannan. We were small parts in the terrible story of Mathuin of Laois; we were parts of the tragic tale of Lily and Ash and the household that had clung on for two hundred years, waiting for us. And when we went back to Cahercorcan, we'd once again be part of the tale of Oran and Flidais and the baby yet to be born, a child who could be king one day.

There was another, older tale. It belonged in these woods, and in the forest all around the Tower of Thorns, and in our own woodland back at Winterfalls. The tale of the small folk, as stoic as Senach and the others. The curse had compelled them to stay and to help. Despite that compulsion, they had tended to Ash with kindness. They had handled his remains, and Geiléis's, with tender respect. Perhaps, over the long trial they had endured together, the wee folk had grown to love Ash, and he them. I found myself wishing I had known him.

The first traces of dawn light were visible in the sky when there was a rustling close by. My fingers fastened around the ax. I rose silently to my feet.

A polite little cough to one side. A clearing of the throat to the other. I lowered my weapon as a group of small cloaked personages emerged from under the trees to come up to the fire. Grim slept on; Father Tomas's mead was potent.

"Don't wake him," I whispered, indicating Grim. "He's hurt."

"We will mend him," said one of the little ones.

"We will dig," said another, who had a tiny spade over his shoulder.

I eyed the lifeless form of Flannan. He had been a tallish man. I looked at the crowd of very small folk.

"We are many," pointed out one of them.

"You rest one day. Rest your horses. Rest the big man. One day, then go on."

Their kindness was overwhelming. Once again I had to order myself not to shed tears. "We owe your folk many favors already," I said. "This is . . ."

"Common sense," put in someone briskly. I guessed her identity before she pushed back her hood, revealing her shock of curls. It was the little woman of the ogham message, the fey healer. "Now don't be stubborn," she said. "Say yes and let's get on with things. Our clan owes you and your man a big, big debt."

"Consider the debt acquitted," I said, failing to stem the tears. "But yes, some help at this point would be welcome. Maybe I can cook you breakfast."

For some reason they thought this hilarious. The gusts of laughter continued as they busied themselves around the place. While Grim slept on, oblivious, the firewood was replenished, the horses were fed and watered, the wet clothing was dried with a speed no ordinary fire could possibly have achieved, and Flannan was covered up with a blanket that had not been among our possessions earlier. Most surprising of all, four of the small men appeared leading a familiar creature on a rope. The dog dwarfed them.

"Ripple," I breathed. "Where was she?" I hastened to fill a bowl with water, to find something she could eat.

"Tied up in the woods, not far off. Not making a sound. Sitting quiet, waiting."

I would not cry again. Grim had commented more than once on what a perfectly obedient creature Ripple was. Through all of it, and she must surely have heard, or sensed, something of that struggle, she had done exactly what Flannan had bid her do: *Sit. Wait.* He could never have caught us by surprise if she'd been free to run about. "Good girl," I told her. "Eat now. Drink. Rest." Did she know he lay dead under that blanket over there? Had she sensed that he was not coming back for her? "Thank you," I said to the little men. "I'll take care of her now."

A group of little folk was working at a discreet distance, digging away with miniature spades. A big group; the hole was growing quickly deeper.

As the sun climbed higher Grim stirred. It was obvious that his head was hurting him, but once he saw the small folk he sat up, entranced, and watched them with evident wonder. Ripple went over to him, shoulders hunched, tail down, hesitant now. He fondled her ears, murmuring, and she settled by his side. I could see where that was headed.

I'd been wondering how we were going to shift Flannan's body to the grave. That, I was sure these folk could not manage, and I didn't want Grim trying to do it. But he was quick with a solution.

"Got a rope, haven't we?" he said, eyeing the shrouded body. "And horses? Just tie the right knots and it's easy. Undignified, yes. But easy. Not planning to damage myself anymore. Not for a man who tried to kill you."

"And you."

"That too. I'll show you the knots now if you want."

. . .

One day of rest. After breakfast the fey healer inspected Grim's shoulder wound and then the swelling on his head. He responded to her questions with a series of expressive grunts, since her presence seemed to render him mute. She told me I'd done good work, then opened her own healer's bag and constructed her own dressing, complete with a mash of various powdered herbs.

While she was applying this I went off, at her suggestion, to gather herbs useful for controlling pain and banishing ill humors. Grim would need a headache draft. By the time I got back the little woman was in animated conversation with Grim. When I came close she waved me away. I was fairly sure they were talking about me.

The small folk finished digging the grave, and with the assistance of the rope, two horses and a lot of conflicting suggestions, we got Flannan into it. The fey ones formed a circle all around. Grim leaned against one of the horses, his arm across its back. Everyone seemed to be waiting.

I was the wise woman. This was my job. But I couldn't find the right words, not this time. I'd lost my belief in gods long ago. And right now, I couldn't think of one good thing to say about the dead man. The silence drew out.

"We give this man back to the earth." It was Grim's deep voice, steady and sure. "He did some bad things in his life. Some good too, maybe. But he lost his way. Could be he'll just rot down and help something grow. Not such a bad end, that. Could be he'll walk down a new path and find a better way."

The wee folk stayed close for most of the day. Whatever the small healer had done to Grim's injuries—I was sure that had been no ordinary dressing—he returned to something like his old self with truly astonishing speed. I made up enough of the headache draft to see us back to Cahercorcan and its well-stocked stillroom.

I snatched an opportunity, later, to speak with the fey healer on her own. Grim was at the center of a group of very small men. They were engrossed in some activity that involved tying knots in stalks of grass.

We were by the fire, she and I. I thanked her for her care of Grim. She observed that he seemed worth saving. I thanked her for the ogham messages and apologized for being so slow to understand. I asked if the king had survived his ordeal in the thorn hedge.

"He did. He's being tended to, back home. Not quite himself yet, but he will be."

"I'm not sure if I should ask this," I said, "but I will. There was a man, one of your kind, who spoke to Grim, soon after we came to Bann. Grim helped lift something. The man gave him a warning. We heard later that there was a penalty if your kind spoke out about the one in the tower."

"That is true. Our king suffered for every word."

"Then we're deeply sorry," I said. "And I hope the one who did speak out, to Grim I mean, was not punished for it."

"The king bore the punishment for us. A long curse, and a cruel one."

"I have another question for you."

"Ask away."

"True love's tears. The herb. You kept reminding me of it. I thought I needed it to break the curse that lay over the Tower of Thorns. So I gathered some and took it with me, but when I got there I didn't use it, because . . ."

"Because you did the deed, and they were back to themselves without the need for it," said the little healer, nodding. Her beady eyes had lost some of their combative look. "And then you were changed."

"I tried to tell Grim about the herb, but I . . . my mouth was odd, deformed, and I couldn't make him understand. And then . . . suddenly I was myself again, and he hadn't used it either. I don't know what undid the spell. Or why the woman who invented the curse didn't make it end with Lily and Ash."

"Her?" The little healer lifted her brows in scorn. "She wasn't only bad; she was as mad as a half-witted dog at full moon. Did what she wanted and didn't give a fig about anyone else. That's why she was so angry when the girl, Lily, crossed her. Angry enough for two hundred years of sorrow and a bit more. Be glad your man broke the spell for you."

"Grim broke it? But he never even touched the herb."

She threw back her head and let out a hearty laugh. Heads turned toward us from everywhere. "For a wise woman," she said, "you're a touch blind about some things. Tell me, did your man weep over you up there? Did he weep over the poor thing you'd become?"

I recalled Grim wiping my face with the red kerchief. Wiping his own. Saying he'd stand by me for two hundred years, if that was what it took. "Yes, but—"

"There you are, then," she said. "Now it's time we were on our way. Your fellow will be fit to ride by the morning. Trust me. And safe journey to you."

"And to you."

I thought about it later, when Grim was feeding the horses and I was readying our bedding for the night. What she'd said couldn't possibly be right. True love's tears? That was just nonsense. It wasn't like that with him and me and it never would be. What we had was far too precious to be complicated by that kind of thing. Grim would have a good laugh when I told him.

He came back. We shared a brew and settled to sleep. I didn't say a thing about true love's tears. In the morning we struck camp and rode for Cahercorcan. I put the herb in the part of my mind reserved for *too hard*. It could wait for Winterfalls and Conmael. If indeed I decided to broach the topic at all. For now, there was court and a royal baby to deliver. I found, to my surprise, that I was almost looking forward to that.